COVENANT

DEREK THOMPSON

Published in the United Kingdom in 2012 by Sixpence Publishing.

Cover design by kind permission of Annemarie Skjold. Final format by Rebsie Fairholm.

Printed and bound in Great Britain by Lightning Source Ltd.

For further information: derek@professional-writer.co.uk

www.professional-writer.co.uk

ISBN 978-0-9569877-3-0

For Anne, who needs no words for magic.

In memory of Kate Beeching, who dared to dream bright dreams.

In memory of Elsie Kerrigan, whose faith never dimmed.

And with thanks to:

Annemarie Skjold, Angela Reeve, Antonia Cardella, Bea Jn. Pierre, Cathy Smith, Colin Lazenby, David Heeley, Dean Ford, Donna Whitewolf, Geraldine Beskin, Grace, Jeremy Faulkner-Court, Jonathan Coward, Karen Deise, Karen Drake, Kath Morgan, Lisa Coward, Lucy Ashton, Lutz Winterfeldt, Mala Harilal, Marion Pearce, Mary Madeline Day, Monica Smith, Nance Zilch, Neil Roberts, Pat Riddell, Pete Adams, Rebsie Fairholm, Renata Caron, Richard Matty, Robert Alderton, Sandie Sedgbeer, Sandra Duvivier, Sara Joy, Sarah Wiles, Scott Schneider, Sheila Moylan, Sheree, Susan Hanson, Teresa Davis, Vara L. Lyngklip, Villayat Sunkmanitu, Warren Stevenson and Wendy Berg.

Covenant is a fantasy, inspired by the Western Mysteries. It can be read as a magical quest without any specialist knowledge, and will also be appreciated by those readers with an interest in meditation, mysticism, the tarot, path-workings and the Tree of Life.

The archetypal landscape still calls to us in the language of visions and dreams. It's a realm dimly remembered, and eagerly sought, where the light of our True Will shines strong amid the shadows of the Unseen.

"Serve the Many through the One and Serve the One through the Many."

— Derek Thompson

PROLOGUE

For an hour Errmoyne had sat, facing the altar where the stone Tablet rested. His patience was at an end; he traced the grooves of the pentagram with his index finger, moving it purposefully to focus his intent. If the Guardian wouldn't come to him then he would cross the boundary by force of will and face it in its own domain. His mouth dried at the prospect and his own dread mocked him – the very thing that he sought above all else was that which terrified him most: communion. He lifted his hand free and turned to each of the five candles that encompassed him within a ring of sacred fire. Then he took a final glance at the Tablet and treasured the image for fear that he might not live to see another. His breathing came under practised control, narrowing his awareness, and the world around him faded like a memory.

Pressure. So much pressure at his temples – a crushing darkness that propels him across the divide. There is no time or distance, only levels of consciousness traversed.

In the stillness that follows, patterns of reality shift to frame this higher world, colouring the terrain in muted shades of indigo and purple. A wall appears, the seamless stones defining the Guardian's domain on this plane of reality. And, as Errmoyne's awareness stabilises, a rainbow-arched gate emerges from the mist.

"Hosanna!" he cries, making a sign of invocation.

"Who calls me from the Realm of Shadows?"

"It is I, Errmoyne – Keeper of the Tablet."

The Guardian approaches, magnificent and terrible. Swathes of energy shimmer behind it like heroic wings; yet whether it is more angel or demon, Errmoyne cannot tell.

"Why have you come here, Keeper?"

He bows low. "For months now I have sought to be your servant, but you have denied me. Am I unrighteous? Have I lost my way?"

"The Way is as it has always been," the Guardian proclaims, dulling its emanations for his benefit. "The Way is Sarrell and the path is founded upon sacrifice."

"Yes, Master," he trembles.

A gate opens and the Guardian bids him enter. Errmoyne crosses the threshold, gazing in wonder as exotic trees and fleeting, morphic creatures burst into colour and form. The Guardian leads him silently, allowing him to glimpse what he will.

They move to an ancient well, where the deep, dark waters touch some hidden part of the physical world, so that Errmoyne may discern the path that awaits him. At first all he sees is his own reflection, for the Gods are content to hide truth in the simplest of guises. Then he stares harder into those limpid eyes and a vision takes hold.

The Guardian stirs and myriad flickers of light bustle around it like attendant flames. They are the slumbering souls of the lost, trapped in this realm – awaiting the second death to another level of existence or rebirth to the one they left behind – as yet denied entry to the Holy City of Sarrell.

"The Enemy knows of my existence," Errmoyne reveals with tempered conceit.

"You see clearly, Keeper. You must leave the life you have known."

"And the Tablet?" he wavers, clinging to his role as if it alone sustains him.

"A successor will be chosen. So it has been, so shall it be again, until one who is righteous claims the Tablet and reveals its wisdom."

Errmoyne kneels before the Guardian and confronts its hollow eyes in realisation. There is no room for compromise in the pattern of perfection. "So shall it be," he defers, humbled by a terrible acceptance. His awareness retreats, cascading back through levels of consciousness, crushed finally into the fragile form that he calls 'life'.

Errmoyne shivered as he awoke. High above the fireplace a small curtain revealed two doors, each adorned with a painted eye. Bridging them was a rainbow, the symbolic gateway to Sarrell. He stared up at those eyes for a long time and it seemed as if they shared his sorrow. The life that he knew and cherished was over – the Guardian had decreed it.

Heat and rage coursed through his body, sharpening his wits. He leapt up like a man possessed, running from room to room, grabbing belongings and hurling them into the grate. Once he'd packed boxes around the base and topped the stack with his beloved books, he paused and breathed deeply.

"Burn! Burn!" he added paraffin in a final rite of observance. "Let every ounce of matter and every trace of spirit be banished from this temple!"

He ignited the pyre, watching as the flames spread to the painted doors and beyond. Then he moved swiftly from room to room, spraying fuel like blessings – every drop an aid to intent. He laughed at himself, the voice scornful and empty. The Enemy would still seek him out; he could already sense the shadow of their presence like the sickly breath of the stricken.

At the front door he tossed three matches behind him. Fire engulfed the space, ripping out the windows so quickly that he felt the heat as he ran. He navigated the alleyways blindly, changing direction at every turn until he reached a main street. Even there he felt echoes of the chaos and fought to shut it out of his mind. He slowed his pace, blending with the crowd. The good citizens of Tarsis City State passed by, unaware.

Once he was free of the Community Zone, he felt the first contact of his successor. Her mind called to him, invading his thoughts in its hunger. She was a Twiceborn – and she was waiting. For a moment he felt confused, paralysed by a lack of understanding, but it was futile: he had already glimpsed his destiny.

He snaked his way towards her, compelled by the instinct to protect the Tablet. Although the neighbourhood was unfamiliar, he could have found his way to her blindfolded. She had become his eyes now, guiding him, drawing him to her like a Siren. She was waiting in the alley, pressed against the wall, eyes like opals. She took the Tablet from him and offered the traditional greeting, kissing him on the mouth and the forehead. Her lips were cold and enduring, more priestess than woman.

When he opened his eyes she had vanished, along with the Tablet. Where now? An image of Keres Park formed, where Ces Frayer's statue stared out across the city of Tarsis like a feudal overlord. He could destroy the monument, send a message to the believers and honour the faith. He reached into his tunic and took out a thin digit of metal, casting his eyes over the Godname along its surface. If he'd been a scholar he would have known the intonation and attributes of the deity, but he was an uneducated man – obedience was all the Guardian had demanded of him as Keeper. He put the device away and smiled; after months of patient submission, he was free to act in accordance with his own will.

A patrol car passed and slowed ahead of him. He crossed the street, walking faster, setting his face resolutely forward. He heard a car door open and an officer yelling like a curse.

"Let the wild hunt begin," he whispered, surging ahead, instinctively drawing them away from the area. He dived down an alleyway that led to the park, his aching heart buoyant on adrenaline. As soon as he reached the trees, he buried himself deep in the shadows.

The patrol car screeched in the distance, up by the far gates. He broke cover, plunging into the undergrowth to flatten himself against the soil. The granite effigy of Ces Frayer beckoned through the foliage. Wait, he told himself – better to take some of them with him. He swore at the idea of it and revelled in the sacrilege.

Heavy boots thundered past. Errmoyne shifted position and crouched low, lunging at the iron railings with a muffled roar. He felt the *crack* as he landed awkwardly on the pavement, and cradled his elbow to stem the blood. Nearby he could hear the clamour as they searched the park.

He staggered through the backstreets that laced the tenements, his heart pounding disobediently in a ragged rhythm of dissent. The pain came in waves and he welcomed it to drive out the fear. His mind played tricks, filling his senses with treachery. He heard voices; a dark whispering that clung to his skin. Whether real or unreal, the voices plotted his demise.

Physically and mentally overwrought, he stopped and spread his arms wide. Gradually, his bellowing breath softened and then he heard birdsong. He laughed – a hollow laughter, borne of arrogance. The Guardian had not foreseen this triumph. He had escaped his fate.

When he turned he saw two Targen officers, watching him with a subdued sense of rapture. Their pace was calculated, like starving wolves moving in for the kill. He wanted to retch or to rage against the faith, and he wished to the Most High that he had never been chosen as Keeper. That was the deepest pain of all.

"Give us the Tablet and it will be painless."

The faith taught that every day should be lived as if it were the last; now his final day had come. The Targen repeated her order and Errmoyne realised that one was female and the other male. Her accent was foreign, from another City State. He tried to distract himself with details, but a jangling dread sliced through his composure.

A baton swung in from nowhere and dropped him to the ground. One thought crowded his mind: could he throw himself on their mercy? He felt the chill of their gaze as he struggled to his knees. They were incapable of mercy – they were the Enemy.

The female Targen revealed a triangular talisman on a chain. Errmoyne was transfixed, drawn to its moulding like a terrible conclusion, even as it blistered his psyche.

"Tell us where she is and we'll let you live."

It was a lie rich with irony. The Guardian had hidden the Tablet from *all* eyes; he couldn't betray the priestess now even if he'd wanted to.

She registered surprise at his stoicism and then contempt, pressing her talisman against his forehead. Something sinister skirted the edges of his mind, intensifying his fear.

"Your life is over," the other Targen unclipped a baton to set about his terrible work. "When you get to Sarrell, tell your kin that this plane of existence is ours."

Impaled upon his agony, Errmoyne felt the woman rifling through his clothes. His lips contorted as he felt her wrench the detonator from his side.

"Looks like Latin," the male snatched it from her hand.

"It's sacred," Errmoyne gurgled, forcing his vocal chords to vibrate through a choking river of blood. A final blow splintered his rib cage and he sank to the ground for the last time.

The two Targen studied the device, relishing the way Errmoyne's blood adorned it. The senior officer ran his finger through the blood and licked at it. The raised letters hissed as they descended in sequence. He just had time to gauge the surprise on his companion's face before the object and everything in its vicinity erupted into white flame.

Errmoyne heard their final cries as the Guardian's arms opened to receive him. He had served the faith well; surely he would attain Sarrell.

chapter 1
AN ACT OF WILL

RAIN FELL like a curse, scattering the inhabitants of Tarsis. Isca watched them from the Library with a dull fascination. From up here she could see across the city, prisoner of all she surveyed. In the distance the pale, grey line of the perimeter wall strained against the populace. Closer in and the central sector lay spread before her like an intricate tapestry, one she could no more understand than appreciate. Nearer still and the rain-drenched streets snared her memory with the day that Errmoyne had called to her. It seemed as though it hadn't stopped raining since then, as if the present still wept in shame of the past.

She stared out beyond the municipal buildings, her eyes settling on where they'd found Errmoyne's remains. A tainted place, where each cry of terror had left a psychic stain as indelible as the scorch marks. All the rain in the world couldn't wash that away.

Isca recalled only fragments of her encounter. She had been meditating and then the spirit had moved her, directing her out into the streets to find him. He had seemed alone and afraid, but the inner voice that commanded her had only been concerned for the Tablet. Whenever she communed with it, she also touched a part of him. Yet despite the atrocity she sought no reprisal. She was a Thaylin Sarra priestess and retribution was not their way. In life or death all that mattered was the fulfilment of their creed and the revelation of their homeland.

Looking back over her life she could trace a thread of coincidences, stretching into childhood. Growing up in the settlements she had heard many stories about the Tablet and its mythology. Fortune and misfortune were said to follow in its wake like hunting dogs. No one knew for certain who had carried the relic though many claimed to have felt its touch and witnessed its wonders. Old Mathia, healed by the Tablet, had changed her name to Maen-Soph – Stone Wisdom in the Old Languages. Isca remembered how keen the woman had been to share the tale when they'd met on the trade roads.

While once they had been dismissed as fanatics, clinging to outlandish tales of Old Earth and talk of the Lost Holy City of Sarrell, interest in the Thaylin Sarra faith had been steadily increasing. In the city of Qayla the faith had even prospered in a limited fashion. There had been allies for a time, isolated study groups who met to share their teachings. But Tarsis lacked even that brief flourish of tolerance. A routine questioning could suddenly escalate to arrest and internment; strangers would appear at a Thaylin Sarra meeting and within a week everyone present had been visited by the Security Forces. Hardly a Thaylin Sarra household remained that had not been scarred by some travesty of justice.

Isca knew now that the Tablet was their true quest and with that awareness came a terrible understanding. For if the Targen sought such an artefact, Ces Frayer   their commander in chief and ruler of Tarsis City State – must be in league with the Enemy.

A bell sounded; it was time to leave the library and face her demons, or more specifically: one demon. She walked down the stairs briskly, steeling herself for a confrontation with the Guardian of the Tablet. It had beckoned to her in dreams since the day that she'd taken possession of the stone, taunting her with an ethereal presence. For weeks she had followed the path her faith dictated and waited in vain for guidance, until she'd reasoned that the answers must surely lie within its domain. But had Errmoyne reached the same conclusion, she wondered, and paid for his insolence?

The streets seemed deserted as she headed home, but she didn't relax her guard. The hood of her cloak flapped about, casting feral strands of red hair to the wind like an offering. Her eyes gleamed and her body thrilled to the delicious stirring of the elements. She drew back her hood and let the tempest grapple with her. Rain speckled her face and ran down her neck like a benediction. It was good to be outdoors again where she belonged. It reminded her of earlier times, before she had surrendered to their way of life. There wasn't another soul around now. How deprived those civilised city folk were – safe behind their walls. She pitied them. Back in the settlements, only the old and infirm sought refuge from the forces of nature.

She crossed the street into an alleyway. Dilapidated buildings smothered the path in shadow and long forgotten posters clung to the brickwork in ragged strips. She took a familiar route, down squalid backstreets where beggars sat and mourned the day. And where, when the night came, the walkways – littered with drug phials and crushed hopes – bore witness to a hidden netherworld where the Targen seldom ventured.

A side alley led to the enclosed courtyard that she called home. As she approached, a large, black dog pricked its ears. Before she'd reached the wooden steps it was at her side, waiting patiently as she twisted an iron key in the door. Once inside she lit a fire and threw her heavy cloak on to a chair. She shook the rain from her hair and moved over to the window. The dog sat beside her and they watched together as the lone tree in the courtyard bent and groaned while the wind used it for sport. She pressed her palm to the windowpane to bless the spirit of the tree and prayed that she might embody the same resilience.

The dog gave a low growl and met her eyes. No more stalling. She pulled the flimsy curtain to and fumbled about in the half-light for a match. One flame became six as she lit five candles and kindled some incense resin. Soon a grey aromatic column uncurled in the air like an awakening serpent, charging the room with potency.

She felt the storm gathering like the onset of passion and arched her back to the flickering lightning outside. The candle flames danced crazily, casting grotesque shadows against the walls. A haze of incense floated before her and she breathed deeply, twitching her nostrils as the fragrance wrapped around her senses. She gazed up at the painted doors above her fireplace and pressed an index finger to the Tablet, feeling a subtle heat as her finger moved along the furrowed star.

The stone responded quickly, absorbing the energy she poured into it and closing off her senses one by one. She felt herself being drawn up and out of her body, and acquiesced without protest. As the vision took hold she found herself standing before two great doors, each adorned with a compassionate and piercing eye. The doors opened, revealing their darkness. She entered and invoked the Guardian. There was no need – it was expecting her.

Awareness flickers as another level of reality unfolds. She is whole and her form is brilliance. Five pillars encircle her, each one topped with a luminous symbol of protection and aligned with her intent. The crude landscape settles into something familiar conjured from tradition. She feels the Guardian approaching and watches as it shapeshifts across the terrain.

The creature charges the circle, but the boundary of the pillars checks its progress; Isca has marked out her territory well.

"Be still daemon!" she decrees, raising a hand to quell the chaos.

The creature cackles, resting on its haunches outside the circle as if it were hers to command. For the first time Isca is afraid, for she must meet the being face-to-face. A word of summoning and the dog appears, sleek and ferocious, prowling around her in a solemn ritual of protection. The Guardian assumes human form, merging into the semblance of an old woman.

"May I enter your sanctuary, my daughter?" The voice is feeble, but even those few words betray a smouldering sense of power.

Isca lowers her hand and a gap appears in the boundary. For an instant she feels a dagger at her belt, an unconscious reaction. She dissolves the weapon and opens her hand. The dog moves deftly in front of her, its jaws gaping at the intruder.

"I bear you no malice, my child."

"And Errmoyne?"

"He was rash, but in his sacrifice he removed two of your adversaries."

"I have no enemies," she counters, realising her ignorance as soon as she has spoken.

"Until the Lock and the Key are united, the enemies of the Thaylin Sarra are everywhere."

"What do you want of me?" she feels her voice wavering, unconsciously according the Guardian respect.

"The Tablet you hold in trust is a terrible burden. What if I could offer you a dispensation, a way out of your trial?"

"Never!" she rises in form amid shards of golden fire.

"Isca," the Guardian's voice assumes authority, "what is the highest law?"

"To preserve the integrity of the faith and to prepare the way for the Restitution," she recites the words, having known them since childhood.

"Look beyond tradition, Isca; search for the higher meaning to the purpose you so willingly serve." There is an ancient weariness in the Guardian's voice.

"Lady?" No, she reasons, it must be a trick; the Guardian means to deceive her. She waits, her head bowed low like a Thaylin Sarra novice.

The Guardian looks at the light around her and discerns Isca's true nature: she is a Hybrolen – a Twiceborn. "Isca, hear me now. Truth and Light are not the exclusive provinces of the Thaylin Sarra. Your people have been blinded by their own vision. You can liberate them and yourself. Answer me this: How can you best protect the Lock – the Tablet that leads to Sarrell?"

"By keeping it safe from the Enemy until a Righteous One claims it, through a sacrifice of a different order. By hiding the Tablet with a messenger who is outside the faith." She is stunned by her own words, but now she understands.

The Guardian stretches a hand to the dog and it lies at Isca's feet, contented; there is no threat here. "This day I relieve you of your faith, Isca, and the constraints it has imposed upon your True Will. It is time to discover who you are, even as I acknowledge you."

She bows once more, watching as the Guardian retreats beyond the circle.

"Mark well the initiate's vow – to cultivate the will, to dare, to use the knowledge gained and to be silent."

"What do I tell the others?"

"Beliefs are powerful things, Isca, but they are not truth. You must find your own way and they must find theirs. The Restitution depends upon it."

She weeps at the enormity of her task, her tears dissipating like fading pearls. She must shake the Thaylin Sarra faith to its foundations and forge a new path, alone.

Isca blinked awake and found herself surrounded by a fog of incense. The five candle flames had held constant through the gloom, steadfastly maintaining their light. She cleared the temple and banished the space. There was no time for delay; she would tell the others of her decision that night and face the consequences.

As evening came she made preparations for the trip across town. A protection ritual sufficed, enough to keep her mind focused and the Tablet temporarily hidden from unrighteous eyes. The journey beyond the community zone was not one she looked forward to at the best of times, but tonight everything assumed a deeper importance. She hoped they'd understand her actions in light of the faith. She smiled, catching her likeness in the mirror and laughing at her own folly. Any blind allegiance to the Thaylin Sarra faith was at an end. Her world had shifted in a moment of realisation, freed from one set of obligations and thrust into a new liberty with responsibilities of its own.

The dog waited by the door as she drew her cloak around her in a final, physical layer of protection. It walked ahead and paused, sniffing the evening air.

"Wish me luck," she whispered, looking up into the darkening sky.

The stench of rotting food carried along the walkways, a sharp reminder of the squalor and filth that marked the zone. Many times she had questioned the wisdom of remaining there, but this part of the city, comprising little more than stacked hovels, had suited her needs well enough. And now that anonymity seemed like a blessing. In the whole of Tarsis City State, this was the closest thing to sanctuary.

It wasn't long before she reached a more affluent neighbourhood and the contrast was painful. Here were brightly lit buildings and clean streets, where the Targen would wait on your doorstep, standing smartly to attention, instead of smashing the door in with a sledgehammer. This district of Tarsis, forced between sections of the poor like a torment, was a monument to inequality. There was even a fountain there. A fountain! Four blocks down and you couldn't trust the water out of the standpipes.

It was as blatant as it was immoral. The faith had taught her that the restitution of Sarrell would reinstate a balance. For the first time in a long while she really believed that was possible.

The front door was just like the rest of the row, but as Isca stepped up she could already sense the presence of her kin. Feren was among them, which pleased her most of all. If anyone would support her tonight it was Feren.

The bell chimed and the heavy door inched open. A few words were exchanged as the host scanned the street behind her. The door widened in one deliberate movement and she was snatched inside before it slammed shut. She calmed herself, asking after the host's family as was customary with benefactors. Then she headed for the backroom. All conversation ended as she pushed the door.

"Welcome, Isca, we've been waiting for you," the Matriarch Etta indicated an empty seat beside her. "I believe you have something to tell us?"

It was more of a statement than a question. Isca's eyes widened, caught in the glare of a dozen faces. Feren stared at the floor – there was no comfort to be found in his gaze. She swallowed softly and took her place at the table, remembering the Old Earth tradition of the Christed One and the Last Supper.

"Have you approached the matter?" Etta asked, avoiding explicit reference to the Tablet or its reputed Guardian.

"I have done much and much have I yet to do," Isca told her, speaking in one of the ancient, lyrical tongues so that few present could take in the meaning.

Etta unlaced her fingers with a look of resignation. "If we are to speak of this we should talk openly. Tonight there are no neophytes."

"Very well then," Isca agreed. "I have determined the way forward. The Tablet makes its will known through the expression of my True Will."

Etta considered her own position carefully before responding. Isca was recognised as a Hybrolen Twiceborn, young in years yet already gifted with soul-memories. And she had apparently been chosen to receive the Tablet. It was also common knowledge that Etta's own soul nature had yet to fully reveal itself. She was a good intuitive and a Matriarch by virtue of age, tradition and acquired wisdom. The Hybrolen, in contrast, walked among the Thaylin Sarra as bright flames clothed in flesh, lest they blind their companions, according to the Books of Law. It would not do to be seen to as either usurper or usurped.

"What do you *propose*, Isca?"

The room died down to a whisper. She took a deep breath and spoke her truth. "A messenger will be summoned to protect the Tablet – an *outsider*."

Feren's chair scraped back like a shriek of despair.

"What heresy is this?" Gev erupted, slamming his palms against the table. "You would take our most precious relic – our greatest hope – and put it in the hands of a heathen! Why not deliver it to Ces Frayer personally and have done with it!"

Isca held firm. "Listen to me, all of you. They know the Tablet is in Tarsis. Who would have another suffer the same fate as Errmoyne? You, Feren?"

He recoiled, as if she had stabbed him through the heart, pained beyond words that she should look for dissent in *his* eyes.

"And what if you are wrong?" Etta's voice pierced the melee. "How are we to know if your claim to the Tablet is even valid? Perhaps the Enemy has poisoned your mind to relinquish our hope of salvation?"

"No, the poison lies in keeping the Tablet and assuming it is for my hands alone."

All eyes turned to Etta.

"As Matriarch of this cell it falls to me to support or reject your proposal. I am not Hybrolen as you are. I cannot pass judgement on whether you are speaking from your True Will. Therefore I must be guided by intuition alone. You have my leave to summon your messenger," she closed her eyes. "But should the Gods fail to meet your petition, within one cycle of the moon, you must release the Tablet into our collective care."

Isca stared back across the gulf between them; the Guardian's words were already coming to pass. "I accept your judgement. It is a sound conclusion," she hid her thoughts behind a face of granite, certain that they had little appreciation of either the forces at work or the nature of the task.

"Isca?" Feren pressed. "How will we know if your messenger is true?" It would have been a worthy question from anyone else, but Feren's lips made it a bitter betrayal.

She settled her mind and faced him. "The messenger will remain hidden from all of you except Etta, unless she or the Guardian decide otherwise. I have no proof to share, Feren. The Ways of the One are often a mystery – even to the Hybrolen."

Etta placed her fingertips on the table; the matter was closed. She picked up a book and found the desired text. "These words were gathered up by Parva Serach the Sage. May they guard us and guide us in the difficult times ahead."

The group bowed their heads.

"The people who walk in darkness will see light, dwellers subsisting in the shadow of death. They shall grow in number and proclaim their freedom from tyranny. Their freedom will be hard won, for my way is the Way of the Spirit and it is a testing one. Therefore build the temple within and fortify it with courage, wisdom and truth."

"So shall it be," they affirmed in unison.

Etta had no difficulty building mental pictures for the others to follow; she always found it easier when Isca was present. Isca focused her mind and fed the Matriarch clarity and devotion – for this night at least. When they had finished their rite Etta knocked on the wall to signal that food and drink could be brought in.

Their host arrived with a tray of delicacies undreamed of in the community zone. They ate and talked freely. There was news of their kin in other cities and lively discussion about The Assembly's latest curfew measures. Feren spoke of the settlements, far beyond the city walls where some, like Isca, had begun their journeys. To hear mention of the fields at harvest again and the cool, autumn winds was almost more than she could bear.

Herbs and healing salts were distributed, and then Etta interpreted dreams in line with tradition. As the final blessing was given, Isca sensed the change among them. Everyone filed out quietly until only Etta, Feren and Isca remained.

"You've been a great strength tonight, Etta," Isca touched her shoulder in an uncharacteristic display of feeling.

"Don't think for a moment that I approve of this," she rounded on her. "You have chosen this path and it would seem that we are forced to walk it alongside you. I pray you know what you are doing," she closed the door behind her, a study in self-control.

Feren edged closer. "Isca, may I speak with you…privately?"

"There's no one else here, speak freely," she blushed; it was still there between them – the dying embers.

"I'm moving on to Sirn City once I've tied up some loose ends," his voice lingered, heavy with longing.

"I wish you well. There is much good work to be done there."

His unchecked emotions swamped her like a torrent. She felt his desire and did not return his gaze.

"I'll wait outside for you, Isca."

She closed the door after him without answering and sat for a few moments, staring at the empty chairs in turn before she realised she had unwittingly chosen the Matriarch's seat. A phrase came to mind: *Let every trace of spirit be banished from this temple.* She didn't say the words aloud, but nodded in agreement, focusing her True Will to erase all traces of their presence from the room. It was said that the Appren initiates, the

Enemy of the Thaylin Sarra, could seek out the remnants of magic like a scent; she left them nothing.

Feren was across the street, head bent low against the rain.

"Come with me," he pleaded, "to another city or out to the settlements."

"And then what, Feren?"

He stared at the ground, as if accused of some great weakness.

"Didn't you hear a word I said tonight?"

"I just want things to go back to how they were," he faltered.

He sounded so fragile that she had to stop herself from reaching out to him.

"Things have changed, Feren – *I've* changed. Even if we were still together the Tablet and the messenger would take precedence. I must meet my responsibilities."

He nodded sadly, backing away. "When will I see you next?"

"Soon," she promised, scurrying into the downpour before she lost her resolve.

chapter 2
THE BEGUILING AND THE BEGUILED

FOR SEVEN DAYS and nights Isca cut herself off from the world. In truth it was no great hardship. Etta had made her position clear at their last meeting and the others there hadn't beaten a path to her door. The Matriarch's concession of a lunar month rankled; it felt like a challenge to her integrity – either prove herself or admit that she was misguided and surrender the Tablet.

She looked up from a pile of charts and glowered. The Tablet lay at her feet and she brushed her hand across it. Perhaps a second communion was needed? "But is that what I'm supposed to do?" she asked aloud.

The carved symbols and glyphs flickered before her inner sight with the promise of revelation. Some she recognised as familiar shapes associated with the faith; others felt brooding to the touch.

The Guardian's response came quickly, building on their previous encounter. She felt the energy of the room change as the barrier between worlds faded. The dog lifted its head, responding to the subtle shift.

She approaches the twin portals and raises her arms in invocation. The painted eyes glow fiercely before the doors yield. She tries to take a step forward, but her progress is checked. The dog at her feet utters a low growl. The sound resonates through her, driving back the lure of the Guardian with a force of its own.

She sat up, stung into awareness. The dog sighed and stretched with a yawn.

"Bless you, my companion; once again you have brought me to my senses," she clapped her hands triumphantly.

Cast aside the traditional Thaylin Sarra teachings – that's what the Guardian had insisted. Her mind floated free, liberated by days of fasting and meditation. As her rational side gave way, emotive force burst through with clarity. If the Gods had seen fit to abandon her then she would take matters into her own hands and summon a messenger by her True Will. She scooped up papers and dropped them behind a couch. Then she turned to the dog and looked deep into its eyes. The beast stood and began to pace around her in a clockwise path.

"Guard me against my own weakness," she commanded.

She heard the rain crash down outside and smiled in appreciation. Her skin bristled; a sure sign that the magical currents were present. Candles soon adorned her room once more, five flames that licked the damp air with ravenous tongues. She chose her incense carefully, spreading myrrh, benzoin and dittany across a heated tin plate in the middle of the floor. The black hound sniffed the air and settled by the candle for Ether. There it rested, blinking slowly, as Isca's form shifted in and out of phase with the room.

When she sensed that the temple was established she lifted up a small bell to waist height. The sky darkened as deep, menacing purple devoured the grey. She felt a pressure at her back, closing around her, trying to contain her. But she would have none of it tonight.

In one great, circular movement she cast the bell clockwise and cried out passionately, "Hekas Hekas Este Bibeloi," translating the words of power in her mind: 'Be gone from this place all that is profane.'

The sounds resonated around the room. In her mind's eye she saw patterns of energy glistening and swirling about her. The dog snarled and stared intently as the candle to Isca's left choked and spat. She stretched out her hand, infusing the flame with energy until it recovered, and drew meaning from it, as all practitioners of magic take wisdom from the world. This was the candle of Earth; her quarry was near and she would awaken them.

She tightened her jaw and took the stance of the magus, summoning energy from within. Her consciousness rushed in upon itself. Everything disappeared: no circle, no dog and no sanctuary. A sound engulfed her like the roaring of an ocean, submerging all sense of identity. She rose from its nadir to become the tide, flowing forcefully into the void. And from out of that eventual stillness an arc of force arose. She knew her art well and rode the current, directing it from dissolution to form. At the apex of her magic, where she felt she might disintegrate within the vastness of it all, she called forth her True Will and released the seed energy to do its irresistible work. An invocation beyond sound or even the essence of an idea: raw, primordial power. A call so strong that the recipient could not fail to heed it.

The next thing she knew, the dog was nuzzling her awake. The candles had burned to oblivion. A vestige of the fire remained in the grate, but the room felt barren and depleted. It took all her strength to quit the circle and drag a grey blanket over her limp body. Then sleep overtook her.

It was late morning when Isca awoke. She drew back the curtain, one hand across her face to shield herself from the merciless glare of sunlight. The remnants of a sound echoed in her mind, steadily stripping away the memory of her dreams.

After a hurried meal and a change of clothes, she gathered her things and headed off for the market with the dog in tow – the usual meditation would have to wait. She enjoyed the spectacle they made as she walked along together. Thaylin Sarra often kept animal companions; strays mainly, often found starving and abandoned. It was a gesture, a way of showing service to all life.

Many of the faith held conventional, menial jobs, but Isca had long since chosen to live as independently as possible. It made for fewer ties and it was easier to move on without complications. So she'd crafted a living for herself, selling herbs and charms and dispensing guidance through divination. Some of the city state folk were a superstitious lot and a reasonable living could be had if you kept your wits about you.

Isca had found the transition difficult at first for some of the teachings warned against providing insight for the curious and sceptical. But what better way to take the light of knowledge to the people who needed it most? And what virtue was there in truth if it didn't feed your body as well as your soul? It wasn't an entirely risk-free enterprise – some of the herbs and plants were hard to come by and carried both strictures and healing properties. You had to know your sciences as well as your suppliers. Officially, traders were limited by what they could bring in from the settlements. There were always ways around that; everyone had a price.

She reached the market and found her usual spot, unpacking her wares and carefully positioning a purple crystal on the table. No other stallholder paid her much attention, which suited her. When she'd first arrived at the market others had been wary, afraid even. Now she took their occasional comments in good humour, convinced that they were secretly pleased to have one of her kind among them even though they didn't always show it.

Once the stall was set up she reached into her bag and passed a bone to the dog. It took the offering in an unhurried fashion, crushing it into splinters to savour the meagre flesh. It was a routine they performed most days, while onlookers watched from a safe distance.

She waited until sufficient interest had built up. "You can go now, I'll be fine," she promised, watching the dog slip into the crowd.

The effect was instantaneous. Once the sleek, black tail had vanished from view the first potential customer approached. The woman examined the sachets and herbs, all the while avoiding eye contact, one hand resting on the crystal. Isca shared her appreciation. In all her travels she'd rarely seen a finer piece; it had come a long way. And she knew that if things ever got desperate she could count on a reasonable price for it.

The smell of bubbling soup and cheap stew wafted across the market, a more tantalising call than any vendor could bellow. It was said that anything could be obtained at the markets. Before the authorities had clamped down on the trade, it had been possible to buy a wife, a husband or even a child. The local working girls still called it the Commodities Market.

A child ran up to the table as a dare, while her friends called and jeered. Isca handed the little girl a flatcake for her courage and watched as she ran back to share it. She loved the waifs and urchins who wandered the market in search of scraps and kindness. They often came up to see the *Keldie* lady – the local slang for Thaylin Sarra – with her dog. Other traders chased away the little brats because beggars were bad for business, but Isca delighted in their irrepressible nature.

The morning passed uneventfully and early afternoon showed no sign of promise. People came and went, much as they always did, seeking mystical solutions to mundane problems and rapid remedies for conditions long in the making. She sat back and tried to intuit some pale clue to the outcome of her work. It was the first time she'd worked magic like that, away from the certainty of books and dogma, embracing a deeper reality where energy and intent were tangible enough on their own.

Her thoughts rebelled and she doubted herself. What if it had all been an illusion of power – a ploy of the Gods to mock her wilful independence? To that she had no answer. Magic was there to be used of course, but outside the bounds of tradition? She sighed, glancing at her reflection in the crystal. It was so different in Tarsis. Among the urban faithful, the small, outward acts of magic such as calling down the rain were discouraged and considered an indulgence. Out in the settlements it was another matter entirely. Such magic was welcomed and expected for the benefit of the community.

Later that afternoon the dog returned. She packed her bags and quit the stall, lingering by the market gate. The dog would not be swayed and nudged her along insistently. With a final, bitter glance behind her, she caught sight of two Targen officers forcing their way through the crowd and manhandling anyone in their path. She bent down and patted the dog, which gave a loud murmur of satisfaction.

At home she boiled up some drinking herbs and cleared space on a low table. She pored over charts to scrutinise the timing of her invocation; later, she would turn her attention to the actual technique. She frowned; nothing seemed contrary to magical practice. The conditions had not been perfect; alignments such as she'd have preferred were few and far between. But she had acted in accordance with her True Will. Better that in unfavourable conditions than clinging to tradition out of habit and fear.

A banging on the door broke her concentration. The dog moved swiftly, putting itself between Isca and the noise. She glanced around and checked that the Tablet was out of sight.

"Isca, it's me – Etta."

She opened the door, one hand behind to steady the dog. Etta staggered inside.

"The Targen visited our benefactor and they've arrested Gev."

"On what charge?" Isca raged, screwing her hand into a fist. "Is belonging to the faith a crime itself now?"

"No," Etta sneered, "but setting incendiaries and other acts of sedition are."

"Gev?" Isca leaned back. "I know he came up from the south after the troubles there, but that doesn't mean…"

"Look," Etta cut her off, "I'm not here because of Gev. I want you to reconsider your decision. I do not see things as you see them but I do *see…*"

"Meaning?" Isca glared at her, piqued.

"I mean," Etta slumped into a chair, "that it is easier to appreciate the actions of another objectively. If they can detain Gev without evidence then they won't be long in picking up the rest of us. I'm begging you – don't bring in an outsider, not now. The threat of exposure is too great. If you persist with your plan there will be repercussions."

"I know the risks," she insisted.

"*Do you?* You can't just hide the Tablet with an outsider and then discard them when it suits you. Have you even considered what magic could do to a Tarsien mind? Any bond you forge will not be easily broken. You might weave such a charm around them that they cannot tell your will from their own. "

"*Understanding* will guide their actions, not my manipulation. Besides," she confessed, "it is done; I invoked a messenger last night."

Etta gripped the chair. "Oh my child, you have taken on a terrible responsibility. I pray that you can cope with the consequences."

"I respect your wisdom in this matter, Sister," Isca addressed her as an equal for the first time. "And I respect my own. All I ask is that we trust one another."

Without waiting for a response, she brought out the Tablet and held the stone by the window, knowing that sunlight and moonlight provoked different responses. When she sensed that the energy of the stone had awakened she carried it over.

Etta's eyes sparkled with reverence at the sight of the holy relic. She cradled it, marvelling at its carved intricacy. Such a light shone from Etta's face that Isca soon lost any ill feeling towards her.

"It is more sentient than I imagined," she whispered.

"Indeed. Its mood shifts with the courses of the sun and the moon."

She sat back and watched, as Etta tilted her head and listened to some inner voice. She smiled; it was the same for her. Often she would gain faint impressions from the Tablet, veiled glimpses of the past or future – but the full meaning eluded her. She had learned to live with that. It was enough to be a Keeper of the Tablet; the Righteous One would take the next step.

After a time Etta passed the Tablet back. She seemed changed, at peace with herself and secure in the strength of her faith. Isca saw the tears in her eyes and embraced her. Behind them the tree rocked in the breeze, its boughs creaking and flexing to a blustery rhythm. It endured – a testament both to its own nature and to that other tree, enshrined in Thaylin Sarra teachings: the Tree of Life.

Isca returned to the market with renewed hope. She saw the people around her with fresh eyes. Their striving, their yearning and even their ignorance – all strands of the complex web of existence; every choice made or negated sending out ripples of consequence.

She gazed at her crystal, enjoying the interplay of light and colour. Maybe today would be different. As she looked out across the aisles she saw two youths approaching, deep in the throes of an argument. She smiled at the sight of them – one tall and the other short – and waited to see the outcome.

"Come on Syriem," Dorron teased his friend as he looked down at him. "It was only a gathering – it wasn't even a very good one! I'll get you into one of the others."

Dorron's promise was a measured combination of mockery and regret, finely honed over the years that he and Syriem had been best friends. Syriem shuffled along, hands in pockets, to the amusement of stallholders with nothing better to do than gawp.

"Look it wasn't my fault; you were the one who struck out. I couldn't leave and disappoint them both, now could I?" Dorron opened his arms and panned wide, taking in the audience.

Syriem seethed, unconsciously baring his teeth as his emotions overtook him. "Dorron, you're despicable!" He stormed off – in what Dorron called *one of his little moods* – and disappeared to sulk in private.

Dorron picked out Isca almost immediately. True she was one of those Keldies, but she was an attractive one. He sauntered over and pretended to be interested in her wares – which he was, after a fashion. Isca maintained her reserve and studied Dorron as he stood there, admiring his own reflection. It wouldn't do to be too forward; she might scare him off – he was a Tarsien after all. Even so, she congratulated herself; lean, young and strong, he would blend in effortlessly. She resisted sensing his aura in case the influx of energy unnerved him.

He glanced up at her in their dance of strangers and rested his fingers on the edge of the table. She held her breath, eager to see how the power of the invocation would shape his first words. He leaned in, placed a hand over hers and whispered furtively, "Do you do fortunes?"

Some time later Dorron scuttled away, his ears stinging from Isca's guidance. He was not the messenger. An intriguing prospect certainly, but his temperament didn't allow for all the development he'd need – and neither did hers.

Syriem had watched from a distance, curious to see what had held Dorron's interest for so long. This time, he vowed, he'd prove that he was Dorron's equal.

Once Dorron had left, a woman rushed in to take the empty seat. Her clothes had seen better days, but she carried herself with dignity. Isca read the scars in her aura and passed her three slivers of wood. She turned the sticks over in her hands, unconsciously infusing them with her own energies.

Isca calmly received them and let the sticks fall on to a blue cloth, embroidered with fine, white stitching like a spider's web. She cast several times for different aspects of the woman's life, describing each pattern in terms of where it fell and the shapes made. Gradually the woman's spirit lifted and she waved her hands around as she verified some of Isca's words and challenged others.

After casting five patterns, Isca summed up. The woman listened intently and Isca noted that the marks in the aura had barely changed; knowledge without action was only potential. Isca declined the payment and deftly pressed a small parcel into her hands as she left.

"I usually charge for spectators," she turned to confront Syriem.

He blushed and edged forward, as though she had invited him in. "I didn't see her pay," he toyed with the crystal while his face burned.

"She's been paying for a *long* time," she snapped, "not that it's any concern of yours."

He pouted and pressed a palm against the crystal's point.

"You seem a bit young for this, but as you're here…" she took pity on him, nodding to the seat. "Which is it to be – sticks or cards?"

He shrugged, but his eyes were on the sticks.

"Come on then," she dropped them into his hands, "let's see what we can see."

He held the strips of wood with trepidation, rubbing the bark between his hands. Always a bit of a dreamer he soon lost himself in a daydream, running through a forest at dawn with the sun at his face…

"When you're ready," she interrupted after a minute of inactivity.

He looked up in surprise and meekly handed the sticks over.

The patterns formed with each descent, yielding their stories. She noted how the shapes were at odds with one another, a common occurrence for someone so young. There was little of substance to tell him, as though his life hadn't properly begun. She sought clarification on minor matters and immersed herself in the process, enjoying the ebb and flow between querent and reader. During the fourth casting, she peered up from the cloth and noticed him staring into space again.

"Look, if you're not really interested, don't waste my time."

He nodded, dimly aware of her words washing over him. She willed herself to pierce the veil and an image formed – of Syriem on horseback, leading a crowd. She shared it with him and he replied that he didn't trust horses and anyway it was probably symbolic. She laughed at that and cast one last time, determined to show him something meaningful. The sticks tumbled slyly onto the cloth, revealing the configuration that she knew as the Messenger. She blinked for a moment or two, mesmerised by the sight.

A wave of emotion swarmed through her, shattering her composure. The dog came bounding through the crowd to her aid. She recovered to find Syriem catatonic. "How can this be?" she whispered to the dog. "He's just a child."

She touched the boy's face firmly, lifting his chin to look him full in the eyes. More impressions came to her – scenes of fear and persecution. It made no sense; he was no Thaylin Sarra yet there was an affinity with the faith and its past. There was something buried there, hidden even from himself.

"Who are you, child? Why are you here?"

"I come because she calls me," he responded, seeing nothing but a formless void, which charmed him like an opiate.

She felt her senses fading and summoned a last trickle of willpower, gently squeezing his wrists. He flinched and looked around.

"It's time for you to go," she snatched her hands back to break the circuit.

"What…happened?"

"Come back in a few days and we'll talk some more," she promised. Before he could protest, she was frantically packing up her things.

Syriem took the hint and went off to look for Dorron, who was nowhere to be seen. He drifted about in a daze, lost in memories that didn't seem rightfully his. He soon gave up on Dorron and wandered off, puzzled and invigorated in equal measure.

By the time Isca made it home, she was cold to the core. The Guardian was absent in a way she'd never experienced before. It was as if it too had lost a measure of its essence to the boy. She dragged herself up the steps and dropped her bags inside the door. All she wanted to do was sleep, but she boiled up an infusion and ate a couple of flatcakes. She knew without question that Syriem would return in a few days, governed by the rhythm she had set in motion. She stared across at the Tablet, consumed by a single thought: her work had begun.

It took Syriem three days to recover. Three days of disrupted sleep and bizarre dreams, of waves of enthusiasm followed by depths of depression; and all of it culminating in a desire for knowledge. Like any good Tarsien he knew only two things about the Thaylin Sarra – there was some crazy belief about a hidden city and they moved from place to place promoting their faith. What he needed were facts and there was one place to get them – the library.

He was no stranger to the carefully controlled rows of books and essays. Here he was free to explore the limits of his imagination, without criticism or ridicule from Dorron. His friend detested the place, calling it a mausoleum for the living.

A crosscheck of subjects and sections rapidly ground Syriem's enthusiasm to dust. Not a single book or record existed on the Thaylin Sarra faith. There was an abundance of works on official history and related themes – stretching back to the Old Times before colonisation, but nothing to tell him more about the mystery woman and her way of life.

He paced the aisles and tried ransacking shelves at random. His persistence was eventually rewarded with three Thaylin Sarra booklets thrust between volumes on cultural change. He found a quiet corner and settled down to read.

The booklets were packed with information, each strand of delicate writing offering an uncompromising and alternative view of the world that he had grown up with. He read the first pamphlet quickly – it sounded like nonsense. Was Tarsis really the *City of Despair*, thriving on the oppression of the poor and the exploitation of the settlements? Could The Assembly, who governed the city state, have actually lied to him since the day he was born? He felt crushed; was Isca that deluded? His mind ached; this would take some thinking about. In the mean time, he conceded, if she wanted to believe all that then it was her business.

The next booklet, just a single sheet of folded paper, was a set of questions about life and purpose. If anything, that made him more uncomfortable than the previous one.

The last booklet was different. It spoke of prophecies and the Restitution – evidently a key tenet of the faith. He didn't understand the references to liberation and righteousness, but the text captured his imagination from the first sentence. Here was a new and intoxicating way of looking at the world, through mythology, shining a light on his life and bringing it into focus.

He took the booklets home, re-reading them repeatedly to make notes and copy out phrases. When he could recite them by heart, he practised arguments with Dorron in his head. And each time he recited the words, he felt a little closer to Isca.

Dorron wasn't big on intellectual debate, but their friend, Athenna, listened with interest to Syriem's borrowed theories on conspiracy and mysticism. She had known both of them for years and although she thought Syriem had sound judgement in most matters, she found his sudden conversion worrying.

Easen, Athenna's father, also listened. A charismatic speaker and wildly outspoken against the authorities, he delighted in sharing tales about Assembly members and their foibles. Once Syriem began to voice his new perspective Easen made more of an effort to welcome his daughter's friends, which led to lively discussions at the house.

Athenna had heard her father's tales many times before, but relished seeing him holding court again. Whatever strange ideas Syriem had taken up with, she could at least thank him for that. Dorron didn't say too much about any of it, which seemed to suit everyone.

After two weeks Syriem felt ready to revisit the market. He was more confident about seeing Isca again, thought less certain about why he needed to it so badly. It was an instinct; something he knew not to discuss, even with Dorron. Had he Isca's knowledge, he would have understood that a lunar rhythm governed his return.

The market was already closing by the time he'd arrived. He dodged through the mass of people and barrows heading out and found his way to the aisle where he'd last seen her. His heart soared; she was still there, sat at an empty table – a model of tranquillity. He moved forward, a deafening pulse in his ears.

"Hello again," he struggled to catch his breath; oblivious to the way her fingers trembled on the table. "You did say I could come back…"

Isca was silent for a moment and insecurity swamped him. Maybe he'd imagined it all and she was waiting for someone else? He sniffed softly, something he always did when confronted with emotion or discomfort – which generally amounted to the same thing. And then he stared up at the sky, catching sight of the moon.

She cleared her throat and smiled, sensing the change in him. She chose her words carefully, speaking to that part of him he was as yet unaware of. "Are you ready?"

He felt a chill down his spine and nodded. They walked in silence, Syriem glancing up at her from time to time. He didn't know a single thing about her or where they were going, and he didn't care.

She kept her focus and ignored his gaze. He had made it back to the market – a good sign – although they were not out of the woods yet. She had to be certain that he was fit for the task; he'd need to be tested.

He noticed they were moving away from the neighbourhood, but said nothing. Then the first alleyway appeared, like an entrance into the underworld. He took a gulp of courage, tightened his shoulders and kept on walking. This was one of those community zones he'd been warned about. The screams in the distance and a dull, echoing roar that sounded like a gunshot did little to soothe his nerves.

She led on, indifferent to the chaos within him. He dropped back a little, absorbed in the struggle to control his thoughts and emotions. She tuned to his mood with ease. It pleased her in a twisted sort of way; he was witnessing a slice of life seldom glimpsed by the fair citizens of Tarsis – a far cry from the safe and sanitised world he was used to.

She took a different route home, along treacherous paths she might otherwise have avoided were she not feeling so confident. Was she being too hard on him? She shrugged her shoulders in the gloom and stepped up the pace. *No*, she told herself as she turned up her collar, *he has a long journey ahead of him.*

Yet for all her concerns, and there were many, she also felt a growing sense of stability. The messenger had been found in all probability, which meant her actions had been aligned with Universal Will. The thought gave her a frisson of excitement. Syriem also felt an inner stirring with a hormone or two thrown in for good measure.

The last alleyway opened out to a cobbled courtyard, where a single tree stood amid a ring of old buildings like the hub of a wheel. Syriem felt drawn to it and ventured from her side while she waited, watching him keenly.

At the stairway a pair of gleaming eyes surveyed him. Isca muttered a word that Syriem couldn't quite catch and a black dog appeared from beneath the steps. He froze as it sauntered towards him and sniffed at his hand.

"What's its name?" he stammered, trying not to look into those gleaming eyes.

"Oh, it has many names," she threw her head back with laughter, "and sometimes it doesn't answer to any of them!"

The dog peered at Syriem, flashing its teeth with a low rumble.

"Don't worry," she promised, as she climbed the steps, "you'll be safe with me!"

And he cherished the words as he followed her.

Chapter 3
RENDING THE VEIL

THE WOODEN BOARDS creaked and groaned, as Isca rounded the stairs. Syriem followed closely behind, almost tripping at the top of the landing.

"This way," her voice trailed along the passage.

She held out a hand in the gloom. "We're here," she opened the heavy door and went inside. "Find yourself a space."

There was no real welcome or invitation, as if his presence were completely incidental and he felt slighted by that. He suddenly remembered the dog. He turned and faced the creature beyond the threshold, its eyes glinting fiercely.

"He'll be fine out there," she called.

Taking her at her word, he slammed the door resolutely in its face. The room looked as if it had only been recently occupied and even then in a hurry. Furniture was randomly deposited around the room – *arranged* would be too strong a word for it – with papers and books strewn everywhere.

He picked his way over to a couch. "Have you lived here long?"

"Long enough," she called, clattering around in the kitchen. "I'm the last tenant. The rest of the building is unoccupied now."

"Condemned, more like," he muttered, noticing a small curtain above the fireplace. He was about to investigate when Isca returned.

She followed his line of vision but said nothing, setting two cups down on a collection of papers. "Please excuse the mess; the maid hasn't been for a while."

After a few seconds she flashed a smile, putting him out of his misery. They talked a little about the market and other places they both knew in Tarsis. He started to relax, relinquishing Dorron's assertions of Thaylin Sarra sacrifice.

As the conversation flowed she went to work on him, keeping things light while she found out what she needed to know. He had no strong personal ties and he lived with his family across town, on the far side of the sector. Dorron, the friend she had already encountered, came up a few times, as well as a girl. Unremarkable details in themselves, but each one a clue to this stranger come into her life. He had a fondness for the girl that his friend evidently shared. And when she pressed him he went off at a tangent, hiding behind Athenna's history.

The diversion paid unexpected dividends. When he explained that Athenna's mother, Buda, had left years before, Isca paid close attention. Buda – a Thaylin Sarra name. So either Buda had been born into the faith or changed her name at some point. She made a mental note to check with her sources and let Syriem ramble on uninterrupted. His honesty was refreshing; he seemed to see his life as an open book and he looked to everyone and everything around him to help fill the pages.

She stoked the fire, breathing life into the iron grate, and watched with satisfaction as the flames crept hungrily over the wood. Even with her back to him she could feel his eyes upon her. "Tell me, Syriem, how old are you?"

He choked, caught off guard. "Eighteen."

She turned to look at him, trying to fit his age to his face.

"Well, seventeen and a half…ish."

"Have you eaten?" she changed tack, thinking more of her dog than her guest.

She left him and rifled through the cupboards for something she thought he would eat. Out of practice with entertaining, and for outsiders at that, she made the best of it with some eggs and a few vegetables.

"You don't eat meat," he announced triumphantly, sniffing at his cup.

"Well, I don't, usually – that's not true for all of us. I'm pleased to see that you've undertaken some research!"

The dog called to be let in and skirted around the room, still undecided about whether he was an intruder. It gave him the benefit of the doubt and lay down by its mistress.

"I've asked enough questions; it's your turn," she challenged him, rubbing a lazy ankle along the dog's flank.

"Where do I start?" he gushed.

She smiled. He was keen. And articulate too, judging by the way that he expressed himself – that could be useful. He wasted little time, seeking out details of her faith, her past and her private life. She told him that she was single and watched as great bursts of emotional energy shot out from his aura, a fair match for the colour that he blushed. Then he sat back and his face grew pensive.

"Why am I here? Is this how you get converts – by befriending them?"

"You're here, Syriem, because I feel we have an affinity. I think we could learn a lot from one another. I'm not looking for a convert; I invited you because I want you here."

He brightened, nodding appreciatively, as if she had brought him back from the brink of some catastrophe. But the silence that followed was a strained one.

"I could show you the sticks again, if you like…"

He blinked slowly and shook his head. "Tell me about life beyond the cities."

She settled in a chair and closed her eyes, concentrating to project the images for him. She soon lost herself in the telling, drawing on treasured memories that she offered to him as gifts. Acres of farmland, ringing with the songs of the land folk as they toiled from dawn to dusk; the great ridges across the hills where mighty oaks and beeches stood their ground against the autumn winds from the north. And further still, more than a three-week crossing by horse, the desert – where only lizards and burrowers survived the unrelenting heat. There were so many places and each so different, and none of them home.

"…And in the seaports a sack of spice is worth more than any of the crew, bar the captain or the navigator. There is delicate web of settlements, speckling the land, every one of them denounced and belittled by the fortified City States of The Assembly."

When she had finished speaking, he let out such a sigh of longing that even the dog stirred from its slumber. She was pleased her heartsong had moved him, but so lost was he in the power of her words that she saw tears in his eyes. Evidence of an emotional nature – a trait she resolved to rid him of at the earliest opportunity.

They talked more of *his* world, of the way that people in Tarsis felt about the Thaylin Sarra. He squirmed when he revealed some of the more outlandish rumours, such as how the Thaylin Sarra stole children to swell their numbers. And then there was a peaceful silence, where nothing needed to be said.

It was deep into the night before he realised the time. "So what happens next?" he broke the stillness.

"What happens?" she rubbed the back of her neck. "You head off home, for that job of yours in the morning."

"No shift tomorrow," he stared into the fading flames. "Just as well, seeing how late it is…"

"Okay," she thought for a moment, "you'd best stay here tonight – I don't rate your chances of getting through the zone in one piece at this hour."

He ventured a little grin, which she didn't return.

"But I want to make one thing absolutely clear – you're here to learn. Don't go getting distracted by any *other* ideas. Incidentally, won't your family be worried about you?"

"I've been out all night before," his voice leapt an octave. "I'm not a child!"

She apologised and managed to stifle her laughter, resolving to keep a check on her words in future. But she wondered why he hadn't questioned her comment about being there to learn – he'd never asked for that. Maybe he was just glad of the attention. She frowned; she was going to have tread very carefully.

Syriem spent a peaceful night by the dying embers of the fire, wrapped in a grey blanket that smelt faintly of the dog. He lay awake for a long while, listening to the tree swaying outside and thinking about Isca, until sleep snatched her from him.

She woke from an unsettling dream during the night. Peering from her door, she watched his body twitching as he mumbled in his sleep; so like a child, it scared her when she thought about what she was asking of him.

A rasping bark dragged Syriem from the comfort of his dreams. He let the dog in and it prowled around the furniture before settling near Isca's door. He shuffled over to the window, still wrapped in the blanket, negotiating the gaps in the floorboards. Outside he could see the lone tree clearly now, adrift in a sea of stone.

The light came on under Isca's bedroom door and as he listened intently he could hear singing. It would probably have disappointed Dorron to know that crossing that thin strip of brightness hadn't even occurred to Syriem in his early morning happiness.

They shared a makeshift breakfast without discussion. Isca was keen not to make any concessions until she had thought things through. She walked him back to a main street with the dog beside her. A terrible longing washed over him as she pointed him home. She sensed his mood and touched him lightly on the shoulder – a simple transference of energy to keep him buoyant – before sending him on his way.

The sun was barely up, bathing the deserted streets in a subdued glow. As Syriem reached his home neighbourhood the first person he saw was Dorron, manoeuvring slowly on the other side of the street. They stared across at one another.

"You look dreadful," Syriem called over.

"Yeah, there was a gathering…" Dorron confided with a weak grin, leaning against a wall for effect. "…And I didn't get much sleep!" His bleary eyes suddenly opened wide. "What are you doing out this early?"

"Oh, you know…just clearing my head."

"I worry about you sometimes," Dorron mused.

Syriem tiptoed up to the front door. His key rattled rebelliously then the door opened with a persuasive shove. He heard his parents as he went inside. The kitchen was a picture of normality – cups and plates neatly on the table, a kettle warming gently on the stove. His mother, Sro, was fussing over pots as he entered the room.

His father, Tem, welcomed him to the table. "Didn't realise you were out last night, boy, not until this morning…"

Syriem ignored him and slouched at the table. Nothing and no one was going to spoil his day. Tem and Sro stood together, waiting for him to say something. When he finally obliged them they wished that he hadn't.

"What do you know about the Thaylin Sarra?"

His parents exchanged a fearful look that barely lasted seconds. "Not much," Tem flustered. "Them Keldies are a strange lot and best left to themselves,"

"I met one yesterday…" Syriem ventured, gauging his father's reaction.

"Oh, you don't want to get mixed up in all their nonsense," Tem turned away. "Brings nothing but trouble, you mark my words. Let fetch you some breakfast."

Syriem dragged his chair to the table and said no more, which suited his parents just fine.

At the next Thaylin Sarra meeting Isca announced that she'd met her messenger. Etta was against introducing the boy to any of the others or exposing him to their practices. He would need to understand how their faith worked in the cities – to increase the opportunities for a Righteous One to make contact; no one objected to that. But if he were to become too enamoured with their ways and especially with Isca herself, Etta had glared ominously, he might never fit back into everyday life after he had served his purpose. Isca felt a pang of conscience upon hearing that. From what she had seen, Syriem didn't fit in much anyway.

"He will do what I ask of him," she insisted.

"So be it, Isca," Etta conceded, "it rests with you now." She didn't understand Isca's intentions fully, especially about how long the Tablet would stay with the boy. Perhaps it was a test of faith for them all.

The meeting assumed a more genial air, almost like old times. Feren seized his chance with Isca the moment they were alone.

"Are you free tonight?"

She smiled and paused by the door to wait for him.

Dorron began to notice subtle changes in Syriem. As the weeks progressed Syriem seemed quieter and more self-contained, but that wasn't the whole of it. Tracked down to the library with the prospect of a double date at short notice, Syriem had barely looked up from his history book to decline. Yep, there was definitely something strange about him.

Isca structured Syriem's visits, teaching him first how to control his breathing and quieten his mind. Despite Etta's views on his education, she sought her own guidance by meditating before and after each session. Drawing upon both inner promptings and his interest, she gave him a grounding in Old Earth mythology and showed him how imagination infused with emotion could form potent mental symbols.

"But what am I doing this for, if the image is only in my head?" he bleated, when she told him again that he wasn't performing the visualisation correctly.

"Inner symbols contain power. Just try it one more time," she coaxed. "The more you do it, correctly, the stronger the symbol will become in your aura. You're find it easier then to connect with it and experience it fully."

She instructed him not to return to the market and to ignore her if he ever saw her outside. He could make up whatever tales he needed to for Dorron and his family, as long as he didn't disrespect her faith or their friendship. Whatever that left.

In between teaching Syriem, working at the market and keeping Etta appraised, Isca carved out a measure of time alone with Feren. In truth she was sometimes tempted by his offers of travel and escape. Her commitment to the Tablet took its toll. Syriem could be joyous company, but he could also be cloying and exhausting. His progress was sporadic and unpredictable; one session he might astonish her with some flippant insight, only to completely undermine it later by an emotional outburst.

She thanked the Gods for Feren's understanding and for a month or more managed a dual existence, secure in the knowledge that everyone knew their place. So it was unfortunate when Syriem chose to disobey her instructions and paid her an unscheduled visit.

The time came for Syriem when the tension between what he desired and what was apparent generated the need for action. He had deliberated on it for two days, contriving dubious justifications to sate his conscience. After all, what harm could it do to drop in on a friend?

He made the journey as late as he dared, hailing a cab and paying extra for someone to take him right into the community zone. The driver seemed genuinely concerned as he took the payment and waited for a tip.

"Are you sure you know what you're doing here, son?" At that moment a red curtain lit up in the building above them. The driver looked to Syriem and smiled. "You take care now and have a good time!"

Syriem waited at the corner until the cab reached the end of the street. He took out a torch, told himself he could use it as a weapon if need be and tried to believe it. The cloudy sky did little to reassure him, shrouding the alleys in shadow. He walked quickly, masking the torchlight in case it drew attention. Once or twice he thought he heard footsteps behind him and didn't wait to find out.

The courtyard had a hollow, depleted atmosphere. He found his way to the tree in the semi-darkness and stood by the trunk. As he turned he could just discern the outline of the dog, lurking by the stairs. It suddenly occurred to him that it might not let him pass. He swore under his breath, distraught to think he might have made it so far only to founder at the last obstacle. In desperation he decided to put his lessons to the test.

He regulated his breathing, allowing his mind to filter out the static of his thoughts, closing off all points of focus except the dog. After a few cycles, with the cold wind grasping at his skin, he brought to mind one of the mental symbols of protection. He poured all his focus and belief into the image of a bright blue pentacle flaming at his heart. A part of him still thought the idea was dubious, but it was a better option than trying to rush the dog.

Gradually the dog turned its head, offsetting its gaze. Syriem held his ground; he wasn't ready to advance, but he could feel the heat in his chest and beads of sweat at his forehead. The dog got up and moved a short distance away.

Syriem crossed the space, looking for some recognition in those pale, jewelled eyes as he passed – a futile quest. He wanted to run, but he restrained himself, mounting each stair deliberately, all the while half-expecting the dog to come crashing after him. He trod with care to dull the sounds; he wanted this to be a complete surprise.

Finally he was at her door. He straightened his jacket and tapped in staccato. Isca was slow to respond, checking his identity and mumbling in whispers before she opened the door.

"*What are you doing here?*"

He stared, tongue-tied, glimpsing the glow of the fire from the doorway.

"Well, you'd better come in," she relented, turning her back to him.

He went inside and closed the door. At first he thought it was the incense that made the room feel different, but he soon realised it was more than that. On the opposite side of the fire, and now in full view, a man was warming himself. Syriem met his smile. Maybe it was a trick of the light, but the features seemed to take on a triumphant glare.

Syriem swallowed. He suddenly felt very small; an insect duly crushed.

"I'll be off now, Isca; it looks like you have things to do," Feren nodded at Syriem, who stood to one side to let him pass.

"You don't have to..." she sighed, her disappointment palpable.

Syriem wasted no time in claiming Feren's space by the fire.

Feren faced Isca at the door. "Soon," he kissed her softly on the lips and the forehead.

"Soon," she reciprocated, with an intimacy that pierced Syriem like a blade.

He held his breath as their lips touched and then looked away. She didn't speak again until she'd closed the door. The light in her eyes had darkened.

"You had *no* right coming here. You were not invited."

"*No right?*" he repeated, enraged by his own insignificance. "Well, I'm sorry if I spoiled your romantic evening. Though come to think of it, aren't you supposed to be single?"

"How dare you, *Syriem*," she fashioned his name into a curse. "What I do with my time and who I spend it with is none of your business."

For a few seconds she felt nothing but a vague sense of contempt. However did she come to live like this? A Hybrolen priestess called to account by a Tarsien! The sooner she completed her work with him, the sooner she'd be free... She cut her thoughts dead, shocked by her own lack of self-control.

"Why did you come here tonight?"

"I wanted to see you..." his voice fell flat. "I thought I'd surprise you."

"Maybe this was necessary," she reasoned; "it's about time we cleared the air."

Syriem sat and braved the storm, listening to her measured tone as she told him the bitter truth. That she was not there to fulfil any romantic fantasy for him, nor was she obligated to him in any way. He was there because he had a purpose to serve, and if he couldn't accept that he'd best think about why he was there at all. But whatever he did, he would not intrude upon her private life again.

Her insights into his shortcomings tore into him. He said nothing the whole time, staring ahead as if he couldn't quite believe it was happening. And when he felt that his heart would shatter, he lunged at the door and ran down the stairs into the courtyard.

His first instinct was to go to the tree, which made no sense at all. So he staggered through the alleyways, tormented beyond endurance. As the rain began to fall all his anguish and pain surged through in a great banshee wail. He didn't care if anyone saw or heard him. She had hurt him – she of all people – and he would never forget it. The weather turned against him, as if to punish his weakness, which only served to harden his soul.

At first Syriem's fury shielded him and drove him deeper within himself. For three weeks he avoided anywhere he associated with Isca, including the library. Dorron welcomed him back with open arms. Syriem didn't say much about the cause, but then he didn't have to. Dorron had heard enough rhetoric over the last couple of months to recognise that his friend had got into dangerous waters.

Dorron had missed him; they shared a common history and you couldn't put a price on that. He took every opportunity to tell him that he'd had a lucky escape from those dangerous Keldies. And, like any good Tarsien, he had a ready-made solution to ease his friend's troubles. "Get drunk and get laid."

Syriem threw himself into the part, accompanying Dorron on nightly forays to the less salubrious Treasure House bars in the sector. His parents breathed a little easier when he came home drunk or didn't come home at all. On the surface, things had settled into a once familiar rhythm. But once or twice, when Dorron was late, Syriem found himself with time to kill. He fell back upon the exercises, controlling his breathing and focusing on a symbol or quality. So that by the time Dorron arrived he'd be in *one of those moods*. It was a warning of sorts; a sign of what was to follow. The first time that Syriem didn't show up as planned, Dorron knew he'd lost him to *them* and that all his dire warnings had gone unheeded.

"Don't get involved, Syriem," Dorron had insisted. "Once they've get hold of you, they'll gnaw away until there's nothing left – remember Sedran."

Sedran had achieved notoriety by joining a Thaylin Sarra sect. It had started with an innocent conversation on a street corner, no more than politeness. And where had it got him? Living as a pauper, his head shaven like a mark of shame – an embarrassment to family and friends. But Syriem wouldn't listen to that, oh no. He had an explanation, said that Sedran had joined an extreme faction. What did Syriem know? They could be fattening him up with lies, ready for the kill. So Dorron mourned for his friend the only way he knew how, with a large drink, and left him to his fate.

Syriem crouched low in the park, pressing his palms into the damp ground as he gazed across at the trees; the same trees that he and Dorron had climbed as children. He remembered one time when he'd fallen from a branch, while rising to a dare. Dorron had brought him home, bruised and bloodied like an honoured veteran.

And what of the present? The last three weeks had tempered his resentment and he was reconciled to the situation. He'd been hasty, turning up at Isca's unannounced; he could see that now. He mulled over all that she had said, reviewing every painful detail. An insight came to him in the stillness of the park, a flash of memory so intense that he stumbled forward to the wet grass – something she'd said in the heat of the moment: *You have a purpose to serve...*

He smiled for the first time in days and wiped the moisture from his face. A vague plan began to form – one that would sustain him until he could regain her respect. There was no sense in going back if things hadn't changed; he needed a means of demonstrating that he'd learned something.

With renewed focus the mental exercises took on an added dimension. Some symbols generated secondary symbols that reappeared in his dreams. He worked diligently, retiring to his room after meals or heading off to the park when the weather was good. Once he felt that his foundations were secure, he wrote an apology and took it to the market. But the sight of the dog reminded him that she had sworn him from meeting her in public. So he ventured into the community zone and posted it under her door. He held back nothing in his letter, acknowledging both his own limitations and his intent to progress beyond them. He hoped it would be enough.

It still wouldn't do though to just turn up on her doorstep again. He needed a sign that couldn't be misinterpreted. And in his own way he wanted to test her. She'd made such a point about the reality of the mental images as *a language for higher consciousness*, something he'd also read in one of the pamphlets, that it seemed the obvious method of reaching her.

The first visualisations were clumsy and poorly structured, leading to an afternoon doze in one case and a rather suspect fantasy in another. He learned from his failures and set aside a regular time when he was less likely to be distracted, preparing himself before each attempt at contact. Here again there was progress, but his untamed body rebelled against the enforced stillness. Then he tried different postures and added a simple candle for focus – never doubting that Isca would receive his contact through the symbols. What he hadn't figured out was how she'd communicate back to him.

The answer came in a dream. He found the courtyard shrouded in darkness, much like the last time he had left her. But now the great tree was in fruit – laden with translucent, coloured orbs. She was standing beside the tree and all he had to do was cross a line of stones. But each time he lifted a foot over something held him back. Three nights he had the dream; three different seasons, but always the same bountiful tree.

He meditated before bed on the fourth night, focusing on a blue pentacle at his heart. This time the dream was different; he found himself trapped in a nightmare journey through the alleyways, pushing past the destitute and tormented as they cried out after him. Then he was racing, faster and faster, almost gliding above the ground. He reached the courtyard without slowing and tripped over the line of stones. As he hit the ground he realised he was dreaming.

He stood up slowly, taking in the dreamscape. All was still. He felt his entire body pulsating and lifted a hand, turning it in the night air to catch the silvery tinge of moonlight. But where was the moon? He looked over and saw it hanging from the tree like a silver apple. Above it was the golden peach of the sun. And then, like a wondrous candelabra, the tree burst into full fruit and all its coloured spheres shone like jewels.

Isca appeared from behind the tree. She said nothing, but held out a hand in invitation, touching her forehead and her lips. He copied the gesture and saw a blue glow at her heart.

The sense of certainty was still with him the next morning. Every fibre of his being told him that his experience had been real. At breakfast, he told his parents that he'd be home late.

Tem nodded, thinking well of their son for his consideration. "You see," he whispered to Sro, "I told you we were worrying over nothing. He's fine now."

Syriem walked steadily along the alleyways, projecting different symbols against an imagined column of light along his spine. In the courtyard, he paused at the tree and let his fingertips caress the bark. A fleeting sense of connection seemed to pulse through the trunk. Then the spell was broken and he could delay no longer, hurriedly climbing the stairs to the thumping rhythm of his heart. A knock on the door drew no response. Bolstered by an unshakeable faith in his dream, he slowly turned the doorknob and entered.

The room reflected a new sense of order, all books and papers tidied away; even the rug had been replaced by a great oval of woven blue.

"Let us continue," she called from the kitchen. "Sit down – I'll be with you in a moment."

He sat and listened for her voice, eagerly anticipating some sort of acknowledgement. She put the cups down and rested her hand lightly on his shoulder, as if he'd been out on an errand and not absent for weeks.

"You got my letter?"

"I received all of your communications," she said, eliciting a broad smile. "It took courage to be so honest with me – and with yourself;

that shows character. And Syriem, you should know that I would never willingly hurt you if it could be avoided."

He blew out a breath. "I probably deserved it."

"Maybe," she narrowed her eyes, matching his tone.

"But maybe not?"

She laughed, her voice rising and falling like the rush of a stream, and the awkwardness evaporated. She begged to hear what he'd been up to during his absence and listened without judgement as he related his adventures with Dorron. For his part, Syriem felt no desire to ask about *her* private life; he was just relieved to find her alone.

"I want you to know that I'm still committed. I realise what I've been missing."

She sat back, contented. It pleased her that he had returned at all, but especially so that he had come back hungry. The Guardian had been right – working on him at a magical level had yielded results.

They talked as they used to, with Syriem asking questions while she gave him the answers she thought he could cope with. Tonight he wanted to focus on the different strands of the Thaylin Sarra faith and the core teachings. She was so enthralled by his enthusiasm that for a while his intentions eluded her. She fell into his plan, explaining how the Thaylin Sarra faith took elements from Old Earth traditions. In the Cities, the symbols of the cross, the stars and the crescent tended to dominate. While in the Settlements, surrounded by the natural world, other symbols held sway: stones, trees and animals, sacred wells and holy fires. She surmised that much of the old wisdom was lost and what remained was at best fragmented. Seldom had she felt so relaxed or so talkative.

"I really want to learn more," he said, accidentally setting a pentagram at his forehead. The symbol flared in his aura for an instant and he brushed at his fringe, unaware. She noted the star without comment.

"Very well; I will teach you more of the Low Arts," she agreed, easing forward in the chair to watch his delight.

His eyes took on the glazed look from the market, as if some deep, dark memory had consumed him. When he blinked back from it, something had shifted.

"I have a proposition for you," he struggled to form the words. "You need me for this *purpose* you once spoke of – I'd like something in return."

She raised an eyebrow at his insolence. "Have I not already offered you more than you are entitled to?"

"We both know I don't belong in their world," he cast a lazy hand to the door. "I need to learn from you, so that when you're done with me I'll have something left for myself."

She wanted to tell him he had nothing to fear, but she'd promised herself she would never lie to him. "I'm not sure I can do that, Syri. Such knowledge brings its own responsibilities." She wondered what Etta would make of *this* development. "Let me consult the sticks."

She passed over the sticks, certain that he wouldn't object. He held them briefly and knelt by the table, content to leave the matter to a higher power. Her mood grew more sombre as the sticks revealed their guidance. Each casting lent credibility to Syriem's petition until, at the fourth, the form of the Messenger lay before her once again.

"It is agreed," her jaw tightened. "I will give you the knowledge that I see fit to teach you, by your readiness, of both the Low Arts and the High Arts. But mark me well, Syriem, there are conditions."

"Go on," he held her gaze.

"Magic – for magic *is* my way – is not for the faint of heart or weak of will. The things that I will share with you are normally passed only between Thaylin Sarra initiates. *No one* must know the source of your knowledge or of our agreement. And you can never be received into the faith – that path is barred to you.

"If you give your consent tonight, your fate will be to become a part of everything, yet belong to nothing. This night you will die and be reborn, if that is what you truly want. Do you understand? Think carefully, Syriem, for I will not offer this pact a second time."

He searched his heart and knew that his place was with her, for however long it lasted and wherever it led him. "I willingly accept that fate," he replied solemnly.

"As you will," she acknowledged, closing her eyes and bowing her head.

"Will I receive an initiation?"

"You just have, Syriem," she said gravely; "you just have."

chapter 4
BEHOLDEN

ETTA AND THE other Thaylin Sarra never learned of Isca's arrangement; Feren too was spared that burden. At times it seemed like madness to Isca, letting Syriem share her heritage with no guarantee of how he would use the knowledge. Still, she had given her word – the word of a Hybrolen Twiceborn – and she was set to that. Secretly, she'd been impressed. He was wise, intuiting that he'd be empty without her, for there *would* come a time when he'd be alone.

Syriem rose to the challenge. Under her watchful tutelage, he learned to develop his potential and began to assimilate the shadow aspect of his nature. She taught him that it was a source of both power and fear, and that each could be a reflection of the other. Pain and joy were neither sought nor avoided; each was simply a path to understanding. She spared him nothing. Every time he set his heart upon her, she broke it. And every time she healed him, he was more complete than the last.

He read voraciously, thirsting for knowledge. She slaked his craving with selected passages and texts, some of them borrowed from other Thaylin Sarra. All fed the flame within him, but nothing hinted at a direction or outcome. That piece of the puzzle lay solely, and tantalisingly, with Isca. As the weeks went by, he filled notebooks with inner journeys, dreams and conclusions. They acted as a bridge between the two worlds he inhabited. The more he immersed himself in the one, the more he found stability and meaning in the other.

Isca sometimes met him in Keres Park, where Ces Frayer's statue loomed over them like a curse. Yet, for some reason Syriem could never fathom, Isca insisted the place was sacred. It was there that she showed him how to make the first elemental contact with Earth.

He'd arrived at dawn and waited by the statue. It had a brooding presence despite the perpetual glow of the lights around it. Only when she emerged from the trees, with the dog at her side, did he realise that she'd been watching him. She smiled, touching her lips to command silence as she drew him into the undergrowth. A circle was already marked in the soil, large enough for two people. He took the space opposite her and closed his eyes, allowing each in-breath to sink deep within, and each out-breath to radiate from him like a sphere of intent. He felt the soft, yielding earth receive him as a prodigal son, reinstating a connection with the rhythms of life and nature.

Isca waited and at some subtle signal placed a crystal in each of his hands: a smooth, round stone in the left and a harsh, angular specimen in the right. He gripped them and straightened his spine.

"Relax," she lowered his hands to his knees. "Let your consciousness take you forward."

He listened for her breathing and adjusted his own to match. The stones vibrated gently or it may have been his hands   he couldn't tell which. His mind conjured up explanations, but he kept the flow and accepted any images or feelings without reacting to them. As his responses subsided, the Earth enveloped him, closing around him in inky blackness. Breath and breath and breath. A slow, steady pulse arose, like the heartbeat of the world, louder and louder, crushing his eardrums until he thought the sound would destroy him. Then he plunged back into primordial stillness; no longer separate, no longer alone...

Snap. A sound broke through. He felt his own frantic heartbeat, shocking him awake. He opened his eyes to find Isca outside the circle, resting against a tree trunk.

"How was that?" she stood up and brushed her hands clean.

"Instructive," he replied quietly, noticing the broken branch by her feet.

They returned to her home, where she gave him some flatcakes and an infusion to bring the heat back into his body. Then he slept by the fire for an hour or so while she sat beside him, making notes and watching over him.

She continued working with the phases of the moon, seeking out opportunities to unite him with the other three mundane elements: a pond for Water, a wasteland pyre for Fire and the library's breezy rooftop for Air. Each served as an elemental initiation, a magical experience without the rigidity of Thaylin Sarra tradition. She found the shift refreshing, trusting her intuition and acting spontaneously to meet her needs as his guide.

Syriem changed almost imperceptibly, as the days wove around their pact like the twin serpents of a caduceus. He steadily gained greater control of his mind and his tongue; only the occasional chaos of his emotions threatened his equilibrium. Yet despite their time together, he still had no inkling of his purpose; and desiring only to serve her, he asked nothing.

The day of Syriem's eighteenth birthday marked a turning point. It started that morning with talk of aunts and uncles and the family gathering that evening. Given the choice he would have skipped the event, but his parents were proud people and he knew that they wanted to do well by him. As he entered the kitchen, his mother was well into her baking campaign.

"I've made special ones for you," she whispered, "without mutton in them."

He was eating less meat now and had cut out alcohol, although given the disastrous effect it had on him that was no great sacrifice. He cared little what conclusions his parents drew from his behaviour though he was certain they disapproved.

Tem cleared his throat – a sure sign that a speech was coming. "From today you are a man in the eyes of the world, Syriem. Make sure you carry yourself with dignity and never bring shame upon us."

An odd choice of words, Syriem thought, and the undertone did not escape him. He nodded agreeably and called to mind one of the power symbols, mentally projecting it. Tem flinched a little and broke eye contact. Syriem returned to his breakfast.

When Dorron had turned eighteen, a few months back, his parents hired out a Treasure House. Syriem had opted for a quiet affair, if he had to endure any festivities at all. It was *their* day really – Tem and Sro – and while he appreciated their efforts, the only thing on his mind was how Isca would mark the day.

He took his time getting to the courtyard, enjoying the delicious sense of anticipation. The steps were unguarded; lately the dog seemed to accept his presence without much interest. He climbed the stairs at a gallop and knocked on the door before he'd caught his breath.

She greeted him with her usual combination of warmth and detachment. On the table was a small package, wrapped in handmade paper and bearing his name. "It's yours," she told him.

He lifted the parcel and turned it over, checking each glyph to see if there were any he didn't recognise. Then he removed the knot and unravelled the paper to discover a narrow, clear shaft of crystal.

"I thought you might use it for focusing."

She shuddered a little as he embraced her, not that he noticed. It was less distinct than a vision, more a sense of his future grief. She broke free and ushered him back to the table. "While I can't compete with your mother's cooking, I think you'll find it's edible!"

"So what's planned for today?" he asked with a glint in his eye, keenly aware that they would be working on the fifth element of Ether.

Isca completed a silent blessing. Syriem had just completed an elemental initiation of Ether, known by some as Spirit, the fifth and final point on the star. He exhaled a long, luxurious out-breath as the subtle energy infused his being. Then she drew him safely back to awareness and sensed his aura. He saw nothing himself, but he felt impulses and patterns moving around him like shifting dances of force and form. When she was satisfied that the final energy pattern had set its reflection within him, she showed him how to re-open the fifth auric seal with an appropriate symbol and then how to close all the energy centres again.

She made him repeat the practice, talking her through what he felt and intuited with each symbol. When the exercise was over, they reviewed his progress together and he read aloud from his notebook. She listened for a long time; her patience and dedication had borne fruit. It was time to reveal the path she had trained him for.

"You know that I have prepared you for a purpose of my design."

He turned the crystal on the table, following the ripples of energy around her as she spoke.

"The path you have followed is of great importance to the faith. I am guided in a way that is very different from other Thaylin Sarra," she explained warily. "Part of that guidance has been to prepare a *messenger* for the coming Righteous One. That messenger is you."

She sank back into her chair, freed from her burden at last. Syriem received her revelation with a look of abject disappointment. She sensed a measure of resistance, which surprised her, and stressed the importance of his role. He heard her words through a fog of indifference; it was far less than he'd hoped for.

"You don't believe me?"

"It's not that…exactly," he squirmed, drawing his hands around the crystal for comfort. "Just…from everything I've learned so far, I could be waiting a long time."

"You are twice blessed," she laughed; "you have the benefit of the teachings without the faith to constrain you. I've never lied to you, Syriem, not even when it may have hurt us both. So believe me when I tell you that the Righteous One *will* come soon; it has been foretold."

He closed his eyes and took himself back to the day in the library when he'd found the leaflets. He knew so much more now, understood their ways better than he understood his own family. Maybe he didn't want to believe in a Righteous One, not if it meant everything he treasured would end. He sniffed, recalling that few Thaylin Sarra settled outside the faith. But if he wasn't an outsider…

"No, it is forbidden," she banged the table. "Look, this may not be what you want, Syriem, but it's what is asked of you. Your greatest strength lies in your *separation* from the faith. It leaves your True Will open to ways of being that would be unimaginable to them."

"*My* True Will?" He relished the idea, imagining himself an integral part of some great plan. An idea surfaced from the mire of his thoughts. That once he'd fulfilled his obligations to this *Righteous One*, he'd be free to do as he pleased. He'd keep his word about never joining the faith, but there was nothing to stop him striking out on his own. Maybe he could use the crystal in some way to find her again. He glanced up as she spread the cards out for another lesson. Had he taken it for granted she would leave him?

She beckoned him over and he succumbed, surrendering to the moment. He shuffled the cards, passing them to her as if he were offering a part of himself. She watched the intensity in his eyes and wondered what the coming months would make of him. They worked on the card spread together, moving through the interpretation; first he shared what he'd surmised and then she showed him how to go deeper.

Mindful of his demeanour she kept her focus on mundane aspects of his life, mentioning a work opportunity that would expand his horizons in the future. He told her that he already knew about a beneficial change to his shift pattern at the Cargo Plant and wondered aloud whether she had worked some magic on his behalf. She denied it and curtly reminded him that the Arts were not to be squandered on worldly needs.

When the reading concluded he sat back and gazed up at the painted doors above the fireplace, lost in his own realisations. Those last few months were the happiest he'd ever known. And she had become such a focal point that he couldn't imagine life without her.

"What are you thinking?" she probed, aware of the auric flashes around his solar plexus.

He glanced back and she shook her head in friendly disapproval.

"Be mindful where you put your focus!" She reformed the pack, giving it a shuffle before passing it over. "Do you feel an affinity with the cards?"

"I think so. I enjoy using the sticks, but the cards speak to me more clearly. I get drawn in by the images."

"Then you shall have a set of your own, some day," she promised, enjoying the etheric display as tiny beads of energy shot out from him in all directions.

He spread the deck, face down, setting seven cards out in a line. Then he let his hand hover above each one in turn, allowing impressions to form, all the while conscious of Isca's scrutiny. He wondered what Dorron would say if he could see him and then decided that he didn't care any

more. In fact, he wasn't sure that he cared about many things except…
He lowered his hand and turned over a card that called to him: it was The
High Priestess.

It was early evening by the time Syriem finally showed his face at home.
The reception from his parents was muted, but he knew they wouldn't
make a fuss in front of guests.

"Too long at the Treasure House, eh?" his uncle bellowed, slapping
Syriem hard on the back. "Still not too tall – and not much meat on you –
that'll be your father's blood. We don't breed 'em big, just wiry!"

Syriem took a drink and turned his thoughts to the day that had been.
Meantime, everyone remarked on how much he had changed. The aunts
chattered, urging their daughters to come and talk to him. They were
more interested in his friend Dorron that they had heard so much about
– Dorron, who hadn't managed to turn up. He marvelled at their dulled
senses; had he come so far from such beginnings?

Tem and Sro glanced over, watching him as he sat among strangers.
When he'd arrived back late, smelling of incense and with his attention
elsewhere, they knew all too well what he'd been up to. They threw him
forced smiles, tipping their glasses as proud hosts, but they knew. And
they dealt with it the best way they could, by not dealing with it at all.

Syriem's new work shifts came into effect within a few days of his birthday.
It meant earlier starts, but the upside was being able to see Isca some
afternoons. A pity then that the job itself was unchanged.

He glanced up at the clock adorning Loading Bay Four, the great casing
shouldered by the words: *Frayer Transit and Cargo – Journeys without
End*. All around him the huge Transvector cargo vehicles waited, their red
and grey livery splattered with mud and filth. Fresh in from the northern
cities and parked up, ready for the next morning when Syriem would
once again begin his shift by cleaning every last one of them.

Finally, the clock chimed; all vehicles accounted for and their transit
teams away to the nearest Treasure House. He touched the body panels and
closed his eyes, running his fingers through lines of dirt that contoured
like the winds that had deposited them. In a few, quiet breaths he opened
his mind to impressions from the journey. He glimpsed foreign vistas in
his imagination, reaching out to a wider world that he yearned for. But
as soon as his concentration dropped, his mind plummeted back to life
in Tarsis.

He opened his eyes and etched a tiny symbol in the dirt with his
fingernail. Time to go – Isca would be waiting for him. He hurried
through the gate and headed across town with a small bag of fruit under

his jacket, purchased from a driver. She had assured him that the fruit had come all the way from Variz City State – a fitting gift.

The dog wasn't waiting in the courtyard, but he didn't feel unduly concerned. He leapt up the loose-boarded steps and tried the door. It was unlocked; the place was deserted and the grate empty. He slumped into a chair; she should have been there – it was *his* time.

He awoke later to the creak of the door and the dull thud of paws. Isca affected a tired, indifferent smile. He could see that she'd been crying; even the dog seemed subdued. She flung a newspaper at him without speaking, her face etched with sadness. He scanned the folded page and thought it strange somehow that she would read newspapers.

A man's body had been found in Sirn City. It had been apparent, the brief column of print revealed, that the victim had belonged to one of the sects that were becoming so prevalent in the city states.

"I knew him," she whispered; "he was someone close to me, once."

He stared back at the page, unable to bear the pain in her eyes.

"Of course they won't find anything," she gulped. "Case closed – another one of our kind for the slaughter!"

He wavered, unsure how to respond.

"Don't you *see*?" she hung her head, weighed down by grief. "He knew better than to attract attention." She steadied herself by the mantelpiece, gazing up at the little curtain malevolently. "This shouldn't have happened, not now we've followed the Guardian's bidding." She paused, aware that it had been *her* bidding too. "The man they murdered…" she choked, unable to name him, "…he knew about the Tablet."

Syriem waited, incapable of understanding and powerless to comfort her.

"Right," she calmed herself to a decision, "you have to go now. And don't give me that look…you'll get your education; my word was not lightly given."

"Nor mine," he replied sharply.

She fetched out a book and dropped it on the table. "Take this; come back when you've read it. It's time you learned about the shadow that stalks us."

Her hand struck the air like a dagger and he leapt to his feet, duly banished. He glanced back at her silhouette against the fire and thought that he'd never seen another human being so crushed by circumstance.

Syriem went straight home. The house was empty and a note waited on the kitchen table: *Gone to see relatives*. He lit a candle in his room and opened the book. It was a handwritten work, a personal reflection on *the past and the present through the precepts of the faith*. There were a few admonitions at the beginning, a call to be resolute in the face of spiritual and physical hardship, and then the body of the text unfolded.

'This book is not the truth; it is my understanding of truth. Ceaselessly have I dwelt on the matter of my faith and meditated on the teachings of my tutors. In as much as I can convey what I believe to be true, I set forth here the knowledge that I have made my own.

'This place we inhabit is the first world colonised by the children of Old Earth. It is known in our tradition as Laurasia, but The Assembly denounces such links with the past and insists on calling our world Triste.

'The past gives us our origins and our roots. This world, Laurasia, was the embodiment of hope for Old Earth and they called her the Firstborn. The Seekers of Light seeded Laurasia with their children, but the unrighteous offspring of ignorance sought to enslave them and pursued them across the vastness of space. Parva Serach taught that they navigated along the limbs of the Tree of Life, but I cannot grasp such a mystery.'

Syriem read on. A whole section was devoted to the early battles for territory and the different factions drawn into the conflict. Old Earth decided to cut her losses and abandoned her children, withholding her embrace until time had matured them. But as the generations passed, so the hostilities increased. The struggles for supremacy and survival eventually engulfed the fledgling world and plunged it into darkness. Disease and starvation followed – the cleansing of the unrighteous. Entire regions were laid waste, forcing the tribes underground or up into the mountains. Those who could not make the journey were left to endure the pestilence and decay.

And from out of the chaos and suffering, an opportunist group emerged. A curious people, who made pacts among their bloodlines and who slowly but definitively became the conquerors, turning tribe against tribe and reaping a harvest of blood – for blood was their covenant. Their ways were strange and they worshipped low forms, always under cover in the secret places. They came together from different traditions with a common purpose – dominion. And they took a new, tribal name to unite them: Frayer.

Under their guidance the first, great City of Armageddon was rebuilt by slaves and renamed Tarsis. Then came the new laws – a bastardisation of justice to exercise control. One of these was the First Criteria – a heinous document that identified the unworthy and the unsightly, banishing them from the cities without trial. A new order swiftly arose.

At a time when the high walls had yet to be secured, the Frayer clan divided and infiltrated every city. There they used hidden knowledge and the sciences, working their way into the heart of each fragile democracy.

Eventually every City State, Territory, Outpost and Protectorate came under their hegemony. The Cuprad Treaty Council, once so instrumental in bringing about a measure of peace, became the Cuprad Frayer Treaty Council. The poison spread deeply and within two generations the CFTC had mutated into The Assembly. No one spoke about the CFTC after that.

There was, however, one City that did not fall to the barbarians. It was known by many titles, including M'Qar, Sarrell and The Blessed. It had long remained hidden, awaiting the Restitution when a Righteous One would lead the faithful home.

Syriem knew of the claims for Sarrell. How it was in the world and yet removed from it, awaiting revelation. He'd learned too of the legendary figures in its history – an account at odds with official records. The book carried its own sparse chronology, referring to envoys from Sarrell who reached the Variz region and the fate that befell them. Then there was a long gap in the years and another reference to Parva Serach the Sage, who formulated the Thaylin Sarra beliefs into the beginnings of a unified faith. Her capture and martyrdom, it was said, had been the catalyst for the spreading of the Word by her four Companions.

He put the book down and rubbed at his temples. His mind ached; there was so much to take in. He closed his eyes, entered the rhythm of his breath and allowed the imagery of the book to lead him.

Faded towers from a forgotten Variz welcomed him. He drifted dreamily above the marbled minarets and watched a setting sun splayed red gold across the landscape. He viewed it from a cocoon of detachment, until he heard the first cries. Then the world below became a grey chasm, pulling him to his doom. He plummeted, twisted and spun by scenes of devastation and massacre – a kaleidoscope of suffering that spanned the generations until the intensity of it all overwhelmed him.

The surroundings gradually come into focus and consciousness is restored. He looks around, mystified. Sheer sides of a cavern have risen up like waves of molten rock, as if to seal the tomb. How did he come here? A dream perhaps? If so, it is more vivid than almost any dream he has ever known.

Impressions flood in. He is Syriem and yet he is not Syriem – both present and witness. Shouting reverberates around him; boots quickstep into the distance. For the first time he sees the lights fixed into the cavern walls, raining down an eerie, jaundiced glow. Water seeps from fissures in the rock, spilling on to the cave floor in steady splatters. The air reeks of fear. He presses himself behind a stone and the moist, glistening rock is cold against his skin. He shivers, touching sponge mould that speckles the rock in tiny, orange starbursts. Other senses awaken. Voices grow louder; a cacophony of tongues in a sinister chorus and a single voice that tugs at his soul. He moves closer, compelled to be near her and unwittingly sets the drama in motion.

She lies on the ground, lost in agonies. Her limbs are outstretched, making a star pattern on the ground; her voice lost in a never-ending rhythm, incessantly invoking a Deity that has apparently forsaken her. He crawls closer, unaware that his movements are silent to all except her. She ceases her litany and turns. Their faces meet and eyes of fire flash back to Syriem in the shadows. For an instant there is an incomprehensible recognition. He flinches, petrified that she will expose him, but she offers only wisdom in the exchange – he need have no fear, save for the past. Her hand stretches towards him, the bruised and bloody fingers pressed together in invocation. He feels her presence and knows intuitively that she is in touch with tremendous forces. That she chooses not to make use of them only deepens the mystery and the tragedy.

She struggles to her feet, uncurling her battered body in an arc of metamorphosis. Then she looks straight at Syriem and smiles. He shrinks from her gaze, unable to receive her love and overcome with remorse. He presses his face tightly to the stone in an effort to shut out sensations, but there is no escape from the final scene. She offers a sign of blessing to the soldiers, which they scorn. Her voice is sonorous and clear, imbued with an unshakeable confidence.

"You have ordered me to speak and I shall. Not because you wish it, but because a higher authority demands it. I bring you this truth. You are blinded by your own vision! In seizing me you have not prevented the Restitution, you have merely become instruments in the inevitable. A tree does not suffer the loss of one blossom; the Great Work will continue through my Companions – you have secured that by my martyrdom. The Covenant will be fulfilled; it cannot be otherwise. Therefore, do what thou wilt."

She crosses her arms over her chest in the sign of the slain, to show that she has accepted her path. But whatever they do now, they do so in awareness of their actions. The soldiers step back and draw weapons; they no more accept the sanctity of her life than they do the continuation of her existence. Still she tries to offer them hope.

"You are inheritors of a dying world. Yet this day you shall commence upon the path of personal restitution. So shall it be."

She looks to Syriem and he acknowledges her, bowing his head low. Then he turns abruptly, aware of other presences behind him in the cavern. She touches her heart and speaks her final words. "The future and the present are met, with the past the womb of all."

The soldiers look towards Syriem, seeing nothing, and the charge is solemnly read out.

"Parva Serach, you are sentenced to death."

She smiles at the impossibility of their decree. Then she raises her hands and faces them defiantly, her head tilted upwards. Sensations overlap. Shots are fired, a woman cries out in liberation and Syriem runs forward, shrieking like an avenging angel. But before he can get to her, white fire consumes the scene.

Syriem wrenched awake in a violent spasm. His breath came in laboured reaches, his heart straining against the remnants of a vision. "*What the hell was that?*" he asked aloud. The candle flame swayed reassuringly. "I should have prepared better," he scolded himself and reached under his pillow for Isca's crystal.

The book was on the bed; its open pages filled with the sayings of Parva Serach the Sage. He closed it sharply. Then he reached for his journal and started making rough sketches in hurried, baroque strokes, augmenting what he'd witnessed with observations and comments. When he reached the part where the woman had died, he couldn't see the page for tears.

Across town Isca closed down the temple and extinguished her candles one by one. She had cleared a path for Syriem and set forces in motion to work their own way through him.

The next morning he was still preoccupied by his dream. He reread his notes; there were specifics about uniforms and colours, even a rough description of Parva Serach herself. His first instinct was to go straight to Isca and share his revelation. But he'd barely started reading the book; better to wait and present her with *all* his conclusions. In the meantime, the library might help him on his quest.

It took a whole morning of researching his notes and sketches, but in the end he found what he was looking for. Buried in the records was an image from his dream. A time period for the uniform was given, along with a region: Variz. A footnote made reference to military campaigns against the *Mazda'an Uprisings*, in what was then known as the Variz Territory.

Syriem returned to Isca's door, two weeks later.

"It's good to see you again," she cupped her hands together, as if she were holding something precious. While she had enjoyed the freedom to continue with her own magical work, she had missed him too. "I trust you found the book instructive," she broke the silence, deciding that he had stared at her for long enough.

He nodded, suddenly serious. "It's given me a lot to think about." He opened his notebook and starting reading aloud.

She leaned back and listened, as he described the sights and sounds of his encounter.

"Your emotional responses tell us as much as your visions. Feelings in dreams both shape reality and reflect it."

He frowned, wary of sounding too self-assured. "There's more; I did some research on the things I saw."

"*Feel* you saw," she corrected him.

He unfolded the ripped out journal papers for her inspection.

"May I keep these?" she swallowed, setting the pages out of his reach.

He smiled at the way that she stared at the sketches, but his composure did not last long. "So the book – is it all true?" he faltered. "Because then that would mean…"

"That things are not what they seem?" she countered, receiving her book back from him. "The contents are true, in the main; certainly everything about the Frayers, though I imagine you find that hard to believe. As for the rest – you'll have to decide for yourself."

"Do you think that Parva Serach actually looked like she did in my dream?"

"Hard to say; no authenticated pictures of her survive. Likewise, little is known about her martyrdom – all the accounts are secondary."

"So it *may* have happened that way?"

She reached over and touched the sketches. "Look, Syriem, it's important that you understand what the Thaylin Sarra believe and why they are persecuted. But there are *many* truths. Don't get caught up in any one view of the world."

Syriem picked up on her reply. "You said *they*."

"Did I?" she coughed self-consciously. "By bringing you into my life I have set myself apart from the faith; I have sacrificed a lifetime of tradition to serve my True Will. And I have since learned that all paths are valid."

"Serve the One through the Many; Serve the Many through the One," he quoted aloud, to her evident delight.

"Indeed," she raised the book in the air. "And now that you've got that clear, this has served its purpose." Before he could react, she took a couple of steps and tossed the book on to the fire.

He watched as the withered pages surrendered to the flames. "Why?" he lamented, catching glimpses of the faded colours as they burned.

"It has served its purpose. Better never to outlast one's purpose."

He stared at the fire, overwhelmed by the implications.

"Always remember, Syriem, that what we do here matters. Everything I have told you is the truth; and when the Righteous One arrives, you will understand that more fully than I could ever show you." Her voice trailed off, smothered by the pain that surfaced whenever he looked at her that way.

"Must you go?" he searched her eyes for a glimmer of hope, but she had none there to find.

"Hush," she touched his arm. "I don't belong in Tarsis; I came here for a reason and I have fulfilled that purpose. My True Will guides me now. But I promise you that you'll be protected in the times to come," she whispered, as if that were some consolation.

"I could still come with you."

"That would do no good, as you well know. You must walk the path before you."

"Who will I share my dreams with?" he closed his eyes against the tears.

She put her arms around him and spoke in a whisper, breathing softly on his eyelids. "I cannot diminish your suffering, Syriem. It will be difficult for you, but I have given you something more enduring than pain. The Unseen Ones will not desert you, not when your True Will burns bright. I owe you a great debt and I grieve at the prospect of our parting."

"Then why leave me?" he pushed against her arms, but she held him fast and they clung together like leaves in a storm.

Stillness descended, cocooning them from the world. It was the closest thing that Isca had felt recently to the Guardian's blessing and she wept for the joy of it, anointing his forehead with her tears. The moment didn't last, for magic is often powerful and fleeting. And when it had subsided, they were just two scared and lonely people holding each other close.

"I'll walk you back," she smoothed his face. She felt confused; suddenly he was more than a mere tool for her Art. "Please," she insisted, "I want to see where you live – just this once."

The night was clear and the waxing moon sat heavy in the sky like a fading lantern. They walked together in silence, the dog a few paces behind her. Upon reaching his door, she leaned forward and kissed him on the forehead and the lips, and he reciprocated. His wounded smile hurt so much that she had to turn away, calling her goodbyes behind her.

He span round and tumbled into some rubbish bins. A neighbour shouted obscenities, but he didn't care – right that moment, he felt liberated. In the distance, Isca pulled her collar up and headed back for another night's work, surprised to find tears in her eyes again.

Etta had made the journey at Isca's request. She was waiting in the courtyard, her face as stern as winter. "So, is it true?" she harried her.

"Have you compromised your feelings for an outsider? Will you tell me that this too is the Guardian's Will?"

"I cannot say, Mother," Isca called the dog to her side. "But I have something to show you that may change your view of our messenger."

"Believe me, my child, nothing will alter my opinion," she followed her upstairs.

Etta pored over the scrawled notes and drawings for a long time. "It… proves nothing," she broke eye contact. "Be certain whose voice you are answering, Isca; the Enemy will use any means at its disposal."

Isca was suddenly struck by a terrible revelation. Faced with the possibility that the Restitution was actually upon them, Etta had retreated into dogma. "I know where my loyalties lie."

"And if it breaks the boy?" Etta locked eyes with her.

"Then so be it. I will meet the debt personally."

chapter 5
INHERITANCE

SYRIEM WOKE AT first light, numbed by the previous day's excesses. He reached for the crystal and laid it flat against his forehead. Suitably focused, he circulated energy through his body by using visualising different symbols – a little ritual he'd made up – and slowly dragged himself from the covers. He was on a late shift at the Plant, but he planned to leave the house early to avoid a confrontation. The night before, when he'd gone inside, the atmosphere had seethed – a brooding pressure that he could only escape through sleep. Now he'd need his wits about him if he wanted to get out unchallenged.

As he pushed the kitchen door, they faced him from across the table like an inquisition. Tem and Sro sat together, hands entwined. Their sallow faces appealed to him to say something, anything to break the stalemate silence between them. He shifted to one corner of the kitchen, marking out his territory, and silently recited a mantra of protection.

"Come and sit down," Sro said, more of a plea than a request. "We need to have a talk."

He recognised the tone from childhood and hunched his shoulders as he drew up a chair.

"You've been associating with Keldies," she confronted him. "There's no sense denying it; folk round here have been talking about little else." She crossed her arms.

He stayed silent, certain there was more to come. His mother didn't disappoint him.

"At first we were prepared to let things lie, figuring you were too young to know better and that it'd pass. We said nothing when you brought home your books and drawings, even turned a blind eye to the candles and all the other stuff that you keep in that box at the back of your wardrobe. We've tried to be patient, really we have; but bringing her to our door and kissing in the street, for the whole world to see, well that's overstepping the mark!"

He rose to protest, but now his father intervened.

"It's got to stop, Syriem. You've no idea the trouble we could all get into.

I told you, those Keldies bring bad luck."

Syriem sat in stony silence, as sealed as a tomb.

"Look," Tem ventured, "I know you're keen on her boy, but that's how they work. You've got to come to your senses. Or before you know it, you'll get so caught up in their ideas that you'll forget who you are. And for what? She'll never be yours, boy – you must see that?"

Syriem scowled defiantly, inflaming Tem's temper. Sro shook her head, staggered by her husband's indiscretion. Tem crossed to the cupboard and fiddled with the crockery, while Syriem's eyes bored into him.

"It's got nothing to do with you!" Syriem roared. "You wouldn't understand!"

"Oh, wouldn't we?" Tem eyed his son in disgust.

Sro began to weep and Syriem looked over, appalled and humiliated.

"I wash my hands of it, you won't be told," Tem ranted. "You do what you bloody well like boy, but you don't know the half of it. And it's time you thought about us for a change."

"There, Syriem," Sro dried her eyes, "it wasn't your doing in the first place." She shot a plaintive glance at Tem and he relented, taking his place back at the table.

"The thing is," Tem rubbed his hands together slowly, "we have a confession of sorts. It's not like we were deliberately keeping it from you, as such. But the situation being how it is, well, you need to know certain things…"

Tem and Sro proceeded to tell Syriem a story – one he could scarcely believe – about meeting a starving Thaylin Sarra priest. And how a few gifts of food and a blanket had led to friendship. Many times they had met him and always, it seemed, by coincidence.

"…He became a Zealot. All he could talk about was his precious calling. When he kept inviting us to meetings and offering to show us his ways, we had to tell him not to bother us any more." Tem fell silent, as if he still regretted it.

"The thing is," Sro continued, "he put a notion into our heads about letting our unborn child feel the world *outside*. He said as how that would be important." She blushed and Tem squeezed her hand. "I admit it, son – we were taken in. It was hard enough not to see him, never mind ignore his words. Your father knew someone on one of the construction teams for the new city walls. The perimeter was being expanded and security was lax. It was a special time for us. We were newly wed the year before and I was carrying you.

Tem cut in. "So we took a chance, especially so in your mother's condition. Returned at night through one of the work routes and paid the Targen off near the border. Others had done it before; where was the harm?"

Sro touched his hand. "Course we'd always been told that the high walls were there to protect us from marauders. We figured we'd only stay a little while, just to see. You can't imagine our surprise though, when we stepped through the fence. It was so peaceful, so beautiful; everything he'd promised us that it would be."

Tem nodded, smiling at the sparkle in her eyes. "Who'd have thought that a wall would have made such a difference? We knew then what our Thaylin Sarra friend had meant; we felt *renewed* – I can't put it better than that. We rested by one of the tall trees and saw the night sky in all its glory."

Sro seemed wistful, but other memories soon returned. "In the blink of an eye, something changed. We felt out of place, like we didn't belong. We realised that we were as foreign to that world, just a few yards beyond the boundary, as if we'd gone to the snowy wastelands of Agnorsteta City State. The wind picked up in a show of spite, the trees stretching and bowing so much we were afeared they'd come crashing down on top of us. Clouds choked the moon and a thick darkness came down. Then it rained, Syriem, and I have never seen rain like that before or since. It was an ill omen and I was so terrified that I went into labour early. We thought it was a punishment and that I'd lose you," she paused for breath, trapped once again in the storm.

"Tell him all of it. It's time he knew," Tem conceded. "Then maybe he'll finally see sense."

"I prayed, Syriem. Despite all the barriers we'd put up against our friend, I prayed to his Gods. I promised that if we were spared we'd lead a good life, but the storm didn't budge. Well, just when it all seemed hopeless, we heard people moving about in the shadows. At first we thought settlers had come for us or that we'd be arrested. There were three of them, two adults and a child; they were more scared than us. On the run they were, heading *into* the city!

"They were Keldie types, no doubt about it, but not quite like our friend. I swear to you now, Syriem, the woman held up a hand – no more than that – and the storm turned. The moon streamed through and at that moment my waters broke…" She blushed, mindful that, as old as he was, Syriem was still her son.

"Fortunately, the woman knew all about birthing and brought you into the world, frail little thing that you were. I remember how pale you looked on that terrible night, with your frightened eyes peering out. Anyway, while the woman was attending to me," she flustered again, "the man with her made a little speech – you probably know the sort of thing.

"I can still hear his voice, Syriem, after all these years; something about peace and darkness and redemption. But the boy with them, he was the strangest o' the lot. He looked down at you lying there and smiled, as if he knew you. Then he slipped something into the folds of the blanket, said as how the gift bonded the giver and the receiver alike. And then he waved some funny looking stick over you and touched your chest. Tem thought they might be after taking you," she shook her head, "but they meant us no harm. They gave me some herbs to strengthen me and dull the pains till I could get to my bed.

"They had people waiting for them inside the boundary and they insisted we were taken home first. They begged us to forget we'd ever seen them. Terrified they were, as if someone was pursuing them."

Tem and Sro stopped talking.

"So your prayers were answered after all," Syriem said. "And what about the gift?"

"All in good time, my son," Tem took over as Sro dabbed at her eyes. "It was a spring night and whatever charm the woman had used must have held because no more rain fell. We were careful because of the Targen, but we saw no one. Once we'd brought you home we just sat there and slept, holding you close. It was well into the morning before we thought to see what the boy had left you."

Sro left the table and lifted a locked metal box out from the cupboard – the box that Syriem had known through childhood as the savings box, never to be touched. The lock gave a satisfying creak as the key turned. Sro handed the little cloth parcel to Tem, who shook his head and motioned for her to give it directly to Syriem.

"A couple of times recently we thought about losing it, but we couldn't do it," Tem turned to the window. "When all's said and done, it's yours by right."

Syriem unwrapped the cloth to find a metal disc, inscribed with various shapes and sigils. On one side was a six-pointed star, encircled by a serpent, with a figure of eight in the centre. "Why didn't you tell me before?" he asked, unable to disguise the trembling joy in his voice.

"I suppose we were hoping we wouldn't have to," Tem sank back in his chair, puffing his discontent. "If folks had got to hear how you were born foreign, outside the city, we'd have ended up in one o' those community slums. As it was, we moved home as soon as we were able; couldn't run the risk that someone might have seen us out with strangers the night you were born. We had to falsify your birth records as well. What we did was *wrong*, Syriem – against the law," he leaned in earnestly. "And now it looks like we're paying the price."

Sro tried to temper the blow. "The last thing we want to do is draw attention to ourselves. So do the right thing, Syriem – for all our sakes – and forget her."

In the space of an hour Syriem's world had changed forever; he'd become a different person, with a past that he barely knew. His first thought was of Isca. Now maybe she'd see that they were kindred spirits after all.

He went off to the station to meet Dorron. He wouldn't say anything yet, not until he was sure in his own mind what was safe to tell. It had been a morning of revelations and while some things he'd heard had delighted him, others gave him cause for concern. He needed to hear a simple, unbiased outlook: Dorron's.

"I thought you weren't on early starts this week?"

"Library," he lied.

The train pulled in, packed with workers making their way across the city.

"Come on," Dorron hauled him in before the door slammed shut, pushing through to a corner of the carriage.

An attractive blonde followed him with her eyes and he nudged Syriem, licking his lips. Syriem took no notice and started off slowly, inventing a conversation with a beggar outside the Cargo Plant. Dorron appeared vaguely interested, albeit still with one eye on the woman. Next Syriem touched upon the issue of immigrants in the sector. So far so good. No more than a few grumbles from Dorron about putting their own people first. Then Syriem pushed a little further about the conditions in the community zones.

Dorron cast around to make sure he had a ready audience and shifted position to face Syriem. He was sweating; he felt exposed by Syriem's politics and tainted by association. He made a derogatory remark about *those foreigners* and hoped it would deter his friend from making an even bigger fool of himself.

But Syriem was not for backing down and dug in deeper. It had become a battle of wills and he trusted that he was more than a match.

"Open your eyes, Syriem," Dorron finally exploded. "These outsiders you're so fond of – they're lucky to have slums to live in. Where did they live before – caves? Huts? They get into our cities by the back door – bringing all kinds of diseases most likely – and then *you* want to give them decent housing!"

A few people around them murmured their approval, which stoked the fire.

"No one invited them here, with their strange ways an' all; and then they complain about being second class citizens. Well, they don't complain – people like you do it for them. As far as I'm concerned, they're parasites and people like you are weak and deluded for supporting them." Dorron felt a surge of adrenaline, aware that all eyes were on him. "And Syriem," he raised his voice for effect, "I hope you're not getting deeper into all that stuff. I hear you've been seeing some Keldie woman!"

Syriem's pupils dilated at the thought of her.

"Mind you, if it's the one from the market," Dorron patted his groin, "she did look good for one thing!"

Syriem longed to retaliate, but he knew that was what Dorron wanted. He focused, blocking out thoughts of such malice that he could scarcely contain them.

"Look Dorron, I hear what you're saying," he spat the words out like poison, "but you can't blame the immigrants or the Keldies – it's not their fault they were born outside the cities."

It was a cheap ploy, appealing to Dorron's sense of Tarsien pride – a last ditch effort to bridge the gap between them. Dorron pondered for a moment then stared back accusingly, as if he'd seen the trap that Syriem had laid.

"I thought your Keldie leaflets said they believe people choose where they're born?" Dorron's voice was slow and delivered, for maximum effect.

The train pulled into the station. As the doors opened and Syriem stepped on to the platform, he turned to see Dorron's checkmate sneer through the glass. He trudged out of the station and made an immediate detour to the nearest park. Dorron had no excuse, but *he* ought to have known better. Habit made him want to seek Isca out, but he felt unworthy.

A group of Targen Cadets were practising a drill on patch of grass, their taut faces etched with concentration. Were these cadets, men and women not far from his own age, really the instruments of a State dedicated to eradicating Isca and her kind? When he looked at them now as they confused right with left, and *stand* with *stand straight*, it made little sense. Nothing made any sense today. He took an apple from his jacket and caressed the skin. Then he thought about Dorron and bit into it savagely.

By the afternoon Syriem had managed to gain a little perspective. Most of the Transvectors were away on long distance runs between the City States, giving him ample time to mull over the morning's conversations. He sat down with a list of cargo sheets to check and tried to picture his birth with its strange attendants, losing himself in his thoughts until the supervisor bellowed his name across the yard.

He edged into the office and loitered by the door. She was back at her desk now, surrounded by paperwork. A large chart behind her showed the vehicle schedules for the coming weeks. She coughed loudly to draw his attention back from the wall.

"My team always outperforms all the others and I expect you to pull your weight. You weren't my first choice, you know, so you better buck your ideas up. I've seen the way you float around this place half the time. At least *look* like you're paying attention."

He nodded methodically and turned his gaze upon her, sensing how much she despised him. Once he might have taken offence, but there was a kind of certainty in the knowledge.

Later, when she ventured back from a break the worse for drink, he stopped her from making a fool of herself in front of one of the maintenance crews. In return she allowed him to finish his shift early. She wished him well as he walked out, slurring her goodbyes. And if the fool wasn't around when some personal cargo was delivered, so much the better.

The house was empty when Syriem arrived home, but it was still felt charged with the emotions of the morning. He opened his journal to the middle and gathered up the disc, holding it to his chest in front of a mirror. Unlike when he was with Isca, he saw no colours around his reflection. He closed his eyes and clasped the disc between his hands, muttering a Thaylin Sarra blessing. Then he rushed to the community zone.

"You won't believe what I have to tell you!" he bounded over, almost dropping the disc in Isca's lap.

She weighed it in her hand. "Where did you get it?"

"It's a long story," he promised, eager to savour every detail again.

She listened as he recounted the story, rocking to the rhythm of his words. Knees clasped, eyes half-closed, she let the pictures form in her mind. "It would seem," she startled him, "that you were summoned long before I called you into my life."

"I don't understand – what does it mean?"

She opened her eyes, catching him off guard. Her expression changed; for a moment she looked as if she might yield him a straight answer. "Why don't you make us both a drink?"

He wandered off to the kitchen. When he had gone, Isca turned the disc in her hand and opened up fully to its impressions. Then she reached into her clothing, one eye still on the door, and slipped a pendant free. There they rested in her palms, two talismans, identical in every respect.

She put her own talisman away and placed his on the table. In all her travels she had only seen one other. So how did he, an outsider, come to possess such a thing?

"Syriem," she called, as he searched through the cupboards, "I want to try an experiment."

As he returned she was spreading out a blanket near the fire.

"When you've had your drink, I'd like to investigate your *history*."

He swayed a little, facing the fire. The rough, grey blanket pressed against his bare soles and the heat brought him out in a sweat. Isca spoke quietly but forcefully, instilling her Will.

He followed her tone as she directed him through the imagery. When he had settled sufficiently, she placed her fingers at the base of his skull and carefully kneaded with her thumbs. Then she worked her way down both sides of his spine, applying subtle pressure in a precise pattern and order. Finally, she knelt behind him and gripped at his ankles then helped him to the floor. In a few breaths he'd fallen into a trance. She called the dog to her, gave it a name and sent it away at her bidding.

It was some time before the dog returned with its quarry. He was a tall, imposing man, whose manner seemed to match the dog's sombre mood.

"You were lucky to find me; I had important business to attend to."

She pointed to Syriem's prone body by way of explanation.

"So, this is your precious secret, eh? He's a bit of a runt," Gev muttered, watching the expression on her face.

"That's unjust," she forced a smile. "We are any of us rarely what we seem." She showed him the talisman.

"Is it real?" he touched the disc as if it were sanctified.

"It seems to be; the more so when I tell you how he came by it."

He handed it back after a few seconds. "If only we had another to compare it with."

She shifted her gaze.

"And could this be a sign of The Restitution?"

"Perhaps. He may simply be a messenger…" she paused, thinking back to her first meeting with Syriem. "Something to give the faithful hope. Or he may indeed be one of the fated ones, returned to us."

"But how can that be when he's outside the faith? And what magic would bring such a messenger to the very group that has the stone tablet?"

She dismissed Gev's questions out of hand. "I take this as confirmation," she held up the talisman. "You must tell Etta that it's time he knew about the Tablet."

"Ah yes, the fabulous stone that will lead us all home…"

"So cynical for the priesthood?"

"I lack your insight, Hybrolen. I'm a realist, not a zealot. The faith saved me from the life I was leading and I am grateful for that. But any talk of

Guardians and Gods is beyond me." He snatched up a piece of paper to take a rubbing of the disc. "I'll show this to Etta and she can decide what's best."

"It is my decision; he will know tonight," she told him calmly, her words devoid of feeling. "And the Tablet will remain in my care."

He touched the talisman again. "What if this is a ploy by the Enemy to deceive us? Remember the discredited artefacts in Variz."

She summoned her True Will and faced him. "I will not be deviated from my course."

"I meant no disrespect, Hybrolen," he lowered his voice. "I will speak with Etta tonight, just as you have instructed."

She raised a serene, implacable smile and closed the door after him. A low groan drew her back to the fireside.

"I must have drifted off," Syriem yawned, rubbing his eyes.

"Tell me what you dreamt."

He smelt the dusky incense on her clothes, but there was something else. Not a scent exactly, more of a feeling – an inner knowing. The dog entered the room and its presence seemed to fill it. Their eyes met and Isca nodded respectfully before turning to Syriem.

"You may begin."

"I kept seeing a pyra…"

"Pyramid," she reminded him. "It is one of the symbols of the Mysteries. Go on."

He bit at his nails. "I dreamt about the woman again."

Isca and the dog shared a glance.

"She drew a triangle in the air and it…started moving. I saw it was really one face of a pyramid. And then…well…a disc appeared at each of the points, like the one given to me. Why would there be five though?"

The dog murmured and Isca hastily cut in. "I look forward to your considered interpretation. Now, I need to say something to you."

He got up and made himself uncomfortable on the couch.

"I think we can agree that your disc changes things," she paused, struck by a question she'd never dared to ask herself. Did the same child mark them both out for a future purpose? Had *he* been the Righteous One?

Syriem was still studying her face.

"Look," she continued, "time is precious and I cannot allow your limitations to dictate the pace of our work. Your desire for me is based upon a misconception."

He fidgeted in embarrassment.

"You feel the resonance between us, but you wilfully distort it into something it is not. We share a *magical* bond, but you insist on trying to interpret it as…" she paused, hoping he would meet her halfway and not force her to say it out loud. "Syriem," she sighed, "I cannot be – I'm not – what you think you want me to be; there are more important matters at stake. Surely the presence of your talisman tells you that?" She glowered, incensed at his emotional attachment; something she had yet to subdue.

He looked away to the dog.

"To continue like this only invites more pain – for both of us. I need you for this work and while I do care for you, Syriem, without the fulfilment of our work you are of little use to me." A first lie, she excused herself, but a necessary one. "In the fullness of time you will come to appreciate the depths of our bond; until then you will have to take what I say on trust."

"I trust you," he insisted.

"Then put an end to these distractions and let's use our time together to good effect."

He unfolded his arms and laced his fingers together.

"Yours is not the first disc I've seen. Would you believe that your talisman might be connected with Sarrell?" She didn't wait for an answer. "We've talked about Sarrell many times now – as a belief and as a myth, about what it symbolises to the world. But I *know* that Sarrell exists because I have experienced it on the astral plane." She smiled nervously, willing him to follow her inference without prompting.

"That doesn't mean it exists physically though," he rationed his opinion.

"That's reasonable," she complimented him. "Some Thaylin Sarra would agree, although few would declare it so openly. I had an awakening as a child – that's why the Thaylin Sarra rank and file declare me a Hybrolen. My True Will has given me levels of understanding beyond this plane of existence. Do you understand?"

"I think so, but then I'm not a Hybrolen; I'm not even a Thaylin Sarra."

There was a hint of self-pity in his voice, which she chose to ignore.

"I was coming to that. If I'm right about your talisman, we may be able to use it to cross the divide between planes of consciousness. Then you will *see* Sarrell as I have seen it."

He set his hands in one of the postures to stave off a counter-tide of questions. Isca passed his talisman to him.

"Will it be dangerous?" he asked softly.

"I believe this is a paradox and that the risk lies in not completing the circuit."

He sniffed aloud. "Then let's do it."

She locked the front door. The dog got up, stretched then lay down, sphinx-like, at Syriem's feet. He remained perfectly still as Isca cleared some space and lit four candles, placing them at the quarters.

"Wait here," she went off to change her clothes.

He didn't know whether she was speaking to him or the dog. His heart raced. This was the culmination of a secret desire – Temple Magic – and he was afraid. He closed his eyes and performed the mental cleansing exercises that he knew she'd be expecting of him.

Isca returned and paused by the doorway. Syriem's breath caught in his throat. However beautiful he had thought her before, she eclipsed that now in a simple grey robe.

"I had always hoped that we would come to this point," she smiled.

He received her accolade without comment and awaited her instructions.

"I have prepared a robe for you," she pointed to the bedroom.

The robe felt weighty, as if it represented the responsibility thrust upon him. He touched the seams, delighting in the notion that she had stitched it by hand. As he brushed his hand against the thick folds, the garment released subtle scents. He straightened the hood and dispelled a sudden, intrusive thought about Feren.

When he felt ready, he joined her in the centre of the room and knelt towards the east. Above the mantelpiece, the eyes of Horus – as he now knew them – looked out upon their work like a watchful guardian. Isca moved within the temple bounds, spreading a fine white powder about them in a circle and chanting a simple rhythm as she went. Then she flashed a dagger full of stars, slashing the air and the ether, to fix names of power with each of four pentagrams. When the room was ritually sealed, she took her place opposite him, facing west.

"Come with me," she whispered, taking his hands gently. "Give yourself over to me and I will take you to another realm."

"I am thy willing sacrifice," he offered no resistance.

It may have been the effect of the incense, but he soon became aware of waves of force lapping against him, eroding his waking consciousness like an ineffable tide. Only an inner voice remained – her voice – leading him beyond the limits of his own understanding.

The painted doors draw him forward. It is a moment before he realises that he is free of his body. She takes his hand and the doors open to another plane of existence. They emerge into a chamber – a cavern formed not of rock but of energy, pulsing and humming like a living structure. They travel together, as she guides him through a shell of transition.

He gazes at the temple ceiling, stretching upwards like the inside of an endless mountain. Colours sparkle and flash to the rhythm of his thoughts. The walls become murals of the past and present combined. He feels constrained, held back by the bounds of his own attainment. In her hand he sees a talisman like his own.

"Bring forth your disc," she demands and he opens his hand.

The talisman appears in his palm. The two objects are matched, symbol for symbol, and his realisation coincides with vibrations that resonate from the walls. Ahead of them a round, flat stone rests upon an altar. He copies her, pressing his disc against it so that two of the pentacle's five points are covered. Light bursts from the stone in a fountain of colour. Time ceases and consciousness accelerates, hurtling them forward like a cataclysmic thrust into the Unseen. Perception dissolves, awareness is negated and self is annihilated in the void.

The light gradually abates and the domain prisms into detail, enabling him to glimpse vistas he could not have invented.

'Where are we?' he forms the question without speaking, but she calls for silence.

Mere words will not give him the answers he seeks. A reverberating tone builds at the back of his mind, forcing its way through. She feels it too; he knows that. He knows so much about her now that he is overwhelmed. His body begins to shake, the iridescent form quivering as the vibrations restructure his form. Once he can safely cross the divide, darkness embraces him.

The seductive scents of a balmy evening greet Isca and her charge, carried on the breeze. Realisation dawns anew; they are not creating reality – they are revealing it. They walk together through a temple garden, hand in hand like lovers. Great statues bear silent witness, each one imbued with the majesty it represents: white marble for the Fair Aphrodite and dark, unfathomable jet for Black Isis.

He wanders free, drawn to the statue of a jackal and touches the smooth, polished stone. It ripples and his hand passes beyond its surface, reaching to even higher worlds. He snatches back his hand to find it unmarred and looks over to his love, wearing his confusion like a veil.

She sees that he does not have sufficient True Will to carry him safely to Sarrell. In despair at his loss she offers a prayer to the Guardian, a supplication that Syriem may receive her aid. The Guardian comes quickly and Isca instinctively shields him as a mother would her child.

"You have returned, my daughter? I had not anticipated your presence again so soon." The Guardian is puzzled, but the presence of the boy whets its appetite.

Isca brings Syriem forward, cocooning him in her aura.

"He bears the disc and he bears the burden," the Guardian concedes.

Isca runs a hand across his face and consciousness dulls, leaving him in a stupor.

"Would that you had not attempted this, my child," the Guardian laments. And for the first time its words are tinged with compassion. "Your actions make you vulnerable to the Enemy."

"One glimpse – it is his right," Isca holds out a hand to the Guardian, while her other hand reaches for Syriem, offering herself as a conduit.

In an instant Syriem opens alien eyes, reflecting the unfathomable truth of All That Is. The ground slips away, relinquished as the last pretence of a temporal domain. A citadel materialises before him, shimmering in the same multicoloured hues as the great arc that spans its borders. He is filled with an ecstatic vision of the Holy City of Sarrell. A choir of voices embrace him, like the prayers of the ages. Isca calls to him, forcing her Will upon him as a screen against the tide of welcome. If he does not maintain his focus the quickening wave of consciousness will claim him and she will lose him for good.

The Guardian stands impassively, unmoved by Isca's terrible struggle to wrest Syriem from sanctuary. Then the moment passes and the cosmic course wanes, freeing him from its bonds.

"He will recover," the Guardian promises and Isca bows with gratitude.

While Isca enters in silent communion, Syriem can only feel impressions – emotional hues and forms that barely convey the exchange. For an instant he sees Parva Serach again, this time with a third matching talisman. Then the vision blurs into chaos.

Syriem opened his eyes, startled by the sound of Isca's breathing. "Who was that woman?"

"Why don't you do the talking?"

Words and images tumbled from his mind, glimpses and distortions of his experience. As Isca's insight pierced the confusion he allowed the unpalatable truth to emerge. He had encountered something inhuman – a being of tremendous power and focus – and it had recognised Isca as an ally.

She listened without judgement or explanation; they were past that now.

"…And a rainbow above the city," he fell silent at his own revelation.

"Yes, Syriem. Each time I have reached Sarrell there has been a rainbow. It is one of the great traditions, the magical arc that is the union of all rays and all understanding. The Many and the One – a presence in the world that is not of this world." She turned to him and closed on his face, filling his eyes with her own. "What you have witnessed in the upper realms may you one day know in the flesh."

She brought out a folded, grey shawl from a cupboard and handed it to him. He smiled at the thought of another test, resting it on the table as he tried, unsuccessfully, to sense the contents. He unwrapped it to reveal a round, hand-worked stone, inscribed on one side with a protective pentagram that formed a continuous groove. On the other side was a Tree of Life glyph, its circles and interconnecting pathways bordered by a scattering of symbols and sigils.

"This is the Tablet known through the ages as The Lock. It is the vessel of knowledge that will lead to Sarrell."

"Can you decipher it?" he broke the silence.

"Me? No!" she almost laughed. "But the Righteous One will know how."

He frowned at the reverence in her voice and seized the Tablet, attempting to pierce the riddle by an effort of will. Isca watched him as he tried to wring wisdom from the stone. He was fortunate, if he but knew it. It was enough to know of the Tablet's existence; that alone would bring consequences.

chapter 6
BANE

FROM THE MOMENT Syriem had first laid eyes on the Tablet he knew everything would change. His behaviour at work cast a shadow and his supervisor was quick to transfer him off her team. Everyone around him reacted unconsciously to the invisible barriers that Syriem fortified himself behind. He varied his route to work and avoided the library altogether. He also lied to his parents about not seeing Isca and they were content to believe him.

Parva Serach the Sage, Syriem knew, had proffered that truth was its own salvation. But then, to the best of his knowledge, she had never had to live in Tarsis. The books and study notes steadily disappeared and there were no more candle marks on his bedroom floor.

Isca never said it directly, but Syriem knew the Tablet would become his responsibility. It filled him with a deep sense of purpose and the greatest of burdens. For if he was now ready to be told about the Tablet then the time for separation must be close. He lived in a world of duality – entangled by the two, irreconcilable strands of his existence.

Time and again, he went back over his journal. Had he imagined that Isca had carried an identical talisman, that night in the temple? He wouldn't ask her though; it was for her to tell him of her own accord. And there was so much that she didn't say. She'd always known the strength of his feelings for her and yet she used that knowledge ruthlessly to hone his inner senses. The situation was hard to bear, without being given meditations such as: *the path of sorrow is the first step to growth*. That was no comfort whatsoever.

Isca paced the room, her instincts awoken by the turbulent shift of the seasons. The lone tree battled against the wind outside, scattering yellowed leaves to the cobblestones like discarded coins. She opened a window, drawing the scent of damp foliage into the room. Nature called to her from its primal depths and she, who had known the vast skies and the mighty denizens of the forests, could offer little resistance. She threw a cloak around her shoulders and ordered the dog to stay put. It glanced up at the sickle moon and grudgingly followed down the steps, watching until her shadow receded. Its eyes glistened in the moist, evening air. The Enemy was on the move.

She meandered through the alleyways, attuned to an unspoken summons, unaware that every step carried her further and further from safety. There was no particular destination, just a craving to be out under the stars. She needed to clear her head. Syriem was on the brink of understanding so much, but she would not give him the answers unbidden.

Did he realise how close he had come to death when he glimpsed Sarrell? Could he even begin to comprehend the depths of their bond? She had once seen a third such talisman, back when the faith was as new to her as the seasons. Why, she wondered in dismay, would a Hybrolen child have given talismans to two strangers separated by culture and place? Might a child from the settlements, a traveller and a boy from Tarsis be connected by Syriem's dream?

She walked on, absorbed in an inner dialogue that provided no respite. What more could she do to prepare for the Righteous One? Surely there would have been a sign by now? Her thoughts detoured. Maybe the talisman *was* the sign, but if that were so then how to interpret it? The Guardian had been so eager to receive him – too eager perhaps? Each dark thought built upon the next. Was another sacrifice due, a clearing of the path to finally usher in the Restitution? Not a physical sacrifice this time, she trusted, for surely enough people had been taken to sate the karma of the faith? She sighed and a thought rose up like a whisper – it would soon be time to leave him.

The evening cacophony grew louder as she reached a main street. She didn't recognise the area; her wandering had led her into unfamiliar territory, but no matter. The heady music from the nightclubs warmed her blood and she found her breathing synchronising to the tempo. Tarsis night folk stood out on the street in groups, waiting for access to the more popular Treasure Houses.

She moved closer to the kerb, seized by curiosity, staring across at their gregarious clothes and brash manners. The moon scythed through the clouds to gleam dull silver in the sky. She crossed the street and walked towards the Tarsiens, guided by an inner voice, forgetting that not all inner voices are benevolent – or invited.

As she approached the crowd she heard a taunt against the faith. Someone recognised her from the market. The rabble spilled onto the road ahead of her, raucous and volatile. The scuffling and pushing subsided as she drew nearer. Soon a wall of murmuring faces confronted her. She shrank before their gaze and pulled her cloak in tightly.

A man stumbled through the crowd. "Come on then," he gurgled, thrusting his hand up to her face, "read my fortune!"

He made a lunge for her breast, but she sidestepped him and his momentum sent him crashing to the pavement. He lay there, bruised and bloody, cursing. The mob closed in and for the first time Isca was afraid. A small group mind tuned only to debauchery should have been little match for her sharpened will, but tonight her senses were heavy. She began to push past the clamour.

"Wait. Reveal *my* destiny," a woman eased her way through the fracas. The crowd backed off, deferring to a superior predator.

Isca turned and a flood of impressions punctured her psyche. She fought to withstand the onslaught, battling against the dark chaos that marked the Enemy. She reeled, her physical and magical bodies so enmeshed that the loss of balance in one permeated the other. The stranger's malign influence threatened to overwhelm her and only a half-forgotten survival instinct compelled her forward.

"Remember me," the woman called after her like a hex. "My name is Ursephal."

As Isca staggered along the street, awareness surfaced from the last of her resolve. She had been in the presence of something malevolent and now she was in the greatest danger. Her mind had been ravaged and laid bare; it was too much to hope that her secret was still safe. She choked back tears, half-closing her eyes against a truth that crucified her; months of work undermined by a simple weakness – her attachment to the natural world.

Somehow she found the strength to keep moving, taking each turning at random so that none could locate her by tracing her thoughts. It didn't matter where her intuition led – anywhere to escape those penetrating eyes. She had heard talk of the Appren all her life – the Enemy – and listened to others petrify themselves with hearsay. But now she knew that the Appren were truly without righteousness; a fruit of the Tree that had soured.

"And how righteous am I?" she scorned herself, as she walked the city streets, alone and vulnerable.

Going home, wherever that was, was out of the question. And besides, there was no advantage. The dog could look after itself and she'd taken pains to put the Tablet somewhere safe, somewhere they could not retrieve it easily without her. She huddled in a shop doorway and wept, drawing her cloak around her like feeble wings. Her mind retreated, seeking out the comfort of childhood.

She remembered it all so clearly, even now. That afternoon, looked back upon with understanding, it had rained. Strangers had come to the settlement amid great excitement and secrecy. They had asked for all the children to be gathered together, but she'd remained in the woods. She'd gone to her secret place, scrabbling through the cleft in the hillock that led her beneath the great beech tree. Old Pan, she had named it. Down she'd squeezed, wriggling past ancient roots as thick as limbs. And there, in the middle of her hidden domain, the boy had been waiting.

He wasn't cross with her for being there; he seemed pleased. He had a wound on his arm, and she dressed it as best she could, for she was only at the very beginning of her healing craft. Then he gave her the bound up cloth and smiled at her, as if he'd recognised an old friend. She cried when she saw the talisman and flung her arms around him; she'd never been happier to see anyone in her whole life. And as she touched the talisman and let him hang it around her neck, she'd called forth her spiritual name for the first time: *Isca*. Then he had showed her his own, identical talisman and called her Healer, telling her that they were linked – the giver and the receiver alike.

Isca glanced at her reflection in the shop front. Was this a Priestess of the Gods? Or, as Parva Serach had once contended, might there be no Gods at all and just the shadows of the adepts?

She needed to weave the tattered shreds of her True Will together. If she encountered another Appren that night she might not be so fortunate. She touched her talisman. There was one person she could draw strength from; someone who believed in her purpose without reservation – and she had the means to find him.

An hour or more she walked, one hand gripped against the talisman to aid her concentration. She caught sight of the glare first, a muted magenta glow that crackled in the damp air. As she attuned her intuitive senses the auric field became as visible as the street signs. Her solar plexus throbbed in a slow, deliberate pulse and her True Will began to reassert itself, reforming energetic pathways within her.

Harsh pink and purple lights flashed outside the bar: Treasure House Cortu – All Welcome. She slipped in unnoticed, swept along with the new arrivals. A couple were busy making full use of their shadowy booth and she watched, fascinated by their lack of inhibition.

Someone took her order, returning with a glass shaped like a naked torso. She sipped self-consciously, wondering if the ice water could be trusted. As she loosened her cloak and glanced around for a free table, a familiar voice caught her attention. She listened quietly, stifling tears of gratitude. The One had not abandoned her; he was here.

Syriem's voice warmed her spirit like an elixir, even though a girl was at his side. She felt a pang of sympathy when the girl dismissed him out of hand. And then other feelings stirred – jealousy and self-assurance. He was hers and their bond was inviolable; she could give him what no other else could come close to. And perhaps, she pondered, as she drained the last of her drink, the same could be said of him for her.

Dorron convulsed with laughter at Syriem's expense. "Why can't you, for once in your life, behave normally? No, I take it back; don't ever change – I'd miss the entertainment! Well, look, I've got somewhere to be – you understand."

Isca felt a twinge in her solar plexus as she left the safety of the crowd; slipping past a drunk who thought his drooling fascination was a form of foreplay. She raised her hand, sensing raw power flowing out in a wave of chaos. The drunkard tottered backwards into a table, smashing his glass on the floor.

Syriem didn't stir; his gaze was rooted on Dorron and his private party, as they forced their way out. Isca closed in and ran a finger from the nape of his neck down his spine.

"Buy you a drink, stranger? Or maybe you could buy me one!"

He wheeled round, half-afraid that he had imagined her voice.

"Well, say something?" she laughed, thrilled to see the astonishment in his eyes. "Come on," she decided suddenly, let's dance," and led him by the hand.

She moved lithely, arching and gyrating around him like a wild creature, as he shifted about in one spot. There came a point where he felt more like a voyeur, so he reluctantly sought the safety of the shadows.

"Don't you *want* to dance with me?" she teased, enjoying the intimacy of the game.

He wondered whether, that very moment, she could read his thoughts. He avoided asking how she had come to be there; as if by asking he might break the spell. She was with him and that was enough.

After dancing there were more drinks and then the sanctuary of silence as they sat in a booth together. No one paid them any attention, which pleased him. As time passed, he noticed a subtle shift in the clientele; more people were arriving, already the worse for wear.

"Come on, it's late – we should get out of here," he whispered, laying a tentative hand at her back and feeling the heat through his palm.

She nodded woozily, resting her head on his shoulder, and followed his lead. Her euphoria evaporated in the chill night air. She looked about herself warily and urged him to stay close.

"I'll find us a cab," he took her into the road to escape the crowds.

At first he thought she was drunk, but the further they travelled, the more she seemed to regain her senses.

"How were you even here tonight?"

"It met a mutual need," she told him, as honestly as she dared.

He told the cab driver to drop them off in a different part of the community zone and navigated their way along the alleyways, each one now a familiar pathway to his *other* life – the one Dorron didn't ask about. The courtyard was as quiet as the breeze and they stood for a moment, arm in arm, looking at the stars over the tree.

She led him upstairs where the dog was waiting by the door, its face stern and chiselled in the shadows. "I know," she admitted, "I was foolish. But see who has guided me home."

The dog approached Syriem's hand and nuzzled it. They went inside and he brought through two hot drinks. She sat close, unable to take her eyes off him.

"Who are you?" her voice betrayed her fascination. "Can it be…" she fell silent.

"You probably know that better than me," he insisted. "Maybe you've always known, on some level." And as he spoke, his sombre tone made her laugh like a melody.

"All I know for certain is that you are a blessing to me in this Great Work. And that I will miss you," her eyes lowered.

"As will I," he resigned himself, struggling with his sorrow. "It's funny," he sniffed, "I haven't been out to a bar with Dorron for weeks. I only decided on that Treasure House at the last minute – maybe we were *both* guided there?"

She smiled faintly; even now he was capable of surprising her. "When you act with your True Will, you will always be guided."

"Will I ever see you again – after you leave?"

"If the Gods will it," she told him, hardening her resolve. "Until then, Syriem, trust in the path." She unfastened her cloak and laid it across a chair. "The fire needs stoking."

He traced her outline as she knelt before the flames. "What if *we* will it, never mind the Gods? What if it is your True Will and mine?" He glanced up at the veiled doors.

She looked over to him, but didn't speak.

"I'm sorry, I shouldn't have said that. It's late – I should go," he added hesitantly, aching to reach forward and touch her.

"Stay," she whispered like a charm, staring into the flames.

Safe within his embrace, she thanked the Universe for such a companion and prayed that he would escape the fate of her predecessor. They talked until sleep overtook him and then she slipped away, returning with fresh blankets to make a bed beside the hearth. When she roused him from the couch, she was naked. And around her neck was a silver talisman, a companion to the one around his. He laid his hand upon it and felt the rolling rhythm of her heart. Soon they moved together as one, merging through the senses, until there was no separation between them. And later, their passions spent, they slept entwined by the fire.

Isca woke him soon after dawn and Syriem sensed the difference in her. She had changed again, becoming once more the priestess he had first loved. She saw him to the door and whispered softly, "Don't forget anything I've ever told you. Never doubt that our bond is unbroken and without end. Come back in a few days – you'll know when."

He kissed her on the forehead and lips. And when he held the kiss and sculpted his hand along her neck she drew him as close as her own breath.

"Soon," he whispered without thinking.

She kissed him for the final time, touched her heart and then touched his.

Syriem's days blurred by and he held the joy of that night like a hidden treasure, little realising the price they would pay.

Mist swirls about him, as he stands conscious in the astral realm. Ethereal minarets curl up in ribbons of grey to mimic image and form, dissolving into the void as he struggles to make sense of them. He is alone; he knows that much, but little else. Someone calls his name and he runs towards the sound, confronting his own terror.

Vision clears within the domain and he opens his senses to a walled garden. He questions his presence there and the talisman around his neck glows like an ember. Up ahead, a silhouette waits; an imposing shadow not even the mist will approach. A hand beckons to him.

A woman cries out again from somewhere in the gloom and his solar plexus cramps up in response. The silence that follows is a far worse torture.

His attention returns to the beckoning figure. He approaches cautiously, swathed in the trust that 'she' will be there eventually. The silhouette leads him to a well, where the murky waters below await his intent. The crone lays a hand upon him, her icy fingers probing his psyche. A tiny symbol smoulders in his aura – a remnant of a magical encounter on the day he was born.

"You have the mark of The Key!" the crone shudders.

He peers into the well, greeted by flickering orange flames and the

cackling chatter of salamanders – creatures of elemental fire. He follows
his instincts and plummets into a chasm of despair, rushing headlong into
the chaos. She calls his name a final time, like a lament. He runs blindly,
shouting, screaming for her, but all he can hear is a dog barking behind a
wall of flame…

Syriem flashed his eyes open. Something felt horribly wrong. Back before
he'd met her, he would have dismissed it as the echoes of a nightmare, but
now he knew better. He was already crying as he snatched at a set of keys
and sent a pot crashing to the floor. It seemed to spin for an eternity, its
rhythmic clatter drowning out the pounding in his head.

At the first alleyway the stench of burning was overpowering. He walked
briskly, fighting to maintain self-control. He talked aloud as he marched,
telling himself, over and over that it wouldn't be her and everything would
be fine. His pace increased to a run, the familiar, squalid surroundings no
more than a blur. He reached the courtyard, gasping wildly as he faced
the debris.

Isca's building was completely obliterated; heat still radiated from the
rubble and charred beams. He hoped against hope to see the dog hiding
somewhere, as if its presence would somehow change things, and realised
that he'd never learned its name. He couldn't speak, wouldn't open his
mouth for fear of screaming, thrashing his head about wildly, unable to
keep his attention on anything except his own, crushing grief.

"The Targen came here then there was an explosion and a fire."

He turned sharply. One of the street people was crouching in a corner.

"What happened to the woman with the dog?"

"Leave me alone; I haven't seen nobody!"

"*Answer me,*" Syriem shrieked, flashing his teeth like fangs.

The vagrant took one look at him and ran off in terror.

Syriem sank to his knees and stared at the smoky shell of the building.
"I should never have left her." As he closed his eyes he recalled that first,
wondrous time he had met her at the market. When he'd heard his own
voice declare, "*I come because she calls me.*"

He climbed to his feet, pressing his talisman to steady himself. One
word reverberated in his mind, a word that would trouble him for a long
time: Targen. He wandered the streets for hours, haunted by all the things
Isca had said about the Enemy and their sinister agenda. Why hadn't she
foreseen this? Why hadn't *he* received some sort of warning?

His drifting brought him to Keres Park, where Isca had taught him
so much. Despite what she had told him it didn't feel sacred now. He
criss-crossed the web of paths to stand before Ces Frayer's statue. The

lights flickered for an instant as he approached. He faced the plinth and summoned what little strength remained, speaking aloud to the damp, dismal air.

"You have taken away the most precious thing in the world to me. And by Horus the Avenger I swear there will be justice."

If he'd had the courage then, he would have invoked the few names of power that he'd made his own. But all he felt was a hollow, bitter fury.

"I call you before me!" he cried, the crackling skies his only witness.

For two days Syriem lay in a fever, crying out for Isca in his delirium. Tem and Sro looked after him as best they could, but the true sickness was in his soul. And though they grieved for his suffering they did not share his sorrow. Now it was finally over and everything could get back to normal.

He surfaced from a fitful sleep and reached for his journal, flicking through the insights and experiences that had shaped him. The last page bore its script in tiny, almost insignificant words. *I never got to say goodbye. I never got to tell her…*

He clenched the pen and scratched out his resolve. *This then is my sacred wound – the thing that marks me. From this day forward my life has ceased to have meaning, save to complete the Great Work. May the Gods pay dearly for my loss.* Then he wrote Isca's name underneath and clasped the book to his chest to try and invoke his True Will.

The lucid dream was swift in coming. Isca had told him that some initiates were capable of communicating through the astral dreamworld. She'd said it was claimed by some – and feared by others – that the Hybrolen could even breach the divide between life and death. Syriem was prepared to accept anything except that she was gone.

She doesn't speak; she walks ahead of him, calmly leading him to the appointed place. The dog is already there, the Tablet resting beside it. Isca bids him pick up the stone and as he does so the world explodes around him. She is wrenched from his sight once more and he screams for her.

He finds himself in the ruins of a square tower, looking out upon an unfamiliar landscape. Beyond the bricked archway a robed figure sits in quiet contemplation. He edges cautiously forward and the figure raises its head, the better to see the boy while keeping its own identity hidden. There is no response to his questions, only an immutable silence.

Exhausted and desolate, he bows in submission and they watch the daybreak together. Dawn illuminates the horizon, framed within a rainbow. And at Syriem's feet, as if in answer to the most painful question of all, the stone Tablet glints in the sunlight.

Syriem awoke, seized by a compulsion – he had to go back. The nighttime streets filled him with foreboding, but what was fear now except another layer of suffering. All that mattered was retrieving the Tablet and for that he would bear anything. As he made his way to the community zone he became dimly aware of another influence, something external to him that bolstered his strength. He received its influx hungrily. The last few days of little food and fragmented sleep had taken their toll, but they had also heightened his sensitivity.

The cold, stale air still reeked of ash and the moon flashed in the sky like a blade. He trembled as he picked his way over the scorched remains, all the while fighting the urge to retch. The sound of footsteps brought him to his senses. He found a hiding place and watched as three people emerged.

"As you can see, ma'am – small device, target specific. But we miscalculated the amount of combustible material. The damage was so severe that we may have lost useful evidence."

"Keep your voice down."

"There's no need," he assured her. "The locals are deaf, dumb and blind. I could drag someone out and beat them to death and no one would interfere – they daren't."

Syriem dug his nails into his palms and concentrated on the strangers.

"I'm sure Ces Frayer would convey his personal thanks," the woman said, with a hint of glee in her voice, "but he prefers to leave the clandestine work to others. A search team will be here at first light. Let's get moving."

Outrage burned away the shell of Syriem's suffering, sharpening his wits by a foul alchemy. Even hatred was a focus and any focus brought clarity of intent. He touched his talisman and called upon the Tablet to reveal itself, certain that its presence in his dream had been an omen. It wanted him to retrieve it and he had answered its call.

He followed his instinct and went out to the blasted tree trunk, narrowing his concentration, staunching the flow, saving precious emotion for his Art. Under a veil of darkness, he stood before the crippled tree and reached for a small, lifeless branch.

"As I live again so shall you live," he vowed, deftly snapping the thin bough free. He took a few steps back, standing amid the courtyard like a survivor from a catastrophe. His mind attuned to the frequency of the Tablet and his breathing obeyed its rhythm faultlessly.

Consciousness searches, seeking the way, ascending the levels through colours of understanding. Resonances stabilise and form into spheres – the ten whirling orbs of luminescence and the one beshadowed. Thought solidifies into structures, working from the crown downward in an outpouring of splendour. Etheric energy flows to fill his spine and form the Middle Pillar. Twin pillars appear to the right and left of him, the white-silver and the black, to bear his weary psyche. Pathways of interconnection radiate together to mesh the spheres coherently, blending distillations of intelligence into a matrix of integration. He has his answer.

Syriem opened his eyes and advanced again on the tree. A Godname vibrated from within; a name of power he feared to utter. His lips trembled and his body began to shake.

'Eheieh – I Am That I Am,' rang forth inside his mind, igniting the uppermost sphere in his vision like a supernova.

Lightning zigzagged before his eyes and he traced the shaft of light as it pierced his aura. He repeated the Godname and its translation, reaching into the torso of the tree to lift the Tablet free. Instinctively he drew a pentagram over the space afterwards, to leave his presence undeclared. In the back of his mind, an old woman's mocking laughter ripped at his resolve – a scornful reward for his efforts. He wanted to say, 'Not Mine But Thine,' but a part of him resisted and he left the courtyard incomplete.

As with his predecessors in the grip of The Guardian, Syriem recalled little of his night foray. Physically he was protected, as suited its purpose. None approached him and those who thought they'd seen a stranger, wandering through the community zone at that hour, soon convinced themselves otherwise. Emotionally he was not so fortunate. The experience set a flame to the untapped energy within him, a psychic fuel that might otherwise have dispersed over time. Back home all his strength deserted him. For whatever good the Tablet might do, Isca was gone.

The days stretched into weeks with Syriem's memories still an open wound. He often found himself in Keres Park, a tranquil setting – as long as he couldn't see Ces Frayer's statue – where his dark thoughts were held in abeyance. He stared at his journal and the blank page overwhelmed him; a dare to release his emotions and become whole again – a challenge he had so far resisted.

He knew the woman was coming, long before he saw her, sensing the approach like a physical pressure. His eyes flicked back and forth from the page, until finally he snapped his head up, meeting her with a wall of ice.

Etta stopped in her tracks. "It's Syriem, isn't it?"

He nodded stoically and made space on the bench. He'd often thought they might be keeping an eye on him and would make contact at some point.

"I've been looking for you. I needed to see you before I leave Tarsis."

A flicker of emotion rippled across his face and she seized upon it.

"Isca talked about you, when it was just the two of us."

"You needn't worry, the Tablet is safe. I gave my word to protect it until it's time."

She smiled; Isca had chosen well. "I know, Syriem, I've no concerns there. I am here at Isca's bidding…"

His eyes lit up, but the slightest shake of her head consigned him back to his grief.

"If ever certain conditions were met, I was to find you and give you this," she took a box from her coat and pressed it into his hands.

He lifted the lid to find a set of tarot cards. Etta gasped at the sight, shocked that Isca would have bequeathed her tools to an outsider, even one made a messenger for the faith. Then she remembered the talisman. "Isca also told me to tell you something," she paused; "she said that you must remember who you are."

"Where will you go?" he whispered, his voice so laboured that she strained to hear him.

"I don't know, other than away from Tarsis. Most of our cell has scattered. I wish there was more I could give you. May you find strength, as you await the Righteous One."

He realised that she was waiting for his blessing, or at least his forgiveness, so he stood up and took her hands, allowing a link to form between them. Soon his tears cascaded like broken promises, until even the sight of her was a blur. Then she was gone and he was alone again in the park, gazing into the distance.

chapter 7
PROVENANCE

"Welcome to Tarsis," filtered through the tannoy, as the train trudged in from Variz City State.

Turor reached for his bags and tied the straps securely, ignoring the attendant who wished him a great day. According to the advertising hoarding through the window, every day in Tarsis was a great day. He spotted two shaven-headed Thaylin Sarra devotees, just beyond the security perimeter, thrusting leaflets at people who paused only to abuse them.

As he shut the carriage door and got his papers in order, the first waft of Tarsis air settled in his nostrils. He pulled his bags close, hunched his shoulders and fell into step with the swarm, glancing at the two Thaylin Sarra sideways on in case they recognised him. It was unlikely, given their sect, but better to be cautious. Good fortune wasn't his strong point.

Having passed swiftly through Arrivals, thanks to some expensive paperwork, he bought the last pie in the kiosk and stood at the station entrance. Taxi drivers were still competing to fleece unwary travellers. He sighed; nothing had changed.

The station hall soon emptied, as the beggars disappeared before the next Targen patrol. He grimaced at the thought and adjusted his focus to block out the sense of oppression that always surfaced in Tarsis. Having found a map of the northern sector, he crosschecked a list of addresses, noting the safehouses nearest to a library. It had been a long time since he'd adhered to the precepts of the faith; any pamphlets would be useful revision material – and safer than approaching the two followers he'd avoided earlier. It was always an option, though. Given the task at hand, he'd take any help he could get.

When Syriem returned to work he found that his shifts had been cut back drastically. There was nothing personal in it, if you believed that, despite the graffiti on his locker: *No Keldies.*

Athenna's father, Easen John Minet, had personally intervened to ensure that Syriem kept a job at all. Guided by both his daughter and sympathies of his own, he also arranged some evening work for Syriem at the house. It gave Syriem a renewed friendship with Athenna and it offered her the opportunity to keep an eye on him.

Dorron was swift to rekindle old ties, taking Syriem out on the social circuit whenever the mood took him. And if he happened to capitalise a little on his friend's recent notoriety, what harm could it do?

Without Isca and her work, Syriem's life had become aimless. He existed as a shell, wandering through calendar days of work and socialising and emptiness. Once, in an attempt to reach out to providence, he'd attended a Thaylin Sarra open meeting. He arrived late and sat at the back, listening as they bludgeoned the truth to fit their preconceptions. Isca would have forgiven them their ignorance, but he hated them for it. He left the meeting, disgusted and despondent, and never attended another. If the Righteous One existed at all, they would have to come and find him.

Isca's death seemed to have served no purpose at all, beyond moving the Tablet on to someone else. If he could see that, he reasoned, why couldn't the Gods themselves? He kept up many of the disciplines that she had set him, dragging himself back, time and again, to the altar of his obligations. Daily meditations served as a bulwark against sweeping tides of despair and sometimes he'd take out her tarot cards – inviting the images to offer such comfort as they dared. But mostly, when Dorron had no need of him, he spent his evenings alone beside the Tablet, as still as death. Many times he wondered if the fates had abandoned him. He should have known better, for magic will always have its way and the marks that it makes are as firebrands to those who have the vision.

Opportunity reached out one evening, over at Athenna's house. She made her excuses and left for a rendezvous with Dorron. Syriem had watched her go; envying a life he felt he could never have. In the silence of his suffering he called upon the Powers to make good his pledge. As he glanced up from the workbench, he caught father's hawkish eye.

Easen fidgeted a little and cleared his throat. "Syriem, can I ask you something?"

"Of course," he felt his defences hardening.

"How well do you know the Thaylin Sarra traditions?"

Syriem put down the papers he was checking. For a moment Easen thought that he'd offended him, but Syriem blinked slowly and broke his stony facade. He'd noticed the way that Easen kept to a prescribed list of conversation topics, doubtless agreed with Athenna. And he had also known that it would only be a matter of time before there were questions.

He started cautiously, referring to a Thaylin Sarra concept of the seven rays or schools of approach. Easen nodded, a tacit sign that he wanted to hear more. Syriem turned next to Isca, revealing how they'd met and the friendship that had blossomed between them. Easen delighted in their discussion, throwing in points of his own to balance the trust.

"Did you know that Athenna's mother called herself Buda?" It was more of a statement than a question.

"It means *Awakener of Light*," Syriem explained, confident that Easen already knew.

"I'll tell you something," Easen's eyes narrowed. "When Athenna was born Buda wanted to call her *Thenna,* but I put a stop to that. I told her *she* didn't belong to them now and neither would our daughter. I wanted no part in her old ways."

"It must have been difficult for you," Syriem stared at him coldly.

"Look, we can leave this work till tomorrow. I don't get many visitors that I can talk to like this…" there was a tinge of desperation in his voice.

Easen unlocked a door that led upstairs. Syriem followed without comment. Grand, burgundy curtains swept down, almost touching the richly woven carpet. He made his way over to an armchair and thought that nothing else that evening could surprise him.

"Drink?" Easen opened a large wooden cabinet. "It's good stuff."

He nodded, gazing at a painting that depicted two doors with eyes.

"Buda made it – I found it among her things after she left, so I framed it."

Syriem received his glass and sipped slowly, trying not to show its bitterness. Easen nestled into a chair and emptied his own glass in steady, rhythmic gulps, filling it for a second time while Syriem was still struggling gamely with his first.

Easen passed him a leaflet. "Should be a good meeting. Someone has travelled all the way from Variz City State to bring news about what's going on there. I could get you an invite if you're interested…" he gauged the look on Syriem's face. "I like to keep an eye on developments – for Athenna's sake, you understand."

Syriem concentrated on the leaflet to deflect Easen's scrutiny. If the Enemy were looking for a spy, Easen would fit the bill perfectly. He changed the subject, for fear of saying something he'd regret.

"Do you ever think about the existence of Sarrell? Your wife must have talked about it," he faced him. "I'll tell *you* something, Easen," he toyed with the name. "If Sarrell were discovered tomorrow, the Thaylin Sarra movement would deny it. They prefer the myth; it dignifies their suffering. While Sarrell is unattainable it offers hope without the need to act."

Easen dived into his glass and clenched a fist to drive the liquid down. "You shouldn't speak about things you don't understand."

The thought of returning to the library, to learn more about The Assembly, had not sat easily with Syriem. He tended to distrust inspirations that came fully formed, but he understood the benefits. Isca's Righteous One would likely be a stranger to the cities, just as she had been. Any assistance might serve the cause and make him indispensable.

He picked up another book and took out his notes, moving to a window that overlooked the alleyways. He read fitfully, flicking between pages.

'Following the collapse of independent authorities the Cuprad Frayer Treaty Council came into being, subsequently evolving into The Assembly. Now that a single, unified organisation was in control significant progress became possible. Through scientific advances and tireless dedication to City State citizens, The Assembly has brought life up to its present mode.'

The chapter ended with footnotes referring him to other publications. He scribbled down some references. "And the rest," he whispered defiantly, "is history – a history of deceit." He started a new chapter, oblivious to the tall, silent figure watching him.

Dorron edged forward, forcing back the laughter as he stretched out and slammed the book shut. Syriem snapped round.

"Now that I have your attention…" Dorron grinned. "Come outside; we need to talk."

He motioned to the door with a flick of his head and Syriem dutifully followed, wary of his friend's motives but curious nonetheless. Dorron checked the stairwell and then waved some tickets under Syriem's nose.

"It's the greatest gathering in the whole of Tarsis. I swear to you, Syriem, this is the place to make connections."

"Where did you get them?" Syriem fingered the invitations, sensing for any impressions. "These must have cost dearly and you don't have that sort of money."

Dorron cleared his throat. "I'm not going to lie to you, Syriem. There's this Targen officer I know – he drinks in the same Treasure House. He's on security at the event and he gave me the tickets as a favour."

"The Targen don't do favours," Syriem froze. "What does he want in return?"

"Okay, "Dorron backed off a little, "now, don't get mad or anything. I might have mentioned that I've got a friend who can read the Keldie cards. The guy is trying for promotion and there's this woman…" he squirmed, "…and I thought we could do a trade…"

"Are you out of your mind?" Syriem all but screamed. "Haven't you understood a single thing I've said about the Targen and their agenda?"

Dorron squared up to him. "What's happened to you Syriem, huh? What have you become? If you can't even meet me halfway, just this once, then I'm done with you." He took a few steps and turned at the head of the stairs. "I know it was rough for you and I'm sorry. But it's over now. Get a life, Syriem; *move on* – while you still can."

"Look Dorron," he sniffed; "I see this is important to you, but I can't do it – I just can't."

"Do you really think she'd want this legacy, to see you like this?"

"No, she wouldn't," Syriem capitulated; "but it's how I am."

Dorron left him to it and wished, not for the first time, that they had never gone to the market that day.

Syriem went back inside. He slumped at the reading table and faced his reflection, framed in the city lights. Such a change from the traveller between worlds he'd once thought himself to be. Flat, blue eyes stared out across the glass until inevitable, heavy tears blurred the view. He thought about Isca and their time together, and how it'd all ended. Was the Tablet really worth that sacrifice? He clasped the disc through his shirt, squeezing it tightly as if he could extract some solace from it. Outside, the Treasure Houses were opening for business; it was probably where Dorron had gone – he was welcome to them.

By the time Syriem entered the gates of the park it was deserted and the clear evening lent the place a sense of tranquillity. He found his usual bench and watched as the trees gradually yielded to the night sky. It took hold then, that same clarity of purpose that only reached him in the stillness of meditation. He paced across the green, treading the unseen path that called to him irresistibly.

The great shadow of the monolith broke his rhythm. Ces Frayer's statue towered above, watching paternally over the people of Tarsis. Syriem touched the great stones of the plinth; each one locked irrevocably into place like the city state citizens under Ces Frayer's rule. He gazed up at the icon and shivered, his mind sinking back to the time when Isca had first been taken from him. As he stood before the altar of his suffering he felt rage in every cell of his body – such fury that he thought it would consume him. But when he snatched his hands back and broke the contact, a strange content crept over him.

A tide began to gather, quickening his heartbeat and extending his consciousness. He felt his awareness expand, stretching out to encompass the entire park. No sound or scent escaped him; the totality of his domain was held *within* him. He had ceased to be Syriem; he became – as Isca had once promised – part of everything and belonging to nothing.

A flash of inspiration won through, scouring his psyche and lifting him free of his torment. He took a step back from the statue, arms outstretched in invocation. And in a voice that was both his own and not his own, resonant and purposeful, he cast four small words like a votive offering into the darkness, knowing as he did so that the wheel would at last begin to turn.

"*Not Mine but Thine,*" he moved his arms, shaping the letters L V X in the gloom, and mouthed the words 'Light In Extension'.

As he folded his arms across his chest, something within him shifted. He joined two fingers of his right hand and pressed them lightly, first to his forehead and then to his lips. Behind him, a celestial messenger blazed a trail across the darkened reaches of the sky.

In another part of the city, Turor glanced up at the sky and cursed his own lack of planning. He watched the comet with an uneasy feeling, sensing he'd missed an important opportunity and that he should have been somewhere else. The seers had been right though, about the comet. Or maybe, he pondered, as he walked back inside the house, it was just comet season.

The next morning he thanked his host for a welcome night's rest.

"What brings you to Tarsis?" the adulation in her eyes shone out with a sickening glow.

"Like all those who seek, I am here to meet my path," he replied coldly. It felt strange telling the truth again, like reclaiming a language he'd spoken a long time ago.

His host placed a hand on his shoulder, as if comforting a child. "May the Spirit of the One guide and protect you in all your ways."

Turor yielded a wry smile. "Based on my experience I think it unlikely, but I appreciate the sentiment." Then he went on his way without looking back.

chapter 8
REVELATION

Turor paid scant attention to the market owner beside him; he had other things to consider. Weeks of false starts and dead-ends, dispatching him out as far as Qayla City. Then, as if he'd passed some subtle test of faith, circumstances had led him to the market in Tarsis. To the uninitiated it might have seemed like coincidence; chance meetings and timing sending him on a random course. He'd like to have believed that. It would have made him feel he had a choice, that there wasn't some agency at work meticulously plotting his path. But he knew precisely which intelligence lay behind his progress. The Holy City of Sarrell called to him in a way that it called to few others – because he carried something that belonged there.

He tried feigning interest as the market owner rambled on. Behind him, he could feel the stallholders eyeing him up like a prize exhibit. He shared their disdain; he didn't relish working there either – too vulnerable, too visible to Targen eyes. But he had to eat and he had obligations to meet.

"I 'ad one o' your sort at my other market," the proprietor confided, grabbing the rent money with his fat little hands. "Didn't last too long though," he grinned. "You'll be all right, so long as you don't cause trouble; you don't look much like a Keldie anyway."

Turor fought the urge to wipe that look off his face. It had cost way too much to acquire the pitch, even though they both knew that a Thaylin Sarra in a market was good for business. City State folk loved their little flirtations with the taboo and the superstitious. He hoped so – he was counting on as much business and interaction as he could get.

The proprietor weighed the coins and surveyed his domain. "And don't be scaring my customers," he warned. "I don't need any aggravation here."

Then he sidled closer and broached the delicate matter of an extra levy to keep the Targen at bay. Turor smacked the coins down so hard that the proprietor yelped.

"Now, if you'll excuse me…" Turor dismissed him, turning to a book.

With the proprietor gone, Turor buried himself in the words of Parva Serach the Sage. Her travel experiences were as rich as they were disputed.

No small traveller himself, he devoured the pages until a sound caught his attention – a sombre, resonant hum. He tilted his head to gauge the direction, but the tone was too subtle. From the corner of his eye he saw a charcoal coloured mass, flitting past, weaving its way through an unsuspecting crowd.

Intrigued, Turor trained his gaze on the herd of people milling from stall to stall. There it was again, slowly taking shape. The pointed ears and snout formed first, followed by the legs and torso, tapering to a black tail that swayed gently. He followed the apparition's progress as it snaked unseen through the throng. The spectral dog searched the aisles in measured desperation, coming to rest at a crossroads. Then it turned sharply and looked straight at him, piercing the distance between them. He flinched as it melted away and faded to two pinpricks of brilliance.

"Are you open for business?"

The first customer of the day had arrived. Turor worked steadily and by noon he'd completed four light readings – to him they were all light – and sold a sachet of herbs to a man with a skin condition. And in between, he went back to Parva Serach's words.

It was a few moments before he realised someone was standing over him and he took a deep breath of perfume as he lifted his head. She was dressed as though she had somewhere better to go and, looking around him, Turor figured that could be just about anywhere. Jewelled rings – fakes most probably – adorned her slender hands and a tailored jacket sat snugly over her shoulders.

The woman smiled as she closed on him and made her pitch. At first he was a little slow on the uptake, mistaking her friendliness, but he soon got the message. She was offering a service of her own that had little to do with fortunes or religion. She leaned in to draw attention to her cleavage. Her eyes sparkled like illicit gems, although her face held a fragile smile. He declined her offer, explaining that he was at the market to make money not spend it, and wondered why she would have singled him out. She dropped a business card on the table and gave him a strange, disappointed glance as she slipped away.

Lunch was a bowl of steaming vegetable stew. At least, Turor hoped they were vegetables. They certainly bore little resemblance to any meat he'd ever seen before, and that included time spent in the desert. He tried to amuse himself by sensing people's energy fields as they walked by. It was an old skill, little practised, and it required a relaxed concentration before he could adjust to their vibrations. Experience had taught him that natives of each city had a certain resonance; he could usually spot the foreigners no matter how they dressed.

Sensing didn't always produce the array of colours that the pamphlets promised; sometimes there were symbols, often just a feeling. It served little purpose in the great scheme of things, but it passed the time and it didn't cost anything. He recalled that in earlier times some Thaylin Sarra had been branded *seers of the soul*. Now that would have really saved some time.

A couple drifted past, arm in arm, with another woman beside them. Turor sensed the tendrils of emotion from the man to the lone woman, reaching across like creeper vines. It was a tragedy played out in silence. *One can know too much*, he reminded himself and wondered whether to pack up and leave. He felt his cargo pulsing against his spine, urging him to be patient. He sat back and flicked through the tarot cards to vent his displeasure. The Ace of Rods leapt to his fingers and he greeted the card with a broad smile. He had his answer; he'd wait all day now if need be.

"Wait a minute, you two," Athenna circled back; "I just want a quick look."

"Come on, Athenna, I haven't got all day," Dorron moaned, turning sharp right a second later, as a attractive woman in a fitted jacket caught his eye.

Syriem stood idly by, gazing out on the world. Athenna lingered by the stranger and coughed politely, waiting for him to speak. Turor offered a seat, but she shook her head and pointed to her companions.

"Could you give my friend a reading? He's had a really difficult time lately and I know he'd be receptive. In fact he used to…anyway, would you speak with him?" She gestured discreetly towards Syriem, as he melted into the crowd with Dorron.

Turor agreed and she chased after them, dragging Syriem back with her. He blanched at the sight of Turor, but she sat him down and fussed over him like a child. Then she laid a sympathetic hand at his back and ran off to join Dorron.

Turor studied the boy; this had the makings of a long and painful procedure. He sensed Syriem's aura, catching glimpses of brown and grey threads that wrapped around him like an oversized shroud.

Syriem stared ahead; acutely aware what was taking place.

"So, my friend, how can I help you?"

Syriem sniffed aloud, tightening his face to a mask. He'd seen Thaylin Sarra at other markets, since the fire, but had never stopped to speak with them.

"I feel you have known great suffering," Turor opened strongly, waiting for an invitation into the walled citadel before him. He handed over the pack, half aware of the boy shuffling the cards, but his attention was elsewhere – the dog had re-appeared. Two sharp eyes flashed for an instant and then the creature drifted into the crowd.

"This might sound a bit strange," Turor swallowed, "but do you know anyone who has a black dog?"

Syriem jolted, sending the cards in all directions and mumbling apologies as he scrabbled after them. Turor bent down to help him, beating Syriem to the last card, which he turned over and placed on the table.

The Ace of Pentacles lay before them, its five-pointed star a cruel reminder to Syriem of the Tablet. He feigned ignorance, hiding his own proficiency with the cards and making Turor work for every crumb of input. As the reading progressed, Syriem felt no better. If anything he felt raw and vulnerable, as if every unspoken pain had been exposed to the elements.

They'd talked for almost an hour now and a heavy tension began to form at the base of his spine, inching towards his skull, numbing his muscles and fixing him to the chair. He resisted, summoning his True Will to counter whatever magic he thought had been used against him. With a burst of breath, Syriem wrestled free. His next movements were a reflex action; he lifted the talisman from around his neck and slammed it on the table.

Turor didn't blink. His own hand followed a moment later, crushing Syriem's fingers. He felt the talisman's presence without seeing it and a wave of emotion crashed over him like a dam breach.

Confused, Syriem snatched back his talisman and stood up. He'd only come to the market at Athenna's insistence and the question about the dog had shaken him. Turor's pulse hammered in his skull; it was now or never.

"Don't go yet…Syriem," he said earnestly. And then he smiled, as if he'd just recognised an old friend.

Syriem sat back down and the fog around him shifted a little. "So you know my name – what of it? Athenna must have told you or you heard it earlier. Or maybe you read minds as well as auras?"

Turor took a deep breath. "I know who you are, *Syriem,* because I was present at your birth. I named you." He lifted an identical talisman from around his neck and Syriem stared at it, speechless.

The Black Rod, sometimes known to the faithful as the Key, vibrated against Turor's spine in satisfaction. It had brought them back together at last, after years – and lives.

"Come on," Turor proposed softly, reading the shock in Syriem's eyes. "Let's find somewhere we can talk. We have a lot to catch up on! I'm Turor, by the way."

Turor took him across town to the nearest park. They found a bench and he tossed him an apple, watching with amusement as Syriem studied it carefully before taking a bite.

"What did you mean earlier, about naming me?"

"What's your middle name?"

"I don't have one." Syriem offered a bite of the apple, but Turor declined.

"They never told you then," he reasoned aloud. "Your middle name is *Taulpiris* – it is your given name. And I was the one who gave it to you."

"Look, I've already said…"

"Ask your parents, boy."

Syriem sat very still, uncertain what to tell Turor. There was an affinity between them; he could feel it now that he'd relaxed a little – and the talismans obviously indicated some deeper connection. But he wasn't ready yet to give away too much, especially about Isca.

"How do I know I can trust you?"

"What would you like to know?"

Syriem uncrossed his arms. "Tell me about the discs."

"Let's see now," Turor glanced skyward for inspiration. "The coin has been in your family for your whole life and you've never seen another one like it. Its design is foreign to you and yet you're drawn to it. You believe it's special, like some sort of talisman, but your family don't like to hear talk of it."

Syriem nodded, in concession to Turor's efforts, and as he did so his emotional aura expanded. Unbidden information reached Turor without censorship.

"You long to see the world outside," Turor looked around, getting into his stride; "and you're very fond of the girl, but you think she doesn't know…"

Syriem shut down the energy centres in his aura like heavy lids. And as each one settled, he sealed it with an appropriate symbol before moving his fingers together in focus.

Turor sprang forward as if he'd been kicked from behind. "Gods," he gasped, muttering half a Thaylin Sarra prayer in surprise, "grant me the strength at this hour…"

Without thinking Syriem completed the piece, "…To live in the light of truth." And though he tried to suppress it, the symbols glowed in his aura like hot coals.

"But you're no Wayfarer?" Turor voiced his confusion, little realising that the boy would know the Variz term for the Thaylin Sarra. "How can you know the signs?"

Syriem blushed and waited for the moment to pass. "What's the significance of the talisman?" he returned to safer ground.

"It links us together Syriem, the giver and the receiver alike."

"Yes, but what are they *for*?"

"It's a way of identifying you – and summoning you."

Syriem held back. There were things to tell Turor, he knew that, but not today.

"One more question," he concealed his acuity like a dagger, "are there other talismans?"

Turor straightened his tunic. "It's time for me to go; I'll see you again soon."

Tem and Sro smiled to one another as Syriem brushed past them, pretending to be drunk. Alone in his room he unwrapped the stone Tablet and lifted it on to his chest. Its weight calmed him and centred his mind. Later, so drained that he could scarcely keep his eyes open, he added to his journal and fell asleep with the name *Taulpiris* ringing in his ears.

Easen stared reproachfully at the clock, watching the minute hand creep around the dial. Athenna was late again. Soon Dorron's laughter filtered through the glass, encouraged by Athenna's many attempts to get her key in the door. Already tense, Easen launched himself to standing and folded his arms to face her. The door slammed hard and Dorron's voice receded.

"I'm home!" she warbled.

Easen glared as she stumbled into the room, one shoe in her hand.

"Don't look at me like that. I've been out having fun. You ought to try it some time."

"Go to bed, you're drunk. We'll talk in the morning."

"Suit yourself," she swung her shoe capriciously and hobbled away.

Once he heard her stumbling about upstairs he went to his basement workshop, locking the door behind him. He'd just poured two glasses when he saw the silhouette pressed against the barred, frosted glass. The handle turned slowly; Easen held his breath.

The visitor inched forward, letting in the darkness behind him. Cold eyes ranged over the room. He lingered by the doorway, scrutinising Easen's domain, looking for clues of the man and his work. Finally, Turor shut the door and mustered a sham of a smile.

It was, Easen surmised, a forced smile – the kind of smile a person used when they dealt with people they didn't trust. Turor extended a traditional greeting to his host.

"It's good of you to see me at such short notice," he eased the bag off his shoulder.

"You were recommended by an associate of mine," Easen took a long sip from his glass. "But my contact said that you asked for me…personally?"

"I do as I am bid," Turor replied, warming to the man. "We find ourselves in a time of prophecy and revelation. The dream of uniting the scattered is almost within reach."

Easen's hand trembled as he put his glass down.

"The Restitution has begun, Easen. I have seen with my own eyes – not three weeks ago – a pathfinder who will show the way."

"In Tarsis?" the eagerness in Easen's voice betrayed him.

"He is known to you and your daughter, although he has no inkling of the part he will play," Turor noted how Easen's face twitched. "But he is not of the faith and that's why I have come to you."

Easen was silent for a moment. "Gods, no; not Dorron. If we are expected to put our trust in him you'd best think again!" His tone soured, bitter that the role was not closer to home.

Turor read him clearly. It seemed strange that a Tarsien wished to serve at the table of the Gods. In Turor's experience the dish was invariably sacrifice.

"No, it falls to another; his name is Syriem Taulpiris."

"Syriem," Easen acknowledged quietly, unaware that his aura revealed his true feelings.

"I have travelled from beyond Variz; my message is clear and irrefutable. It's time to prepare an exodus."

"*Exodus*?" Easen shrank back. "We wouldn't get out of Tarsis alive; and even if we did, where would we go? We'd be dead before we reached the nearest settlement."

His words were so final, so embedded in hopelessness that a lesser man than Turor would have given up on him. However, he reached into his bag and touched the Rod. "You were not always a believer; I see that. Why are you one now?"

Easen slumped across the bench, one hand clinging desperately to the edge. Turor wielded his True Will like a blade, excising Easen's defences until the truth was laid bare. If he'd had the choice Turor would have tried to comfort him, but the Black Rod held no such intent.

"Buda?" Turor said, surprised by the clarity of Easen's thoughts.

"She left me because the faith demanded it; she had no say in the matter," Easen railed against him. "Your people took her from me."

"What if faith could ease your suffering?"

"You'd bring her back to me?" Easen schemed, ready to make any bargain.

"No, not that. But I could tell you if she still lives."

"And what use is that to me?" Easen scorned him.

"It would be of benefit to your daughter, for the times to come." He sensed that Easen was ready for the next step – receptive to a second revelation. He deftly lifted the Black Rod free. "This is the Key to Sarrell."

Easen saw the object in blurred shades of mystery. It seemed to cast a shadow in all directions like a parody of a flame. The Rod became first one colour and then another, each hue merging into the next as energy rippled across its gnarled surface. He touched the Rod and his mind embraced it hesitantly. Then his fingers closed around it and a seductive intelligence slithered inside him. He resisted at first, fighting his own repugnance and fear. Then finally, the exchange complete, he opened his hand and flexed it slowly.

Turor smiled fleetingly, a warm, human smile.

"So this is the Key without a Lock that Buda spoke of, years ago?" Easen covered his face. "I forbade her from teaching her faith to our daughter. Will this be my punishment now – to be shown that Buda was right all along?"

Turor shook his head. "The Rod has drawn us together for a common purpose, as it will others. I cannot speak for your past." He sheathed the Black Rod; his work was done – the seeds had been sown.

As he opened the door and faced the night, he heard Easen's farewell. The man sounded edgy, desperate to be rid of him. "I make him uncomfortable," Turor concluded as he pulled the door behind him; "good."

Turor paid Easen several clandestine visits, to receive updates from supporters and to gather intelligence on Syriem. His daughter believed that Syriem had got mixed up with a Thaylin Sarra priestess named Isca, and had even considered running away with her. Somewhere at the back of his mind Turor dimly recalled a child of the settlements, also called Isca. But the Black Rod had drawn a veil over the memories.

And what of the boy? They had a bond; they were kindred, after all. Why else would the Black Rod have urged him to pass on a talisman all those years ago? Then there was the matter of the symbols. Whenever Syriem's awareness faltered, the symbols in his aura flickered into life. He was certainly no Thaylin Sarra, which left Turor with only one plausible explanation: Syriem must have attained the knowledge in some previous incarnation. That would also explain why the boy had apparently thrown in his lot with a priestess so readily.

The Thaylin Sarra teachings on reincarnation were at best contradictory. Some said that a soul would always return to the faith – and clearly Syriem had not. That left another, darker possibility that Turor shunned. Could Syriem have picked up his knowledge in the past service of the Enemy? The Thaylin Sarra faithful were not the only custodians of magic – Appra also had its servants. The Black Rod was silent on the matter, revelling in Turor's turmoil. Forced back upon his own resources, he referred the matter to a higher authority.

Syriem was thrilled to receive Turor's invitation to a Thaylin Sarra house; it was something Isca would never have done. Clearly, the bond with Turor was different. There was the talisman of course, but also the matter of his middle name. He had only brought it up once with his parents and never mentioned it again. He'd heard his mother Sro crying that night, as Tem tried to soothe her; cursing their luck and asking forgiveness from Gods they were too frightened to believe in.

Turor had made him memorise the address for security. He walked mindfully, sifting through his thoughts. He had met Turor several times now and while there had been no formal tuition he always came away with new insights. Those discussions seemed to be the spark that ignited his True Will, shaping his dreams in the days that followed and honing his perception. Soon he'd have to discuss the stone Tablet with him. *And then what?* His mind stalled at the edge of the abyss; it seemed too vast a question to contemplate.

He arrived at the house and rapped three times on the iron knocker. The door glided back and a girl greeted him as Syriem Taulpiris, which made him laugh out loud. She invited him in and then kissed him on the forehead and the lips.

Everyone was assembled in a back room. Turor was already there, although he looked out of place surrounded by their formal attire. Syriem crept in and took an empty seat; no one paid him any attention. The girl sat demurely beside him, pointing to Turor and whispering.

"The Watchers wish to share their presence," Turor declared, sensing the onset of trance.

The group settled to give him their energy and attention. He closed his eyes and felt his palms press against the chair. One arm twitched in a staccato rhythm. It was like being drawn out of his body – no light, no colour and only the sound of his own thoughts. His breathing came in gasps, like the dying breaths of some ancient beast, each rise and fall of his chest threatening to be the last. The sounds subsided to clicks and sighs until his head dropped forward. Slowly the body – for it was no longer his body – composed itself and gazed around the room with closed eyes.

"I greet you and your purpose, which is Sarrell. The Holy City sent forth vessels of righteousness to redeem the land and the people. When the seekers find the way the fruits of the tree shall flourish together. When the last is returned the temple of the arc will be realised.

"The one who is lost will be found; the outcast shall be redeemed from the wilderness. The Key seeks the Lock and all things seek their resolution."

Syriem shrank back in his chair.

"Know that we are with you and that the Watchers guide your actions. Go to your children and ready them. You need wait in the shadows no more – the Restitution dawns. I bid you peace."

Turor felt himself spinning downwards, wrenched back into his body. "I'm sorry," he slowly raised his head, "I couldn't maintain the link for long with such a strong contact. Pass on what you have heard here to the other circles, but tread carefully. The Black Rod holds a fascination for the Enemy. The means must be found for our departure."

He gulped at a glass of water and the girl turned to Syriem.

"He tried to wait for you, but the Watchers were insistent. This is the third time they have come through today. I've have written down the other, longer scripts. Turor told us that his guest would want to see them."

Syriem drew a sharp breath. Isca had demanded that he keep his distance from the Thaylin Sarra yet here he was, sat among them.

"You're probably wondering what you're doing here?" Turor called across, indicating a vacant seat. "We need to move things forward," he said, noting the concern on Syriem's face. "I was hoping for more direct guidance."

"What's this Key that the voice spoke of?" Syriem broke the silence, hiding behind a veil of wilful ignorance.

Turor placed a bag on the table and addressed the room. "Our honoured guest has asked about the Key to Sarrell. Who here will answer him?"

Pupils looked to their teachers and the initiates looked to Turor.

"Surely the Key is the Black Rod?" a brave soul ventured from the back.

"Is that an allegory?" Syriem deflected the question back to Turor.

Turor smiled; Syriem had done as expected. "The Black Rod *is* the Key. It is a vessel of Ruin and Sacrifice, of Dissolution and Loss. All things bear the seeds of their own destruction so that they may begin anew. That principle is embodied in this artefact before you."

For a heart-stopping moment Syriem thought they meant him and flashed his eyes wildly to the door. Turor didn't help matters by passing the bag to him.

"The giver and the receiver alike, Syriem," he nodded in encouragement.

Syriem lowered his hand into the bag. A presence seemed to rise up and reach into the heart of his being, stripping away his pretences. He told himself that it was an illusion and drove out the fear with a silent invocation, unconcerned by what his aura might reveal. With a slow, emphatic breath he withdrew his hand and held the Rod out in front of him. A low thunder seemed to reverberate around the room, rippling outwards from the Black Rod. Tears streamed down his face, overwhelming him. He had met Isca's task and had found the Righteous One she had prophesied; he had fulfilled her purpose for him.

He glanced around the room. Did any of them realise they were in the presence of history? No one else moved; even Turor seemed bound by the moment. As soon as Syriem put the Rod down it relinquished its hold on them.

Turor placed the Rod on a table in the middle of the room. Some fell to their knees and he grimaced as he passed them. "You must be hungry," he drew Syriem to the back of the room. "Feel free to engage with our hosts; I need to attend to some private matters."

A boy led Syriem to the kitchen, where a series of small meals had been prepared. His presence aroused a great deal of interest. They asked about Tarsis – few of them had lived in the area for long – and teased him about the prejudices of the city folk. When he returned to the main room, the table with the Black Rod had been decorated with flowers.

The group shared a round of stories and myths, stretching back to Old Earth and the Great Religions before the First Exodus. Syriem listened, enthralled, reining in his enthusiasm for fear of revealing too much. There were also recent tales of healings and visions, isolated incidents throughout the cities and settlements that made up a constellation of experience.

Turor caught up with him later, as he stood alone in the backroom. "It's getting late; you should stay tonight. We can talk again in the morning."

It was a sparse and tidy room, more suited to contemplation than comfort. Squeezed in behind the door were a bed and a table. Syriem opened a drawer and found a candle and a small pile of leaflets. He lay in the darkness, listening to the hubbub of the house, and tried to reason out his next move. He could get it all over and done with the next morning; simply announce that he'd been protecting the Tablet and give it up to Turor. But wasn't it partly Isca's too, in a way? Maybe he'd keep it for just a little while longer, at least until he understood more about the talismans. He breathed in the faint scent of incense and closed his eyes, imagining that she was beside him again.

chapter 9
REDEMPTION

N O ONE HAD spoken for several minutes. Syriem hunched forward, staring into space, his mind clouded by the past.

"You're very quiet," Turor studied him carefully.

Syriem looked up. "Who are you, Turor, and why are you doing this?"

"That's difficult to say and harder still to understand. I believe that there is an intelligence guiding my actions – so my mother always told me. And I do as I am bid. I once gave you a talisman and now I am leaving the Black Rod with you while I go about its business."

"So what do I do with it, while you're away?"

"Nothing, I hope," he smiled for an instant. "Just keep it safe from prying eyes. It's a great responsibility; I know that. But you're the only one that I'd trust – I can't explain why."

Syriem chose not to pursue the point. He had his own opinions, faltering guesses at a truth that he shunned. And as long as he told himself they were only that – guesses – he could sleep at night.

"You *are* coming back aren't you?" After all, hadn't Isca left him? "And what about them?" he gestured towards the Thaylin Sarra at the far side of the garden.

"I've said you're not to be approached outside this house. And that they are to extend every courtesy to you as a messenger of the faith, should you visit. The Matriarch of the house knows more, but no more than is good for her."

Syriem brightened at the mention of *messenger*.

"You're late," the proprietor scowled. "I can't have customers thinking you're unreliable."

Turor staggered to the table, having run all the way from a meeting with Syriem. "I don't see any queues," he met the market owner's face.

"Just…see it doesn't happen again," he blanched. He remembered how some Thaylin Sarra were said to carry the evil eye; as far as he could tell, he'd just seen it.

Turor called out a blessing as the man hurried off; couldn't very well have his employer scaring himself to death. In the absence of any business, he worked alone with his tarot cards, clearing a space for a full spread.

The first card was the Page of Pentacles and he laid the Wheel of Fortune across it. Above them he drew the Four of Rods and below them the Six of Rods. For the past he dealt the Nine of Swords and for the future there was Death. He spent a while looking at the card, drinking in its symbolism. 'We die to live; we live to die' – the Ancients had said. He felt he understood; he'd known many sacrifices for the promise of a greater life – his own and those of others. Four more cards joined the pattern, building upwards from the base to form a pillar beside the rosette: The High Priestess, The Hermit, the Six of Swords and Justice. His lips curled to a thin smile at the figure's sword and scales in divine equilibrium.

He put the card back down and placed his fingertips at the edge of the table, viewing the spread in totality. Then he drew an eleventh card to seal the matter. The Magician took its place beside the grand design, as Revealer of All. The central figure stood poised at his altar like a living conduit, one arm to the upper realms and the other drawing upon the physical plane. And before him were the four hallows of the mundane elements, with the essence of the fifth symbolised by eternity.

Turor closed his eyes and visualised the figure, clothing it in three dimensions. Then he used his creative imagination to enter the design and *became* the Magician, bearing the Black Rod. After a few breaths he opened his eyes to a decision – he would go out and seek the Lock for the Key. He made the sign of the star over the spread – a little theatrically, in case there was an audience – and pushed the cards back together. Before he'd finished reforming the pack a customer was on her way over.

When he'd finished for the day he thanked whichever Gods he thought had smiled upon him – more out of habit than devotion – and wandered off through the market. Remembering that it was as blessed to give as it was to receive, he handed a jingle of coins to the huddle of people gazing forlornly at the soup stall. Their soul-less eyes received his generosity with subdued gratitude.

Two Targen officers ending their shift did not appreciate the stranger's kindness, not when they had a commission from the owner to clear out drifters from the market. They stood nearby, tracking Turor's departure.

"Here's how I deal with beggars!" one motioned to the other, passing him her unfinished beer. She stepped forward, swinging her baton wildly. Two of the hapless vagrants crashed to the ground with their meals. The stallholder hurriedly secured his pots to the barrow and was off, trundling his goods through the market as fast as he could manage.

The second Targen followed suit and waded into the fray, scattering gaunt bodies in all directions. Then he lifted a boot that stank of day old stew and wiped it on the nearest torso.

Turor heard the commotion behind him and curbed his rage. The Rod taunted him, whispering that he had only to ask and its justice would be enacted more swiftly than his charity. He resisted and kept walking, while memories of other incidents gnawed at his conscience. His Will and the Rod's Will, like Mercy and Severity, bound together around a single purpose. He sighed, burdened by his path. Once again his actions had created unforeseen consequences for others.

A pressure settled at the back of his head, the comforting grasp that heralded the out-reaching of the Black Rod. It was more of a merging of awareness than an overshadowing, but he was under no illusions as to which consciousness was the dominant one. He increased his pace and impressions seeped through the waking landscape. As he paused at a street corner, struggling to maintain focus, the Rod burst through.

Instinct kicked in, painting the world in primary shades of danger and shelter. He launched himself across the main street and into one of the alleys, where sunlight gave way to pale, otherworldly shades.

The Rod released its hold on Turor abruptly, deep into the alleyway. He stopped in his tracks and attuned to the sounds around him. He heard voices – a baroque duet of predator and victim. At the end of the trail he saw a huddled figure and her assailant.

"Did you think I wouldn't come looking for you? Now where's my money, bitch?"

The woman shrieked as a gargantuan arm hoisted her up and swung her against the wall.

"Shit," Turor muttered. Already seen, too late to turn away. At the back of his mind he heard the heavy, empty rattle that passed for the Black Rod's laughter. "Can…can I help you?" he faltered, advancing steadily towards them.

"As it happens you *can*, citizen," the thug sneered. "You can piss off and mind your own business." He gripped the woman by her hair and held out his arm as a dare to the challenger. The woman pleaded with her eyes, staring at Turor in the semi-darkness.

"Look, I really don't think…" was as far as Turor got.

A fist shot out so quickly that Turor barely had time to register it. He took the punch full force and crashed to the ground, spraying blood like a sacrificial offering. In all the commotion the woman seized her chance, twisting her captor's wrist back. As he screamed and released his grip, she thrust a knee into his stomach and scurried away.

Turor opened his eyes and felt the ground pressed against him. A giant of a man came into focus, smouldering like a furnace. He climbed to his knees and felt the sticky mess where his head had made contact with the brickwork.

"You're going nowhere," the thug assured him, one hand over his tender abdomen. "I went to a lot of trouble to find her and you've cost me. I want compensating for my trouble."

Turor fumbled about in his pocket for banknotes, murmuring an apology as he tried to stand. It was a wasted effort. The assailant struck his ribs and sent him sprawling.

"Not so brave now are you? I'll teach you to keep your nose out of other people's affairs."

"Just take them…" he waved the notes frantically, crawling back along the alleyway.

They were snatched away and a knuckle caught Turor across the face, flooring him again.

"Let's see what else you've got," the thug laughed, grabbing at Turor's bag.

"Don't touch that," Turor warned, struggling to regain equilibrium.

"I'll do what I like!" he raved, kicking him to reinforce the message.

"Alright then, do what you will…" Turor groaned and something in his delivery caused his attacker to pause. "Do what you will and let justice take its course."

"Don't mind if I do," the man grinned inanely, opening the bag. He discarded a rolled up cloth containing the tarot cards, along with charms and sachets of herbs. "A bloody Keldie – I might have known," he snapped. Then he found some metal trinkets, clipped them on his wrist and held them up to the light. "Might fetch something."

Now the bag had only one treasure remaining. He reached in feverishly, driven by a lust that was only partly his own. The Black Rod shuddered as it felt the touch of the unrighteous fool who now laid claim to it. The would-be thief lifted the sheath out into the dank air and his hand shook as his fingers coiled around it.

"Now this…" was all he could utter before the Rod claimed its spoils.

Several lights along the alley fizzled with an eerie hum and then dwindled to malevolent coals. The thug darted his eyes about in the gloom, almost as if he knew what was coming.

Turor scrambled clear of the choking atmosphere, a cloying astral fog that his assailant had barely begun to register. He looked away as he heard the Rod being slid from its cover. The shrieks of pain exploded in his ears and despite himself he now turned to the source. In near darkness he sensed the semblance of a great winged creature towering over the man. In his nightmare vision Turor saw the Rod gleam with a furious light, shrouding its victim as the daemon moved in for the kill.

Turor garnered his will, seeking to lessen the effect. The Rod paused in its frenzy and confronted Turor.

'Would you rather I had not intervened, Hybrolen?'

Scenes unfolded in Turor's mind, reminding him of when the Rod had acted on his behalf in the past. 'Then do it swiftly and let all things be brought to a state of balance,' Turor replied mentally, recognising that perhaps Mercy was twinned with Severity for its own protection.

When the Rod was sated it clattered to the ground, rolling obediently to Turor's crumpled hand. His swollen fingers curled around it, the whitened knuckles suckling energy into his battered body. The thug tumbled back against the wall, his face a mask of terror.

Turor steadied himself, surprised to find the man still alive. "I warned you," he hissed, laying a hand on the wretch's head to offer what little healing he could.

The electric lights crackled in unison, bursting into life like a false dawn. The man screamed, shielding his eyes from Turor's shadow.

"The debt is settled," he conceded, sensing the lacerated psyche, which ebbed away like a spectral haemorrhage. After reclaiming his possessions, he searched the man's jacket for the money. He found it next to a Targen badge and took what was his.

A new instinct took over. He touched his ribs carefully, surveying the damage; it felt bad. His mind was clouding over. If he fell in the open, he'd stay there and bleed to death most likely – a fitting sacrifice to uncover the Lock. He closed his eyes and felt a savage caress of blood as it ran across his face. He sifted through the sachets for any herbs that would aid him and came across the woman's business card.

The journey took an eternity, every movement demanding a force of will that was less his own than he realised. He kept to the shadows and emerged from the network of alleyways to find two tenements in a landscape of decay. Shattered foyer windows adorned the entrance of the block, like webs drawing in prey.

He pushed the main door, gritting his teeth to stop himself screaming. Then he made a slow ascent up the stairs, hoisting first one side of his body then the other in a gruelling rhythm. Crimson letters of hatred greeted him at the top floor: Tarsis is for Tarsiens. He pulled the door behind him, closing off the stench of urine from the stairwell, and staggered towards a nameplate. As he slumped against the door, an echoing clamour reverberated through his wounds. Someone dragged him in, stirring up pain beyond endurance until finally there was nothing but a welcoming casket of silence.

"You shouldn't have come here," she helped him drink. "If he finds you, we're both finished."

"You left me for dead," Turor choked. "For all you knew he'd killed me."

"No, Rysenn always stops when he gets what he wants."

"Well, you can relax for a while; he won't be going anywhere…" Turor broke into a coughing fit and rubbed an eye with the hand that was least damaged.

"How *did* you get away?" She rinsed out a cloth and watched as the bloodied water cascaded into a bowl.

"Like you said – I gave him what he asked for," he sucked in a breath as the cold water found his wounds. "What is he to you anyway?"

"A business acquaintance," she replied flatly. "Try not to talk – save your strength."

"I really need to be somewhere," he murmured and then closed his eyes again.

It was late evening when he awoke. Memories swarmed around him, vivid flashbacks flickering in time with the pounding in his skull. "What time is it?" he called, trusting that she was still there.

She moved the curtain a little. "It's around nine. I'll get you some more water."

"Wait," he raised an arm from the floor; "I don't even know your name. I want to thank you – you could have turned me away."

"Gisellan – it's on the card. And why would I turn you away?"

"Because of Rysenn. He's a Targen officer – from a local precinct?"

"No, not from around here. He's been after me for old debts from Sirn City. Anyway, I should be thanking you." She sat beside him, placing her hands together in supplication. "I prayed to the One for a sign that I had not been abandoned. And you came to me."

Turor hauled himself to kneeling; he felt like a poor instrument of deliverance. "I don't want to be in the way; you're probably expecting… visitors."

"I didn't always live like this, Hybrolen," she lowered her eyes.

Turor saw faded symbols rise to the surface of her aura and recognised her as his kin. He touched her cheek. "In the eyes of the One, we are all children. Who can know the true path for another?"

"There are few in the faith who would see my life now as a service to the Great Ones!" And then she laughed, suddenly comfortable in his gaze. "I won't burden you with my journey; it involved the drug Nepenthene and my own weak will. I'm not looking for pity; I made my choices and I suffer the consequences."

"What is your true name, Daughter of the One?"

She smiled, warmed by the title of an initiate. "When I lived within the faith, it was Alda. And now I am Gisellan."

"The door is always open, *Alda*."

"Would that such a thing were possible," she sighed.

He put an arm around her, wincing as she crushed her tears against him.

"Forgive me, Hybrolen, it has been a long time since I talked like this."

"I meant what I said; if you have someone coming round, I'll leave."

She shook her head and he didn't pursue the matter.

"Alda, I need some materials if you have them. Some salt, fresh water, a candle and some incense. And a space where I won't be disturbed."

She left him for a short while, returning with a small box. "I hoped I'd see a use for these things again."

Turor hobbled into the little room, groaning as he bent down to place an offering at each of the cardinal points. From Alda's box he found four triangular cards for the mundane elements and positioned each one at the appropriate direction. Lacking a dagger for the working, he drew the Black Rod from its cover and mumbled his apologies aloud.

His performance of the banishing ritual was lifeless and perfunctory, hampered by a mind as bruised as his body. Only the Rod's reservoir of power lent the proceedings any magical authority, conjuring his flimsy words into vortices of force on the inner planes. He kneeled at the east and closed his eyes, bringing both hands around the rod. Then he lay down and held the rod along his chest. Pain drained from his body, as his mind soared free.

He wakes, misshapen by his injuries, on a round plateau of stone. Dull reds and oranges glow through the grey at his solar plexus. He uncurls himself like a newborn, offering his naked body up to the Gods. A shape blocks the horizon, swooping down at him with the speed of an eagle. He thinks of mythical Prometheus, whose liver was repeatedly torn out for daring to steal fire from the Gods. The shadow descends and covers him with its wings, drawing off the worst of the damage. Then he sleeps, or so it seems, for when he opens his eyes again the terrain is bathed in a new light.

Her emanations are so strong that he feels her presence before he can see her. Memory recounts their first encounter – for this incarnation at least.

"Isca?" he asks, sitting up to face the arch. "Can it be you?"

"Am I not the Healer?" she replies softly. As the piercing blue glow around her fades, a black dog appears and circles him protectively. It completes its circuit and waits at her feet.

"Where is this place?" he asks, grateful for the company of a companion.

"Somewhere safe," she smiles, "where the Guardian could oversee your healing."

"The Guardian? Then the Lock is close at hand?"

She does not answer, but leans towards him, touching his head and lips. "Remember me to him," she calls behind her. "Tell Syriem that I have not forgotten him or our pact."

Coldness…damp…confusion. Turor's dull eyes searched the room. The candle had melted completely; the incense was now just a memory. He heard the muffled sound of the front door closing. It was none of his business – best not to get involved. Only he *was* involved now; the Rod had ordained that from their first meeting in the market. He closed down the temple and placed a pinch of salt in his mouth to sharpen his wits. When he felt ready to face her, he opened the door to a crack of light and listened for voices.

"It's okay, there's only me here."

"I heard the door…"

"Someone came round with news of Rysenn. He's had some sort of trauma – they took him to a hospital. They're going to question him tomorrow if he's well enough."

"So, you have friends…"

"I'm not an Assembly informant, if that's what you're implying. My loyalties haven't changed, whatever else has happened."

She felt crushed, as if Turor had somehow coaxed out the best in her only to smash it before her eyes. "I had forgotten how hard the ways of the Thaylin Sarra are to bear."

"I need to do something, first thing tomorrow and then I can take you somewhere safe."

"I've no money," she scorned him. "Why do you think I live like this?"

He revealed a wad of banknotes. "Some are from Variz so they won't be worth as much. Even so, there's enough here for travelling and I'll get you more tomorrow."

She turned sharply, tears welling in her eyes. Then she pushed the money away – gently, for fear of hurting him – and felt the hot whispering of his breath. His lips were soft despite their appearance, yielding to hers as her mouth pursued him.

"I didn't mean…" he eased back as her arm slipped around his waist.

"I am free to choose my own path now," she drew him close, spurred on by the heat of his body close to hers.

Turor yawned, shaken by a noise at the window. He saw the crow now, tapping furiously against the pane. He freed himself from the covers and pulled back the flimsy curtain, allowing light into the room by degrees. It was just after dawn and the bird behind the glass weighed him up with beady, onyx eyes.

"Carek," Alda called from the bed.

The bird stamped its feet and Turor wrenched the window open to see what it would do.

"My one concession to the past," she held out a hand to the bird, which flew around the room calling its name before settling on the bed.

She slipped from the blankets and stood before Turor, a vision of abuse. For a moment he couldn't bear to look at her, to confront what life and men like Rysenn had done to her. And he silently thanked the Rod for its mercy.

"Not so pretty, eh?" she reached for a dressing gown. "This is what you released me from."

"What you have liberated yourself from," he corrected her.

"Indeed," she yielded a fragile smile. "Last night was the first tenderness I have known since…" she stumbled at the words and turned to the bird. "Come and say goodbye, Carek. Today we are both free of this place."

The crow hopped along the floor and flapped a jump to the window. She stroked its beak, catching her reflection in its bright, dark eyes. Then she clapped her hands and it flew off, soaring over the rooftops to announce the day.

"What now, Turor?"

"We need to cover your tracks; after that the choice is yours."

They gathered up *Gisellan's* few possessions in boxes and took them downstairs, behind the building. Then she offered a half-remembered blessing to the life that she had led and lit the pyre. They stood together, waiting until the flames took hold.

"I'm free," she whispered quietly, turning to face the sun.

The Thaylin Sarra house received them warmly, despite the hour. Turor introduced Alda and asked for assistance to take their sister away from her persecutors. He also talked privately with the Matriarch of the house, relating as much of Alda's tale as he needed her to know. He was more reticent about the Black Rod.

"You are to keep it safe until he comes to collect it. This is a private matter between you, me and the boy."

An hour later, bolstered by food and funds, Turor and Alda sat in a taxi. He gazed admiringly at his reflection. Some of the bruising had come to full glory, giving him a weathered, no-nonsense appearance.

"Where to, sir?" the driver asked curtly, glancing at Turor's swollen jaw.

"Station," he snapped, with a wink to Alda. The driver took another look at his face and pulled out into traffic, with scant regard for his own safety.

chapter 10
THE POINT OF RETURN

SYRIEM ARRIVED at the Thaylin Sarra house two days later. The Matriarch invited him into a tiny room where she was editing a set of Thaylin Sarra pamphlets. Her desk was covered with papers, whose titles meant nothing to him: Koran, Sephirah Yetzirah and Vedas.

"The Teacher left this for you," she carefully opened a cupboard. For a moment, as the cloth bound Rod rested in her grasp, she stopped and her grip tightened. Then she passed the bundle to him with a stifled sigh.

He forced a bow and stuffed the cloth into a bag. He could feel her need to understand, but he didn't have an explanation to hand; at least, not one that he could yet come to terms with.

"Can I ask you something?" he felt her trying to sense his aura.

"Of course, my child, although you may not fully comprehend my response."

He accepted her conceit as the price of his anonymity, and drew his chair closer.

"Have you known Turor long?"

The Matriarch smiled at him and tried to sense Syriem's auric patterns again. Finding her efforts rebuffed, she hid her failure in a blanket of words.

"In one way I have always known him; in another, only recently. He is a Hybrolen, a Twiceborn. In the Variz Territory they still talk of a child, born almost thirty years ago and fated to usher in the Restitution. Strangers scoured the settlements when he was still young. Some say the riders came from Sarrell itself; others say they came from Appra. All we do know is that the child, this great hope of ours, was taken from us. He emerged, years later, clear in his purpose."

"If you believe the child *was* Turor, what do you think happened to him? Where could he have been all that time?"

She looked to the door, momentarily distracted by noises in the house. "In Sarrell, of course, to receive the Key and the guidance to lead us all home." She lent back in her chair. "You sought to test us for the Hybrolen. I hope my answer was sufficient."

"It was," he replied dutifully, intent on getting out as quickly as possible.

He didn't breathe easily until he'd reached Keres Park. There was always something welcoming about the great deciduous trees that lined the park, improbably fenced in by the iron railings they dwarfed. He followed one of the paths that converged like threads of a web, confronting Ces Frayer's concrete effigy. The Rod, unused to the lack of restraint offered by Syriem's wavering self-control, sifted his emotions and burned against his spine.

"Me too," he glared at the monument.

For the first time in a long while he was clear about what he had to do. Once he got home he lifted the Tablet from the bottom of the wardrobe and placed it on his bed, beside the Rod. After checking again that the house was empty he returned to his room and heaved a cabinet across the floor, setting it tight against the door.

He was sweating now, the exertion and anticipation dappling his body like anointing oil. He took off his shirt and stood at the bed, feeling the heat of the talisman against his sternum. In a series of controlled breaths and visualisations he formed the required magical symbols in his aura, imbuing them with his intent.

First he unwrapped the Tablet and laid a hand flat against it, conjuring up vivid memories of Isca. The sadness passed, but no current stirred in him – not a tremor of power. He turned to the Rod and unsheathed it, forcing his breath into a deliberate rhythm. His heart throbbed through his body in a hypnotic cadence.

With his left hand still on the Tablet, he lifted his right into the air and brought it down on the Black Rod. It felt neither warm nor cold; only the rough texture of its carvings reminded him that he was touching something separate from himself. For a while it seemed inert and then he felt his fingers instinctively negotiating the grooves and score marks. His mind became the observer, registering the shapes and sigils as he probed the Rod's surface.

A shudder rippled through his body like an invading parasite, with callous disregard for its host. He pressed his hands down, spreading his fingers to dissipate the charge. Whatever happened he did not want to break contact. The surge of energy steadied, bringing with it a warm, seductive confidence. He smiled to himself as he gazed at the Lock and the Key, side by side. Now that wasn't so difficult.

He closed his eyes in relief and in that second of unawareness, something snapped – deep in the centre of his being. The blast hit him full force, sending him to the ground like a corpse. He couldn't move or voice his terror. He didn't remember *before*; there was only *now*, a frightening immediacy that engulfed him. His throat constricted as air was squeezed from his torso. Then a hideous cackling drowned out the last of his thoughts, as he was dragged from his form in screaming silence.

Oblivion. The bliss of non-existence, remembered as a yearning after the descent into incarnation. Mind forms a body to house its splendour and with Mind clothed, identity unfurls. Life-force seeps in, allowing him to ingest colour and texture. Sensory information floods in. Objectively he comprehends nothing, but he feels with a depth of understanding that renders reasoning irrelevant.

He rises from the stone plinth and takes in an impossible vista. Around this circular table of sacrifice, five great pillars mark out his domain, each blossoming into some feature of deity: a black-headed jackal, the head of a lioness, a hawk, a sacrificed God and the Goddess of All. The pillars are frail and flawed; dust spills from their cracked veins. He stands with effort, resting against the pillar of the dog. Light issues from his hand, flowing across the pillar to sheath it in electrum. He adapts quickly to the laws of this plane, touching the four remaining pillars to set them ablaze with light.

"Why am I here?" he calls to the etheric wilderness beyond the circle. Outside, there are only shadows, nameless forms that move unhindered in the ever-changing grey. "Why have you called me to this place?"

The words echo back and forth, regurgitated by the dense fog in dark, cynical waves. In the instant of a thought the Black Rod appears in his hand, casting a dull glow against his skin.

"Who are you, child?" the voice calls from the nebulous, swirling masses beyond the pillars.

"I am Syriem Taulpiris," he declares, as if it is of some consequence.

"What is your purpose here?"

"I don't know." He wonders how to make sense of his experience and then realises that Isca would have understood.

"You have neglected her memory!"

He doesn't think to ask who is speaking or how his thoughts are so easily discerned. All he knows is the blistering heat at his heart. "I have not," he roars, radiating tremors of discord.

"Be still, child," the old woman soothes him, parting the swirling mists as she approaches. Her face is lined with ancient creases and her eyes shine an iridescent blue-grey. He sees himself reflected in those eyes, a trembling network of flickering brilliance.

"I saw you before. Are you...human?"

"In this domain, all is consciousness and projection. Even those great pillars are simply the work of your predecessor, an imprint to create an enclave on this plane."

"Why have you brought me here?"

She smiles and reaches a hand to a pillar, which hums resonantly under her touch. "I merely answered your call. Pass me the Rod so that I may commune with the presence behind it."

"Wait," he backs away, cradling the Rod to his chest. "Tell me this – has Isca reincarnated?" he snatches at ideas, consumed with a desperate, distorted notion of reunion.

The Guardian is bemused by his ignorance of the way of things and chooses to leave him in his darkness. "No, child; she has not reincarnated."

His glowing form dulls to a flicker of light. And though he feels his heart will burst, no tears elect to leave him. The Guardian reads him clearly and does not torment him. He has come here seeking only understanding, while others before him had sought a far less worthy quest.

"I could bring you a vision of her, but it would only be that. Her presence is hers alone to govern. If not the cause of love, what then?"

He looks beyond the five columns, knowing that to step through would be to embrace death – a painless, effortless transition. And if Isca existed on that plane at all he would be free to find her. In the midst of his confusion, a new awareness dawns: there is another way to honour Isca and his pledge.

"If not love," he vows, "then understanding and justice. I want to know who I am and I want to change the balance."

His eyes betray the hidden fire he has nurtured so diligently since Isca was taken from him.

"Very well, Syriem Taulpiris," the Crone concedes. "The bargain is met. When the time comes, you will be the instrument of our justice and we the instrument of yours. But hear me, child, it is Sarrell that is the final justice and understanding."

"Is this not Sarrell?" his consciousness is fading and the pillars are already shedding their glamour without his attention.

"Quickly, release the Rod to me," she urges, losing the gravelled tone of age to a voice that strikes him as familiar.

He pushes the Rod through the boundary and as she grasps the other end a connection is made. A great, dark creature manifests suddenly on the plane and countless eyes look back at him. Then it is gone. The one has met the other and between them an accord is restored.

"It is done," the Crone returns the Rod to him to reanimate his weary soul. "Go back to the world that you know, child, and prepare for the Exodus."

He lies down on the plinth, trembling like the unstable pillars that surround him and witnesses the disintegration of Isca's portal. Sight is the last sense to fade and the final vision, as all else fails him, is the black dog as it comes crashing down.

"Turor – come back to bed, it's cold here on my own!"

He stood in the darkness of the forest, at the centre of a marked out pentagram, gazing up at the starry heavens. And although the universe seemed to be moving in silent harmony, disquiet chilled his bones.

"There's been a change of plan," he announced, standing witness before the constellation of the flame. "I have to return to Tarsis immediately."

"But I can't go back yet – my work is here," Alda patted the blanket beside her.

"I'm relying on that; we need support from the settlements."

"There won't be any safe transport for over an hour…"

"Then we have time for other things," he concluded. "I'll set up a full temple."

"Are you in there?" Sro rattled the doorknob.

Syriem made a feeble lunge from the floor and crawled to the door.

"I'm here," he mumbled, gripping the cabinet to stand up.

"Someone from the plant called round – you didn't turn up for your shift today."

"I've not been myself," he forced a weary grin. "I'm going back to bed now. I'll speak to you this evening," he called from the other side of the door.

"Syriem, it *is* evening."

"So I'll see you tomorrow then, goodnight."

The Rod lay across the Tablet on the bed, shimmering in the half-light. He approached them with trepidation and lifted the Rod clear. Then he eased under the covers and let sleep enfold him.

It was deep into the night when he awoke. Pale moonlight had crept through the curtained window, illuminating the small, round disc as it lay on the carpet. He left his refuge and scrabbled about for the talisman, turning it slowly in a silvery caress. Then he placed it back around his neck and went to sleep, unaware that the Enemy had once again been denied.

The harsh light of dawn punctured Syriem's slumber. His cabinet resisted to the last as he dragged it back across the floor. Then he pulled on some clothes and made for the kitchen, consumed by a raging thirst.

Tem and Sro stopped mid-conversation as he appeared. "You want to be careful wearing that thing," Sro pointed to the talisman. "It's probably making you ill."

Tem rallied to his defence. "Nonsense. Just a touch too much of the grog, eh?"

Syriem nodded in a daze and filled a glass. He squeezed a broken smile and gulped down the cool, soothing water. "I think I'll give work a miss today as well."

"As you like, boy," Tem agreed, following him back to his room and closing the door behind them. "Look, Syriem, I know we haven't got on lately, 'specially after that tragic business with the Keldie woman."

"*Isca* – her name was Isca. And they're called Thaylin Sarra."

"What I'm trying to say, Syriem, is that I'm not as daft as I look. Your mother, see, she likes to pretend; I don't kid myself so. These days you're rarely here and yet I haven't seen Dorron for weeks or smelt the drink about you. Is something going on? "

"Everything's fine; I just need time to myself."

Tem left him and went back to report to Sro.

At mid-morning, Syriem broke off from his meditation to put his body through some gentle bends and twists, wringing out the lethargy. He lay there afterwards, listening to the world outside. Maybe he'd visit the Thaylin Sarra house – they might have a remedy for him. He killed the thought in an instant; what if they discerned the cause? He fetched out the three sections of stick, salvaged from the courtyard tree, and asked a question.

Syriem watched the line of people stretching back beyond the platform barrier. They shuffled slowly forwards, in marked contrast to the City State citizens who breezed through the statutory checkpoint. The Station Hall endured the foreigners like a penance. They queued quietly, over-awed by the ostentatious splendour of the station terminus. Sleek, architectural lines of steel curved high into the upper reaches of the building, bubbling down in molten flows of gold, scarlet and lapis blue. Every spare inch of wall that wasn't covered by a poster or city ordinance bulged out in basalt relief, depicting scenes emblazoned with titles such as: Endeavour, Industry and Fortitude.

A crumpled orange slip of paper blew across his feet. He knelt down and rescued it, carefully smoothing out its creased edges. One side showed a comely figure on a couch, in the style of some ancient civilisation. He stared at the image and mentally ran though a litany of goddesses who might fit the design. He turned the piece of paper over, still pondering Diana as the likely image when he read the words:

Treasure House Carbul – Temple of Delights! He ripped it up and headed outside, cursing the Gods for their indifference.

It was a long journey from the station to Keres Park, but still not enough time to shirk the mood that dogged him. He reached the railings and surveyed the area, as if it were his personal domain. From the gate he could see a lone figure, crouched beside the state of Ces Frayer. And though he told himself it could have been anybody, he knew it had to be Turor.

"You're back sooner than I expected."

"I didn't much choice," Turor lifted his head slowly. "How are you?"

"Me? I'm fine! Why wouldn't I be?"

He looked through him. "Fetch the Rod and meet me back at the house."

Turor handled the Rod cautiously, touching the object as if he were receiving it for the first time. It felt distant and aloof; their brief separation had disturbed him more than he'd anticipated. He closed his eyes and focused, mentally reaching out to make contact. The symbolic gateway that heralded the link with the Rod's intelligence slowly emerged. In his mind's eye he approached the portal, pacing out the steps until…he halted in his tracks. The magical seals were broken. Somehow the boy had achieved communion – a contingency he hadn't allowed for. He closed down quickly and sat, eyes closed, listening to Syriem's erratic breathing. The sound irritated him.

Syriem remained still, frightened to move in case he disturbed his mentor's work and equally petrified that Turor would uncover his secret.

Turor opened his eyes and carefully laid the Rod aside. How had the boy done it? What work of Art had enabled Syriem to breach its defences, cross into the Rod's domain and return unscathed?

"Well, you appear to have accomplished the impossible."

Syriem smiled – a fragile, placating crescent that failed to convince either of them. In the candlelight, each bruise and blemish on Turor's face assumed malign importance.

"You went in search of the Lock," he lowered his head.

"Yes," Turor nodded slowly. "I've set forces in motion to aid us."

"Do…do you know what you're looking for?" Syriem's eyes blazed from the shadows.

Turor exhaled a plume of mist that almost smothered the candle flame. "The Lock is an encoded stone tablet; that much I know. The closest I ever came to it was at a settlement on the edge of the Variz Region. I was there for a few days when a travelling woman claimed that a magical stone had healed her – she'd been struck down by blindness as a child. She also spoke of visions.

"I met with her privately, certain that the Rod had drawn me out of hiding to fulfil its prophecy. I couldn't have been more wrong. Her eyes were still unaccustomed to light, just beginning to register colours. I don't know why I did it, pity I suppose and maybe arrogance. But I felt I could improve her condition.

"I laid the Black Rod in her hands and she wept. Then I placed my palms over her eyes. But as I stood beside her all *my* pain was drained away, as if it were being poured into a bottomless cauldron. She told me that she had now encountered both the Lock and the Key, prophesying that I would bring them together. When I took my hands away I saw that her eyes had cleared."

"When was this?"

"About three years ago, I think. And now here we are. The Rod has an affinity with you, Syriem, perhaps because it was present at your birth. I can feel it – and that's more of a rarity than you can imagine. It was the Rod that guided me to bequeath you your talisman – and the others. But the Rod is only half of the puzzle; we need the Tablet."

Syriem finally yielded, his shame wringing out the words that he'd held back for too long.

"I think we need to have a talk…"

Turor listened in disbelief, as Syriem made his confession. Years of searching, of evasion and subterfuge, only to come full circle to the boy.

"…Isca hid the Tablet with me and paid a heavy price to keep it safe," he cracked. "She entrusted it to me because she knew that we'd meet."

"Aye, she saw the light within you – and much more besides."

"I didn't even know about my talisman when I met her and nor did she," Syriem blew out the candle and pulled back the curtain. "Is everything out there so wrong?"

"No, not wrong," Turor consoled him, "but incomplete – out of balance."

"What do you mean?" Syriem's eyes blazed again. No allegories this time, just the truth."

"As you wish," Turor clapped his hands together. "I'll give you an example. Nothing new has been made in the City States for at least three hundred years."

Syriem shook his head, thinking of all the changes he had seen since childhood. And yet, another part of him never doubted Turor for a second.

"It doesn't make sense, does it?" Turor headed for the door. "But there it is."

Syriem arrived at Easen's house early, hoping to catch Athenna alone. He rapped on the great door and rejoiced as he heard the clip, clip of Athenna's shoes across the finely tiled hallway. She seemed distracted, whispering, as they walked through, that it really wasn't a good time to talk. As they entered the lounge, Dorron lifted out of the chair.

"Can we go now?" he dismissed Syriem's presence with a sneer. Then he swung an arm around Athenna and squeezed her to him, roping in his chattel. Athenna struggled, but not too vigorously, feigning outrage. Dorron shot Syriem a final, triumphant glance and slammed the door after him.

Syriem was still seething when he went downstairs to Easen's workshop.

"Is there a problem?" Easen paused from pinning a blueprint to the bench.

"It's nothing – just Dorron," Syriem stared at his feet.

Easen nodded. So, Turor's understudy had a weakness after all.

"Drink?" he rattled a glass to get Syriem's attention.

Syriem kept his head down and concentrated on the design, carefully logging the letters and numbers, as if it all meant something to him. He heard Easen lift a bottle from under the bench and tried not to judge him for it.

"When Athenna was born," Easen waved his finger like a cudgel, "I gave Buda a choice; I told her straight – it was her faith or me. I wasn't having any child of mine brought up as an outcast," he puffed out his chest and drained the glass. "She gave me her word," he sniffed, "but they drew Buda back into old ways. She said she'd leave me if I set foot in Appra City again – and take Athenna with her; can you believe that?"

Syriem shook his head on command.

"I couldn't let her do it."

Syriem tried to find compassion, but the mention of Appra turned his gaze to stone.

"Who are you to judge me?" Easen screeched, his bloodshot eyes the colour of hate. "You think that you're something special just because *he* says so?"

"I think I should go," Syriem edged towards the door.

"Wait," Easen relented, raising his hands. "I'm sorry. If you're everything he claims then prove it – bring Buda back. You do that and I'll follow you anywhere."

Syriem faced at Easen, fixing him with his will. "Everything *who* claims?"

"Turor, of course. I know all about his quest for Sarrell – and we're with you."

Syriem left without another word. This was madness and it was Turor's doing. And though the thought of travelling with Turor thrilled him, it also terrified him.

Turor watched the boy leaving and checked the time – earlier than expected, but no matter. He entered the basement and closed the door behind him.

"I trust you have some useful information for me…" he stopped short at the sight of Easen, sprawled over the bench. "What have you done?"

"I told him about Buda," Easen wailed; "I wanted him to know…"

"He'll know what *I* decide," Turor pulled a small flask from his jacket, scarcely able to contain his rage. "Drink this. You have compromised our arrangement and betrayed Syriem's trust."

Easen murmured an incoherent apology, but Turor was unmoved.

"Again," he pushed the flask on Easen. "Syriem can no longer work for you here, so you will compensate him. And you are forbidden to speak of these matters, to your daughter or anyone. Do you understand? Now, gather your wits – we have work to do."

Two hours on, Turor stood pensively in the cold night air. He would have to rethink his approach; Easen's meddling had complicated matters.

chapter 11
THE POINT OF NO RETURN

O NE OF Parva Serach's commentaries stated that the Thaylin Sarra should be like unto shadows, passing through the waking world without substance or form. When word got out that the Righteous One had been proclaimed, it spread like wildfire through the Thaylin Sarra communities. And like shadows they moved between the cities, hastening back with tests of faith and requests for an audience. Most had long anticipated one who would confirm the prophecies – an individual to heal divisions within the faith and reinstate orthodoxy. In short: someone who wasn't Turor.

He faced all their challenges, keen to move the faithful beyond the dry, dusty canons of the past. A practical plan was needed to get people safely out of Tarsis. With that single concern, he met circle after circle to muster support for the journey.

"Only the ignorant would interpret Sarrell purely as a physical place," they told him as they rested serenely in their robes, oblivious to the filth and poverty outside. "If you were truly who you claim to be then you would understand that."

"What if Sarrell is both place and presence?" he tried a different approach. "One requiring us to first find liberation within and then seek it out in the world?"

The Matriarchs and Patriarchs smiled generously at the upstart pretender before them, treating his ignorance with the pity it deserved.

Elsewhere, Turor accepted the accolades of Hybrolen and Righteous One ungraciously. It was a prop at best, a cloak reluctantly donned for ease of identification. If the believers needed a framework of understanding in order to commit their support then so be it. For without their support it was meaningless, and without meaning he would fail those he was tasked to serve. But he was sure of one thing – if need be he would make the journey with only the boy beside him.

Even those closest to him could not be relied upon to keep his confidences for long – Easen was proof of that. And once the Targen took a keen interest, the Appren initiates would be swift to follow. Faced with such a dilemma, he turned to Easen's circle of supporters, bearing the fragments of a plan forged in a moment of revelation.

Turor and Syriem had been in Keres Park, idly passing the time, watching the inhabitants of Tarsis drift by like caricatures. Syriem had fixed his discussion on Athenna, in that guarded way of his. Turor had listened to Syriem's self-inflicted suffering for as long as his patience held, and then looked for another topic to distract him. Syriem took the bait, seizing on the chance to vent his frustration about work. How he loathed his supervisor and couldn't see what spiritual benefit there was in bearing the scorn of fools.

Turor laughed with him, drawn into Syriem's wicked parodies of his co-workers, as he went into an elaborate performance of cleaning down a cargo vehicle, each action accompanied by a whining supervisor's voice insisting that every inch of the truck was spotless.

As he listened, Turor felt the Black Rod's presence bringing itself to bear and paid closer attention, sifting Syriem's words for gold. When inspiration came it struck him like lightning, framing the future in violet brilliance.

"Tell me more about the Transvector cargo vehicles, where you work," he glanced up suddenly with a half-smile. "Exactly how big *are* they?" And then he pitched Syriem a frenzy of questions, jotting down notes and calculations on sheets of hand-pressed prayer paper. "Could we get schematics?"

"The supervisor's office holds all the engineering and repair sheets," Syriem said, watching Turor's lips curl. "But if I got caught I could lose my job…"

Turor cocked his head on one side and raised an eyebrow.

"Oh yeah, I see what you mean," Syriem grinned sheepishly, sprawling on the grass like a vagabond. He looked up, suddenly overwhelmed. "You're serious?"

"Deadly serious," Turor replied without looking over. "This is the breakthrough we've been waiting for."

"Well, if I get a late shift next week and the supervisor leaves early again, I could have a look round the office…" his voice fell away.

"Do what you can," Turor urged. "And let's keep this just between us."

In Sirn city they mocked him and called him *Sarrien* – a mythical Protector of Sarrell. To those willing to hear him, he offered hope of the Restitution; but to those who would not listen, he was just another misguided soul trapped in his own delusions.

Syriem did what was asked of him, delivering three diagrams that told Turor lamentably little – information he could have easily acquired by other means. Still, it had served as a test of the boy's courage. Esoteric allegiances were all well and good, but the ability to turn intent into action would be the strongest link in their chain – or the weakest.

Easen fussed over the last few details of the meeting, adding two more items to an already burgeoning list. Everything had to be right, with so many representatives from the other circles all in one place. Bench tops, usually home to laboratory equipment or engineering tools, had been meticulously scrubbed and shrouded in great, embroidered cloths. Food – and expensive food at that – was separated into two groups, in deference to those who abstained from meat and fish.

Athenna was away until the morning; in the absence of voices, memories resounded through the cavernous house. He ached for the comfort of a full glass and a world blurred at the edges, but Turor had forbidden it and he knew better than to cross him again.

The first visitor arrived early, tapping on the window with bird-like timidity. She extended the Thaylin Sarra greeting, as he stood in the doorway. Her thin lips tasted of some exotic spice and he reddened, shocked by a fleeting charge of desire. She smiled and followed him to the tables, her scent wafting around him like a lure. And although he tried to make small talk, she picked at the food without speaking.

Within the hour more than a dozen guests had arrived, some unmistakably Thaylin Sarra and others allies to the cause. Easen performed his duties as host, but whenever he was free from his responsibilities he returned to the woman's side like a lost child. She watched him carefully, aware from his demeanour that he had long since given up on a personal life and that he was finding the thaw more painful than the rigour he had buried himself in. Their hands brushed for an instant and she sensed a part of him long dormant reawakening.

Turor arrived last, slipping inside with feline stealth. The room hushed to silence. "Why wasn't someone guarding the door?" he clicked the lock behind him and went over to Easen, shaking him warmly by the hand.

"I've collated the feedback from other circles," Easen handed around papers.

"We'll burn these before we leave, " Turor insisted. "Close the blinds and dim the lights."

"Is that necessary?" a friend of Easen's protested. "This is a respectable neighbourhood."

"It's not the neighbours we need to be concerned about," the woman near Easen opened her bag and took out a small radio-set. "Now we can eavesdrop on the local Targen."

"Let us make a beginning," the Matriarch Nessa proclaimed, rustling her papers to get everyone's attention. "Item 1 – Appeal to The Assembly for a larger community zone that we can transform into a homeland – that's from a cell group in Sirn City."

Turor held his tongue while they debated the point to an ignoble end. Four more points were also dismissed without his involvement. But the fifth item, debating the meaning of a particular prophecy, could not go unchallenged.

"We'll get nowhere if we waste time on matters of little consequence."

The silence in the room was deafening.

"We have only one thing to decide. Are we committed to the path that leads to Sarrell?" One or two looked eager to respond. "Before you quote Parva Serach, I don't want to hear it. We need to focus on the present, not the past. The only way to Sarrell is out of Tarsis."

Patriarch Verif cleared his throat. "And how do you expect to get out of the city?"

Turor turned to one side. "Easen?"

He stepped forward. "We'll take people out of the city in Transvector haulage trucks."

Turor smiled – succinct and factual, just as they'd discussed.

"How would such a thing be possible?" Verif gasped, sensing Turor's aura. "Are we to ask the authorities for these vehicles? What makes you think the Way is shown to you when others have searched their whole lives in vain?"

Turor judged that the moment had arrived and brought out the Black Rod. In the dimmed light, a vibrating shimmer cocooned the Rod, refracting light to seven principles. Then, while all eyes were on the Rod, he lifted the Tablet from the bag.

"The Lock and the Key are revealed – and through *them* the Way will be shown.

"Salaam al Shaddai, Verif cried. "May I live to see that day." Yet something in his voice held an inestimable sadness.

Turor laid the Tablet on a bench and crossed the floor to embrace Verif, keeping the Rod in his left hand. It sought out the weakened energy field around Verif and, in keeping with Turor's unspoken wishes, directed its current of force towards him. Then the Rod's revelation collided with Turor's mind and grief numbed him.

Verif held him close and whispered, in one of the ancient tongues, "I know now that I will not see Sarrell in this world. But I will be a shepherd to the fallen."

Turor returned to his seat, shaken, aware that the flame had now been lit.

"Which names go on the list? Who has the right to share in this covenant?"

"I don't know," he admitted. "It all depends on how many vehicles we can get."

"How do we choose? Poets, healers, scientists?"

"What use are men of science in the Promised Land?"

"I think," the woman beside Easen spoke up, "we should stick to the practicalities tonight."

"Agreed; we need a tangible plan if we're asking people to commit themselves to…"

"Sedition," Easen gave a long sigh.

"Then our next objective is clear," Verif laid a hand on Turor's shoulder. "Before we leave here tonight we must determine when this great journey will take place."

Nessa stepped forward, bowing to Verif. "We consulted our greatest astrologers…" she unravelled a pile of charts.

Easen stared at the Rod, resting next to the tablet, and glowered. Religious aspirations were understandable; he could even respect them to a certain extent, but the notion of fate offended him. It happened slowly, like the first, shy kiss of lovers. He peered into the misty halo around the Rod and a tumbling sense of heaviness overtook him. He followed it in his mind, circling down, each spiral of consciousness drawing him deeper inward, until…

"*Easen!*" Turor barked, aware that he had felt the Rod's touch.

He recovered his senses, but his face betrayed the exchange. "I think I have it – the date of departure: Ascension Day."

Nessa waved a piece of paper in the air. "We have a chart for that," she said, deftly tucking other charts into her robe.

A brief show of hands sealed the fate of the chosen. The streets would be clear for the annual parade, commemorating his ascent as head of Tarsis City State. The timing would be both symbolic and practical.

With the main business settled, talk fell to other subjects. Turor allowed them the inevitable dissection of prophecies in relation to their scheme, listening politely as the religious and the secular negotiated a meeting of minds. And as he listened, he found himself drawn back towards Easen's companion.

Nessa offered a prayer for the endeavour in the hope that it would save more lives than it cost, for to be certain there would be losses. Then Verif presided over the Eucharist, passing around salt, flatcakes and water. When the last had drunk from the cup, Turor moved aside the table that had served as an altar. He stood in its place, grasping the Rod at the centre of its gnarled length. One by one they moved in close, so that each could touch some part of the Rod together. And it, in turn, could touch a part of each one of them.

"We commit ourselves to the Great Work: the attainment of Sarrell," Turor affirmed, and they repeated his words for their own.

Syriem received both the Rod and the Tablet from Turor, a few days later. He set about building understanding with the Rod. Its mind-voice was an undulating whisper that called to him in the deepest recesses of his dreams. Sometimes it took the form of a snake or a bird, always as dark as an eclipse. He wondered if Turor still heard that seductive call in his dreams, but the Rod itself counselled against discussing it. Whatever they shared together, it promised Syriem, would be his alone.

Turor had cautioned him to allot his time with the Rod wisely – invasive, he had called it, like the Nepenthene peddled outside the Treasure Houses. Too little and no benefit was derived, leaving a hunger that gnawed at the soul. Too much and the Rod would smother his will with its own. Only the middle way would suffice and it was for Syriem to determine it.

He put Isca's training to good use. A protection ritual preceded every contact with the Rod. And every night, before sleep, he effected a magical banishing of his room. Whenever he dealt with the Rod, it would be on his own terms. The Tablet, meanwhile, lay hidden in his wardrobe, waiting until Turor was ready to claim it.

Turor had conceded Syriem the date of their departure, but little else; and that was how Syriem preferred it. Whenever they met, Turor would ration information, measuring Syriem's progress against some private scale he had yet to divulge.

The more Syriem tried to fathom the Rod, the more it drew him into its domain – a visionary world of wonders and excesses. Sometimes he would finish his inner journeys in the early hours of morning, so invigorated that he was beyond sleep. Or else debilitation would send him to his bed for a day and a night. It promoted intense dreams – sometimes of Isca. It was a cruel irony that the image he sought so desperately was plainly a façade. Yet the more the Rod tested him, the more he clung to the conceit that he was piercing its boundaries.

Only once did Syriem seek to profit from his True Will, for once was enough. After weeks without Athenna or Dorron in his life, he had begun to crave the company of his friends. Not the unspoken bond that Turor offered, but a more emotional attachment, borne of shared years and experiences.

Athenna and Dorron were waiting at the bar, eager to see what had become of him. At first glance, he was the same old Syriem; shoulders bowed, glancing surreptitiously at the exit.

"Anything you'd like?" Dorron pulled Athenna closer to provoke him.

"Whatever you're having," he headed off to find a table.

Dorron ferried his drink over like a servant. "So, how have you been?"

He smiled, and something in that smile unnerved Athenna. In all the years she had known Syriem, there had been a certain emptiness about him – a sense of separation that in some ways she could relate to. But now, as he turned to her, she saw that the void had been filled.

Dorron waited until they were settled before he played his ace card. To celebrate Syriem's return to the *real* world, he'd had arranged a blind date for him.

"Good, I could do with the exercise."

"That's my boy!" Dorron roared into his beer, slapping Syriem on the back.

At that moment, and for entirely different reasons, Athenna hated them both. The girl soon arrived and looked around for her prize. Dorron called her over to join the party.

"Let me get you something," Syriem leaned across, touching her hand.

She followed him over to the bar, intrigued. Dorron sat back to watch the show and reached for Athenna's hand, which wilfully eluded his. She narrowed her eyes and, as had happened in recent months, faint clouds of light appeared around the people at the bar like a mirage. The girl shone misty pink, flecks of red sparking off towards Syriem. His aura was more guarded, but Athenna persisted. Waves of dissonance rippled around his outline, fending off her will until she focused on his solar plexus, the emotional seat where she instinctively knew he'd be most vulnerable.

He turned to her slowly, drawn by the intensity of her gaze and wilfully lowered his defences. The union with the Rod appeared to Athenna as an apparition – dark, malevolent bulges at Syriem's shoulders like folded wings, distorting his shape into a hobgoblin.

"It's amazing, isn't it?" Dorron nudged her. "I'd never have thought they'd get on so well."

Syriem remained at the bar with his consort, laughing and joking. He was more tactile than ever, repeatedly touching her, reinforcing the link between them. Finally, as the first tendril of energy spiralled out around the girl like a suffocating vine, Athenna could stand it no more.

"Wouldn't you be more comfortable over here?" she called.

Her insistent voice spoke to a buried fragment inside Syriem. He released his prey for a moment and turned towards her. Athenna met his cold glance with a look of fury. *Don't think that I don't know*, her eyes told him, but the expression of his face was equally unambiguous. He didn't care that she knew. In fact, it pleased him.

"We're going on somewhere," Perrani called over. "Are you coming?"

Athenna shook her head before Dorron could speak.

"You're right," he agreed, "Best leave them to it. Syriem's got a lot of living to catch up on."

Syriem slipped an arm around Perrani and together they squeezed through the door. Dorron waved his glass in a salute of honour.

"You look pleased with yourself," Athenna fumed.

"I can't wait to hear Syriem's story tomorrow. A shot of Nep will open his eyes up to something more meaningful than philosophy!"

"Nepenthene?" she gasped. "You don't mean…she's a junkie?"

"Keep your voice down," Dorron shushed her. "You're starting to sound like your father. She uses a little now and again – what's the big deal?"

"Perrani, Perrani," Syriem whispered, nuzzling her neck as he unbuttoned her jacket. The brisk night air was cold against her skin, but all he felt was fire.

"Hey, take it easy now," she restrained him as his hand rounded on her breast. "Let's go somewhere more private."

She smiled in the glow of a streetlight, pleased that she hadn't followed her first instincts and left straight away. Maybe Dorron had steered her wrong about him, but that just added to the mystery. He seemed so different from other people, with a definite presence about him.

They made their way far into the southern sector. She mentioned a flatmate, who worked nights, but Syriem had stopped listening to her; all he could hear was the rasping voice within him. As she opened her door he pinned her to the wall, feasting on her like a parasite.

"Mmm, you don't waste time," she yawned, suddenly drained of energy. "Why don't I rustle us up a little something to heighten the experience?"

She disentangled herself and slipped past him to get to the bedroom. He was keen and no mistake – a wild one. She just hoped that his stamina matched his interest. "Won't be long now," she called from the bedroom. "Just doing what a girl's gotta do!"

Music blared out along the hallway in a primitive, sensuous beat. The combination of sound, alcohol and Dorron's chemical surprise ran riot in Syriem's chaotic consciousness. He licked his lips as he squinted at the lights. Water – he needed water. He stumbled along the corridor to the bathroom.

Dull eyes reviewed him from the mirror. The *voice* resumed its chatter and his reflection distorted into something hideous. He reacted instinctively, lashing out with his fist. The image smashed into a hundred splinters, but each fragment multiplied the grotesque apparition. Blood trickled into the sink, coiling slowly down the plughole like a bloated worm. As he tried to wash the mess away, his sleeve brushed scarlet against the tiles. He felt a wave of nausea and lurched backwards. He had to get out, had to escape from the mirror and its secrets. His stomach tightened and bile clawed at the back of his throat.

He made a dash for the front door and retched up a flood of steaming discharge on the step outside. The cold air slammed into him and he staggered into the night.

Perrani listened hard. What was keeping him? Maybe he wasn't so keen after all? "You okay out there?" she crouched over her apparatus. "Do you want me to come and find you?"

She took the flame away from the tiny crucible and blew on the liquid. A milky layer formed on the surface and she skimmed it off carefully. The taste cavorted through her senses. She was hot and hungry now, aching for his body while this other, subtle seduction endured. She let her skirt slip to the floor and eased out of her remaining clothes, touching her palm against her breast and delighting in the sensation. Then she put on a sheer, translucent dressing robe.

"Are you still there?" she giggled, stroking the top of her thigh and thrilling to the possibilities it suggested.

She loosened the robe, so that every shift of the fabric rippled through her body as she moved. The front door lay wide open, a thin trail of blood leading back inside. At first she panicked, fearing that she'd find him slumped outside. But as she drew closer, the stench overwhelmed her. She slammed the door against it and staggered into the bathroom. The tap was still running, its hiss blending with the roar in her ears. And as she looked up at the mirror, myriad distorted faces screamed back at her from the glass.

Easen sat in his workroom, staring into space. His case lay at his feet and the notes he'd presented to the honourable members of The Assembly, not two hours before, were still curled in his hand. He had done it; he had convinced them to accept his proposal.

'Hi-jacking losses are not only expensive, but a challenge to the security and authority of the City States. In the past two months there have been several lucky escapes and one entire Transvector taken – it was a miracle that the crew made it to an Outpost alive.'

How Turor had known about the incident was a mystery; he'd been right though and the information had definitely helped win them over. There had been those who pointed the blame less at the settlements, who were said to lack the resources for piracy on such a scale, than at elements within other City States.

However, irrespective of the opinions that Assembly members voiced privately, the official line remained. Marauders were a threat to commerce and they needed to be dealt with. Firearms were already standard issue to the long distance crews, but it wasn't enough. Easen would undertake a study of all vehicles and transport procedures to identify any weaknesses. Then he would make his recommendations and oversee the necessary changes.

Soon after the plan was sanctioned, Easen disappeared. By the third day, without word, Turor feared the Targen had spirited him away and broken a confession out of him. Syriem's visit to Athenna yielded little information, other than that her father was on a research assignment in Appra. Syriem thought twice about visiting again after that.

Turor's dreams were empty; the Black Rod was silent to him. He wondered if it too were preparing for the journey. It was the first time in many years that he found himself before an altar with a direct petition. He chose the Gods of the starry deserts, seeking the protection of Sekhmet for the travellers to come, and the wisdom of Tehuti to guide their actions. The Gods, in their way, contrived to give Turor some of what he desired – but at a cost.

Had the Rod not have touched Easen, that night of the meeting, he might have been swayed by his three weeks in Appra. Back amongst the favoured elite, he relished the attention they heaped upon him, finding only reassurance in the presence of armed guards at every turn. Little had changed at the Research Facility.

Every courtesy was extended to him during his stay; nothing was too much trouble. He was still a loyal and valued servant of Tarsis City State, despite that terrible business some years before with his errant wife. Under close scrutiny and with the blessing of Ces Frayer himself, Easen set about his work. He was to start with an exploration of a new alloy for the Transvectors, in the deepest recesses of the Garrison. New, in the sense that the Appren High Command had now seen fit to release the formula.

At the start of each working day he was escorted across the compound, like the category 'A' prisoners that they occasionally brought in for interrogation, flanked by officers who neither spoke nor acknowledged him. Many times during those first nights on the base he laid awake, convinced that his true work would be uncovered. Three weeks, he told himself; three invaluable weeks where he could learn far more than in months on the outside.

He bore his responsibilities stoically, tempering his labours with unexpected pleasures. Soon after the great gathering, where Turor had revealed the Lock and the Key, she had come back to him. At first he didn't even know her name. Now the thought of her soothed him like a charm: *Alda*. But to the guards, who brought her in through the reinforced gates, she was Gisellan. And if her embrace was sanctuary, who could call it betrayal?

Turor received Alda's intelligence reports every few days. Their meetings were cordial now, but free of judgement. What had passed between them, joyous though it had been, was an interlude – nothing more. At least, that's what he told himself.

Easen returned from Appra to find that Athenna was growing ever closer with Dorron. Which, aside from depleting his drinks cabinet in circumstances he preferred not to think about, made him realise it was time to tell his daughter about their plans. He had convinced himself that the Exodus was some time in the hazy future. But the days were creeping by and he knew that the longer he delayed, the harder it would be. An opportunity soon presented itself, for the Universe does not discriminate in how it bestows its favours, so long as action follows intention.

Athenna came back early, following a row with Dorron. Easen started cautiously, dwelling upon the past, on things she already knew. Then he spoke about Buda, of life since her departure and his unhappiness since then. And gradually, stealthily, like a spider cocooning its prey, his tale of melancholy and disappointment held her fast, until he felt confident enough to go in for the kill.

She blinked slowly in disbelief. "*Leaving?* But you can't – you'll ruin everything."

Her selfishness stunned him; somehow he hadn't anticipated that. "I know this must be hard to take in. But if you understood what's at stake, you'd realise it is the only sensible course of action."

She studied his face for signs of sobriety. "Sensible?"

"It's the right thing to do, believe me. Maybe Dorron..." he stumbled on the name, "...wouldn't appreciate it, but if you talked to Syriem..."

"Syriem?" she blanched. "Don't say you've got him involved in this."

"He is a servant of The Restitution, as am I. If your mother were here today, she would make you see..." he looked away quickly. "I used to scoff at the things Buda believed, Athenna; I see it all differently now. I only wish to the Gods that I'd opened my eyes before. Then maybe…" his voice subsided again.

"How dare you bring her into this!" she screamed. "Maybe she saw a side of you that I'm only beginning to. First you vanish for three weeks and then you come back to tell me that you've seen the light. Just listen to yourself; who are you trying to impress – me or that woman you've been seeing?"

He shrank before her like a guilty child.

"You think I didn't know about the two of you? It all starts to make sense. I bet she's the one who's put you up to this."

He wanted to tell her that to stand against him now would break him, but he held on, knowing he needed her consent. And he knew exactly how to get it. He retold the story of when he and Buda had met and the life they'd planned together. Soon the tears were rolling down her face.

"You really loved Mum, didn't you?"

"She was everything to me, Athenna, just as you are now," he leaned forward and took her hand. "There's nothing for us here. But *outside*…we can make a new life."

"All right," she relented, "tell me exactly what you intend to do and I'll think it over."

He crossed the room to hide his smile. Just a little further to go. "There are dozens of us – Thaylin Sarra and city folk alike. We want a new life, away from The Assembly and its control. Sarrell will set us free."

"Sarrell's just a myth. You've told me that yourself, countless times…"

"It's time you knew the truth; Buda left us to seek Sarrell."

Athenna stared hard at him. "Is that what this is really about – finding her?"

He didn't answer straight away, but waited until her face had softened, excusing himself the final manipulation. "This is something she would have wanted for *all* of us."

Athenna wiped away tears. "Supposing I did agree to go with you – what about Dorron?"

He opened his hands wide; the choice was hers.

"I'll talk to him. It's okay – I won't tell him everything; I know I can trust him."

He reached for a bottle as soon as she was out of the room.

It was the first time that Syriem had ever seen his parents afraid. They had shown concern before, over his association with Isca, but this was different. Their ashen faces tore at his heart. They talked to him in low voices until the early hours, desperate to turn him from his decision. And when they found that he could not be swayed by fear or guile, Tem made it easier for all of them.

"The time will come soon enough. Let's say no more on the matter until then and get along as best we can."

Syriem lay awake that night, tortured by the knowledge that he'd be leaving them behind. The Rod offered poor solace, its realisation like a wound – they were as set to their path as he was to his.

A few days later, Syriem caught up with Dorron in the street. A mixture of affection and resentment welled up inside him; he'd miss Dorron most of all.

Dorron waved him over. "Athenna has told me what you're planning; she wants me to join your exodus. Surely there must be another way. Some sort of reform?"

Syriem looked up at him calmly. "There is no other way."

"Look, I'm not against what you're doing – in principle," Dorron chuckled nervously, his sharp, discordant shrills rising up like cries of pain. "But hiding in ditches for the rest of your life is not my idea of freedom."

Syriem searched his heart. All he found there was the realisation that he was born outside the cities and he was going home.

chapter 12
EXODUS

SYRIEM STRETCHED OUT in bed, keeping his breathing slow and regular. The day that he had hoped for – and suffered for – had finally arrived. The Rod lay by his side and he touched it affectionately, activating the energy nodes along his spine. Waves of vitality circulated through his being, sharpening his awareness. Before the day was out he would be sleeping under a foreign sky. Or else, as the Rod whispered spitefully in his mind, he would not be sleeping at all.

He lifted the Tablet on to the bed. He'd neglected it of late, too enamoured with the Rod's seductive tone. Today he would cede the Tablet to Turor, honouring his pledge to Isca. And how long ago that seemed now.

As he leaned back, his talisman bounced against his collarbone, clamouring for attention. He lifted it free and laid it on the stone. There they rested before him, three objects unified by the changes they heralded – three symbols of Sarrell. He could hear his parents making ready for the day and was glad of it.

Sro pulled out a chair as he entered the kitchen, as if it were any other day. But when they had finished their breakfast Tem laid a fatherly hand on his shoulder.

"Find time to come back today, before you leave."

The gates of the Cargo Plant rattled like a jailor's keys, as a Transvector rumbled through. Syriem nodded to the driver, who barely acknowledged him. Soon he would to be free of that place. By the time Ces Frayer's Ascension Day Parade was ready to begin, everything would be different.

Civic decorations were already dangling from the gates like rags, flapping in the truck's slipstream. He gazed at the gold and purple pennants, Ces Frayer's colours of office, and spat at them. Ces Frayer was a man he had never met and was never likely to meet, but in a time of helplessness and despair, Syriem had learned the architect of his suffering and would never forget it. He was still muttering curses as he crossed the loading yard.

"Syriem," his supervisor bellowed, "get in here."

He started to make his way over then stalled, half-paralysed at the sight of Easen.

"You're assigned with Mr Minet for today and it'll be an extended shift."

He nodded dumbly. The supervisor carried on talking as if he wasn't there.

"Yes, of course, Mr Minet. Well, if you insist – *Easen*. Your latest materials have already been delivered. I'll see to it that you're not disturbed. We're delighted that our vehicles are being used for the trial and it's a privilege to have you here."

Syriem went outside and waited. Easen soon followed.

"It was Turor's idea, for the final preparations. I've managed to avoid all your other shifts."

"Whatever you say, Mr Minet"

Easen broke the rhythm of their steps. "Athenna will be pleased to see you."

"I'll bear that in mind," he slowed up to let him lead the way.

"It'll all work out; you'll see," Easen promised, pushing past.

Time weighed heavily. Easen had little work for him to do, but needed him to stay near.

"You don't think very highly of me these days," Easen muttered, as he made adjustments under a dashboard.

Syriem passed him an instrument. "Anyone who travels to Appra and comes back unscathed is not to be trusted."

"And would that include Turor?"

Syriem shut the cab door and drew his knees up to his chin.

"Has he told you what we can expect – out there?" Easen probed.

"You would serve us better if you concentrated on the task at hand," he glared, but he wondered what else Turor was keeping from him.

After another couple of hours, confined with Easen, Syriem needed some air. He'd only been out at the front gates for a short while when he saw Turor approaching. Wandering Thaylin Sarra sometimes resorted to begging, so no one paid him much attention. Syriem reached into his pocket in a show of charity, as Turor drew close.

"Go home now and prepare the Tablet the way I instructed. I will not see you again until tonight, with the others."

Syriem pressed a few coins into Turor's hand and announced that he was going off-site for Easen. As he passed through the gates, the enormity of the situation swamped him. His future and everyone else's now rested on Turor's audacious plan.

His heart was still pounding when he reached home. Tem and Sro stood in the doorway, as he turned his key for the last time, the resignation on their faces a flimsy canvas against the coming storm.

"So, time's come, eh?" Tem crushed Sro to his side.

Syriem nodded and went to his bedroom. For a moment his mind went blank and panic set in, warping the memory of the symbols that Turor had so diligently programmed into him. Then he calmed himself, reasserting inner equilibrium to meet the task.

He knelt towards the east and invoked the image of a guardian dog, pouring his True Will into the operation to produce an expansive version of Isca's companion. He visualised the creature's snout with dagger teeth and emerald eyes. The muscular form rippled into being in his mind's eye, filling the space before him. He heard a rumbling snarl in his imagination and his body trembled in accord. When his nostrils twitched at the dog's presence, he repeated the procedure at the remaining compass points to secure the room with four creatures.

Now he positioned the Tablet in the centre of its cloth and laid it on the floor beside a burning candle. He brought to mind each of the five required symbols in turn, picturing them glowing iridescently against the complementary colour.

Then, in the prescribed manner that Turor had taught him, he folded down a portion of the cloth at a time, sealing it with wax before inscribing a magical sigil with his fingernail. When the last fold of cloth had been set, he poured wax over the union of the five points, pressing his birth talisman into the centre to leave its mark.

"It is finished," he declared, dissolving the four dogs in one firm breath.

He picked up the Rod and traced a pentagram in the east, imagining the etheric lines of force that he knew Turor could see without difficulty. With the star completed, he stabbed the centre with the Rod and felt a charge activate the symbol. He treated the other three compass points identically, then above and below, sealing himself in a chamber of visualised pentagrams. He saw as if through a mist, as though the environment were foreign to him – had always been foreign. He wavered, both hands grasping the Rod, and felt the potency of the moment. Reality was poised, volatile, needing only a spark of True Will to ignite it. He smiled – a fierce, joyous acknowledgement of the journey that he was committing to – and struck the Rod against floor with a resounding crack. It was over; his time there was done.

Tem and Sro were stood in the kitchen. He embraced them together and told them that he loved them. Then he collected his things and said his goodbyes.

"Syriem…" his mother wavered, as he stood by the open doorway.

"I have to go; I will see you again." Then he remembered that Isca had said much the same to him, the last time he ever saw her.

"Travel well, my son," Sro whispered, her proud tears etching the scene into memory.

Syriem reached the Cargo Plant and slipped through the wrought iron gates. The rest of the decorations for Ces Frayer's parade had been set in place. Lanterns anchored to the gateposts would be lit the next morning, as was the tradition. He rapped a knuckle against a casing and smiled. This year Ces Frayer would get a tribute he'd never forget.

He returned to Easen, running errands across the Plant whenever they'd had their fill of one another. Crews came and went around him; cargo was despatched and received. There was an air of unreality about the place that made it hard to focus on anything. He took to meditating in short bursts, communing with the Black Rod in a cargo hold while Easen worked away in the front.

As the hours passed, the transit crews began to disappear. He watched them as they signed off for the day and heard their rambling chatter as they made for the nearest Treasure House or for home. A part of him almost envied them.

Once the place had quietened he left Easen to start the refuelling. He stood by the fuel lines, watching the counters as they poured potential distance into the Transvectors.

"Syriem?" his supervisor's voice cut through the air. "What are you doing over there?"

He stopped the pump and went across. "Mr Minet wanted the fuel gauges calibrated."

She nodded grimly and tightened her coat, her face like thunder. No one had discussed fuel checks – so typical of Syriem to make her look bad in front of their visitor. She'd make him sorry the next time she drew up the shift rosters.

When Sro heard the knock at the door, her first thought was that their son had returned. Then a stranger called them both by name. Tem opened the door cautiously.

"I am Turor," he said, projecting his True Will to stave off their fear.

As they wavered, he slipped past them into the kitchen.

"It's you, isn't it?" Sro skirted the room. "After all this time."

He nodded. "This is a momentous and difficult day. I come to offer our gratitude. You have raised your son well."

"And you've taken him from us!" Tem banged his fist on the table.

Sro sniffed, her eyes raw from crying. All she felt was pain; a lesion so deep she thought she might never recover from it. But at least she was beginning to understand; her only son had always been *theirs* too. Perhaps that was the price for his safe entry into the world. She reached out and gripped Tem's hand.

"What will happen to Syriem?" she broke her silence.

"He will not join the faith; his separateness is what makes him special to us."

There was affection in Turor's voice and that pleased her. At least Syriem would be with people who cared about him. She raised a fragile smile and laid out some plates; they were not enemies after all. The three of them talked for a while, sketching in the years since Syriem's birth. Then Sro went to fetch some pictures, leaving the two men together.

"There's still time to change your mind and join us."

"I don't know about all that," Tem flustered. "We're too set in our ways to go chasing after some old place that probably doesn't exist."

Turor saw the fear in his eyes and let it pass.

"Here we are," Sro bustled in, spreading out the faded photographs. "He never was one for pictures; such a serious child," she touched the frame affectionately.

Turor put a small bag on the table. "Look, this might prove useful in the times ahead."

Tem glared. "You think your money makes everything right?"

Turor ignored him and turned to Sro. "If they come here – for they will surely come for others – this will protect you from the worst of it. Should it get too dangerous to stay here, I've listed some safe-houses where they will look after you." He reached out and touched their hands. "We honour your sacrifice and the things it makes possible. As does Syriem."

Maybe it was their desperation, but they took strength from his words.

The travellers appeared in small groups and were ushered through the shadows. Names were checked off lists and new ones added, as they massed together in the loading yard. Some had come with only the clothes on their backs and whatever food they could carry; others had brought along keepsakes and family heirlooms too precious to leave behind. Conspirators at the Plant welcomed one and all, directing them to the back of the vehicle blocks. Some acted as sentries, marshalling everyone together, armed and ready to defend their new clan.

A man crossed the yard and stopped halfway, lifting his arms to show he wasn't a threat.

"You're the driver, Cordal?"

He nodded curtly, looking for his crew. "Where is the Righteous One? Why isn't he here?"

By the time Turor arrived, the steady trickle of people had grown to a crowd. They all fell silent as he approached; some of them bowed. He called for the drivers to come forward and issued his instructions.

Easen wove his way through the throng, allocating people to vehicles and settling disputes with an arbitrary wave of his hand. He ran a finger through the lists, worrying his way down until everyone had been accounted for. But there were still faces before him.

"I can't accommodate them all, Turor."

"Anyone who has come seeking a new life will not be turned away – see to it."

Easen raised his papers in despair.

Turor walked off, trailing his voice behind him. "We'll find space somehow, Easen, even if it means taking more vehicles." He walked among the people, reassuring them, and went in search of Syriem.

"I trust you did as I asked?" he welcomed him, reassured to feel the vibrations of both the Rod and the Tablet.

"It is done," Syriem picked up on his mood. "Is everything going to plan?"

Turor's face tightened. "One of the Transvectors is delayed – no one knows why. Matters have been arranged so that they'll enter through the side gates; they shouldn't be aware of us when we exit through the front." There was a hint of uncertainty in Turor's voice.

"Do you know who you're waiting for?"

Turor unfolded a slip of paper almost creased to oblivion. "The driver is Garrin Noch."

"I wouldn't worry too much," Syriem relaxed a little. "She'll be with her crew at the Treasure House Pergata by now; they're habitually late."

Turor patted his shoulder. "Ever the messenger; bless you, Syriem. Where would I be without you?" He pulled a flask from his pocket. "Now, I want you to drink some of this."

Syriem lifted it to his nose warily.

"I promise you that it's safe."

"No point in my asking what's in it?" he stalled, gazing at the mouth of the bottle.

"You know you can trust me," Turor insisted, which was no answer at all.

Syriem grasped the bottle firmly and let the viscous liquid flow down his throat, warming his insides like an elixir. He began to feel sublimely at peace, with everyone and everything. The melee of voices faded to the background and a higher sensory awareness replaced it. He was still fully conscious, still able to appreciate everything going on around him, but all that was less important than this other, deeper understanding. He looked at Turor, tilting his head as if to catch some whispered thought.

Turor left him and went to speak to Easen nearby.

"They are at a Treasure House," Turor told him. "We can delay no longer."

Easen sent the word round. The stragglers passed up their belongings and clambered into the cargo holds. A steady pile of discarded property built up against the far wall. Syriem stood beside the mound of belongings, watching as Cordal set the timer for the incendiary. Turor told him to get in the Transvector and he ambled off obediently, bags in hand.

Once everyone was on board there was a moment of absolute stillness, as if they all shared the same, single thought. This act of defiance was also an act of faith. Everyone held strong, clinging to loved ones or to strangers. And those who believed prayed to the Most High that they made it to the dawn.

A radio handset crackled. "We have to go now, Turor," Cordal demanded.

"As you say, Cordal." His thoughts turned to Patriarch Verif's prophecy.

Six vehicles growled into life – four Transvector cargo trucks and two smaller Scouts. Easen stared out at the street entrance, torn between what he knew must be done and what it would cost him. Still no sign of Athenna… His soul screamed for her, but he wouldn't be swayed – there were too many other lives at stake.

As the first Transvector edged forward, Athenna suddenly appeared and Easen began to breathe again. She staggered, clinging to Dorron as if he were a hard won trophy. Dorron hoisted himself up in the cab after her, glancing around in the shadows. Syriem made space for them and the full flood of their emotions washed over him like a cruel wave. Dorron said nothing and pressed his face against the window.

Just as Easen edged the convoy out to the street, the late cargo run returned and crossed their course at speed. The Exodus wrenched to a violent halt, hurling the hapless travellers around like scattered offerings. Once he'd heard there were no serious casualties and that the vehicles were undamaged, the fear left him. He was grateful now for the tonic that Turor had provided earlier. He looked ahead and the dark streets stretched away like possible futures.

The radio crackled again. "Which City Gate do we head for?"

Dorron seized his moment and wrenched at the door handle, launching himself on to the pavement. "I'm sorry, I can't do this – you haven't a chance!"

Athenna wailed in anguish, but Syriem laid a hand on her arm, settling her to an eerie silence. The Black Rod's influence had awoken within him. He felt the heat rising in his belly, radiating out and spiralling along his limbs. Then a sense of heaviness descended, slowing his movements and intensifying his thoughts. He pulled in the door, unmoved by the sight of Dorron running into the night.

Turor turned to him, but he held his tongue when their eyes met. Syriem reached for the handset and Easen jerked back at the coldness of his touch. Syriem turned to Turor for an instant and then his face grew stern.

"It is time for the children of the lost to make the journey home. Go now!" he commanded, and they obeyed him without question.

Turor flinched as he heard the voice.

"We're too vulnerable," Easen protested. "Six vehicles together and all they have to do is block one road."

The driver of the fourth vehicle seized the initiative. "I'll take the two vehicles behind me to the Southern Gate and leave you the East, Turor," Cordal swung the Transvector hard left.

"The Gods be with you."

The streets were largely deserted on the way to the Southern Gate, much as Cordal had anticipated. It was a longer route out of Tarsis, but they were less likely to be stopped. Which was all to the good, as he planned to drive through without incident.

"We'll be beyond the city before you know it," he promised the crews. "You do as I say and we'll all get out of here alive."

He tapped his breast pocket for his lucky cigar. Maybe later, when they'd cleared the border. First to business – Easen had promised some modifications, but Cordal placed little faith in science. Guile would be their greatest ally and he had plenty of that. He smiled as they drove on, mentally assessing the border guard on the eve of Tarsis's greatest civic occasion.

Eventually the three vehicles skirted the South Exitway and the twin sentry towers of the Southern Gate stained the horizon.

"This is it," he warned, pressing his pistol against his leg.

A solitary figure stood in the road, with a rifle slung over one shoulder. Even from a distance he looked like a boy in a man's uniform. He gestured to the tower as he walked towards them, and then waved them down. Cordal slowed the Transvector.

"Must be his first posting," Cordal told his team, deciding he would kill him if necessary.

The vehicles pulled in twenty yards from the exit gates – standard procedure so that the guard could clear them through. Cordal wound down the window and poked his head out, blinking as the drizzle spattered his face.

"Nice night for it!"

The soldier grinned inanely. "I'm supposed to ask…" he groaned, straightening his back.

"I think you'll find everything's in order," Cordal passed down his cargo dockets.

"These aren't the specified vehicles?" the soldier mumbled, staring at the papers.

Cordal laid his hand on the pistol and felt the cold, inviting handle. "Yeah, last minute change; usual team's still out on the town. What can you do, eh? So they draft us in, offer me extra pay for leading the crews on Ascension Day and tell me to haul the cargo down south."

The soldier looked up at Cordal, desperate to be convinced.

"This your first detail, son?"

He nodded dumbly, sagging a little as if his cover had been blown.

"Well, look…" he leaned right out of the window, "I'll bet those lousy bastards up in the tower are itching to see you screw up?" He smiled at an infinitesimal nod. "Why don't I step outside, as if you're giving me a hard time, and we'll come to an arrangement? You don't want to look stupid if we have to drag them down here, now do you?" "He wound up the window and turned to his co-driver. "I'll be five minutes, maximum. Any longer, or if you see activity from the tower, kill the cadet – run him down if you have to – and just go; you got that?"

He stowed the gun in his jacket and ventured outside. "Walk with me around the rig like you're doing an inspection," he instructed the guard, leading the way. "And point a few times to show you're paying close attention."

They completed the circuit and Cordal passed a small roll of notes, palmed in his hand. "For your trouble, son. The quicker I get away from here, the more chance I have of a fat delivery bonus."

The soldier took the money and grinned, stuffing the notes in his tunic with his back to the tower. Then he turned and saluted up at his superiors, mouthing an obscenity that he knew they wouldn't be able to see.

"Have a pleasant night," Cordal called and climbed back on board.

The soldier waved his hand and signalled for the gates to be opened. Cordal took the wheel and nudged the Transvector forward, breathless at his own daring.

"This is cargo leader J24 – prepare to disembark. All crew report."

The drivers and crews called back a series of names, each as false as their travel documents. Cordal clicked off the radio and turned to his co-driver again.

"Now, who has the rendezvous co-ordinates, or has Turor kept that a secret too?"

Just a few miles across the city, the weather had turned against Turor and his people. Easen stayed hunched over the wheel, terrified in case he lost sight of the road, telling himself that everything would be fine if they could just make it to the Exitway. Turor laid a hand on his shoulder and shook his head. Easen yielded and nodded slowly.

"Glast," Turor called out over the radio, "take the lead position."

Easen watched with relief as the other Transvector moved past them. But Glast, more used to driving a Scout along border roads, overtook at breakneck speed. They soon heard the plaintive wail of a Targen patrol car as it picked up the pursuit. A few blocks later they saw the barriers.

Glast hurled the Transvector through makeshift barricades, scattering Targen in all directions. Further on, oil drums had been rolled into the street. They smashed on impact, oozing fluid across the carriageway. Little practised with manoeuvring a Transvector – and in such treacherous conditions – Easen wrestled with the steering, roaring at Turor to do something, anything, to steady their course.

If Turor heard Easen's abuse, he did not acknowledge it. When Syriem looked to Turor for guidance, he saw that he had closed his eyes and retreated within himself. Syriem stifled a cry of despair and promised the Gods if they delivered them from catastrophe he would serve them forever. And then, as if to mock him, the rain crashed down again in a furious torrent.

"It's a bad omen," the third driver declared, as the swish of the water carried over the radio like a wraith's cry.

"We'll be off the Exitway soon," Easen mumbled, as if he didn't rate their chances at all.

Targen troops had taken up defensive positions along the perimeter wall and two field guns from a nearby garrison were angled towards the road. They had been warned to expect a settler raid, but nothing prepared them for the sight that met them.

Easen gripped the wheel harder, yelling defiantly as the Transvector pitched and swayed. No matter what, he swore aloud, he wasn't coming back; whatever the destination, this was a one-way journey.

The Exitway widened and the twin towers of the Eastern Gate appeared before them, blurring in and out of focus through the rain. Easen waited until the last possible moment and then gave the order to activate the modifications. The troops opened fire and bullets streamed in all directions, thumping against the vehicle shielding.

"It won't hold for long, but it should buy us a little more time…" Easen explained to anyone that would listen.

Athenna screamed and buried herself in Syriem's jacket, dragging him below the window line as bullets fractured the glass. He grimaced as the chaos threatened to consume them, closing his ears to the downpour and the gunfire.

A shell from a field gun slammed into the first Transvector, catching it broadside on. It lurched on the bend, screeching a death call as it overturned and slid into the barricades. The two vehicles behind it – Easen's Transvector and the Scout – could only swing wide, spraying up leaked fuel in their wake. Easen snatched a glimpse of bedlam in the mirror. Targen troops quickly surrounded the blazing heap and dragged out the living and the dead alike, throwing them down on the pavement together. And then he heard more gunfire.

Syriem clung to Athenna, trying to shield them both from the maelstrom. An insidious pressure was increasing in his head the closer they got to the Eastern Gate. He drew his arms away from Athenna and pressed against his eyes. The pain pressed back, numbing his senses and shutting down his awareness.

"Focus your mind," Turor urged, desperate to reach him while he was still conscious. "Around every City State…powerful…barrier…means of control…worse going out…"

Syriem slumped against the door.

"It will pass," Turor promised, clawing back focus by degrees. He took the Rod from Syriem's bag and it seemed to pulsate in the flashing dread of the storm. He arched his back to the sky and a guttural cry rang out as he struck the Rod against the floor of the Transvector. Lightning flashed, carving up the sky with iridescent daggers.

He formed a picture in his mind, ruthlessly willing it into being. A single shaft struck at the City Gates, obliterating the left watchtower. It ignited with a roar, casting the troops from the gantry like fallen angels. The steel plates twisted and buckled, causing the left gate to lurch to one side before it cracked from top to base. Easen reacted instinctively and pressed another button. A fiery orange trail shot out, bursting the debris into a thousand smouldering fragments as he drove through.

Turor seized Syriem. "This moment you have been reborn, *Syriem Taulpiris.*"

He smiled for an instant and then faded to the void.

chapter 13
AFTERMATH

Eastern Sector Assembly members held an emergency session, to determine whether any of them were brave enough to face Ces Frayer. But, as none dared sully Ascension Day and the great parade, a cover story was put out that outsiders had attacked the Eastern Gate – aided and abetted by conspirators within Tarsis. All raiders had been killed in the assault and several Targen soldiers died in the valiant service of the City State. A memorial plaque would forever grace the Eastern Gate in their honour, just as soon as it was rebuilt.

The initiates of Appra didn't need The Assembly for information; they had other means at their disposal. The truth emerged among the chosen few, that the Exodus had carried the Tablet to the Outlands. Fortunately, contingency measures had already been put in place.

Dorron was transferred to Sector Headquarters for interrogation. After surrendering to the nearest Targen patrol, he'd wasted little time in fulfilling his civic duty. Central Intelligence had taken a keen interest in his testimony.

He sat alone in a cell, awaiting his fate. No one knew he was there; he could easily disappear without a trace, just like Syriem had told him. He breathed into his hands and recalled the night's events in disbelief. At first, all he could think about was Athenna. He wondered whether she'd made it to the Outlands – that lawless wasteland those religious fanatics were so keen to reach.

The Targen would be back for him soon. So far he'd only told them part of what he knew; at least, that's how he remembered it. Perhaps he could still extricate himself from the whole affair. Fragmented images crowded his mind, each one a pivotal time where he might have said or done something to divert events from their disastrous outcome.

He closed his eyes and tried to ignore the pleas and threats of prisoners along the corridor. As he sat there, shielding his face from the sickly pallor of the ceiling lights, an impulse took hold. He bowed his head and squeezed his hands together, driving the knuckles white as he said a silent prayer – for Athenna and Syriem, and all of them. In the hope that they made it out safely and found whatever they were looking for. Then he rolled back on the wooden bench and tried to lose himself in sleep.

The opaque hours of darkness carried the Exodus far beyond Tarsis. There wasn't one among them who did not offer a private thanksgiving to the Gods. When the two vehicles from the Eastern Gate rejoined the convoy there was rejoicing, and then came the solemn task of identifying the lost. True to his vision, the Patriarch Verif had not survived past the city gates.

Turor waited until the roll call of the dead was complete before he gave his instructions – head southeast, away from the city, until dawn. He said no more than that, watching the sky anxiously as the convoy pushed into the unknown. The first of the Tablet's five seals had to be released at first light, but before then he would need to make contact.

Syriem and Athenna were nestled in a heap so he lifted the Tablet free, careful to keep the wax seals intact. His mind embraced the stone's imprint through its glyph of the Tree of Life. The spheres on the tree turned in unison, activating interconnecting pathways. The vibrations stabilised until only the colours remained, merging and arcing out into seven distinct layers. As Turor loosened the bonds of consciousness to enter the domain, the rainbow reared up like a serpent and swallowed him whole.

Awareness blossoms like a lotus. Land stretches in all directions. To the north, a wrought iron entrance appears in the mist. A vengeful breeze crashes the blackened gate against its post, clanging like a death knell. Words from the waking past resonate within him: 'We die to live, we live to die.'

The gate is cold to the touch, as if the metal itself bears some terrible sadness. The design on the frame is exquisite, its molten teardrops cascading in a procession of sorrow. And through the curves, Turor sees the faces of the dead – pale hollows of humanity awaiting their shepherd. A man comes forward, his face shining with an indestructible faith. Verif offers Turor a silent blessing before leading his people away.

The landscape feels both familiar and archetypal, with all seasons converging and overlapping. A shrub before him is in first flower, while a mighty oak basks in the majestic throes of summer. At the first turn of the path he sees a dense army of winter trees, their limbs stark and unyielding against the greying sky. A castle rises up from marshland and he moves towards it in earnest, wading through mud and silt.

There is a throne beyond the marsh, set within the forest, where a young woman waits. Moonlight glints off her crown like flashes of hope. She does not stir, but she watches as he presses on to the trees.

"Isca, is it you?"

She touches her lips to command silence. Her face as pale as ermine; it is not Isca.

"Who are you? Why are you here? Are you righteous?"

He stands before her, childlike, devoid of authority. The questions resonate through the cold air like a raven's cry, calling him to account. Before he can answer, his body draws him back, fading the land in a blanket of forgetfulness. But the words burn into his memory and insight survives intact: something has changed – the laws of reality have shifted. And his people need him more than ever.

Ces Frayer was frequently underestimated, as was his intention. When his spies brought him news of the Exodus, he said nothing. The Ascension Parade went ahead as planned, with all due ceremony and occasion. But once the marching troops had returned to their barracks and the cheering crowds had dispersed, he called his minions to him. This enemy incursion had unsettled the good citizens of Tarsis. They needed reassurance that order prevailed; a show of strength was required.

The Targen Security Forces moved quickly, carrying out raids across Tarsis, Qayla and Sirn that same night. Syriem's parents escaped the first trawl, huddled safe in their beds as the sirens wailed in the distance, but their time would come.

Each raid was the same. Targen troops arrived in force with armoured vehicles and dogs. Searchlights drenched the streets in scathing brilliance, as the snatch teams flitted through the neighbourhood. Known dissenters and their families were chained together and sped away; men, women and children – young and old – no one was spared. All were herded into holding pens for processing, which could mean different things depending on what they suspected you of knowing.

Dorron wasn't officially listed as a prisoner because he'd volunteered his statement, not that his treatment was any better for it. Light erupted around him in his cell, consuming the room and everything in it.

"Get up!"

Sleep died. Dorron buried his face in his jacket, but it made little difference. Even with his eyes shut he could feel them staring at him, sifting through his thoughts.

"Who is behind this insurrection, Dorron? Where are they heading for?"

The room spun and the floor slammed into him. He yelled in despair, pressing his temples to drive out the clamour.

"Come on now, Dorron, tell us what you know. Then we can straighten this mess out and *all* get some sleep."

Sleep; he yearned to never feel anything again – a desire his Targen captors were quite capable of accommodating. He raised himself to sitting and began his betrayal.

"If I tell you, will you let me go?"

"Of course," a voice soothed him.

He looked his interrogator in the eyes – where he thought her eyes lay behind that mass of light – and gave her six words to conjure with: "They are going to find Sarrell."

There was a chorus of whispering then the light receded; a welcoming blanket of darkness enveloped him. He closed his eyes and sank to his dreams.

Dorron's interrogator cut the lights, leaving her prisoner in peace. He'd earned it, and she would gain a promotion from his confession. She called along the corridor for her superior and waited by the door. The senior arrived and listened as the officer shared her revelation. The suspect was telling the truth, she was certain. Given the medication running through his veins, it was a wonder he could speak at all.

"You have done well," Senior Haric congratulated her. "I'll see you are rewarded." Then she made a mental note to get her transferred off the base at the first opportunity. "Keep this door locked and stand guard *outside*." Gods forbid she should wring more information from the prisoner in her absence. "Don't let anyone enter until I return."

Senior Haric wove her way through the maze of corridors. And as she passed lines of cells, the inhabitants screamed for mercy, or liberty, or they just screamed. She was oblivious to their concerns, lost in a seductive, internal dialogue. Tonight might very well be the turning point in her career.

She knocked at the door and Ursephal opened it without warning, startling her.

"Ma'am," Senior Haric saluted sharply, taking refuge in formality. "We are holding an informer, a witness to the hi-jacking."

"What concern is this of mine, child?"

"The prisoner indicated that the incident could be connected with the Thaylin Sarra."

Ursephal's eyes flickered, dull browns warming to amber. "And?" There was menace in the word, a dare to speak the unspeakable.

"The prisoner believes they are heading for Sarrell."

"But Sarrell is a heresy that doesn't exist."

Senior Haric felt Ursephal probing her. She dug her nails into her palm. "No, Ma'am," she lowered her eyes to the amulet at Ursephal's neck.

"Then we shall have to see why the prisoner is mistaken."

Senior Haric suffered the solemn journey with Ursephal beside her. Every movement felt under scrutiny. As they walked their silent walk, punctuated only by Ursephal's rhythmic breathing, the noise from the cells ceased. Ursephal charged the atmosphere, subjugating them with her presence, casting an invisible influence over everything in her path.

Senior Haric breathed a sigh of relief when they reached the cell door – her obligation was over. "General Ursephal," she announced.

The officer guarding the door mouthed the rank silently and swallowed. Ursephal dismissed them, instructing the senior to return in one hour. She walked her subordinate out of the prison block and gave her some advice.

"Forget whatever you've heard here if you value your life. I'll see to it that you are transferred at dawn." Only this time she meant it for her own good.

Dorron drifted back and tried to focus. He couldn't see the woman clearly, but he sensed she was there. Ursephal waved her hands over his tattered aura and then administered more drugs, checking the dosage – no point killing him before she had what she needed. He made a grab for her leg and slumped back. She glared, her face bitter as poison.

"Be careful what you wish for," she warned, as the last vestiges of consciousness receded.

She added material to a crucible, mixing in the powder. Soon it frothed above the flame, a sulphurous blend to stir her jaded senses. She stroked Dorron's brow mockingly and ran her hands above his prone body in circular passes, feeding on the chaotic energy around him. She could leave him as a half-wit shell, as an example to others. Or, more tantalisingly, she could make him into a slave to do her bidding. She considered that for a moment. He had a fine body – a shame to waste such promising material.

Unbuttoning his shirt, she salivated at the taut chest muscles and trailed her index finger across his torso. Then she pressed until the surface gave way and her talon pierced his skin. He stirred, writhing on the bench, as she twisted the nail in further. Then she snared a shred of flesh with her nail, which she savoured.

"Now, my pretty one, what shall we do with you?" She ran her finger back and forth along his chest so that blood and saliva swam together. The connection had been made.

Dorron's subconscious offered no resistance; he was hers for the taking. How should it be, she asked herself, as she lay down beside him. A temptress? An innocent? Or perhaps a harridan? Which guise should she wear to his astral nightmare?

Ursephal finds Dorron easily – in a Treasure House, holding court. Women surround him; all kinds of women – clothed, naked, available. Before he sees her she deliberates her form, slipping through a dozen wavering changes until she settles on an image.

As she crosses the room, his eyes fall upon her in rapture. He opens his mouth to speak, but her mind touches his and turns his thoughts to stone.

"Tell me everything," she whispers.

The doors bolt theatrically to emphasise his helplessness. His entourage clears a path, sweeping back like welcoming thighs. She glides through the cleft, her movements heavy with desire. She closes upon him, laying bare his chest, digging in her nails until she can feel his heart through her fingertips. Then she suckles at a wound for sustenance.

"Tell me everything and then I am yours."

He is slow to respond, his chest heaving as he gathers the energy to speak. She wastes no time, clawing at his mind and mauling his memories. A faded six-point star rises to the surface of his aura, flickering with the remnants of power.

"What?" she bellows, livid that she did not recognise the Thaylin Sarra mark before.

She discards her temptress form and an ogre rises up to fill the void – a monstrous deformity of life. A single curse shatters the room, smashing the harem wenches to crimson. Her talon rips at the Thaylin Sarra seal. It burns to the touch – an old auric amulet, the faded work of a high initiate – but it does not impede her. Dorron cowers.

"You," she commands, "are mine!"

She wraps a tentacle around his throat and pulls him spluttering towards her. A sucker fastens to his face, then another and another. Slime gurgles through the pores to drench his torso in rhythmic, foetid pulses. The bubbling mucus clings to his skin; as it pops, tiny mollusc-like creatures emerge to drain the life-force out of him.

Her True Will ravages his psyche, sifting information and scarring his mind in a frenzy of revelation. And then she has it, the architect of his protection: an adept worthy of respect. The image of the priestess dissipates and a man's face flickers before her.

"Speak his name, dearest; it will help you breathe," she promises, wiping away the mucus.

He looks upon her with no will but to obey. "Turor."

"No!" she screams, transfixed by a fleeting image of the boy who left her behind.

For a moment she is consumed by her own torment, rending scars from the past that she had sutured so well. In a domain of shifting realities, her agonies rise up and take on substance. They come from the place of soul-less shells – demons by any other name.

Hideous laughter echoes around her purgatory – hell, they are saving for later. They approach and retreat in a fluid motion, so that one of them is always touching her. Each sickening caress weakens her, reducing her to the girl she once was. And that is their mistake.

She stands before them as a child, reciting the barbarous names over and over to draw upon the might of her heritage. Raw power spirals towards her, channelled though the Appren necklace around her neck; the pendant stones of orange, red and black begin to glow. She raises a hand, twirling her nail in the air like a sabre. Faster and faster, summoning energy and will.

They watch her, sniggering and bickering, gazing at her with a hunger that surpasses lust. She works on, driving primordial hatred into the nail, extending it, fortifying it, until it becomes a silvery blade. Then, as she regains her authority over the plane of reality, she reforms her monster, adding her disgust to its armoury. By the time her tormentors realise her strength it is too late. She slices the first creature in two with a wide, sickening swish, stamping the quivering corpse to a pulp.

The second creature backs away. Ursephal directs the blade and a ring of flame scorches off its tail. It retreats to the wall, surrounded by fire and the stench of burning.

"What do you bargain for your life, demon?"

"He fears you still," its voice is as dry as sand.

"Fear is only the absence of Will," she stares the creature down, her own face a mass of broken, gleaming fangs.

She lifts a lobster-like pincer and frames the demon within the claws. The creature shrieks for mercy, but her eyes take on a cold, satisfied lustre and she snaps the claw shut. The wretch is instantly engulfed in mustard flames.

One look at Dorron reanimates him and he falls to his knees.

"You have served me well. And now you shall have your reward."

She seeks out an abomination from Dorron's mind, wedding his lust to his repugnance. And though he cries out, simultaneously repulsed and driven mad by desire, he is mated to his nemesis. She utters laughter that would shatter worlds, as his sweating, fevered thrusts are accompanied by the choking splatter of vomit against her skin. When she has had her fill of him, she discards him to endure the hideous copulation alone, his rampant body left to penetrate empty air.

She is weakened, both by monsters of the past and Dorron's revelations of the present. Each has struck her, deep as daggers, and she must recover in another domain.

Ursephal shuddered as she became fully conscious. Dorron lay next to her, twitching as the drugs and his nightmare endured. She traced a sadistic finger over his groin. When she was strong enough to stand, she reached for a glass phial and swallowed the contents, shaking out every drop. Heat returned to her body, seeping steadily from her stomach to warm icy limbs. She flexed her hand, marvelling at the nail that had been her salvation.

After removing her instruments, she pressed the candle into Dorron's wound and inhaled the rich scent. Then she closed his aura with a sign of her own and smoothed his clothes. She heard footsteps outside; perfect timing.

"I'm finished here," she pushed past Senior Haric. "He's all yours."

A car was waiting outside, the driver beside it pensive and watchful. He saluted smartly as she emerged from the building and straightened his tunic before opening the door.

"Ma'am?"

"Eln Border Garrison, Eastern Sector."

Ursephal reviewed her astral encounter in a series of flashbacks. Later, she would gain deeper insights – there would be time enough for that on the long, subterranean journey to Appra. She glanced up, catching the driver's fixed expression, and breathed easier at the thought of returning to the citadel.

Appra, the place of secrets, the real power base behind the Frayers. Appra, the true child of Old Earth shaping the future in its own ideals. Appra, mother to the city states, suckling her children with a bitter milk to make them strong.

She had learned of Sarrell too, after being brought to Appra as a child. And of its people, who had spurned Old Earth and fled across the stars, damning those who were sent to punish their heresy. And somewhere, driven back to the very edge of memory by denial and punishment, there had been a settlement and *different* tales of Sarrell. Tales of abandoned goddesses and gods, who in turn had forgotten her when the slavers came.

She shook her mind free and returned to the fruits of her interrogation: Turor, still alive after all those years. Sustained by the Black Rod, no doubt. The Appren High Command could have Sarrell – if it existed at all – but Turor would answer to her.

Syriem woke suddenly from the throes of a nightmare; he could still hear Dorron screaming. The Transvector cab was empty and there were muffled voices outside. The Rod rested beside him, pressing into his body, and he instinctively reached for it to steady himself.

Through the glass, he caught sight of the tallest tress he had ever laid eyes on; giant denizens of the forest that would have dwarfed the trees back in Tarsis. He stared awhile before the wan glow from the East caught his attention. Time to go. He coughed out stale air and stretched; his throat felt like leather, his back as if it were stone.

As he lowered himself to the ground, dizzying forest vapours overwhelmed him. Easen called across and Athenna embraced him.

"Isn't this wonderful? They'll never find us here."

He glanced around and wondered whether anyone else realised this was only the first stage of a long journey. Turor wasn't difficult to find once he'd shifted his focus. Turor's vibrations, like the individual vibrations of everyone around him, were unmistakable. He found him alone, leaning against an oak tree. The sun was already bathing the land in subtle, flaxen shades.

"There are things you'll want to know," Turor contended. "There'll be time for that later, but first there is the first seal to attend to. Let us make a beginning," he said solemnly, walking off through the trees.

Syriem followed at a distance and his feelings betrayed him. For all the training Isca had given him, he felt vulnerable in the open forest. The ground had already been prepared and he approached the circle with reverence, standing outside the earthwork until Turor gave him permission to enter. He trembled as he stepped into a quartered circle, aware of a mirage glow of black, olive, citrine and russet.

Turor took his mark, nodding for Syriem to join him in the very centre of the design. They stood, back-to-back, a foot in each of the four segments. Once Syriem indicated that he was ready, Turor faced the east and intoned a call to the elements. Then he presented the Tablet to the sun, using it to shield his eyes.

Syriem pressed against him so that their spines touched, and drew the Rod, lifting it high. Now, for the first time, he noticed the small candles at the circle's perimeter, tiny flames thrust into the good earth to honour the task. Turor took a long in-breath and tightened his leg muscles, sinking into his pelvis to make the stance solid. Syriem brought the Rod level with his chest, mentally feeding its power into Turor and the Tablet, so that knowledge might be wrought from it.

Turor cradled the Tablet in his left arm, easing one finger under a fold of cloth, then another, gripping securely as he invoked the sacred name on the wax. Then in one deft movement he ripped the cloth free and broke the seal. The wind whipped up and the trees seemed to bend in supplication. Intuition slowly trickled through, teasing his senses. He closed his eyes and directed Syriem to do the same.

Finally, as Turor stood before the dawn, with Syriem shrouded in his shadow, he delivered the words of power proper to the design: *Adonai ha Aretz*. The ground pulled at his feet, anchoring his body to let his spirit soar free.

The gateway of many names is quickly dispensed with. She waits once more upon her rock-hewn throne, a symbol of permanence on the plane. But the journey is less challenging this time; the marsh has become meadow.

She is smaller now, a goddess in human proportions: Virgin, Bride and Queen. She lifts her gleaming crown aside, as if to reveal her humanity, and her eyes shine like jewels.

"Approach me with your petition."

He advances steadily, mesmerised by her.

"Come, embrace the gifts of earth," she guides him to the throne.

He kneels and stretches forward, touching the ancient carvings to partake of her mysteries. The land shifts and changes as a living form around them. She repeats her questions, so that he may dwell upon the answers.

"Who are you? Why are you here? Are you righteous?"

A question forms in his mind: 'What now?'

She smiles without speaking; his audience is at an end. The knowledge has been instilled within him and he must nurture the insights to manifestation. The circuit is discharged.

Syriem eased away from Turor's spine. Vague impressions of a forest and its ruler loitered in his mind like some Thaylin Sarra legend. He opened his eyes slowly and saw the glade illuminated in sunlight. As he gazed around his half of the circle, tiny, glowing spheres coalesced briefly into forms, masking their true nature in fleeting guises of his imagination.

Turor stirred beside him, blinking against the light. "It is done."

"I thought I saw something, just at the edge…"

"Elemental creatures of earth." Turor didn't elaborate.

As they turned to face one another, Turor's head was haloed in sunlight.

"Do you feel different out here?" Syriem carefully put the Rod away.

"In what way?"

"I'm more in tune with myself and my surroundings, but also more susceptible. I'm the same person I ever was, but…"

"Are you sure about that?" Turor cut in, his tone so emphatic that Syriem stopped to consider the question.

"This felt different to Tarsis; out here, something else was in control."

They quit the circle and collected the candles. Syriem echoed some of

Turor's inner journey, tentatively offering his own thoughts and meanings. Then he stood back, watching as Turor methodically erased the markings on the ground. Afterwards they sat on the dew-drenched grass together.

"I have some questions…"

"I expected as much," Turor returned the Tablet to its bag.

"What happened, back in Tarsis – when we reached the border?"

"You mean the pain you felt?" Turor rubbed his hands self-consciously. "This will require a leap of faith; it's not part of the orthodox Thaylin Sarra view."

Syriem settled on the ground, letting the sun warm his face.

"Each city has a particular resonance, like a key note. It's especially strong in Tarsis, due to the work of Appren initiates, and it's augmented by technology – designed to suppress certain levels of consciousness. Some say that's why so few Hybrolen are born inside the cities."

Syriem was on another train of thought entirely; he pressed his forehead to squeeze the ideas into words. "If, as a Hybrolen, you have access to higher levels of consciousness…then does that mean you already know the route to Sarrell?"

Turor looked over at Syriem, aware that the boy's auric symbols had come to life again. "It's complicated," he said. "The knowledge is shaped by understanding."

Syriem opened his eyes. "You're not going to give me a straight answer, are you?"

"It's for your own good," he replied without malice. "Wisdom lies in asking the right questions and then acting according to your True Will."

Syriem left to join the others, determined to speak to the Thaylin Sarra; maybe they'd know more about his part in Turor's great scheme.

They received him so warmly that he wondered why Isca would have left him so unprepared. Then he listened as his companions told him how the dead would be honoured when they reached Sarrell. It was too much to bear and he broke free, back towards the trees.

He found his way to the oak and leant against the trunk, closing his eyes, drawing upon its stability to re-establish his own. Gradually, his breathing calmed; he managed to dispel the sense of loss that always seemed to be on the periphery of his thoughts. When he opened his eyes, Turor was standing in front of him.

"Are you okay? It will take some adjustment, being outside like this."

"How did you know about the design of the seals?" he found his focus again. "Tell me that at least. Where did you learn to construct them?"

Turor looked towards the camp and, in a voice that sounded as old as the world, conceded, "I have always known."

"So is it true, what some of them are saying back there? Are you really the Righteous One, sent to protect the faithful and lead them to Sarrell?"

"If you want expedient answers," Turor chided him, "be patient – as they are."

Syriem felt the heat rising across his face. "No, what I want is the truth. And from what I pick up elsewhere around the camp, I doubt all our companions will wait indefinitely."

Turor stared implacably. For a moment Syriem thought that he would fly into a rage. Then Turor's face softened and he laughed.

"So you think their trust in me is misplaced?"

"I just sense that you know more than you're saying – and I think you ought to trust me. After all, you sought me out. The giver and the receiver alike."

"I promise you, Syriem, when I can be sure that what I say will serve you more than it will harm you, I'll confide in you. In the meantime, try not to become too enamoured with the Thaylin Sarra – their path is not your path."

Syriem sniffed and looked into the distance, remembering similar words from Isca.

"Come on," Turor started walking. "Let's get back; I have a proclamation to make."

chapter 14
SETTLEMENT

EASEN CALLED Turor over. "Fuel stocks are as expected and the vehicles are performing to my specifications," he paused, waiting in vain for some acknowledgement. "Food and water supplies will last us for the time being, but people are on edge; no one really knows what to expect. Your disappearing act doesn't help things – you and the other Thaylin Sarra should take your responsibilities more seriously."

"You are right, Easen. Gather the people together; it's time to do just that."

As Easen went off about his task, Turor sought out the Thaylin Sarra elders. Some were reluctant to join him at first. He felt how the mood had shifted now they were out of immediate danger; clearly, still some saw him as a dubious prophet. He understood, to a point. The Black Rod was a facet of the faith that did not sit comfortably with many. For him to be the bearer of the Rod, he must be either a Twiceborn or a thief.

The elders stayed close as he walked to the crowd. He praised their faith and the courageous step they had taken towards the fulfilment of Sarrell. Suitably placated, they awaited his guidance, but could scarcely have guessed the message that he brought them.

"There is a settlement a few miles from here. We can either make contact or move on and they will respect our decision." He sat and let the flame burn.

Easen immediately voiced his support for the venture – hopeful for word of Buda – and the Thaylin Sarra sided with him, eager to seek out any settlement kin. Freedom of movement between the Outlands, Settlements and the City States was a foundation of the faith, no matter what measures The Assembly tried to enforce.

Many of the city folk were resistant, fearing conflict or capture in the settlement. Easen insisted it was an opportunity to show that a blow had been struck against The Assembly. The elders found a resolution, encouraging a democratic debate and a show of hands. Ultimately, Turor and Easen had their way, albeit with conditions.

Eight people were selected to make the journey: Easen, Athenna –

who would not stay without him, four city folk, and two Thaylin Sarra
to represent the faith. Turor stood his own rejection stoically, accepting
their plea that he was needed at the camp, even though he didn't believe
it for a second.

Easen organised the loading of a Scout; cramming in anything they
were willing to trade. He also added three of his sealed containers,
checking the security tags as he placed the boxes among the cargo.

"What *has* he got in those?" Cordal nudged Turor as Easen passed
nearby.

"Whatever it is, I'm sure it's for our benefit," Turor reassured him,
stressing unity with Easen – at least until he knew exactly what they were
carrying.

Easen fired up the engine, shattering the stillness of the forest. The crowd
watched as the Scout departed, negotiating a makeshift path through
the trees. Once the deputation had disappeared, people split into work
groups. Fires were lit and food prepared; a self-appointed watch mapped
out a perimeter to patrol. Others located a water source and attended to
the basic needs of the people, gathering fresh water and digging latrines.

The entire camp was a hive of activity and that pleased Turor. While they
were occupied, they were manageable. How much time had been wasted
just picking eight people, to say nothing of the animosity generated? No,
the people of the Exodus needed leadership and he intended to see that
they got it.

He joined some of the Thaylin Sarra, taking a seat beside the shrine
they'd created. The questions started before he had swallowed the first bite
of a flatcake – eager, forthright explorations of the Exodus in the light of
the faith. Unaccustomed to such a receptive audience, he invited anyone
over who wished to know more about their traditions. Some came almost
reluctantly, charmed by the stranger from the Outlands. Others declined,
happy to leave the Keldie folk to their own business. Turor called Syriem
across too, although it was less of a suggestion than an instruction. He
made space for him by the fire, watching as the branches crackled in the
flames.

Someone struck a small prayer bell and its high, clear tone seemed
to settle the people. Turor smiled graciously, clearing his throat and his
thoughts.

"We need to go back into ancient history to understand the origins of
our ways. In the days of Old Earth…" he looked to the Thaylin Sarra who
sat together, wearing the different coloured bands of their rays, "…there
were many faiths and much antagonism between them. But the division

of truth is like unused grain, hoarded for no purpose. In time it will spoil and become fit only for vermin."

He made a rat's face and the children sat before him squealed with laughter.

"There were also teachings that acknowledged all creeds of the Light, however it was expressed. When great hardships fell upon the children of Old Earth, these groups forged a common destiny. They were not in complete accord, but they recognised their intrinsic value, as different facets of the one jewel that is *truth*.

"But there were some ideologies that could not be integrated; those of dominion and subjugation   those that perpetuated chaos and hatred. These unfaiths took many guises, sharing common intents: to silence the heart, to crush the spirit and to break the will. Often a faith would find itself split between the Light and the Darkness, so that its teachings were brought into question. That is one of the ways that chaos works, separating us from the source and blinding us by our own vision."

More city folk had grown curious and drifted across.

"These unfaiths banded together in a powerful alliance. They wanted to rid the peoples of Old Earth of their free will, imprisoning them through the same approaches used to seek liberation and enlightenment: religion, philosophy and science. This reminds us that the means always serves the morality.

"About this time, astral travellers discovered new worlds and their presence was confirmed by scientists. Those of the Light saw an opportunity to seed humanity among the stars. They formulated this great work in two ways, through physical colonisation and the establishment of future lines of incarnation."

He paused and wondered how many had grasped the deeper meaning of the words, which had only now entered his consciousness. Even the children sat quietly, lulled by the flowing pitch of his voice. A good sign, he felt.

"Of course, these truths are no longer taught, even as the population of Old Earth remained ignorant of such things. Great vessels were created for the journey, while those with sufficient knowledge worked on the inner planes. The light ships took the travellers from Old Earth, just as some said the teachers of humanity had once arrived. They were righteous, tempering the manifest laws of science with the subtle harmonics of the living Universe."

He took a sip of water and gazed into the flames, aware of all eyes upon him.

"Their intent was the founding of a new Eden, maintaining the bond with Old Earth. But the unfaiths pursued them across reaches of space, set on their destruction. Fate was merciful for the first ship arrived a half a century before any that followed. Where it landed is the place we know as Sarrell. Others call it M'Qar, or Achth, or The Blessed. By whatever name, the One saw its reflection in a solitary beacon for there were no other light vessels. The children of Old Earth established their colony on this fledgling world and they named her Laurasia."

The influence behind his words changed. Parva Search had said that where there was shadow, there was also strength; it was time to put that to the test.

"Where the oppressors of Sarrell first landed is the citadel we call Appra. Other craft followed, bearing colonisers with no knowledge of the hidden struggles between the Light and the Shadow – folk who had left Old Earth behind at the will of their masters. The Appren initiates manipulated the leaders and their clans like a trance poison, corrupting the truth, turning kin against kin to profit from the bloodshed. Even now Appra continues its heresy, twisting the authority of The Assembly to meet its own ends. And the people of the city states continue to live in ignorance."

Some rocked in silent agreement with his revelations. There were none now who labelled him as a madman or dismissed his wisdom as the rantings of a fool.

"What will Sarrell be like?" one of the Thaylin Sarra children came forward.

"Sarrell is beyond explanation," he rested a wary hand on the child's head. "It is the answer to all your questions." He felt that the moment had passed and raised his hand in blessing to the crowd. "Know that our journey prepares the ground and heralds The Restitution. Now, I have said enough; who here has tales to tell?"

A Matriarch called Verrsa took the lead, corralling the children together. With skilful ease, she wove them a tale of the Ancient Ones and their efforts to guide fledgling humanity from chaos to order. Turor listened awhile, as enthralled as everyone else with the telling. Then he walked off to find peace in solitude.

Syriem was slow to notice and then he raced around the Transvectors to head him off.

"Wait! What you said back there," he panted for breath, "is that what you believe?"

Turor closed his eyes for an instant. There was that feeling again, as if the sky had narrowed in. "I neither believe nor disbelieve; I accept the symbolism of what I tell them. My actions are governed by the purpose I have aligned myself with. All else is secondary. The time will come when you will need to make your own choice."

"*Choice*? I'm here, aren't I? I brought the Tablet to you – the one thing you say will lead us to Sarrell – and I bear the Rod. What other choice is there for me?"

"Calm yourself, Syriem," he picked up a twig and held it in front of him. "Your loyalty is not in question, only your mastery."

Syriem paused mid-thought and dropped his hands to his sides.

"In order to be the master of yourself, you must know two things: what aligns with your True Will, and what does not." He carefully peeled away the twig's bark to expose the bare white flesh, retaining the strips in his other hand.

"To *become* that master, you must embrace the one and discard the other!" He tossed slivers of bark in the air, indifferent to the frustration that played across Syriem's face. "If your need is for a messiah, Syriem, I'll endeavour to play that part until you're ready to see beyond it. But my patience is finite."

Athenna looked on in wonder, as the trees receded and the land opened out to fields and trackways. Her mind raced, conjuring ideas about the settlement and drawing on what the Thaylin Sarra had told her. She wished Syriem were with her – or better yet, Dorron. It felt like days since she had last seen him and back further still since they'd been truly close. She sighed; Sarrell had driven a wedge between them just as it had her parents.

Easen deftly handled the vehicle over the dips and ruts of the terrain. He wondered if Athenna were thinking of Buda, as he was – and whether she had travelled that same track, years before.

Up ahead, a figure waited. Easen stopped the Scout. The engine hummed impatiently; he felt the dashboard throbbing under his hand.

"Now what?" he snapped, turning to the Thaylin Sarra woman beside him for the first time. He'd tried to accept their presence, but something in their manner always made him feel unwelcome. As if the journey to Sarrell was *their* quest while he and the others were just an encumbrance. Turor was different, he gave him due credit for that; Alda had been too. And where was she was now? He hadn't seen her at the Cargo Plant that night, but she could have been a late arrival. She might also have perished at the roadblock…

He noticed the settler approaching steadily – a staff in her hand, which at first he mistook for a weapon. As she drew closer he saw that she was dressed little differently from some of the travellers. The two Thaylin Sarra beside him shared a private comment and motioned for him to move the vehicle forward. The settler's pace was unhurried and formal, as though she were measuring out the dwindling space between them.

"I bid you welcome," she drew alongside; "we've been expecting you."

"You know about us?" Easen instinctively looked beyond her to check she was alone.

"We've had trackers in the forest since your arrival. We could hardly miss your vehicles entering our territory!"

She turned and led them further along the trail. As Easen drove past the stockade gates that marked the settlement entrance, he caught sight of older City State vehicles. He stopped where directed and got out to wait for their guide.

"I am Gallo, a sentinel here at Esilmeor."

She looked carefully at the travelling party. Almost as if, Easen thought, she were expecting to see someone she knew. A crowd gathered at a distance. No one spoke for a time; only the Thaylin Sarra seemed comfortable with the situation. Verrsa was first to step forward, offering the traditional greeting to one of her kin. The others stayed close by her, Easen watching nervously as the Scout attracted interest.

"You are safe here," Gallo promised, which felt like no reassurance at all.

Athenna turned sharply at the sound of thundering hooves. The crowd parted to let the rider through and he pulled the horse up, its flanks dewed with sweat. As Athenna gazed up at him, she thought she had never seen anything so beautiful.

"Forgive me," the rider caught his breath, "I did not expect you here so soon. I have been away in the company of our neighbours. Gallo will no doubt make you welcome. But…perhaps your youngest companion would accompany me?"

Athenna blushed and, by the slightest of smiles, consented. The rider dismounted in one smooth movement, walking beside her as he led the horse to stable.

"Be careful, Athenna."

Gallo took Easen's hand. "She'll be fine with my brother, Orn."

"Your…brother?" he noted with interest.

She showed him to a timber structure in the centre of the settlement. "This is where we settle our laws and share the ceremonies of life, bonding, separation and death."

"And what does a sentinel do, exactly?" he touched a post carved with names.

"We patrol the ways into the settlement and keep its laws," she turned to him and smiled. "Orn and I will serve for a year and a day, then others will be chosen and we'll return to the work of the fields and orchards."

He listened with a wary eye on the doorway. In the distance he could see Athenna surrounded by local girls. Orn cut an imposing figure beside her.

"Where will you and the other travellers go?"

"To Sarrell, of course," he said, amused at how quickly Turor's words had become his own.

"Why not stay awhile? We could learn much from one another," her fingers touched his hand. "There is no danger here; we monitor the Targen radio transmissions. And in any case, we are more than a match for any patrol that might occasionally stray into our territory."

He flicked her hand away. "How do you come to have City State vehicles?"

"Did you think to find us living as primitives? We trade with the cities to get what we need, but that's all – you'll find no support for The Assembly here. Come, sit with me."

He didn't look convinced, but he took his place at the table.

"It would serve neither of our peoples if it were otherwise; without all the settlements, the cities would go hungry and we would face a bleaker future."

"You sound as enslaved as we once were," he sneered.

"There are many kinds of slave, Easen."

He launched from the table, almost toppling a wooden beaker.

"Wait, there's no reason for conflict," she retreated. "We have much common ground."

She dropped the matter and instead regaled him with the history of the Variz territory, as her grandparents had heard it from their grandparents. It was a detailed account that Easen had never learned in any of the books he'd left behind. Of how a great settlement had resisted to the last, until finally it had been first annexed and then subsumed into a new city state. She also told him about the dissidents exiled to the wastelands or sent to labour camps.

"So the settlements are all allies?" he changed the subject, finding talk of internment and uprising too close to Buda's memory.

"Some..." she drank deeply, as if to avoid the rest of her sentence. "Alliances can be both fluid and fractious, but it's in our interests to support each other. Overall, the settlements are less isolated than The Assembly might believe."

Easen picked at his food, basking in the intensity of her gaze and pushed his empty plate forward in appreciation.

"How large is the settlement territory?"

"Aside from the forestland and the pastures, Esilmeor's fields cover many, many acres. There are outlying buildings to the furthest reaches, though not as it was in times gone by. The old folk die out and the young tend to live more centrally. It's better for defence, and it helps for organising planting and harvest. If you have the time, I can show you around…"

"I'd like that," he stood up. "I'll send someone back – to let the others know we are safe. Now, I had hoped we'd be able to trade…"

Gallo leaned in and the scent of the wine carried on her breath. "I'm sure we can come to a mutually satisfactory arrangement."

The Scout arrived back at the encampment, stocked with supplies and – to almost everyone's surprise – a type of fuel. Syriem rushed to pitch in with the unloading; anything was better than sitting around wondering what Athenna was up to. Turor worked alongside him, stacking up containers to divide between the vehicles.

"Have you ever considered that Athenna is in your life for a *specific* reason?"

Syriem turned towards Turor, brandishing his petulance like a sword. "Go on then, you've obviously got something to say on the matter. No doubt your prophecies have some insight."

Turor squared up to his insolence. "Leave this – someone else can do it."

"There's work to be done," Syriem protested.

He shook his head and called for someone to take over, walking away to the trees. Suddenly panicked, Syriem abandoned his task and followed him.

"Where are you going?" he called after him, determined not to concede any weakness. "We don't know our way around out here…"

Turor led them into the heart of the forest, following an impulse he was unable to articulate. Syriem couldn't tell if Turor were in a trance or simply ignoring him; he struggled behind in silence, attempting to dodge the branches and roots that Turor seemed to know instinctively. And the further away they got from the camp, the more uncomfortable Syriem felt. When it all came down to it, just who was Turor anyway?

"Here will be fine," Turor stopped abruptly beside a beech tree.

Syriem caught up and sat down in a heap, letting the thick roots cradle him. "Look, I'm sorry," he mumbled. "It's just that sometimes, when I'm around you, I feel all this energy stirring up and churning inside me," he searched for the right words. "And then I get this impulse to say something or act, almost before I'm even aware of it. I'm not blaming you…"

"Perhaps the fault is mine, Syriem. I demand too much of you, expecting you to behave like an initiate." He waited to see whether the boy would reveal anything more about Isca.

"No, you're right, I need to make more effort," Syriem played it down. "I just want to know what you're keeping back from the others – I think you owe me that."

Turor smiled; so secrets didn't bother Syriem as long as he was party to them.

"What if I *did* know what lay ahead? Supposing I could tell you right now the part you are here to play?"

It felt like a dare, a blatant test of courage.

"Then tell me," Syriem defied him and his eyes took on a hungry glint, as the Rod invaded his mind. "After all, who are you to say what I can and cannot know? Perhaps you fear a challenge to your role, Holy One?"

"The voice of dissent? I wondered how long we'd have to wait. *That* is the Black Rod speaking," Turor cut him down. "Believe me, I know its voice. I could tell you much, Syriem – it's true – but it wouldn't help at this point. It's better to prepare you, by stripping away your resistance until your True Will is fully revealed. Only then will you fully understand."

"Try me," Syriem seethed.

Turor paused, weighing up Syriem's hunger for knowledge against his own considerations. He sighed; he had a message to deliver, so why not now?

"Your path is inextricably linked with the quest for Sarrell, and it goes beyond the talismans. The answers will come on our journey, if you can face them." He brought his hands together and ended his deliberation. "I encountered Isca on the Inner Planes. She wants you to know that she has not forgotten you – or your pact."

Syriem trembled, tears blurring his face as he reached out to the Rod for comfort. "No, you're lying! Isca would have come to me herself," be backed away. "I don't understand you," he covered his face, choking back his grief.

Turor sensed the chaos growing around him. "Listen to me, Syriem. Now that we're free of Tarsis, every day you will feel stronger, more complete. You'll think it is your True Will, but it is the Rod's influence and it comes at a price. The longer it takes us to reach our destination, the greater the risk to you and to everyone. The Rod is an unbalanced aspect of the Absolute. Mark me well – you will not be safe until you are free of the Rod's power over you."

At first, it seemed like the Rod was lost for an answer. But, with Syriem's subconscious such a chasm of resentments and grievances, it wasn't silent for long.

"Why not release the remaining seals now, Turor – why waste precious time?"

There was malevolence in Syriem's voice, and Turor recognised it from previous times when the Rod had sought out other voices.

"And call your Appren servants to you?" Turor spoke directly to the Rod. "I think not."

Syriem charged forward, knocking Turor to the ground. Turor saw the etheric bind-mark on Syriem's chest flickering with the rhythm of his breath – the auric scar that Turor had inadvertently inflicted upon him at their first meeting.

Turor instinctively drew in his awareness. But as he brought his hands high to invoke protection, Syriem grappled with him and snatched the Tablet. Turor let out a roar of fury and struck Syriem across the face. He lurched backwards and the Tablet flew from his grasp, crashing to the ground. Turor dived across him in a manic effort to reach the Tablet, but it was too late.

The stone came to rest a short distance away, the cloth flapping plaintively in the breeze. Turor gathered it up with shaking hands and examined the cloth. The second seal was rent, its force released prematurely.

Syriem staggered to his feet. "What have I done?"

"We must get back to the others," Turor cradled the Tablet. "They will be safer if we are among them." He sensed Syriem's aura, checking that the chaos had passed. "The magical seals are in place to limit the interaction between the Rod and the Tablet out here. That way, energy can be released under control – through ritual and invocation – so the map is gradually deciphered, leading us stage by stage." He stopped him in his tracks. "You need to understand something: the Rod *will* find its way to Sarrell. The issue is how many of us will last the course to see it."

Syriem offered the Rod up to Turor. "I'm not fit to carry this."

Turor waved it away. "It is your part to play, Syriem; remember this and learn from it. Don't let your focus become clouded again – the consequences could be dire, for all of us."

Turor was relieved when the perimeter guards spotted him and escorted them back. The provisions and fuel had been carefully stowed away; most people were gathered around Easen, Athenna and the others, listening to their account of the settlement. Athenna looked up when she heard Turor's greeting.

"Syriem," she rushed over, "what happened to your face?"

"It's nothing," he replied in a hollow voice; "I fell."

Easen strolled across to Turor with his entourage trailing behind him.

"You were wise to tell us about the settlement, Turor. We could hold up there for days, hiding the vehicles on the far side of the farms. Or maybe just rest for the night…"

Turor glanced at the sky, watching as the clouds began to mesh together. The energy released from the second seal would seek equilibrium. And the further they were from the settlement when that occurred, the better. He summoned his True Will, drawing on the life-force around him, sensing the vitality as an emerald glow. He touched an ancient yew, pressing his fingers into the bark as though a current had passed through him.

"You have three hours," he faced him, furious at Easen's lack of foresight. How could Easen not realise that the Targen would search all the nearest settlements? And Turor knew only too well what they would do to any settlement proven to have aided the Exodus.

"I told them we were grateful for their hospitality," Easen protested.

"And so we are, Easen. Go back to Esilmeor and give them our thanks. Tell them that Sarrell will not forget those who have supported us. You have three hours and then we are leaving – with or without you." He thought for a moment. "And bring back more fuel."

Easen started up the engine and bellowed, venting his anger and humiliation. Then he drove towards Esilmeor, alone, where he knew Gallo would be waiting for him.

Syriem edged around the outskirts of the camp until he found a clear vantage point, making sure he hadn't been followed. He put his bag down and projected symbols of protection around him to try and claim the space.

The soft, pungent soil came away easily at first, but he carried on until his fingers ached and his nails were caked with dirt. He worked methodically, stacking the stones he'd unearthed, using the flattest to form the base of the little cairn and packing in soil to keep the mound solid. With each stone added, a memory surfaced and he let his tears become part of the design. When it was finished he was silent for a time, gathering his intent. Then he knelt before the cairn, folding his hands in prayer.

"This is for you, Isca, to honour your sacrifice and our pact. I will remember who I am, and I will remember you." He took the crystal she had given him on his birthday and used it as the capstone, gazing at the refracted rainbows through the shaft. "Until soon."

chapter 15
RECOMPENSE

TUROR FOUND IT hard to escape a feeling of dread since they'd left the settlement. He had tried to view Syriem's lapse of awareness without judgement; after all, the boy was not of the faith. But that only resurrected other questions. How had Syriem had ended up with the Tablet? Why would Isca have chosen him, *before* he had even known about his talisman? Was she directed to Syriem even as he had been? Perhaps the Rod was working out its own agenda with the three of them as mere instruments of its art. He hoped not. He had seen the fruits of its intent before, and still bore the scars.

Outside the window, even the landscape seemed dispirited. The forests had given way to endless stretches of scrubland and barren soil. Above it, in the distance, a barrage of storm clouds stained the sky. Turor understood the omens; the boundary between internal and external experience was steadily eroding.

Syriem sat in solemn contemplation as the Transvector rolled on, consumed by his own thoughts. Athenna looked on sullenly. Despite her efforts to communicate, he was evidently in as foul a mood as his teacher – jealous no doubt because she'd been to Esilmeor and he hadn't. She smiled, allowing memories of Orn to warm her blood, and decided that she didn't care what Syriem thought or did any more.

Turor quit his isolation and moved to help Easen with the driving, adjusting their course periodically as if to outwit some unseen predator. It looked, to Easen, as though he were steering them directly into the storm's path. Turor didn't react to Easen's comments, mindful of the Rod's attraction for such phenomena.

"I thought we'd have seen at least one of the cities in the distance, by now," Easen struggled to concentrate.

"The elements are not favourable."

The terrain opened up like a carcass, the parched ground cracking and yielding beneath the weight of the Transvectors. Turor slowed the convoy to a dwindling speed.

Syriem peered out at the windswept landscape in response to an unidentifiable, inner voice. Pale recollections of the carnage back in Tarsis arose to taunt him. He felt impossibly, irredeemably accountable, and turned to Athenna for support. One look told him he'd best think again.

He wondered how many more lives the journey would cost. The Rod's consciousness awoke, sending a shock wave through his body. He shot an anxious glance at Turor before sleep claimed him; the Rod was about its work and Turor was the quarry.

Time and space mesh together. Swirling waters unleash upon the mind's eye. Vast, eternal spins of the ocean wrap around a tiny craft. Turor is alone, adrift from everyone and everything, clinging desperately to the battered timbers of a boat. The cruel waves pitch him high into the night sky, as the swell rolls on. He knows that he can turn away from this nightmare – a simple banishing and he will be free. But he would learn nothing from it and his quest is knowledge. Yet to remain on this plane is to be subject to its laws – he can still drown here if he loses focus.

He summons his True Will, driving all thoughts and emotions away except the one intent – to keep the vessel afloat. Intention manifests as magic, infusing the boat with protective pentagrams and binding the flimsy craft together by a craft of his own. The wood begins to crackle and cobalt stars radiate through the grain.

The vessel stabilises and proud lunar crescents appear at stern and aft, a symbolic resonance with the domain. It has ceased to matter whose creation this seascape is and whether he is the instigator or the witness; it must be endured. Each elemental blast pummels him, but he resists, drawing upon reserves of will to clothe his tiny ark in a luminous, magenta sheen. Ahead of him he can see a vast grey monument, subdued by the ocean, disappearing and reappearing in an endless rhythm. The boat changes course, heading towards the granite effigy.

"Enough!" Turor calls to the elements, raising a hand in invocation, matching fury for fury.

The thunder subsides and battalions of clouds retreat to the distance. The sea rebels, frothing and bubbling like an ancient cauldron. He clings steadfastly to the sail rope, one hand still raised against the onslaught.

The wind caresses the granite statue and the facade disintegrates, revealing a living colossus. He rises from the sea like Aphrodite, birthed by the waves and stretching into the sky.

Turor looks on as the leviathan towers above him, salt water coursing down the naked body like the rivers of the world. The giant's grey pallor changes, his beautiful form glistening blue-green in the spin of countless lunar phases, which whirr on through eternal night like a dance out of time.

Turor abandons his defences and the same three questions roar in the storm.

"Who are you? Why are you here? Are you righteous?"

He screams into the clamour, "I am that I am," in answer to the first, putting all the strength behind his voice that his vitality will allow.

The statue turned flesh kneels down, scooping up the boat in one immense hand to lift it level with his face. Turor stands before the eye that shimmers like a great scrying mirror, and watches as light drains into the purple void.

"You are off course, mortal. What has been released must be discharged."

"Yes, my lord," he answers, humbled before the almighty living one. Then he adds the invocation that will draw the veil back further: Shaddai El Chai.

"Well it is then, child of the light. Time and tide are my aids to balance; ebb and flow; flux and reflux. What has been taken must be returned. Your work is done here."

The boat is lowered to gently lapping waves; the storm has passed – on this plane at least.

Athenna nudged Syriem awake. He flashed a tired smile and she burrowed under his defences with consummate ease. She wanted to talk and he had little choice but to listen. Despite himself, he held her close as she wept over Dorron, and did his best to soothe her. She was scared; they all were. Small wonder that she should seek security in the past.

She dabbed at her eyes and nestled close, asking, in a broken voice, whether he knew where they were. He smiled to himself; she was testing him, trying to discover how much Turor had confided. She was every inch her father's daughter.

The Rod hushed its charge. He needed to rest, and trust to greater powers to work out the tangled pathways of the future. So he turned his attention to the others around him – their psyches suddenly as open as the road ahead. Most of the travellers looked to the Thaylin Sarra for protection. But now that Syriem had experienced a glimmer of the Rod's potential, he wasn't sure that was such a wise thing.

When the storm hit, it caught everyone unawares. Even Turor seemed unprepared for the wall of force that met them. The vehicles rocked and strained against the deluge; static muffled the radios and the relentless dust and wind blinded them. Easen pleaded to set up camp, at least until the weather had subsided, but Turor refused.

"How can we carry on if we can't tell where we're going?" Easen reached for a compass.

The engine whimpered at the tempest. Turor moved in close beside Easen and peered through the windscreen, facing an impenetrable curtain of rain.

"All things are possible to those who believe…"

"I don't want to hear it," Easen snapped.

Buda used to talk to him about magic. Not the petty deceptions that the Thaylin Sarra liked to entertain one another with, but real power – authority over the forces of nature. If magic had separated them, drawing Buda far from his reach, then it too was an enemy.

The Rod throbbed with anticipation at the joyous potential for chaos – that sublime state where the vulnerable fell prey to its designs. Turor's mind ached. The Rod tormented him with flashes of what might happen. Progress demanded sacrifice, an Appren maxim that he had heard many times in the past. If he acted quickly, he could be outside to face the storm alone – or take the boy with him. The others might be left in peace. Now whose voice was that? No, he must be strong, devoid of feeling. He was not responsible for anyone else's choices; he couldn't allow himself the weakness or the arrogance of thinking so.

Syriem eased away from Athenna's warm body and moved to Turor. Easen glanced over at Athenna then back at Syriem, saying nothing.

"Something's building up," Syriem's eyes widened, as if to cope with the enormity of the vision. "I can feel it."

"Yes, so do I," Turor nodded, adding quietly, "let them not suffer."

Thunder bellowed, like a prelude, and then a scream cut through the radio static, jolting Easen to his senses. He slammed on the brakes as the terrible news came through – one of the two Scouts had run off track and plunged into a crater.

"Where are your gods now?" Easen railed at Turor.

He ignored him and turned to Syriem. "Stay here; keep the Lock and the Key safe."

Easen called for the strongest among the Exodus to meet at the crater's edge. Syriem watched from the cab and felt their hatred directed towards him like a dagger. He sensed, for an instant, how the Rod gloated, and turned his face from the window.

The wind whipped up, as though the elements were at war, but everyone outside stood their ground. Cordal pushed forward and roped himself up for the descent, along with two others. Tortured cries rose up from the chasm. Turor waited beside the crowd and Cordal touched his arm, a blameless recognition of his need to be there.

Rope teams fixed their faces against the howling gale and took up the strain, lowering the rescue team by degrees. Torches swayed like pendulums, lighting up the rocky crags that marred the way.

"Lower, to my left – there's a body," Cordal's voice reverberated through the gloom.

The torches converged, outlining the bloody form draped over the rock. As Cordal looked on, discipline took over, damming his psyche against the horror. "He's dead, there's nothing we can do. I'll go further on."

Up on the surface Turor saw fleeting trails of energy, reaching out from the crater to infect those around him.

"Take me down!" Cordal screamed.

Below him, he could hear the gurgling spew of water rising up to meet them. He turned to companions on adjacent ropes, adjusting the torch beam to direct his way in the darkness. Tentatively, he undid his rope and stepped onto a ledge, checking in stages that it would bear his weight. He saw the vehicle ahead of him, twisted and rent like a spiteful child's plaything.

Torch beams rained down, criss-crossing the cavern, so that he could drag out the living to a harness. He held three fingers up and shook his head; of the eight passengers, only two adults and an infant would continue the journey.

The rest of the Exodus waited stoically, fending off the wind and rain. The harness reached the surface and was met by a legion of willing hands. Athenna looked across at Syriem, who had disobeyed Turor and stood alone by one of the Transvectors. Verrsa reminded Turor that Parva Serach's prophecies spoke of the separation of the wheat from the chaff. He listened without reacting, but inwardly he was sickened.

Cordal could hear the water more clearly now as it relentlessly swallowed the rock below him. He reached for the baby and prised it from its mother's final embrace, carefully tying the bundle to the harness. Then he went back and lifted the third passenger free of the casket that had so nearly claimed him.

"Pull evenly," he bellowed, as the last survivor disappeared up into the light. He readied to make the ascent, but an impulse seized him. "You go up," he told the other two and pulled three times to stay the rope. "I'll make a final check."

He watched them depart like returning angels and waited until he was alone. The sound of rushing water soothed him as he lowered himself back into the wreckage of the Scout. The metal hull resisted, creaking and bowing to warn him off, but he would not be deterred. He slid inside and felt the moistness against his skin. He told himself it was only fluid from the fuel tanks and reached his hands down. A severed limb pressed against him and he heaved it aside quickly, listening as it bounced into the blackness with a comical splash. He felt himself grinning in the darkness. Something glinted in the frantic arc of torchlight, a gleam of metal on one of the bodies. He grasped the pendant, lifting it away from a once beating chest and pulled to the full length of the chain.

At first there was resistance, where the links dug into flesh. Then the chain broke and the bounty was his. He dropped the pendant into a side pocket, stuffing the trailing chain in after it, and glanced back at the corpse. The face was serene, the eyes retaining a limpid depth that death had not managed to veil. Seconds later he felt the rock shift beneath him and scrambled out of the Scout, roping up and tugging frantically to be pulled clear. As he looked back through the swinging light, the water burst through and claimed the ledge.

Above ground he off-loaded the equipment he had managed to save: a torch, a clip of ammunition and a pistol. But the pendant was his alone, a just reward for his courage. A surge of exhilaration coursed through him and the crowd unconsciously cleared a path – in the midst of death, he'd never felt more alive.

Verrsa walked to the crater's edge and made a final blessing. She glanced at Cordal and quickly averted her gaze, touching her Thaylin Sarra pendant self-consciously. Back in her vehicle, she sat and offered prayers for the dead.

"That's not going to help them," her husband derided her.

She paused and opened her eyes. "It's the only thing that will help them now," she said, remembering how her family had warned her against marrying outside the faith.

Turor, Syriem and Cordal remained outside, among the elements; everyone else had taken shelter. Cordal chose his moment well.

"If you were truly the master that your people *claim* you to be, you would deal with this," he gazed skyward. The words lingered in the air, suffocating Turor's sense of equilibrium.

"As you wish," he conceded. "But know this – if I were a true master of the Higher Arts, I would not deign to deal with it at all."

Turor walked off into the storm, reaching for his talisman and exposing it to the sky. Syriem naturally followed him. In truth he felt safer with Turor than back with the others, but safety was only a matter of degrees now. He sensed that something had changed in Turor – as though he had summoned a part of himself and now presented it to the powers before them.

"You can still walk away now, Syriem," Turor called behind him.

He reached for his own talisman. "The Giver and the Receiver alike?" he reminded him.

"Very well," Turor agreed. "But this will not be…pleasant."

It was the only warning Syriem got. Turor stretched his hands wide, casting a field of energy around them. Syriem felt the life-force being drained from him by degrees. His sight began to fade, along with that other awareness he had learned to put so much trust in. Hands that were not his own lifted the Black Rod to the storm, confronting one power with another. Then Turor was mouthing words – silent gestures, which Syriem could no more hear than comprehend. This magic was not a kind he had ever experienced with Isca, which was as it should have been. For few outsiders had taken part in Appren rituals and lived.

A rocking motion brought Syriem's mind into focus. He became aware of Turor's shoulder digging into his abdomen and saw the ground bouncing before him. He gasped and closed his eyes to stem the nausea.

"It is done," Turor approached Cordal, who was still outside, smoking a cigar.

He waited for Cordal to return to his Transvector and then passed the boy up to Easen. The storm had started to yield. He decided to make the most of it, certain that it wouldn't last.

"The weather will be less of an interference for the time being," he climbed up, indifferent to Easen's nods of gratitude. If they wanted magic, then magic they would have. He felt his skin bristling as the words formed.

"I purify with water."

A sudden, intense burst of rain crashed down around them, scouring the edges of the crater. The ground beneath the vehicles stirred like a waking dragon.

"I consecrate with fire."

In keeping with Turor's words, as if some dark pact had been struck in the thick of the storm, the belly of the crater ignited, sending up a plume of smoke and crimson flame. The travellers stared in horror, certain that Turor and his charge had brought about the fireflood by some baneful sorcery. Then, as if to complete the spectacle, the underground rivers devoured the flames in one almighty hiss.

Only Athenna dared approach Turor. "What's wrong with Syriem?"

Her tone was conciliatory yet wilful, Turor noted; she would be a great asset to the faith.

"Syriem will recover," he assured her. "Right now he needs rest."

She searched him for a flicker of emotion, and found none. "I'm sure you did your best for us, out there, but was it best for Syriem?"

There was a time when Turor would have baulked at that. But he had long ago crossed the line between initiate and initiator, between the one who receives and the one who receives in order to give. In that moment he was the embodiment of one role and Athenna another. Her path was to challenge just as his was to act. So he offered a half smile and let her make up her own mind.

They travelled on until sunset and set up camp on a ridge. Turor assured them they would be safe there, though none questioned how he could be so certain. And with the weather much improved, many looked to him with a cold respect.

Cordal stood in the fading light, scanning the sand that stretched out like an umber tapestry. The fear returned – that terrible sense of isolation. There were no landmarks, not even a distant sign of a city or an outpost. How could that be?

The Thaylin Sarra held a service for the dead. Verrsa dedicated a fire, showering herbs on the flames. And when she judged that the influences were at their fullest effect, she danced through the smoke and sent her song across the ridgeway. Yet for all the otherworldly peace that she sang of, there was little of it around the camp.

Syriem wandered off in a daze. He wasn't as drowsy, but he still felt depleted and incomplete. Whatever Turor had done, back in the storm, had caused him to touch something vast – a glimpse of totality where he was no longer merely Syriem, but had become part of a greater presence. He longed for it now like an elixir, desperate to return to the void. The wind blew softly around his ankles, drawing him to the edge.

Each star, each perfect point of light fixed him with its radiance. Only once before had he felt so abandoned, and the memory of that terrible day did nothing to calm his spirit. If the breeze had demanded it he would have trod those final few steps over the precipice. He would have gone silently, joyously even, to meet whatever fate awaited him beyond the tragic world of the waking. But he teetered at the edge, damned by the knowledge that he had neither the strength to go forward nor the courage to step back.

"Believe me, Syriem," Turor's voice was quiet, almost loving in its own way, "you won't find your answers down there."

He was sat a little way off, facing that same dark expanse.

"You're sure of that?" Syriem challenged him, wearied by the burden of living.

"By all means, try it and see. The Rod would find some way to preserve you – the land would slide in the final moment, or a tree branch would grasp you. Make no mistake Syriem, we are in *its* power."

His chest heaved with emotion. "Why did those people have to die, Turor?"

"All I can tell you is what I know – we should never have been there."

"And all this just to reach Sarrell?"

"So it would seem."

Turor clapped his hands and the sky echoed with thunder. At the sound, Syriem managed to free himself.

"Is any of this *real*?" he sat beside him.

"Will you wake up tomorrow and find that you are still in Tarsis? I doubt that. Yesterday I thought this to be a dream, but this morning I awoke to find myself still here. So, for the time being, this is reality."

"I'm not sure I understand."

Turor continued, regardless. "Is this real for any of them? For the most part, I think not. They exist as if in a dream; we cannot allow ourselves that comfort."

"Blinded by their own vision?" Syriem said without thinking. "Tell me this," he spoke so quietly it was scarcely words at all, "what would happen if I took the Rod and hurled it over the ridge, and never looked back? Would we be free?"

Turor breathed in the dark sky above them. "You might return to the camp to find them all dead, the Rod having lost its use for them. Or you'd go back and when you next checked your belongings, the Rod would be there. And you'd feel such fear in its presence that even sleep could not hide you."

Syriem drew a long sigh. "So what awaits us next on this journey?"

Turor sighed. "The purpose is fixed, but its expression is not. However, be mindful that the Rod is not an evil thing, although in the past…"

"How did the Appren come to possess it?" Syriem interrupted, sharpened by the insights that flooded his mind.

"Of that I'm unsure – I think they had it long before they laid claim to me."

Syriem felt suffocated by the need to know more, but the Rod silenced him.

"What if…" Turor faltered, "what if the Appren had foreknowledge of our escape? There was no way to check everyone's credentials – we took people on trust."

Syriem shrugged, unable to make the connection. Turor looked to the stars again for inspiration, and his intuition flowed fast and free.

"Don't you think it strange that we've had no sightings or reports of any patrols? Not even immediately after leaving Tarsis. Perhaps that's deliberate – if they had another way to monitor our progress, they could follow our trail and march right into Sarrell."

"Assuming we actually find it."

Turor gave him a sideways glance. "Think about it. All they'd have to do is hide one of their own among us. An initiate – someone well shielded. Or maybe an unwitting spy – there *are* those among us who had links with The Assembly." He paced about, ensnared in his own thoughts. "Or maybe this is a higher justice."

Syriem leapt up, brushing the dust from his clothes. "So the Rod created that accident to aid us?" he raged. "Then what about the other people in the Scout – they can't all have been spies. Even if you're right and the Rod was somehow responsible – call it fate, if it makes it easier – what does that make you for bringing them here?"

"*We* brought them here," Turor reminded him coldly.

"Then what are we going to do?"

"Continue, so that their sacrifice and every sacrifice means something. That way you'll receive the understanding and justice you asked for in the inner planes temple."

"But how could you know that? I never told anyone."

When Verrsa's final song subsided and the echoes of a solitary flute faded into the night, she sought anonymity beside the flames. Easen was staring at her with such intensity that she found it uncomfortable. She felt the images rising up in her mind and the fact that he wasn't even seeing *her* made her shiver.

Easen sat, entranced by Buda's faraway voice, reliving a scene when Athenna was just a child. Had it ever been that idyllic? No, it had never been enough for Buda – and apparently neither had he. He hadn't insisted that she break contact with the Thaylin Sarra at first; he had welcomed her *kin*, as she liked to call them, as long as her first loyalty was to the family.

All that changed on the night of the riots. She reneged on her promise, begging him to allow the injured into their home and to hide them from the Targen. Things were never the same after that; he could never really trust her again. The cause still burned strong in her heart – the undiminished fire that razed their future and reduced it to ash.

His covered his face with his hands. Athenna approached, aware of his pain from the distorted colours that danced around him. He threw his arms around her and drew her close. So much for Buda's gods.

chapter 16
A DARK SECRET

"WE CAN'T continue like this," Easen protested to the Thaylin Sarra. "We recharge the batteries during the day, but they're soon drained by the travelling. And the fuel is dangerously low, even after ditching the Transvector yesterday. We're just roaming around in the desert…"

Turor sat among the priesthood, anticipating their support.

"He's right," Verrsa said. "We have already wasted a day, circling this way and that for you to get your bearings. The vehicles are more cramped now; people are hungry and tired – they need proper rest. At this rate, the desert will claim us long before the Enemy does."

He stood under the blazing sun and squinted, his hoarse voice barely a whisper. "Have you abandoned your faith so soon?"

Verrsa stared at her feet. "And the water rations…" she glanced up, hoping to catch him unawares, but his eyes were on her like cudgels.

"I know," he drew the cloth back across his mouth.

"We were better off in the forest," Easen sided with her; "at least we were safe."

"If you've nothing more to say," Turor rasped, "give me peace."

The Thaylin Sarra drifted away, but Easen remained. He could see that Turor was coping badly with the desert, intent as he was on walking across the sand to determine their next course. The poor man's skin was red from the exposure; his mind was probably scarred too. Maybe it was time for someone else to take the lead.

He touched Turor's shoulder, creating a plume of dust. Turor grabbed his arm.

"I require your assistance…"

Easen felt Turor's words tightening around him like a noose, remembering Syriem's condition when he'd last assisted him.

"…A portable radio and aerial – with the best compass you have."

"And that's all?" Easen sagged with relief.

"Not quite," Turor leaned in closer. "I want some of the gold you've brought along – the payment for your work in Appra."

"I meant to tell you," he stammered, wiping the sweat from his brow.

"See that you fetch me a fair amount," he prodded Easen in the chest, "that can be carried on foot."

"You're not going off alone?" Easen asked, cold eyes gleaming at the prospect.

Turor unravelled his cloth and smiled towards Syriem, who immediately left Athenna's side and came over.

"Where are we headed?" he asked warily.

"I'll tell you when we get there."

Athenna embraced Syriem tenderly, certain that she was sending him off to his doom. The Thaylin Sarra withheld a public blessing for fear that it might antagonise the others. Even so, they mingled with those city folk who had gathered to watch Turor and Syriem depart. Easen raised a hand to bid them on their way. And should they not return by sundown, he knew exactly what to do.

Syriem narrowed his eyes and coughed out sand, as he trudged alongside Turor. He had resolved to follow him anywhere, in his pledge to Isca's memory, but he hadn't bargained on this. He twisted round for a final, fleeting glimpse, watching the vehicles manoeuvring to form a triangle. He also saw how their tracks from the camp were vanishing beneath the sand. The way he figured it, they had as little chance of finding their way back as reaching whatever unnamed destination Turor had set his mind to. He swore and bent his head forward, concentrating on each loathsome step.

Turor was too caught up in his own thoughts to bother responding. He slid out a dry, cracked hand that gripped the compass like a claw. The needle slowly turned and Turor shifted position to keep the sun's glare from the dial. With nothing else to judge distance, he paced his steps and veered off in a different direction, while Syriem struggled to keep pace. The boy waded over the dunes with the radio on his back, just beside him, taking it all on faith; he drew courage from that.

Eventually, Turor stretched an arm out to halt him and carefully set the apparatus down.

"Here should be fine," he knelt in the baking heat to set up the aerial.

Syriem dropped to his knees, letting the sand bear his aching body. When he felt able to move again he rolled to one side and crouched low, using Turor's body as a windbreak. He lifted the canteen from his belt. The water was tasteless, but he took a long gulp and then offered the bottle up.

Turor welcomed the gesture, having already finished his own supply. He took a few sips to moisten his lips, more of a comfort than a necessity.

Then he carefully tipped the rest of the water over the radio casing and covered it with his head cloth.

"I think you've just killed us," Syriem mumbled in disbelief.

The radio squealed into life, whinnying and shrieking as Turor adjusted the settings. He pressed an earpiece against the side of his head, and cupped two hands to capture the precious signal.

"Turn the dial," he said without moving. "Slowly, until I tell you to stop."

Syriem shifted his back to the wind-borne sand and did as he was asked. After a few minutes, Turor nodded his head vigorously. A little fine tuning of the signal and there it was, a regular pulse. A notch either way and the beacon was lost; a signal so rhythmic that it had to be deliberate. He looked to Syriem, smiling.

"Now what?" Syriem shouted over the wind.

Turor sent out as brief a message as he dared, in feverish clicks. Then he repeated the sequence over and over again until Syriem felt the rhythm lulling him into submission.

Time passed slowly in the desert. Syriem watched the sun consuming the sky and burning away his resolve. He resigned himself to their fate, hunching up tight as if to disappear.

Turor maintained his vigil, searching the horizon. Finally, something startled him in the distance. He closed his eyes desert and when he opened them again the mirage persisted. Beyond the veil of flying sand, something was moving. As it drew closer, the blurred outline became twelve legs lifting and falling in unison.

Syriem gripped Turor's arm and pointed. He ignored him, calming packing up the radio and securing the cloth back over his head. It was the largest creature Syriem had ever laid eyes on – the three largest creatures, in fact. They dwarfed him as they approached, bellowing a strained, guttural call that was the least welcoming sound he had ever heard. It was only when he saw the legs dangling down from one of the animals that he noticed the rider, swathed in cloth from head to toe and drawing three bridle ropes in one hand. He looked at Turor for an explanation.

"It's a Gimel-beast – a camel," Turor motioned towards the spitting creature. "Now, mount up," he said, beside himself with laughter a moment later when Syriem meekly asked how.

The rider clung tightly to her animal and twirled a stick high in the air. The two riderless camels bellowed again and then sank to their knees. Syriem clambered up quickly to avoid the snapping teeth. Once he was firmly in the saddle, he watched in fascination as Turor took his turn.

Turor bowed graciously to their companion and then hoisted himself high on the camel's back, sliding forward a little once the creature stood to its full height.

If walking in the sand had been unpleasant then a camel journey made that memory seem luxurious. Syriem thought his bones would shake apart long before they reached their destination. Ahead of him, all he could see was miles of endless sand. He closed his eyes to narrow slits and hung on for grim death, cursing as the camel jolted and jarred his weary body. At least it couldn't get any worse, he told himself, just before the camel broke into a frenzied gallop across the dunes.

A sheer wall of uncompromising rock faced them. The rider drew her camel up and put a horn to her lips. At the sound, a man appeared from an opening in the rock and drew back a vast, heavy cloth. The camels moved in single file, bowing their heads as they entered.

The flap closed behind them, holding the torturous wind at bay. Then the camels knelt together, throwing Syriem so far forward that he almost lost his balance. Turor dismounted and unravelled the scarf from his head. Syriem copied him, shaking out his hair and rubbing his face. Attendants rushed forward with water.

Their riding companion slid down from her beast and brushed at her clothes. "I am Agnis," she said with unseen pride. "Come this way."

Turor drew Syriem's attention to the high, sloping roof of the passageway. Agnis waited, enjoying their admiration for the architecture of her forebears. The rugged, asymmetrical red stone had either been carved by nature or excavated by hand – Turor couldn't decide which – opening up the chamber. Water had been made to run through the cavern in broad flowing channels, servicing a profusion of plants that grew in carefully positioned pots. A fire crackled in one area of the chamber. The desert dwellers around it stood up to greet their guests.

"I am Kennaz. We welcome you, travellers of the inner way."

"We are grateful, but time is against us. I trust my presence here is understood?"

"Your kin have told us what you need," Agnis's father replied. "Everything is prepared."

"I am Turor," he sensed the recognition in their eyes. "And this is Syriem Taulpiris."

At the name, the desert people bowed their heads or touched their hearts. Syriem edged towards the fire and its delicious aromas.

"How do you survive out here?"

"We live as we have to, Syriem Taulpiris," a voice called from behind him.

As the turban and swathes of cloth were removed, Syriem saw a young woman, small of frame and with a look as fierce as any camel. She joined him by the fire.

"Will you eat with us?"

He waited eagerly while Agnis hacked away at the long, dark hunk of meat on the spit. No one spoke; all eyes were on him. He received the food eagerly and ripped at the tough, sinewy flesh that dribbled over his chin.

"It's very good," he mumbled as he chewed. "What is it?"

"It's desert fish," Turor answered, raising a chorus of laughter.

"Desert fish?" he paused between mouthfuls.

"Take no notice of Turor," Kennaz replied, "he's making fun of you. It's lizard."

Syriem looked down at his plate.

"When our children are old enough for solid food, we tell them that lizard flesh is desert fish, so they won't think they're eating their pets. If you don't want it, pass your plate to someone who does."

"No," Syriem recovered his appetite, "desert fish is fine by me."

A Thaylin Sarra priestess drew Turor to one side. "I have consulted the runes. You are safe from the Enemy for as long as you remain here."

Syriem's heart sang at the ecstasy of water on his skin again. He rested his arms on the rim and closed his eyes. Images of the past rose up, so he banished them by submerging his head, surfacing in an explosion of water at a rapping on the door.

"Just come in," he called, expecting Turor on some errand of purpose.

Agnis stood at the doorway, the light behind her outlining the muscled curve of her legs. Turor, it transpired, had chosen to spend his time in what she termed *private negotiations*. Syriem smarted at that, though he tried hard not to show it – kept in the dark again, albeit in comfort this time. He sat upright in the tub and locked eyes with her.

"I brought these – you're to put them on when you are ready."

She put the clothes down, exposing one of her legs through a long skirt. He smiled, comfortably aroused in the water, and splashed about to cross his legs. Agnis looked across at him as if she might say something more, then changed her mind and closed the door.

He dunked his head again, shocked by his desire for the girl. Sex wasn't a problem for him – it was *the* problem. Every natural inclination seemed like a betrayal of Isca. He distracted himself with the birth name *Taulpiris* that Turor had apparently chosen for him. And as he pondered the riddle, glancing down at his reflection, other concerns rose up from the depths.

Was Isca's soul at peace now, traversing some plane of existence beyond his reach? Had she forgiven him for abandoning her in Tarsis? And could he ever forgive himself?

"You are an exceptional man, Turor, to attempt this. Your mother must be proud of you – how is she these days?" Kennaz put him on the spot.

"She was well, the last time I saw her," Turor replied curtly. Rarely did he talk of his past and rarer still was the experience a pleasant one. "May I make use of the chamber now?"

"You may!" Kennaz mocked his formality. "It has been ready for days, since our seers first felt your presence in the desert. Whatever we have here is yours – we do not forget. Do you wish us to fetch the boy?"

"Let him rest; he has had a long journey. He'll find me when it's time."

A silence hung over them that only the Black Rod could conjure. They knew it was with him, that mythical harbinger of doom. Those aware of his history knew little else about him. Legends had attached themselves to Turor like curses. Once, it was said, Appren spies had discovered him as a boy, in Variz. Cornered and afraid, he had called out instinctively in one of the Ancient Tongues – to make a demonic pact. And in the morning, when they found the boy insensible, there was not a mark on the Appren corpses. Who could forget a tale like that?

Turor left the main hall, guided by the subtle perfume of Frankincense – a scent he felt he had known his whole life. It seemed to him, as he walked, that a pale shadow followed. He sensed that the Lock was eager for its next encounter with the Key – another seal to be released, and another part of the journey revealed.

The chamber walls shone with the glow of candlelight, lending the rough stone a warm radiance. He closed the door behind him and rested a hand on it. Craftsmanship of the highest order depicted some of the same glyphs as those carved on the Tablet. And above them, in a matrix of spheres, interlinked by delicate channels of inlaid wood and bone: the Tree of Life.

A censor funnelled up sweet smoke from the centre of the room. He sat down beside it to await the boy. The aroma was intoxicating, transporting him to far-flung memories of the Variz territory – of markets, where spices spilled out of sacks and mingled with the dry, dusty air to flavour the day. He smiled; there were few childhood memories that he cherished. With little effort he heard his mother again, singing softly as she led him through the crowd…

The past yielded to the present; he opened his eyes, each breath permeated by the sultry perfume. Frankincense had clouded the room, blurring the candle flames to flickering bowls of light. The third seal called to him feverishly and only the sound of Syriem's heavy footfalls outside brought him to his senses.

Syriem rapped six times on the door and Turor ushered him in. The boy was robed in a white tunic with a sun design emblazoned on the chest, equalling his blond hair, so that it looked as though he were made to fit the garment. It seemed, to Turor, so like a robe that *he* had once worn that for a moment he was lost in memory again, conjuring faces from the past. Syriem said nothing; he picked up the Rod, unsheathed it and held it at arm's length. One end disappeared into the aromatic haze.

Turor worked around him, blessing and securing six directions with etheric stars of blue fire. When the circuit was completed, he stood beside Syriem, waiting for an inner prompt. The Rod flickered into life, yielding him shards of awareness. An urge arose, to remove Syriem from that holy sanctuary. To cast forth this uninitiated, unrighteous one, so that he alone – the Hybrolen who had carried the Rod out of the foul reaches of Appra – could reclaim the knowledge of Sarrell. His arm wavered in the mist.

"It is thine," Turor swallowed his shame, placing the Tablet at Syriem's feet.

Syriem blinked in surprise and offered the Rod in return. Turor took it and stretched his arms wide, visualising the Rod as a mediator between the higher and lower realms.

Syriem reached for the Tablet and turned it slowly, bearing the weight in the centre of one palm. He placed his other hand over the third seal. Had he looked down, he would not have recognised his own artistry on the wax seals. Consciousness was drawing back its gifts and removing all traces from memory. He dug his nails under the cloth, pressing his thumb against the wax. His sinews tensed and his arm began to shake as the Tablet made its presence felt. He tilted his head back at the point of release and wailed like a newborn. The room exploded into light, an engulfing brilliance saturated by ambient Frankincense and the mournful caress of Myrrh.

"Where are you, Turor?"

"I am here, Syriem," he forms on the plane an instant later, angles of light veering towards him like perfect lightning.

The boy hardly dares move, but he feels the intensity behind him. As consciousness shapes the environment, so the tender, scented haze gathers about itself, coalescing into a vehicle of manifestation. Incense merges into a single column of essence. It billows up, higher than the ceiling, flowing out into vast wings that outshine the candle flames. Syriem knows, this moment, that they are in the presence of something sacred.

Unlike Turor, Syriem does not recognise the Being. Even so, he receives its Grace. Light infuses the boy; somewhere – within or without, he cannot tell – a voice commands him to be whole, to end his grieving and seek equilibrium. And though his heart strains to hear a woman speaking, the voice is male. It talks, not of love sacrificed, but of a transcendent fulfilment – the completion of the Great Work.

A fiery wind descends, the white, translucent flames coursing around them. Now the Being stands before them in a simplified form, as elemental ruler of Fire, bidding them return to their own plane where there is work to be done. The boy looks on in silent awe.

Turor calls the intonation, "Jehovah Aloah Va Daath," releasing the Tablet's knowledge.

Syriem opens his mind to share the blessing and a stream of disparate images form, mapping out a direction and a purpose.

A sudden breeze breached the room, extinguishing all the candles bar one and scattering the incense. As the misty haze cleared, a cubic altar became visible; and upon it were the Rod and the Tablet.

"Jehovah Aloah Va Daath," Syriem repeated softly, opening his arms wide.

As soon as they'd vacated the chamber, Turor made preparations to leave. He received their gift of water as keenly as the information that would aid their cause.

"This map shows your nearest water sources," Kennaz handed him a shred of papyrus. It has been some time though – you may have to dig deep! Or perhaps you will conjure an earthquake to aid you!"

"A few shovels will be sufficient," Turor replied, uncomfortable in the boy's presence.

"What now, Hybrolen?" Kennaz's tone became more serious.

"We return to our companions and travel on. Everything else must take its course."

Kennaz called for fresh camels to be readied. His eyes were upon Turor, capturing the sight, so that he might one day tell his grandchildren of the time when two wandering Hybrolen sought refuge on their way to the Holy Land.

Turor unclipped the back of the radio casing, revealing several gold pieces. He turned them in his hands, watching as they flashed against the candlelight.

"This is a token of our pledge. While gold shines, we will ever honour your service. As we have sought the hidden sun, so this is the sun's symbolic wealth."

Kennaz waved them off at the entrance, puzzled that Turor had chosen to travel back by Gimel-beast when other, more comfortable modes of transport were at his disposal. He touched the hull of an old Scout – traded from another settlement – and shook his head. The Hybrolen were known to be creatures of purpose, so there must have been some wisdom to it.

Turor and Syriem rode alongside Agnis. She pointed behind as they travelled, reining in the three camels for a final view of the settlement. From one angle, when the wind and sand permitted it, the outlines of the pyramid-like structures were unmistakable. But a slight shift of vision and there was nothing to see but empty desert.

Syriem's spirits soared. He felt reborn, unfettered by the past and unafraid of the future. He and Turor had shared a communion and the balance had shifted. The sight of the dwellings, nestled against the elements, evoked a tide of emotion. He felt compassion for their harsh existence and an empathy that transcended his own suffering. They had received them as kin and asked for nothing, and he would never forget their kindness.

"Let them see you!" Turor motioned to Agnis, as they neared the Exodus camp. "Then head towards the Transvectors."

She nodded, although she wasn't entirely sure what a Transvector was. Her life had known only the desert and those few brave souls who had ventured there. Of course, her father had told her about the Holy Land and its magical city of M'Qar. He had explained, as she'd readied her camels and pack-sleighs for the journey, that the travellers called the city by another name and that all its names were holy.

And here she was, representing her clan again by escorting the Hybrolen Twiceborn – those who were called, in the Old Tongue, the *Taulpiris*. She would have her pick of the men folk now; any she desired would be hers. But another path had captured her imagination, an alternate destiny that conspired to shape her future. One day she would go to their great city of M'Qar and in turn receive their hospitality. The idea fastened itself as tenaciously as a camel tick and she nodded in time with the camel's bobbing head.

Cordal stood vigilant at his post. There was nothing to see, but he was glad to escape Easen and his machinations. Easen had taken him into his confidence early on, with talk of a contingency in case Turor and Syriem didn't return. He knew well what Easen was about, asking him to head up the watch out on the periphery, so that if the time came he would already appear subordinate. Cordal had accepted the bait, deploying a sentry team to different points beyond the camp, but all of them were loyal to him.

He took out the pendant from the crater and stroked it with his thumb. It spoke to him in subtle impressions, releasing fragments of emotional memory from its former owner. When the alarm call went up he jolted to attention, gripping his rifle excitedly. The pendant slipped from his grasp, into the sand. He panicked, dropping to his knees in a frantic, scrabbling search. At last he recovered it and gazed in rapture at the three sparkling stones – the black, the red and the orange.

The alarm sounded again. He thrust the treasure away, retrieved his rifle and ran back to the Scout vehicle, taking up a command position on the roof. Back at the Cargo Plant, the drivers used to swap tales of strange animal corpses seen along the desert routes. Nothing though had prepared him for the sight of the camels. It had to be Turor – no one else could have managed such an entrance. Even so, he raised his rifle.

Athenna gasped at the sight of Syriem on the Gimel-Beast. He waved, lost his grip and tumbled. Turor introduced Agnis and released a dozen water gourds to the ground.

"Will you rest awhile with us?"

She hesitated and then shook her head. "I must return to my family, but I bid you a safe journey, travellers of the Exodus. We await news of your quest."

Cordal heard her voice elongate into groans. He had a sense of time slowing down and movements hampered by gravity. Before the girl's words had faded, a bullet ripped through the encampment, scattering people in all directions. Somewhere, amid the chaos and screaming, time sprang back and a second shot thudded against the side of a Transvector. One of the camels broke free and fled across the desert in terror, dragging the pack-sleigh behind it. Agnis wrestled with the remaining beasts, struggling to steady them as they strained against their ropes and snapped at the air.

Syriem looked towards Cordal. The Black Rod understood what had to be done, just as it knew that Syriem was incapable of the task. But Cordal would serve the part well.

He gripped his rifle and dived forward, shifting to a kneeling position in a sandbank close to Syriem. Without a word, he cocked the trigger in one fluid movement, adrenaline flooding his senses. His body tensed, but inside was absolute calm. Someone called for him again – no matter. He squeezed the trigger, crushing his finger hard against the metal, exactly how they'd taught him not to during his military service.

Turor had already started running, but it was futile. Cordal loosed a second shot and roared, speeding the bullet home with a primitive incantation to the kill. Turor charged headlong into the fray, screaming like a banshee as he collided with him.

Cordal hit the sand seconds before an incoming bullet skimmed the air above them. He lay there, panting furiously as Turor pinned him down. The sentries returned fire in a blaze of retaliation until, as if by some subtle signal, they all fell silent together.

Agnis backed away. "I swear to you, this was not the work of our people."

Turor waved their weapons down. "Are the tribes at war?" he asked, remembering the treaties he had witnessed on his travels.

"There has been peace among the tribes for a long time. This is the work of outsiders."

Cordal turned to Easen. "I say we make sure that's the end of them."

"Go then, "Turor spoke for him. "Take the Scout, and be on your guard."

Cordal summoned volunteers and Turor wondered just how long he'd been a driver.

"One more thing," he insisted as Cordal readied his team. "If you find any bodies, bring them back – I want to see them."

"I will wait here with you, Turor Taulpiris," Agnis said, "so we all know the truth."

Syriem jerked his head up and stared, open-mouthed.

"As you wish," Turor relented, facing Syriem with a blank expression.

Agnis remained by the camels, holding them still so the travellers could exercise their curiosity. Athenna hurried over to see Syriem, irked by his indifference.

"It must be a drab existence, living in the desert," she glanced at Agnis's clothing.

"The water is always hot and we make what pleasure we can!" she smiled at Syriem, and Athenna stormed off to join her father.

Cordal's team returned in less than an hour, the Scout banking and sliding as it powered over the dunes. They stopped a little way off from the camp, and he called Turor and Easen over. Agnis tethered the camels, collecting Syriem on her way over. They arrived to see Cordal opening the rear door of the Scout; a body rolled out, exposing the skill of his shot.

"Do you recognise him?" Turor turned to Agnis.

She shook her head. He looked too athletic to be one of the desert people; plus, he was clean-shaven – almost unheard of among their menfolk. Cordal checked under the clothing for identification and his hand knocked against body armour.

It confirmed Turor's suspicions. "Targen. Would he be alone, out this far?"

Cordal thought for a moment. "It seems unlikely, judging by his age. The others were probably downed in a sand dune, buried beyond trace."

"Or else they escaped," he watched for Cordal's reaction. "Have you found anything else?"

Cordal shook his head, unaware that Turor was sensing his aura. Musty reds and browns congealed around his outline, stifling a darker resonance. He was lying; Turor knew it. Cordal grabbed a shovel and went off to see to the burial.

"What does it mean?" Syriem stared down at the body.

"It means we are not alone out here."

Easen waited until Agnis and her camels were well into the distance before he started up the Transvector. It grumbled into life, spewing sand from the tail pipe. The fuel gauges veered towards empty; he tapped the glass for Turor's benefit and gazed across the desert. Without a word spoken, he led the convoy out from the camp. For the first time since leaving Tarsis, they knew that Targen troops had been in the vicinity. How long, Easen wondered, before they encountered them again in numbers?

He slipped the vehicle roughly on to solid rock. There had been no discussion, no decisions; he just followed their previous heading. His eyes hung heavy and his spirit heavier still. First there had been rich forest, but that hadn't been enough for Turor; then it was scrubland, and now relentless desert. He glanced in the mirror, eyeing the sweat on Turor's brow as he twisted the compass round. It seemed the desert would freeze over before the so-called Righteous One revealed his secrets.

It had to be in accordance with the needs of the Thaylin Sarra, Turor reasoned. He couldn't simply give out the details and expect them to accept his word. It had been a hard-won treasure and he needed the maximum gain from it – he owed that much to the settlers. He closed his eyes, allowing the motion of the Transvector to draw him inward. In the background, he could hear Syriem weathering a barrage of questions from Athenna. It stood to reason that she and Syriem had some deeper connection. No doubt, before their journey was out, that too would come to a head.

He directed Easen on to a new bearing with well-chosen, ambiguous words. They ought to stay on the move; that way there was more chance of completing the Rod's bidding without a massacre. He paused in his thoughts, aware that a malign influence was around him again. Not the Rod, baneful though that presence could be at times; this was different – a presence he thought he had put behind him: Appra.

He glanced around the Transvector cab, tuning his insight. His mind gathered speed as it sifted energy patterns. Either Appra had always had an infiltrator in their vehicle, and he'd been unaware of it, or else an agent had been appropriated. Neither explanation sat comfortably with him, but he trusted his intuition on the matter.

The desert was now a dangerous place, even though weather conditions were in their favour and military outposts were generally ill equipped for major conflict. Could the settlement defend itself? Maybe. And what about Esilmeor, back in the forest? Was it still standing or had it been razed to the ground – that favoured Targen retribution – as punishment for aiding the Exodus? It didn't bear thinking about, but, as he sat next to Easen, Turor could think of little else.

"Stop here," he commanded. "And raise an aerial; I need to send a message."

Cordal brooded at the back of the cab, watching Easen bend to Turor's will. Where before he'd felt a sense of power, now there was only despair. He had taken at least one life; worse than that, he'd felt good about it – enriched, as if some buried aspect had been reclaimed. He relived the scene over and over, finding refuge in rationalisations. And as long as he kept it that way in his mind, he didn't see the face of his victim: a smooth face, forever rounded in the soft features of youth, marred only by a perfect circle that burrowed into his skull. He gave up the struggle and slept, unaware that the Rod had spread its influence a little further.

A crimson sky beckoned, causing many to retreat into petty superstition and call upon the Thaylin Sarra to protect them. None though called to Turor; he had become an outsider again, he and his apprentice.

Turor watched the fading light turn through shades of ochre; now was as auspicious a time as any. "Verrsa, what guidance can you give us for our journey?"

She produced three sticks from among her few possessions and cleared a space in the Transvector, passing her hands lightly over the floor to dedicate her art. Syriem watched keenly to see how she worked.

After the four directions were summoned and cleared, Verrsa spread out a green cloth that bore faded traces of its creator's devotion. She worked methodically, aware that all eyes were upon her, casting the first pattern as she had countless times before. Easen readied himself at the radio to share her words.

Turor listened to her counsel without comment, giving her insight careful consideration. Five patterns were cast, each bearing a piece of the challenge: strife, seeking, bridge, movement and communication. Then she fell silent to allow him to respond. He gazed down at the last pattern, recognising it as the form of The Messenger.

Despite her blushes, he praised her skill as a seer. She had said in allegory what he dared not profess. Her guidance was true; how could it not be? Their path had been set – one way or another – from the moment they'd left Tarsis.

While everyone around him settled, Turor watched the sky drain purple. Lengthening shadows raked the land like the spreading talons of chaos.

"Can't you go any faster, Easen?"

"We need to conserve fuel; as it is, the batteries are doing much of the work. And who knows how safe this terrain is?" He glanced in the side mirror, catching sight of the convoy as it kicked up dust in its wake.

Turor watched their progress through narrowed eyes. As the minutes ticked by, the presence of the Enemy grew stronger. He glowered, his patience at an end.

"Here," he reached over to take the wheel; "I'll take over."

Easen yielded, staring daggers at Syriem as he took his place beside his mentor.

"Where are we headed, Turor?"

"Not now, boy," he increased the speed.

Syriem picked up the handset, unaware that the thought was not his own.

"Tell them they must keep pace with us," Turor insisted. "If we lose them now they are *dead*." He hunched over the wheel, crushing his hands against it. "Damn you, where *are* you?" He swung the vehicle erratically, using the headlights like search beams.

Syriem closed out the commotion around him. Perhaps Turor was even now wrestling with the Black Rod's influence? He had to say something, if only to let Turor know that the burden was not his alone.

"What can I do?"

A feverish smile lit up Turor's face; maybe there was another way. "Can you drive?"

"Yes, I think so…"

"Good; I need the Rod."

As Syriem took the wheel, Turor placed the compass on the dashboard. "Northwest."

When he lifted the Rod from the bag, its consciousness stirred, embracing him in emotion and thought. Its tone was conciliatory, but he closed out its influence, stalling until he was ready to deal with it. His breathing became strong and steady, primed for the confrontation.

He clenched a fist around the rod, squeezing it ever tighter. The co-ordinates eluded him – precious details that could aid them. Only one explanation made sense. His mind swept away the present and marched towards the past, ruthlessly exhuming memories. A catalogue of injustices, all to protect the Rod; a childhood sacrificed to a legend. It wasn't hate, but it was close. He dispensed with the protection of an inner temple; there was no time for that. He saw his consciousness as a single shaft of light, projecting force and focus to make the connection. Somewhere within, he felt the swirling, cloying energies of a realm to which he was alien.

'Listen to me,' he called mentally, 'you know what I seek and I know that you have it. I swear, whatever befalls me, if you do not yield it I will snap the Rod in two and bury it so deep in the sand that a century of digging would leave it undiscovered.'

The Rod seemed to twist in Turor's choking grasp. He held it fast, calling upon ancient powers to aid *him* for once. The Rod relented, searing his hand as it conceded three words like a hex: *As you wish.*

Syriem turned his head sharply, as a hideous laughter receded from his mind – a haunting, mocking sound that fastened him to the wheel. He hit the brakes without warning, punching down with all his might as he tensed up for the impact. The vehicles screeched and lurched to a standstill. Miraculously, there were no serious injuries – except Turor knew it was no miracle. The Rod had heard him and granted his petition.

Syriem stared at the silhouette before them, waiting for someone to say something. At first they were too busy squabbling among themselves. Then a silence descended as they looked out upon an impossibility. Easen pushed to the front and peered through the bullet-scarred windscreen. To their left, a gaping fissure slithered across the ground. To the right, a lone, abandoned Transvector cast a formidable shadow.

Turor ordered everyone to stay inside. "Except you," he told Syriem, his grip on the Rod so tight that his knuckles were still white.

The night air carried the distant scent of the mountains. Turor approached the vehicle warily, brandishing the Rod like a beacon of darkness. When they drew level with the truck, Turor returned the Rod, and Syriem felt its icy touch as he placed it back in the bag. Turor flexed his knuckles, examining the burns. Then he cupped the palm of his left hand over the right, covering the swollen skin. After a minute or so he removed it, bending the fingers slowly. In the fading light Syriem could see the swelling had subsided.

"How did you…?"

"Listen, Syriem, the Rod gives nothing without exacting a price. Never forget that."

"What was your price?"

Turor turned to the veiled horizon. "I yielded the last of my protection."

And although he could not sense Turor's aura, it seemed to Syriem that the Hybrolen had somehow become diminished.

Turor recovered his composure, patting the boy on the shoulder softly as they examined the Transvector. "Go back and tell them it's safe. And make sure they're unarmed, just in case there are settlers in the vicinity – we don't want another incident."

"Settlers?" Syriem mumbled as he scurried off to fetch the others.

Athenna could feel Syriem's need as though it were her own hunger. He was nowhere to be found though and the Thaylin Sarra showed little interest. She reflected on their attitude as she wandered through the camp, calling out his name like a lost child. They seemed to respect Turor and they accepted Syriem as a part of his plan, but they didn't trust either of them.

She was glad to be free of the Thaylin Sarra for a while. Once they'd learned of her heritage, sooner or later every conversation came round to the faith or the significance of he heritage. How strange now to be forging a similar path to her mother. She remembered something Syriem had quoted from Parva Serach, that history only repeated itself where there was unfinished work and the pattern remained incomplete. She considered that, following the trail of her thoughts, and found him at last in the shadows.

Syriem stared ahead, gripped by the same unreasonable melancholy that always afflicted him after the Rod had been active.

"Mind if I join you?"

He didn't answer so she sat quietly; whenever she looked right at him, his eyes chased hers away.

"I'm sorry I've been distant; I haven't been very fair to you since this all began, have I?"

He sniffed disconsolately, uncertain if she meant the journey or even further back.

"Anyway, I'm here if you need me…"

She felt his hand against her face and masked her smile. She could sense the moisture on his lips and imagined the pounding of his heart like her own. But when she opened her eyes he rested his head on her shoulder.

They stayed like that for a long time, watching the teams that systematically stripped the Transvector. The workers moved under the pallid glow of field lamps, scurrying back and forth like insects, salvaging fuel and dismantling parts. And all the while they sang to raise their spirits, certain that providence had favoured them.

Easen waved to his daughter from the fire, disturbed by the sight of Syriem draped over her like a cripple.

"Looks like it's been out here a while," Cordal kicked the sand that had gathered against the wheels. "The tanks were about three quarters full. It will make a difference, but we'll probably have to ditch another vehicle at some point."

"If that's what it takes, so be it," Easen ventured, as if he had a foresight that Cordal lacked.

"It's already too cramped in the cargo holds. Maybe we should ask Turor…" Cordal's voice tailed off.

Easen called him up into the cab and closed the door. "I think we can handle this by ourselves, don't you? Leave Turor to cater for their souls – it's what he does best."

Turor walked beside Verrsa, content to let Cordal and Easen supervise the work crews. As they moved through the camp, he felt her husband's eyes upon him.

"He doubts me?" Turor nodded in his direction, intrigued by their marriage of opposites.

"My husband lacks the stability of our faith," she searched for a worthy response. "He fears what he does not understand."

"And you?"

"I am content to be guided by the traditions, whether I understand them or not." She looked to the distance. "There's something I've wanted to tell you. I knew Isca, briefly; we met through the Matriarch Etta. She told me what happened to her, but I didn't know Syriem by name then. It's only since speaking with Athenna…" she paused, reading Turor's blank expression. "I'm surprised you've not heard of Etta; she was well known in the district. Ah, but you aren't native to Tarsis…"

Turor yielded a smile and little else.

"So," she continued uncomfortably, "about Syriem. Etta felt that Isca had become enamoured with him."

Turor cast an eye to Syriem, still motionless with Athenna. "I'd prefer it if you did not discuss the matter, Verrsa. It would serve little purpose other than to re-open old wounds."

"He grieves for her still – even I can see that," she protested. "Might it not ease his suffering a little to know how deeply she felt about him?"

"Who among us has not known loss?" he rebuked her. "Syriem is coming to accept things as they are – let that be enough," he turned to leave.

"I've seldom heard so many teachings from one person," her voice followed him. "It must be rare, even for a Hybrolen, to have been so blessed."

"Yes, I have been…*fortunate*," he contorted the word.

"Indeed, I think only Parva Serach herself would speak with such authority."

Turor had heard enough. Parva Serach's reputation had dogged him for the whole of his adult life. And there was that other word: Hybrolen. It crushed him with its expectations, dredging up childhood memories of seekers prostrate before him, seeking knowledge and absolution. They'd professed that he was indeed one of the shining re-born, a redeemer of souls. Yet who had been there for his soul?

Athenna saw Turor heading off alone into the darkness. This time, she resolved, she would have it out with him and get some answers – no more riddles.

Syriem watched it all playing out before him. He was tired, a weariness borne of isolation and powerlessness. If this were all a dream, some kind of delusional realm, then he wanted it to end. He remembered a technique from one of the Thaylin Sarra leaflets he'd found in the library. The same question, repeated three times: 'What do you believe in?'

"Not this," he whispered to the shadowy outline of the mountains; "not this."

Athenna cornered her quarry. "Turor, tell me about Syriem," she garbled the words as she raced over. "Since he's not a Thaylin Sarra, what purpose does he serve? And why do the rest of your people accept him so readily?"

Turor sighed wearily. "Maybe you should ask yourself the same question?"

She stalled, caught off guard.

"How long, Athenna, before you acknowledge your mother's influences?"

"What right have you to tell me who I am and what I need to do?"

Turor smiled ungraciously. "Who am I? I'm a Hybrolen Twiceborn," he mocked himself. "More than that, I am apparently the Righteous One. Yet, while many look to me as the pathfinder, few want to walk the path with me. But *he* does."

She glanced over at Syriem, wishing she had never left his side.

Turor moved in close and followed her gaze, "He is more than he wishes to be – and less, because he has *chosen* to forget the past. Until he confronts that, he will never be free."

Easen had avoided Turor since the refuelling, busying himself any way he could. However he looked at it, there were too many coincidences. If The Assembly wanted to send them on a fool's errand, they could have chosen few better than him.

But he needed to know; it gnawed away at him and he would not rest that night until he had some sort of answer. He found Turor amongst the Thaylin Sarra and waited while they discussed fate and freewill. Turor was silent, as though listening for something important.

"Can I speak with you?" he gestured to one side.

"You can say whatever you need to," Turor offered him a space.

The Thaylin Sarra carried on talking, only now they shifted towards him.

Easen took a breath. "The course change, and the fuel – how is this possible?"

"How else could we continue our journey?"

Morning framed the carcass of the abandoned Transvector. Sunlight skimmed along its sides, flooding the gaping holes left by the previous night's work. Turor stared at the hull, absorbed by the interplay of light and shadow on the chassis.

Behind him, he heard the camp stirring; it was safe now to wander around without starting a panic. He stood and stretched, lifting his arms out to the morning sun. Then he turned the disc around his neck to angle the sun's rays against his forehead. "Not mine but thine," he whispered and tried to sound sincere about it.

It was time to be about his work. He tiptoed around the sleeping hordes, amused to find Syriem and Athenna together; her arms around him like a child. He roused him with his foot, leading him out through the sprawl of bodies and tents.

"Are you going to tell me where we're going? That's not too much to ask," Syriem felt the Black Rod digging into his ribs, and wondered whether Athenna would notice his absence.

"Up," Turor replied. "We're going up."

He made swift progress towards higher ground, scaling the steep face without too much difficulty, while Syriem lagged behind. And every time Turor's footing slipped, a shower of dirt and small stones rained down upon Syriem, covering him in debris.

Syriem paused periodically, to splutter out dust or avoid the stones as they skipped past him. Turor reached the ridge, noting the faint petroglyphs of sky gods and fantastic animals. The vista swept away, up to the mountains and down to the dry, dusty plains. He turned back, unable to see the markings again, and faced the sun, giving thanks in the silence. Syriem eventually arrived, his skin the colour of the land.

"So, what are we looking for?" he destroyed the serenity of the moment effortlessly.

"You tell me."

Syriem surveyed the territory. Below him he could see the camp coming to life. Easen, marching about and giving out orders, though he would have called it organising, and some of the Thaylin Sarra performing devotional postures. It reminded him of poses that Isca had showed him once and he smiled at the memory. Closer to the vehicles, people were arguing over the containers and Cordal was in the thick of it, trying to keep control.

Turor picked up a small stone and flung it at Syriem. "One of the secrets of focus is knowing where to focus in the first place."

"Huh?"

"You're concentrating in the wrong direction. Up, not down!"

He grinned, rubbing at the dirt on his face as he redirected his attention to the mountains. It was a trick of the light perhaps or the sun reflecting off the rock face. "I can see small beacons, almost *sense* them – are we being watched?"

"They were there yesterday too. If they're signalling, I don't think it's to us."

"Targen then?" Syriem warmed to this new equality.

"I doubt it; they would have made a move by now. One heavy artillery attack while we slept would have taken care of most of us." He judged Syriem's mood by the colours around him. "Go on then, you have a captive audience now – ask what you want to know."

Syriem tried framing the words first in his head; he didn't want to waste the opportunity.

"You want to know about the Transvector…" Turor began for him.

"Not exactly," Syriem countered. "I want to know *how* we managed to find it."

Turor congratulated him with a nod. "Ah, but is it the only Transvector?"

"What, so there are Transvectors hidden all over the place?"

"No, not everywhere, but some hijackings were a long-term investment." He waited, to see if Syriem grasped the full implications.

"Tell me again how the Tablet works," Syriem's voice took on a sombre tone.

"The Tablet contains the knowledge; the Rod activates it and makes the knowledge available. The Lock and the Key – each requires the other, because of how they were created."

"Are you speaking in metaphor?"

"It's a metaphor, yes, and it's also true. This environment around us," he opened his arms wide, "isn't the product of that interaction, but our experiences within it are – to a point."

Syriem bit at his lip, conjuring ideas. "So you know what lies ahead?"

"It's not how you think, with me holding back information and only revealing it as and when I see fit. It comes to me as *awareness*. Once I know it, well, I know it. There's no before or after, there just *is*."

"All right, different question," Syriem paused while the Rod's intelligence consolidated the essence of the thought. "What is the link between us – why were you at my birth and why am I part of all this?"

Turor closed his eyes and was silent for a while. "There are four of us," he blinked at his own revelation. "And we were together a long time ago. There is a debt to be settled among us, for the good of the fifth."

Syriem sat down and turned his gaze inward. There were no symbols this time, no conscious act of focus – just an opening to awareness. "I see a cavern," he said. "I've been there before, in dreams."

"Who else was there?" Turor tried hard not to project his own ideas upon him.

"Isca!" Syriem twitched excitedly. "She was there; one among us." He opened his eyes with a sad smile. "So who is the fourth person?"

Turor paled. "It's complicated, Syriem; we'll save that discussion for another time. Right now we need to report back to the others."

"One last question then…which is the nearest city state to our present position?"

"Variz," Turor replied without thinking. "Why?"

"I just wanted to confirm that, on some level, you know exactly where we are."

Cordal didn't like what he was hearing about signals and settlers. His first instinct was to prepare for the worst, and he was a man who listened to first instincts.

"How many people are out there?"

"We've no way of knowing. My best guess," Turor managed an infinitesimal gesture to Syriem, which seemed to suggest *disregard what I'm about to say*, "is that they're nomads. Or most likely from a settlement; we could be near the Crail Settlement."

Syriem blushed; he'd been so enamoured with his cleverness about

Variz that he'd forgotten about settlements. Verrsa weaved her way through the mob to stand shoulder to shoulder with Turor.

"The Crail settlers are known to be peaceful. They have welcomed many of our people and they have no love of the City States."

"What would they want with us?" Easen rounded on Turor, stood before them like a condemned man.

"Consider this," he spoke to the crowd, "we are the outsiders here and we travel in city state vehicles. Perhaps they want to be sure of our intent."

"Let them come as they will," Cordal lifted his faithful rifle into the air. "If they want trouble, they can have it."

Turor placed a hand at Cordal's heart. "Think carefully before you make any rash decisions. You won't be up against a group of adolescents this time."

Cordal squared up to Turor in a battle of wills. But all he found in Turor's gaze was an age-old, impenetrable darkness.

chapter 17
PERICULUM

E ASEN TOOK a break from driving and switched places with Cordal. He stepped over Syriem and Athenna, and squeezed his way through to the cargo space. The connecting door offered scant light. Eyes flashed back at him from the shadows; hardly anyone spoke. The air seemed thick with apathy. He found some space and sank down on a piece of sacking, deciding there and then to draw up a roster so that everyone got to a window regularly.

"You're Easen," a Thaylin Sarra woman turned towards him in the gloom.

He nodded, pressing his shoulders against the metal panelling as he dropped his hands into his lap.

"Let me help you," she took one of his hands and cradled it in her palms, flexing and massaging his fingers.

She reminded him a little of Alda, drawing him back to stolen intimacies in Tarsis. He couldn't understand why Alda had chosen to remain in Tarsis and risk the wrath of the Targen. He'd wondered whether Turor was behind it, punishing them both for their liaison. Surely Turor couldn't that cruel, to deny one of the faithful passage to Sarrell? He offered up his other hand and let his thoughts drift, inevitably, to Buda.

The next thing Easen knew, the woman was gently waking him for his water ration. Everyone had their water at the same times of day now, to make sure none were left out. He welcomed the event as one of the few, bright moments in an otherwise thankless day. The meagre offering slid down his parched throat quickly and did little to satisfy him. He glowered, dimly glimpsing the back of Turor's head through the doorway, and wondered when the great messiah would earn his keep and deliver them all to a lake.

Arkastrell Frayer waited impatiently as her fawning attendants brought out platters of food. She glanced briefly at the sodden mess and sent the servants away. Raw meat had lost its appeal; her palate demanded another kind of sustenance.

She opened the file again and flicked through the pages. She had followed the progress of the Exodus with great interest, receiving the brief, coded reports with a conceit that matched her cunning. As High Dominus of Appra she had been privy to covert intelligence, aided by a loyal faction who pledged allegiance to her as they had done to her mother. Ever since the *accident* in Agnorsteta, where her mother's body still lay buried beneath a ton of ice and snow – ever since that day when she had become the High Dominus in her mother's place – she had sought ways to consolidate and maintain her position.

Opposition to her authority was minimal because of the shadow her mother still cast, but among the murmurs of dissent one fearsome voice loomed large. She stuffed the papers back in the folder and slammed it on the table. That murdering bastard of an uncle, Ces Frayer…once her position was assured, she would avenge her mother. After the subjugation of Sarrell – for no doubt there was some substance to the legend – she would eradicate all opposition, starting with him.

She cared little for those conflicts between Appra and Sarrell, which had supposedly been maintained on the inner planes since the exodus from Old Earth. It was beyond both her understanding and her interest. They could all believe what they wanted, as long as they worked towards the greater plan – the recreation of a Nation State like those of Old Earth. Then she would rule as none had ruled for centuries.

Safe within her chambers, she called her retinue to account and scorned them for their incompetence. The messages from the travellers had ceased, leaving her at the mercy of seers who had sought in vain to contact the lost. She endured an underling's excuses, rubbing her temples to contain her frustration.

"And what of the patrol?" she knew the answer already by the look on his face.

"A specialist cadet unit was sent out, on a training exercise, as you commanded."

"And?" she lashed him with a single word.

"I regret to advise that the unit is missing, ma'am."

His words offended her all the more because it was evidence of her own failing. Inwardly, she seethed. How unprepared she'd been to carry the family honour – her mother would have dealt with this without blinking. She tapped her cheek, mulling over her contingency plan. So far, only her confidantes had shared her true intent; now, she would have to trust another. If, as she suspected, the Black Rod was a factor, there was only one option open – short of sharing her knowledge with the vermin she was forced to call family.

"You may leave," she pointed to a side door.

Soon after he'd gone, a waif-like creature disturbed her. "She has arrived and awaits your instructions, High Dominus."

"Very well; delay her a few more minutes and then send her in."

Arkastrell took the time to compose herself, attempting to shield her mind behind an array of supposedly magical symbols that did little to bolster her confidence. When the door swung in, there was an audible gasp around the room – a palpable reaction to an unholy presence. Arkastrell watched keenly as all other eyes turned from Ursephal's gaze.

Ursephal approached the High Dominus slowly, her cold demeanour mocking Arkastrell without effort. She stood, ramrod straight and hands folded, reading signs that High Dominus could not have hidden even if she'd wanted to.

Arkastrell sized her up. The Appren High Command regarded Ursephal as a unique asset. She was that rare combination, skilled in magic and ruthless in its application; both respected and feared.

"You sent for me."

Arkastrell paced the silence, as one would expect from the High Dominus, and looked her in the eyes. Few people trusted Ursephal – it did not do to get too close; it invited contamination from the other, sub-human company she was rumoured to consort with. Legends had flourished around Ursephal like bindweed; they said she had mated with a demon to learn its arts. Another tale, uttered by one who later wished that he'd held his tongue, told how she had spawned a half-ling now imprisoned in some deep recess of Appra. Arkastrell knew all this and fought to banish such tales from her mind, determined to deal with the woman before her and not her reputation.

The servants vacated the room, leaving just the two of them. Arkastrell offered a seat at the table near the fire, sensing the coldness in her but misjudging it to be something physical. Ursephal took her place, running a finger through the spilled blood that had gathered in the table grooves. She waited without any show of enthusiasm; her passions, such as they were, were reserved for other endeavours.

Arkastrell came straight to the point. "I am aware of your affinity with the Black Rod, which was taken from us. Are you in a position to assist me?"

Ursephal smiled; she liked that: *assistance*. Humility was seldom found among the Frayers. "I am willing to petition my sources for a way forward."

"Then I await a positive outcome."

Ursephal took her leave, bowing low to hide her smile. How strange to find that the High Dominus of Appra was no more skilled in magic than a novice. "Mark my words," she whispered to herself as she returned to her chambers, "there is capital to be made from this."

"Can I get you anything?"

"Yeah," Dorron rested against the bar, "something to make me forget." He flashed a sham of a grin and pointed.

"She must be some lady," the bartender commiserated, unnerved at the way Dorron's hand shook when he reached for the glass.

"You don't want to know."

He sought out a booth and stirred the cocktail, watching as the thin line of froth spiralled into itself. Then he sipped at it in harsh, gasping gulps, dredging up the jellied fruit so that it teetered on the rim. His hand twitched at a flashback and the red, gooey mass submerged beneath the foam.

"Get a grip," he muttered, as if it was that easy.

Glancing around, he took a sachet from his jacket and poured the contents into the glass, swilling it slowly. Immediately he was soothed by the piquant scent of Nepenthene. Tonight, unlike every other night since he'd left Targen custody, he would sleep soundly; she would not be waiting for him in his dreams. He took another sip and tried to ignore a rolling tear as it trailed down his face.

Ursephal always felt a thrill at the prospect of ritual work. A disciplined mind, and a talent for fusing emotion with imagination, had ensured that the doorways to perception were open to her even before she'd been captured and taken to Appra. And if Magic were second nature then an iron will was first. That strength of purpose had allowed her to survive in Appra when so many others had perished.

She knew that the High Dominus gave little credence to Magic, dismissing it as secondary to the pursuit of power. That she had still asked for assistance, in spite of her prejudices, could only mean Arkastrell was desperate.

As she entered the chamber, a dire scent wafted towards her – a blend of Acacia, Rue, Turmeric, Artemisia and Myrrh – the perfect complement to an act of sacrifice.

"That will be all, Narl," she gestured to the door.

The servant woman nodded obediently and left the room, dragging her withered limb behind her so that it looked like something separate from the rest of her body.

Ursephal waited until the sound of Narl's movements had faded and then took a series of conscious breaths. She unrolled a cloth on the altar and placed two wooden objects upon it, one at either side. Next, she turned to each of the four quarters in turn, tuning her astral vision to confirm that the correct sigils and signs had been put in place – Narl would be well rewarded for her efforts. She bolted the door and stood before a full-length mirror, loosening her clothes to the floor. The incense gathered around her pale flesh like gossamer robes. She licked a finger and traced it across her breasts, watching her reflection. Energy centres within her aura began to swirl and pulsate, forming the three great pillars of light that were invisible to the uninitiated.

She heard a commotion from a small cage on a podium, a frenzied curiosity given voice. Her milky limbs drifted through drapes of incense, closing on the rodent like a predator; her presence antagonised the creature, which began to gnaw frantically at the bars. She picked up the cage and pressed it against her belly, feeling the chill of the metal. The rat raked at her skin and she allowed it to draw blood before lifting the cage to eye-level.

"Tonight you shall travel the unspeakable journey, my servant of the ways."

The rat circled in its cage in a deosil dance. She placed it squarely upon the altar, before kneeling solemnly to kiss the triangular stone. A glass philtre rested at the edge and she reached for it, pouring the contents down her throat as if it were ambrosia. With each swaying movement she could feel the caustic liquid seeping deeper inside her. She smashed the empty bottle with the palm of her hand, smearing blood across the stone.

"I come to this altar to fix my work of art," she declared, pressing against the shards. A trickle of blood ran down a central groove to drip lazily into a shallow, lunar dish. "In Dark of Moon I call you, oh Fallen Ones. Draw close that you may serve *my* bidding."

The incense merged with smoke from trance herbs to wrap a pungent veil around her mind. She stared ahead; willing the departed to attend and calling them back by all the Barbarous Names at her command. The candle flames contorted in the choking haze, spiralling up to ignite the mist and give it substance.

"Come to me, my kin," she invoked, teetering at the edge of reason. "Come to me that I may avenge your deaths." She took a last, rapacious breath and cast the physical world aside.

Twin candles burn, illuminating two hollow forms. The faces twist in torment, caught between worlds, unable to pass beyond the currents of her work and some other, hideous magnetism. Each cause is a powerful polarity, drawing and then repelling the trapped spirits. In her mind's eye – for all is mind in this enchantment – she grasps for them, plucking them from their containment to deliver them into another of her own making.

"Arix Vel, reveal to me knowledge of the Exodus."

At the calling of his name, his colours burn brightly, gathering essence into a body of sorts. He looks across at her naked glory, seeing her clearly for the first time, and opens his blackened mouth to speak. The terrible extent of his injuries – imprinted upon his consciousness at the point of his demise – manifest before her eyes.

She is shocked and he reads in her repulsion confirmation of his demise. Now his nightmare imaginings begin to make sense, in a world shielded from true light. He has no tongue with which to speak and, unaccustomed to his present reality, he can only stand mutely before her as her luscious form fluctuates in and out of perception.

"Obey me, spirit," she commands, furious at the lust in his eyes.

In response to her presence, his astral form mimics the body he once inhabited, swelling his erection in charred twists of flesh. His form, while repugnant before, is grotesque in arousal. He is useless to her now and his companion, whether by art or exhaustion has dissipated back into the void.

"Wretch!" she screams, arcing her Will like a scythe to drive him beyond the veil.

The rat stirred, agitated by shadows in the mist. Ursephal rose from the floor and lifted the chalice, tilting the base so that the blood ran fluid. She snorted, drawing up mucus thick with bile. The viscous froth flowed down her milk white chin, the globules cascading into the blood. A crude wooden yoni sat to the left of the cage and a stone phallus to the right. Her eyes wandered over her symbols of force, but she could see no further than her own intent. All else, to any other purpose, was lost.

She moved about the altar, sweeping over the rodent's cage in invisible strokes of power. The creature ceased its clamour and circled slowly, fixated on her pale hands. A few more circuits and then it slumped, dead to the eye yet potent nonetheless.

"Sekha!" she hissed, staring at the rodent as if she could ignite it. From the corner of her eye, there was a flash of activity, flitting behind the altar. "Sekha," she called, sounding out guttural syllables that belonged to some forgotten stage of evolution, back when humanity had more in common with its reptilian forebears.

She smiled, relishing an unspoken request by the spirit; a petition she was happy to meet. She lifted the chalice and pressed it tight against her leg, careful not to spill the precious contents. The cold rim excited her as she held the vessel, sliding it slowly along her thighs. She paused, looking first at the dish then out to where the Sekha waited in anticipation. The dish glided to her genitals, daubing her pubic hair with blood and phlegm. She parted her legs a little then squirted urine into the vessel, spilling it down her legs.

"Feast, my lord," she lifted the chalice high for the Sekha to imbibe the vapours. The ghoul floated above her, shimmering through a haze of malevolence.

"Why have you called me?"

"I have determined a way forward," she answered proudly. "The Taulpiris child has come to light once more. The Exodus draws ever closer to Sarrell, but…" she gauged the spirit's interest by the intensity of its emanations, "a *powerful* being could mar their course, giving me time to intercept them. I can make the link for you – I already have a willing conduit."

"Then proceed," the Sekha instructed, each groaning breath tainting the air.

"Dorron," she invoked aloud, clothing herself in astral substance. With an exertion of will, she leapt from her body, abandoning it trance-like before the altar.

She focuses, allowing the astral currents to settle. Within the temple, the energy is brilliant and nebulous – a place where sound, forms and ideas interpenetrate and separate ceaselessly. But there is work to be done elsewhere. She leaves the confines of her chamber to prowl the astral wastelands, with the Sekha's presence beside her like a powerhouse.

Countless dreams pass by her like the mirages they are – an indistinct chorus of chaos. She weathers the tide and touches solid ground – solid, at least, for this plane of reality – building the Treasure House from memory and populating it with stilted, catatonic figures. Soon everything is in place for the guest of honour. The Sekha shudders with anticipation.

With the Treasure House fixed in the dreamworld, she leaves to find her prey. Her astral form crosses back to the mundane plane, hovering over Tarsis like a wraith. She descends into the Central Sector, stalking Dorron, augmenting her senses through her desire for him. It does not take long to seek him out. Soon he lies just beyond the door; she need only move towards him and he will be hers again. She pauses momentarily at the threshold. Is it compassion, she asks herself, or a sense of pity that stays her? The dilemma is fleeting; whatever the reason, her work against the Exodus takes precedence.

The room is sparsely furnished and anonymous. She studies him in the darkness, her senses ranging over the athletic form that houses his soul. The traces of fear and trauma show as residual distortions in his aura; his astral cord pulses and throbs, extending out a short distance from his physical body. Now to entice him away.

She animates the Treasure House by an act of will and his astral form quivers in response. Yet somehow he continues to resist, anchoring the grey husk above his body. Soon she perceives the cloud-like swirls around him, a key to his state: drugs. She returns to the Treasure House and the stage is set, ready for the leading man.

The Sekha appears, impatient to have its needs fulfilled. "Summon him," it demands, and Ursephal begins to wonder which of them is master and which the servant.

She will be gentle, she decides, calling out to him in the girl's voice from his memory. The tone is anxious, a note of distress that only he can resolve.

"Dorron, where are you?"

Thrice she sings her song, like a temptress, imprinting her will. At the third call, a grey shadow coalesces, and slowly, slowly, the semblance of Dorron appears. His consciousness wavers, Nepenthene warping his awareness even now.

Onlookers appear at the edges of the room, drifting entities that have been drawn to the energy and activity in an otherwise barren region. Dorron's eyes open and for a moment he sees Athenna before him, shaping his own illusions to meet his desires. The scene shifts and the Treasure House becomes a park, silvered by a melancholy moon.

She cannot take Athenna's mask for long, relinquishing the facade when the strain becomes too great. Dorron knows that something is amiss, but he cannot grasp the truth of it. Then Ursephal yields, standing beside him like a coy bride. He gasps, retreating in terror. The Sekha cackles, its guttural call rumbling across a false sky, so that Dorron believes he is in the midst of a terrible storm.

"I will not harm you," she promises, stepping back from him.

Confronted by the memory of his abuse, he becomes paralysed with fear. The Sekha spurs her on, desperate to feed on his emotions, and Ursephal recognises the extent of its power here. She too is a pawn in a situation without redemption.

"Dorron," she dulls her own emanations, making herself as approachable as possible. "Focus on the girl – she can bring you peace if you find her."

Her words have the desired effect, calming him, and he opens his mind to Athenna's presence.

"Where is the Exodus?" Ursephal beguiles him.

His gaze becomes ecstatic as he links with Athenna for the first time.

"Where is she, Dorron – where is the girl?"

He smiles, drawing strength from realisation. "She is standing behind you."

Ursephal turns and the Sekha turns with her. The girl is calm and composed, a tiny auric symbol glows at her chest. Ursephal recoils at the sight of her.

"What do you want from us?" Athenna moves to stand beside Dorron.

He reaches out to her and they touch, radiant joy speckling his body.

"I'm here now," she soothes him.

Ursephal senses no threat from the girl and advances for the kill. Athenna stands her ground, unaware that this is someone else's dream and she is subject to their effects.

"Look at me child; open yourself to me," Ursephal warps swathes of energy around her, cocooning Athenna like a spider's meal.

She complies, powerless to resist, but Dorron knows the horror awaiting her.

"Give me what I want or I will take more than my fill," Ursephal insists, piercing the sheath around Athenna with insect-like feelers.

In a sickening slithering of limbs, living tubes burrow into Athenna, feeding on her memories and experiences.

"Tell her," Dorron pleads.

Athenna feels the parasitic invasion writhing through her, laying bare her defences. Then something gives – a subtle surrender that grants her safe passage from Ursephal's fateful grasp. She begins to reclaim her True Will and connects with another Hybrolen.

In the moment of transition, it is a new voice that Ursephal hears – a child who utters a solitary word: "Mother."

Ursephal's tendrils wither away. The cocoon breaks, but the young girl who emerges is her own daughter.

"Why did you abandon me, mother?"

The Sekha is indifferent to Ursephal's agonies and manifests on the plane in all its profane glory. It moves towards the girl and she bars the way, but it strikes her down.

"You are weak, Hybrolen. While you have wasted time and energy here, I have made the link already. The location of the Exodus is veiled from her – but you will pay me my due nonetheless. Or perhaps your daughter will honour your debt…"

"You touch her and I swear by all that is unholy I will destroy you, even if I have to side with Turor to do it."

The Sekha rises, drawn to her hate, and studies her carefully.

"The next time you threaten me will be the last."

She regains her composure, adopting a more conciliatory tone. "We have a bargain, my lord and I serve you willingly," she fashions a lascivious smile.

The Sekha ponders her words, raising a rodent limb to her. "When I have dined on your degradation and depravity, I will infest the minds of the travellers and subvert their course."

She concedes. What is a body anyway but a plaything for the soul? Notions of dissension rise and fall like the tide, but a realm where thoughts take on form is no place to plot and scheme.

"Alazne, you must leave this place," she says, stone-faced against her daughter's tears and her own.

"Will you ever come back for me?"

"Yes, my child," she banishes her from the realm. "I promise I will come for you."

"Your emotional nature will be your undoing," the Sekha mocks her.

She closes on Dorron, methodically preparing him for the performance.

And although he sees the woman this time, and not some hideous deformity, he still screams at her touch as the monster looks on.

"Forgive me, Dorron," she whispers; "forgive me for my sins."

Ursephal woke the next morning, cold and bruised. The wooden phallus lay on the floor beside her – a testament to the way the Sekha had abused her. She lay on the floor and cried, feeling along the purple abrasions on her thighs. The rat squeaked, as if to taunt her. She struggled to her feet and approached the altar. She wanted nothing more than to smash the rat's skull and cleave the flesh from its filthy body. But the Sekha – if it did indeed dwell within the body of a rodent – would be free. And before she finally freed it, she would have to be strong enough to match its power.

When she returned to Arkastrell Frayer, she sensed the change in her host's attitude. The High Dominus now felt it prudent to disassociate herself from the endeavour. Ursephal would be working alone, at the mercy of her wits and whatever powers she could call to her aid.

She fingered the package, touching the official seal that granted her co-operation from all military quarters. Whatever colony or settlement she encountered, she was to treat any Thaylin Sarra obstruction as a direct threat to the High Dominus herself – and act accordingly.

Ursephal tasted the air as Arkastrell delivered her sermon. *The High Dominus fears them.* They were a strange pair together, the General who had never seen a battlefield and the High Dominus who, incredibly, was restricted to the earth plane. Perhaps they had both missed their vocations.

"You have not asked for anything in return?"

"I serve the greater plan," she nodded curtly and Arkastrell responded.

Back at her chambers, Ursephal held the envelope above a candle. She twisted the burning paper until the pain became too sharp and then cast the tiny inferno into a vessel, watching as the flames consumed themselves. She had no need of Arkastrell's instructions; her desire for vengeance had been years in the making, gnawing away at her soul. She would trace the travellers, follow them into Sarrell and end the matter. But Arkastrell's seal of office – a talisman by any other name – could be very useful.

"Besides," she told herself as she placed it around her neck, "it will be good to see Turor one last time, to take back what is mine and then kill him."

Easen spent the whole day in the Transvector cargo hold, learning about the lives of his fellow travellers. There were other tales too. A wave of nightmares meant that the Thaylin Sarra priesthood were pressed into service, interpreting dreams and offering guidance.

Athenna kept to herself, plagued by memories of a dreamscape so vivid that it still haunted her, hours later. Dorron had been there – she was sure of it. Somehow, finally, she had managed to get through to him.

She wanted to discuss the dream with one of the Thaylin Sarra, but not with Syriem around. She sat in contemplation, expanding the scene in her mind so that she could explore it fully. Dorron had been terrified; she'd heard his call from somewhere across the reaches of darkness. Had they been alone together? No, wherever they were, others had been present too. She felt a sudden chill at the realisation and looked up. There was Syriem, facing the window, locked in his own thoughts. He might well be an intrinsic part of the Thaylin Sarra's quest for Sarrell, but it didn't seem to sit well with him.

She slid back the cargo door and called for someone to take her place; a young girl eagerly stepped forward and a spark fired in Athenna's mind. A girl had been in her dream, looking through her eyes – and a woman too. A dull bulb flickered in the gloom and then faded. A Thaylin Sarra priestess called out to her, and she followed the voice, smelling the perfumed oil before she saw her. Then she sat and presented the dream in hallowed whispers.

Cordal had barely slept. In truth, he hadn't slept well since he'd picked up his souvenir from the crater – the angular pendant of metal and stones. He felt trapped and fractious. It seemed to get worse with each passing day; and the more disturbed he felt, the more others flocked to him as a source of strength. Sometimes he truly believed that they would follow him back to Tarsis, if he ordered it. But where *was* Tarsis? Come to that, where were they now? He scowled at the horizon through the windscreen and veered a little to the left.

The slow, deliberate rumbling of the Transvectors and Scout, as they inched through the narrow passes, contrasted with the stillness of the mountain region. It was a subdued land that even the desert could not tame. In the distance, Turor's mystery lights flickered provocatively. The Tablet's fourth seal waited for his attention, and the steep-sided valley walls, constricting them like a tomb, threatened a sinister retribution should he answer the call unprepared.

He gave up counting the lights, imagining them as the eyes of the Unseen observing their progress. Higher up, he could see huge outcrops at the jaws of the valleys. A few well-placed explosive charges, he mused pessimistically – that's all it would take.

The path thinned and widened at its own bidding, while Cordal matched it for unpredictability. His disposition flickered from sullen to talkative and back again without warning. Turor knew it was a bad omen when someone as closed off as Cordal had become receptive to the psychic landscape.

The route into the valley system receded behind them like a distant memory. They may have travelled two days or three, trapped so long in that damned abyss that time seemed to hold no sway. Whenever the path diverged, Cordal invariably chose the left, responding to an inner prompting so subtle that he didn't even register it.

They travelled on until the evening. Cordal had shown no signs of flagging and no one else had been keen to take the wheel. Light drained from the gorge like an ebb tide, smothering everything in shadow until the campfires took hold.

Talk of the mountain people had spread through the Exodus; wild tales of kidnapping, torture and cannibalism. City folk, united by the propaganda they'd ingested from birth, threw in their lot together, vowing to protect themselves to the last. They slept with knives in their beds and fear in their hearts. The braver souls huddled outside around the campfires, while most sought sanctuary in the cargo space. Not for the first time, many wondered if life back in Tarsis City State had really been that bad.

Cordal eased back in the driver's seat and watched the campfires through the windscreen, pleased with his work. The night watch looked back at him from their posts, keen-eyed and diligent, and prayed to make it through till the morning.

It was some ungodly hour of the morning when Syriem awoke again. Sleep held few enticements and the Rod's silky voice had resumed its whisperings. The freight space was filled with people – a heavy chaos of snoring and groaning. He wondered what time it was. Time – he had almost forgotten what it meant; he knew only dawn and dusk and rations. As he got to the cab door, he saw Cordal in the driving seat, with an extra blanket over him.

Syriem swung the door wide and jumped to the ground, slamming it shut after him and prompting a chorus of abuse. Outside, some of the sentries were playing dice, hunched over a dancing fire. He joined them, watching as the embers pirouetted in the wind.

"Has anyone seen Turor?"

One or two muttered jibes about the *Righteous One*. Away from the camp, a small fire burned brightly against the night sky. A solitary figure knelt beside the flames with his back turned. Syriem paced across the distance.

"Syriem?" Turor called out without moving.

"Are you starting your own settlement now, or won't they let you share the fire?"

Turor glanced over his shoulder. "I thought it best to choose somewhere we wouldn't be overheard. Besides, they're happier with me here. They think they're using me as bait!"

Syriem sat down, warmed by the flames and the prospect of conversation. "You sounded like you were expecting me."

Turor gave him a quizzical look and kicked Syriem's foot back from the shapes he had drawn in the earth. Syriem turned his attention to the design. He saw three columns of circles, two outer columns of three and a middle pillar of five.

"Do you know what this is?" Turor questioned him.

"It is The Tree of Life," he replied reverently.

"Now," Turor raised a finger to his face, "I want you to watch this closely."

In twenty-two deliberate stick marks, Turor connected the circles to make one glyph, with some spheres linked directly and others only reached through an intermediary.

"What do you know about these pathways?" Turor's tone grew serious, for Syriem's knowledge – or lack of it – would dictate the course of the conversation.

"They're on the Tablet and my talisman, but I don't know their full meaning."

"You may find this instructive then."

Syriem peered closer, realising this was the first time that Turor had shared any kind of formal teaching with him. Turor drew out a distorted version of the first matrix, stretching the design lengthways, varying the distance between circles, and altering the connecting lines. When he had finished, he moved his hand away to let Syriem view his creation.

"It looks like the same blueprint, only disproportionate?"

"Very good," Turor praised him. "Now, come round this way and observe," he lifted the Black Rod and pointed to each of the circles in turn. "Here," he indicated the middle circle of the central column, "is Tarsis. Just above and to the right, we have Qayla city; over to the left, we have Sirn."

He touched each groundmark with the Rod and the names of the cities seemed to linger in Syriem's mind. When Turor had named all eleven cities, he waited, keeping the mental projection strong.

Syriem looked first to one set of circles then the other. "I don't understand."

"And nor does anyone else. The one is a distortion of the other, but maybe they couldn't control exactly where the cities were founded after the Great Wars. Well, apart from key sites like Tarsis and Appra."

Syriem nodded, remembering schoolbooks that proudly proclaimed Tarsis as the oldest city of all. He looked up and suddenly Turor seemed like a man apart, someone out of step with the general march of evolution.

"What does it all mean?"

"My best guess?" Turor shrugged. "An intent to map out The Tree physically – the macrocosm in microcosm. It may even be that that the design came later, once they had built a few cities and rediscovered the knowledge…"

"But why do it?"

"That's where I'm in the dark. And note the interconnections between the circles on our Tree," he pointed to the precise drawing. "Most of them correspond to the principal routes between the cities, more or less. The pathways have meaning: a power, intensity and influence of their own. Which all suggests that The Assembly has been encoding the landscape for a long time, to embody the entire glyph; perhaps all the way back since colonisation."

Syriem reached out to the Rod, but shied away from completing the contact.

"Here's the real mystery though," Turor picked up the Rod again. "Let's say for argument's sake…" – which Syriem took to mean *don't question me on this* – "…that we are here, geographically speaking." He prodded the dirt, far outside the pell-mell scattering of circles and lines. "Where would that leave us?"

"Nowhere," Syriem suggested lamely.

"Exactly! Don't you find it strange that the Appren and their Targen servants haven't caught up with us yet, for all their resources? Maybe we're no longer on the map."

"And you're sure about this?" Syriem stared at the two designs in wonder.

"Of course not!" Turor laughed so hard that the guards looked over to see what the commotion was. "It's just a theory; but as theories go, it's an interesting one."

Syriem collapsed to the ground, rocking with laughter. Turor, left without an answer – now he really had seen everything. Only the Rod understood both the irony and the tragedy. Turor had grasped precious wisdom without the requisite understanding to make use of it.

Turor waved to the guards, who acknowledged him briefly and then returned to their games of chance. His mood hardened. "I believe we are in the grip of a subtle chaos. Somehow, we've lost the trail. It's not the Rod; another intelligence is directing us."

"The Tablet, alone?"

"I think not, Syriem. Let me ask you something…"

Syriem settled on the ground, hands clasped together in a pose that Isca had taught him. Turor watched and it still concerned him that an outsider should be so comfortable with the ways of the faith.

"What have you noticed since we left the desert settlement?"

"Well, some of people are becoming more and more isolated – especially Cordal and Easen. I can't really say about the other vehicles because, whenever we make camp, the groups tend to keep themselves apart. Only the Thaylin Sarra make an effort to mix."

Turor nodded. "There are subtle changes there too, believe me. I want you to watch Easen and Cordal carefully from now on," he paused, "and me."

"Turor?"

"There are malign influences among us and worse is to come. The Lock and the Key are your responsibility now. Don't let them out of your control – they are our only hope of reaching Sarrell."

Syriem felt his throat tighten. "What's happening with us?"

"We've lost our way and I'm not sure how to take us back."

Syriem picked up the Tablet and the Rod. "Why don't we get the Thaylin Sarra together for the sunrise?"

"Good idea," Turor scuffed his heel across the dirt to destroy the pictures.

Grey clouds masked the Thaylin Sarra's dawn observance. They persevered, dipping and stretching their bodies in tribute to the living light that brought everything into being. Syriem joined them in their exercises, his bag never more than an arm's length away. He called on Athenna and others to pick the sequence up by rote, and one by one they swelled the throng, until most of the Exodus fell into a rhythm of adoration.

Verrsa walked up to the front and turned towards the gathering. As she raised her head to speak they all stood silent.

"We bring ourselves to the Mind of the One; we open ourselves unto the heart of the Many; we walk in the blessed path of Truth." She brought the first two fingers of her right hand together, touching first her forehead and then her lips. "Are there any among us who wish to share a revelation?"

Cordal exited the Transvector, dressed in military fatigues. "Last night a spirit came to me, in my dreams, and blessed me with knowledge…" His eyes shone with emotion and in a few, short sentences he had concocted a tale, omitting the promise of power made by the Sekha.

Syriem looked to Turor for comment.

"Remember what I said," he cautioned him.

The Exodus broke an entire day's rations in celebration. The musicians among them played, and the people danced at the prospect of their deliverance.

"Oh, Syriem," Athenna held out her hands to him, "soon we shall be in Sarrell."

He saw her aura clearly; he didn't even have to try. For a moment her manner changed and a fleeting sense of uncertainty swept across her face, like a passing shadow. Then it was gone and so was she, off to dance with someone who didn't need to be asked.

He wandered out of the camp to escape the noise and confusion. Once he'd found a suitable boulder, one he could climb safely with his bags, he found a place to sit in solitude. He opened his journal and removed the three divination sticks, wrapping them carefully with Isca's tarot cards.

He breathed deeply, drawing light down through the Middle Pillar in a series of visualisations, just as Isca had taught him during their first meetings. Then, opening his eyes, he drew eleven circles on the page, before adding lines of connection to create the matrix of the Tree of Life. Once he'd completed the task, he stared hard at the design, absorbing it into his consciousness. Breath followed breath, as he closed himself off from the drama of the morning and the stirring of the mountain breeze.

It is dark, a land where light fears to trespass. He feels the glow of another presence, but he cannot see beyond his own imaginings. Undeterred, he turns in the blackness, conjuring east for his work. One pentagram becomes four, mapping the quarters to mark out his domain. Secure within, he builds the middle pillar again, vibrating imagery and Godnames to sanctify the inner temple. There is a faint glow to the east now, a pale rendition of a forgotten sun.

"Where are you?" he calls to the Rod, resolute in his belief that it will hear him.

"I am with you; I am always with you."

"We need your help."

Scornful laughter echoes around him, as it gradually reveals its form.

"You come to this realm asking for my aid – what will you give in return?"

"I offer you the way back to Sarrell."

"You are a fool, Syriem Taulpiris," the voice seethes. "I am beyond the petty limitations of your world. I exist in dimensions you cannot begin to comprehend. Your journey and the welfare of your people mean nothing to me."

He stands in non-space, occupying a chamber maintained by True Will alone. It seems to him then that everything is a dream, no more and no less than the extent of his acceptance. The arrogance of that perception lends him a confidence he would otherwise be afraid to claim.

"Show yourself, spirit."

Darkness descends so completely that what little was seen in manifestation is annihilated.

"This, Taulpiris, is my nature in as much as you can comprehend it," the creature becomes a shadow without causality. "I am the Eternal Night without respite. I am the Omega of form."

"Whatever you are, you are denied entrance to Sarrell. Otherwise you would have long since returned there."

The creature dims in abject grief, the exile too great for such a soul to bear. A female form manifests, an indigo skin encasing her like a sheath. "I was once as you are, Taulpiris. Beyond now, before comprehension, I attained liberation from the wheel. It was my glory and my journey to ascend the Tree. In my dark and terrible aspect I have become sacrifice and ruin personified. I have no capacity for conscience. My existence is forfeit until the doorway is once again open to the righteous."

"How long have you waited?" he asks, touching its sorrow with his own.

"Too long," the creature shrinks back to a thin line of indigo light.

His instinct is to merge with it, but the pressure at his chest, where the talisman rests, keeps him safe.

"This time we have met and by providence you have been protected. Do not rely on the same conclusion in future. I must be true to my nature and

you, Taulpiris, must be true to yours."

"Wait," he pleads, as the shimmering line of light begins to fade. "What should I call you?" He knows that the first step in exerting influence over something is to name it.

"When the time comes, to you I am Khorsia. Beware though, Syriem Taulpiris, for when you call I will exact a price – I can do no less."

"So be it," he responds, accepting the pact.

The darkness swallows itself, funnelling back into the great vortex from whence it first emerged. He turns, and there before him in non-space, a ring of light evolves. It spins around itself, counterbalancing the revolutions in the manifestation of a second ring, to quarter an empty sphere. Within this hollow orb he sees the passage of particles drawn first in one rotation and then the other. And as each narrow band expands in its orbit, a third and final ring forms, constraining the first two.

"What are you?" he asks, reaching up to touch the orb.

"We are as we have always been," the voice resonates within him. "The Tablet is our conduit, just as the Black Rod is Khorsia's."

He convulses, scattering focus. Shapes appear and distort, blurring into residual energy. Light is and is not. Consciousness fragments, along with the reality he has glimpsed. He is drawn back, plunging through nightmare realms of non-existence; down through denser and denser levels of reality until only the shards remain, like the scars of a long forgotten injury. But, though much is lost, there is also something gained.

"Syriem!"

The sound reached his dulled senses. He opened his eyes slowly, blinking in the harsh light of day. Below, at ground level, a man came into view.

Turor sensed the jagged anomalies in Syriem's aura. "Where have you been?"

"I communed with the Rod and the Tablet; I think I understand them better."

Turor flinched. "We're moving soon – we can talk about it later," he guided him down.

"What have I missed?"

"Cordal is still holding court and he's won over most of the Thaylin Sarra."

"Not you, though."

"As far as I'm concerned, none of this is real. But I can't do anything about it until I know what we are dealing with – and when I am guided to act."

Cordal had the Exodus travellers lined up by their vehicles like a passing out parade. Easen walked behind him quietly, hands clasped at his back in military fashion. As Syriem and Turor arrived, Cordal was completing a rousing speech about the final leg of their journey. He walked the line a final time and then commanded them into their vehicles, smiling paternally as they obeyed him.

Syriem watched in a daze, repulsed by what he saw. "Now what?" he whispered as they climbed up into the cargo hold.

Turor sighed uneasily. "We wait," he said, seeking a place in the dark.

chapter 18
CROSSING THE DIVIDE

SINCE THE ONSET of his dream, Cordal had seen no more than he was meant to see – blinded by a vision that was not his own. He didn't flinch as he directed the ailing convoy along a treacherous, ever changing route that snaked into the far reaches of the valley. A puppet to his unseen master, he played his part faultlessly, leading them to a desolate plateau.

He turned off the engine, waiting as the series of tremors died away. No one spoke. Ahead of him, two wooden gates hung limply from enormous posts.

"This is the place – I'm going in."

He opened the cab door and jumped to the ground, landing in a cloud of dirt and dust. As he approached the gates, the wind rasped through cracks in the wood like a dire warning. He flinched – an instinctive reaction that he banished with a flick of his rifle, cleaving the left gate's remaining hinge in three hollow shots. It lurched sideways and crashed to the ground, laying the citadel open. He turned back to the vehicles with a look of triumph.

"It's safe – get out here," he mouthed to Easen, raising his rifle over his shoulder as he disappeared though the entrance.

The great archway led to a forgotten settlement. Cordal turned, at the other side of the gateway, and saw a faded rainbow spanning the doorframe. He traced the line of the ramparts, marvelling at the resilience of the structure. Ancient stonework seemed to extend around the entire settlement.

"Anybody home?" he called at the top of his voice, wandering up the main thoroughfare. He checked left and right, swinging his rifle as he walked; nothing stirred. Many of the buildings were still intact, testament to a superior architecture that had withstood the ravages of time and the elements. Exquisite stone tiles adorned some of the smaller streets, leading off in patterned trails. All around was evidence of artistry and endeavour, but not a living soul was there to receive them.

The vehicles thundered in, squeezing through the archway, like a great asp. Cordal returned from his foray when he saw the crowd massing.

"Behold," he announced as he neared them, with the light of the Sekha burning brightly in his eyes, "I have delivered you to sanctuary."

Turor waited for someone to speak, unwilling to be the first voice of opposition. A deputation of the Thaylin Sarra approached Cordal. Turor made a mental note of how many people he thought were armed and caught sight of Verrsa; she looked concerned. They exchanged subtle glances and he knew then that he could rely on another ally besides Syriem.

After some coaxing, a Thaylin Sarra child steeped forward and presented Cordal with one of their treasured books. The crowd erupted into wild cheering.

"You have to do something," Syriem nudged Turor.

"I'll speak to him tonight," he promised, "for whatever good that does."

Verrsa gathered the Thaylin Sarra together in an old barn, the whitewashed walls suiting its new function as a temple. Candles had been fixed into wall recesses and the floor swept clear for the sacrament.

She secured the doorway to give them a sense of privacy and drew everyone close. When they had settled on the hard, dry earth, she called the meeting to order. Upon her arm was a blue band to denote her devotional path. Others had followed her example; some bore several colours. She gazed out with a heavy heart.

"Open my eyes to Truth, so that in all things I may behold the Law."

The congregation repeated her words.

"We who have been delivered from the cruelty of the unrighteous, let us turn our hearts to those who yet still suffer."

Everyone bowed their heads, as she completed the prayer and remembrances. She touched eyes with Turor at the back of the room and noticed the absence of any colour band on his arm. He nodded gently, silently urging her to do what she must.

She asked if they truly believed their journey was over – whether this was the sanctuary foretold for The Restitution. At first there was silence, as if the question could not have entered their minds unaided.

"How could this not be Sarrell?"

"But do you see any of the Great Ones here to greet us?" she persisted. "Do you see *anyone* – why are we alone?" But her words were as seeds in the breeze.

Outside, the people of the Exodus swarmed through the empty buildings. Cordal claimed a villa for himself, appointing a guard to stand outside. Others copied him, rooting through neighbouring dwellings in the hope of finding something of value.

Turor stood at the back of the temple, watching through a gap in the door. How could they have come to this? He closed the door behind him and ventured outside.

He sought Cordal, later that evening, and found him alone, looking up at the stars.

"They're beautiful, aren't they, Turor?"

He came straight to the point. "Do you know where we are?"

"What's in a name?" Cordal raised his hands. "The most important thing is that we can stop running – we have somewhere to call our own," he babbled on, enthusing about the power of the stars and the destiny that guided him, struggling to mediate the Sekha's influence.

"This place is Dastala. It was the scene of a massacre by Appren forces, generations ago."

Cordal turned to him with a twisted smile. "You know your history, Turor. But then, you have a rich history of your own," his dry voice rattled like a dying breath.

Turor caught the faraway look in Cordal's eyes; a stream of thoughts flitted through his mind, ending with Cordal's rifle and his own chances of ending the conversation alive.

"You're thinking of leaving?" Cordal gave voice to his intuition.

Turor backed away a few steps at a time. "*Who are you?*"

"You do not remember me, Taulpiris? Think back – you called me into being from beyond the divide, torn from my own realm and doomed to remain here."

The words became a powerful incantation; engulfing Turor in the Appren ritual they had forced him into as a child. He smelt again the terror and the blood, when Appren initiates had sought to release and control the Black Rod's power. The shard they created had manifested as the Sekha and wreaked havoc in the Sanctum. Only the High Dominus herself had brought the creature under control, earthing it in the nearest living receptacle – a rat.

"Do you think that Ursephal has forgotten you – or forgiven you?" Cordal snarled. "I know her…intimately. When she comes for you, I will gather up your soul and watch it *burn!*"

Turor felt his senses closing down, numbing his thoughts. Even breathing took a concentrated effort.

"Ah, Turor, there you are!" Syriem appeared with Athenna. "Sorry," he paused, "I didn't realise you were talking."

The Sekha looked at Athenna through Cordal's eyes and averted his gaze. Syriem touched Turor's shoulder, releasing a surge of energy. He recovered, ushering Syriem and Athenna down one of the side streets, spurred on by the pounding in his heart.

"Syriem told me about this place," Athenna repeated the tale of Dastala.

Turor listened with a wry smile; certain he had never mentioned any of it to the boy. It seemed that Syriem was ever more receptive to insights of his own.

"How did you find Cordal?" Syriem asked.

"Unhinged and dangerous," he lowered his voice abruptly. "I can't see it a way through this without bloodshed."

"All things are possible to those who believe," Syriem assured him.

And there was something in the phrase that spoke less of any bright optimism than of a higher wisdom, unfettered by rational understanding. Athenna held on to Syriem's arm and leaned forward, lightly touching Turor's hand.

"I have faith in both of you to do what is right."

Turor joined the watch that night, out by the main gateway, taking the first shift with a pistol cradled in his lap. He stared up at the arch, picking out the faded rainbow colours by firelight. Beyond it were stars and the eternal mysteries, but no answers.

"That's enough!"

Turor awoke suddenly; Verrsa's voice had cut through his sleep like a cry of anguish. He leapt up and ran towards the mob.

"Heresy!" they screamed at her. "Only an outsider would question the nature of Sarrell."

"Since when have we opposed open thought?" she retaliated.

Turor felt overcome by a sudden lethargy and put a pinch of herbs in his mouth to counteract it. The first stirrings of chaos were gathering, the tension before a storm.

"Very well," one of Verrsa's critics relented. "We'll ask *him*."

Turor prepared to receive their question. But no one called his name.

"Cordal," they cried. "Is this place Sarrell?"

He walked into the throng, clearing a space by the power of his presence. "What is Sarrell?" he challenged them. "Can it be proven? Are there not some Thaylin Sarra who say that Sarrell is merely a state of consciousness?" he opened his arms wide to encompass his flock. "Is this not sanctuary?"

"Aye!" they shouted in an ardent chorus.

"But wait," Cordal's voice plummeted, stilling the crowd. "Let us hear the words of one more knowledgeable than I – a Hybrolen. Turor, what is this place?"

The air became stagnant. Cordal smiled, fixing him with the eyes of one who had the mob at his command. Had there been any other way, Turor would gladly have taken it. In times gone by, he would have found some clever way to defuse the situation, but he could see this delusion was a cancer that needed excising. Truth, like all the other virtues, came at a price.

A thin smile of resignation crossed his face. He had become the very thing that they'd mocked him for in Tarsis – *Sarrien* – Protector of Sarrell. He cleared his throat and looked around at the travellers, making eye contact where they would allow it.

"We have travelled a long way together, have we not?"

The crowd murmured; they were still responsive, but barely.

"We have all lost loved ones – in our journey from Tarsis, and back even further in the lives we once led. When I first came to you, it was at the behest of a prophecy – a promise stretching back into antiquity. It told of a place where the children of Old Earth had first touched the soil and made it blessed. That place is Sarrell."

"Answer the question," a voice called out at Cordal's prompting.

"Is this Sarrell, you ask me?" Turor's voice boomed like a fury, unnerving them with its intensity. "No; this is a sanctuary, right enough, but it is not Sarrell."

"Deceiver!" Cordal raged.

The crowd wept, throwing themselves in the dirt and calling upon the Gods to ease their pain. Turor felt nothing except contempt; they seemed ready to stampede, like the cattle they had become. He warned Syriem to get clear, intent on protecting the boy at all costs. But Syriem stepped through the writhing bodies to stand beside Turor, facing Cordal. Turor took one look at him and made a sign of blessing.

The boundary between inner and outer realities rent and unravelled. As the sky darkened, seething and bellowing in elemental wrath, people scattered in panic. Cordal stood his ground, shaking, unable to articulate his hatred. Syriem drew closer.

Move, Turor silently pleaded, watching the scene unfold. Cordal's eyes invaded Syriem, burning through with a message of subjugation.

"*I am the Sekha and your life is mine.*"

Syriem felt a pressure, squeezing him free of his body. There was momentary fear and then the rush of liberation swept him up like the flight of angels.

The instant he whispers the name, he feels the presence enfolding his psyche in great wings of darkness: Khorsia. Senses fade in a strangled scream, dragging him to the place that he fears most of all. He sees the fire raging around his love, imagines her judging him, and hears the echoed agonies of his own grief.

Yet, while the pain threatens to consume him, he does not falter; his torments are merely layers to be discarded before True Will can be fully revealed. Fragmented images flash by – of family, of a life in Tarsis that was never meant to be, and of a birth attended by a forgotten companion. All tiles in the mosaic, and each one a part of The Restitution.

The kaleidoscopic journey ends and reality condenses to form a cave. A black, putrid river runs at his feet, coursing its way through the netherworld of his imprisonment.

"You shall answer to me," the creature calls from the shadows, feeding on his responses to bolster its reserves. "Do you know who I am?"

He does not respond beyond a flicker of a smile, aware of the eyes behind his own. The two, the Taulpiris and Khorsia together, gaze about his personalised hell. Tendrils of power filter through his Being as he advances to the middle of the cave.

"Do you fear me so, that you cannot show yourself?" he reaches for the Rod, which has entered the realm undetected. His fingers touch its surface and he lowers his guard.

"Fear, boy? I fear nothing!" Blood spews up from a fissure in the floor, spraying the cave walls. "I," the word resonates like thunder, "am the Sekha, formed out of living hatred from a shard of the Great One whose very name is Ruin and Sacrifice."

He is silent. An invisible hand stays him until the Sekha has laid itself bare.

"You will submit to my will," the Sekha rises from a pool of filth. "And when I escape this rodent curse, your living corpse will fit my purpose."

He grips the Rod, ready to strike, given to the moment. "Ensoul me!"

The words pulsate around him, and the source of his strength gathers momentum. He lifts the Rod high, unleashing its authority and shattering the cave walls in gleaming rays of darkness. Khorsia enters Syriem's body wholly, extending its force through him. The Sekha falters, gyrating and spinning as it tries to re-form on the plane. Khorsia advances to absorb its renegade aspect, but the Sekha resists at the last.

Syriem witnesses the scene as something apart, experiencing it through a distortion of perception. The Sekha focuses its battered will, reappearing for an instant. In a fit of vile rage, it calls upon its own powers, puissant forces cultivated since its separation – and directs them at the boy. He cries in agony, yet The Rod does not intervene. The astral plane gives him up like flotsam, discarding him back to physical existence.

Turor looked on as energy discharged between Cordal and Syriem, blasting the two of them apart. He heard the boy squirming on the ground, but knew he had to attend to Cordal first.

Cordal lay insensible, a look of dread etched upon his face. Turor tried to make him comfortable and saw the chain around his neck. He recoiled in horror at the same pendant they had forced *him* to wear as a child – a penance of control. The insignia seemed to fester in his hands, its angular edges driving deep into his flesh.

With a tremendous effort of will, he lifted the chain free. Colour started returning to Cordal's death mask. The pendant swung hypnotically, inviting Turor to place it around his own neck. He closed his eyes to the hideous prospect and flung the object high into the air.

"Hekas Hekas Este Bibeloi," he called out to the sky.

The chain twisted and turned in the purple air, and as the words rang out, lightning found its target, smashing the pendant and atomising the metal. Three stones scattered by his feet: black, red and orange.

Cordal stirred and the enormity of his actions overwhelmed him. He fell back to the ground, retching up tears of remorse at his betrayal. Turor went to the boy.

Syriem laid very still, a terrible heaviness at his chest. To Turor's eye, Syriem's auric lesion had extended.

"How bad is it?" Syriem asked, as if he knew how close he'd come to dying.

"You took a grave risk," Turor touched his forehead.

Athenna ran towards them and then stopped as the glistening stones caught her eye.

"Don't touch them!" Turor roared.

Syriem buried his face in his hands. The past, that cruel tapestry he had worked so diligently to evade, now shrouded him once more.

"Turor," Cordal called out, like a child in the dark; "I wish to be accepted into the faith this day – it is time I walked the path in earnest."

"Then speak to Verrsa or one of the others; I cannot receive you," he replied, confirming what Syriem had long thought, that Turor was no more a member of the faith than he was.

The sky cleared to a celestial blue and the mob found its voice again.

"What now, Hybrolen? If this is not Sarrell, how much further must we travel?"

Turor searched his heart. These were his people, those who had garnered the courage to follow him. What solace could he offer?

"We no longer suffer under a City State yoke; you are free to live as you choose."

"Free to make a life here?" Verrsa's husband ignored his wife's steely glare.

"If it is your will, yes. You must each decide what is best for you."

A steady trickle of individuals stepped over to one side, away from the Transvectors.

"Then it is here I make my home," one of the Thaylin Sarra women declared, joining them.

Turor marvelled at her sacrifice, knowing she had chosen to stay for the good of others. He gestured to her in blessing and she nodded back with tears on her eyes.

"We will be with you in spirit, always," she said.

"When we reach Sarrell," Verrsa promised the crowd, "we will send you a sign. Then you will know."

"And what about *him*?" the mob looked to Cordal.

He stood before them, saying nothing, submitting to their scorn as his first step in the faith. Turor stood beside him, like a guardian. Only the Thaylin Sarra did not condemn Cordal – because they recognised that his weakness had also been their own.

"He will travel on with us," Turor rested a firm hand on Cordal's shoulder. "But do not judge him too harshly. In as much as he was tested, so were you all."

They faced their own hypocrisy in silence, and Turor continued.

"If we all agree, those who wish to travel will leave in two days. We'll divide the supplies. Until then, we should work on repairing the main gate and making this settlement habitable."

Syriem sought out Turor and together they set off to explore part of the citadel. They wandered through empty streets, drawn by intuition that masked itself as faded memory. Turor led him up a row of steep, broad steps that narrowed in and spiralled upwards to fill an ancient tower. Turor walked purposefully, attuning his breathing to the rhythm of his thoughts. Syriem followed, his conscious mind denying a truth that had already begun to taunt him.

"I've been here before," he said, as Turor disappeared up the tower.

Turor paused, watching the pale wisps of breath rise in the damp air. "We both have," he said without further explanation, resuming his course to the summit.

From their vantage point, the citadel spread out before them to reveal a purposeful design, the trails converging in a mandala design.

"What took place here, Turor?"

"Something terrible. Dastala was once a seat of learning and commerce, but you don't need me to tell you that."

Syriem felt the damp stones pressing against his back. "Will they be safe here?"

"Hard to say. Are any of us safe? What matters is that they live by their own will." He opened his left hand and held out the three stones from the Appren pendant. In his right were similar pieces of green, blue and pale grey that Verrsa had given him. He placed the stones into narrow recesses in the wall,

As Syriem drew nearer, he recognised the feature as a stylised version of the Tree of Life. Turor lit a candle at the base of a central channel, between the lines of stones. The flame sparkled into life, climbing a carved pillar of quartz that magnified the light.

"When do you think you last did that?" Syriem asked, kneeling before the altar.

"I'm not sure I ever have," Turor replied, "but the rite is familiar to me today."

He closed his eyes and let the scene unfold in his mind. The fragrance came first – a tantalising blend as evocative as anything from Variz. Next he heard the echoes of chants long forgotten, a sacred worship lost to history. He waited to see what else his senses would claim from the collective memory.

Each breath drew him deeper into the vision, uniting past and present. He heard a great bell being rung – *invaders* through the gates, intent on pillaging the Holy of Holies. Two guardians kept the flame alive, while others gathered up the treasures – the sacred line of darkness and the stone tablet protector – and took them away. Now they would be separated, so that the Enemy could never breach the sanctuary.

"Turor!" Syriem shoved him hard, freeing him from his stupor.

He rubbed his arms to stave off the cold in his bones. "Let's get out of here."

"Shall I dig the stones out?" Syriem leaned across to the wall.

"No, leave them. I'll bring this though," Turor snuffed the candle.

The crystalline rock retained an eerie glow as the light gradually faded. He trusted that the Gods would look well upon his brief act of observance, and perhaps remember it in the future.

The morning of departure came swiftly, gracing the dawn with a wide-open sky that promised fresh horizons. True to Turor's word, no one had tried to influence those who had chosen to stay in Dastala. A life in Tarsis City State had shown them all what it was to live under someone else's dictates.

They left the Scout to the settlement. And, under pressure from Verrsa and Turor, Easen bequeathed the new settlement some of his sealed containers. Inside, the travellers found stores of seeds and nutrients as well as designs and components for machinery. Some were strange devices, power cells – like those on the roofs of the vehicles – needing only the light of the sun for energy. It was a bewildering technology and Easen had spent the past two days writing out reams of instructions.

"Where did these wonders come from?" Verrsa asked him.

Easen's ashen face yielded no secrets. Turor withheld comment; he knew they could only have come from Appra. He watched Easen as he fended off Verrsa's admiration and questions. Plundering material from Appren laboratories could not have been easy – no wonder Easen had been so keen to bring the containers out of Tarsis.

They broke bread together around the fires, sharing their hopes and dreams. Once more a litany of names was read out, commemorating all those whose sacrifice had made the journey possible. Other names had been added to the list this time – Easen had done his research well. Distant loved ones were mentioned, as well as friends and ancestors. Alda's name graced list now, as well as two that Turor had not expected: Buda and Isca.

Upon hearing her name, Syriem closed his eyes. He cast his mind back to the previous evening, when he'd stood before the standing stone in the middle of the square. He had called her to him, imagining their hands touching. And never realised that Athenna had watched unseen and silently wept with him.

Turor sensed the minds of Sarrell reaching out in beams of consciousness. The Exodus was closer than they had ever been to the hallowed place and he knew it. The Tablet was impatient, forcing its will upon him whenever he dropped his guard, seizing every opportunity to impress its own sense of urgency. He recognised the mountains from dreams, not by sight but by resonance, from that rarefied realm where the difference between truth and imagination was just a shift in perception. Awareness was the thing that guided them now; and whatever else Sarrell was or was not, it was the coalescence of awareness.

Whether they had managed to faithfully retrace Cordal's route, or had forged a fresh path, Turor couldn't say for certain. But on the second day, both he and Syriem saw the flickering lights again.

At the next camp, Easen called Turor over on some pretence, keeping his emotions in check for fear of provoking him. "Back in Tarsis you spoke of finding Buda…"

Turor drew in a sharp breath. "I said I could find out information about her."

"Can you still do it?"

He hesitated for a moment, giving Easen the chance to strike.

"Of course, I could always ask Syriem."

"No, there's no need for that. Leave it with me; I'll do what I can."

Turor found Syriem with Athenna, sat together by the glow of the flames. She looked up, smiling, and let go of Syriem's hand.

"I'll leave you two in peace."

"What can I do for you?" Syriem welcomed him.

Turor joined him, bemused by their change in roles. But before he could speak, Syriem's face clouded over.

'*More and more I dwell in him, and he in me. There will come a time when I can no longer safeguard him from the path he has chosen – you must then protect him.*'

Turor received the warning though neither of them had spoken. He closed his eyes and attuned to the stream of consciousness that emanated from the boy.

'*The gap between what is his by attainment and what he receives through my will widens with each passing day. I would fear for him, but I am incapable of fear.*'

Turor held Easen's petition in his mind and released it to the Rod and the Tablet.

"Buda is alive," Syriem revealed without thinking, indifferent to the revelation.

By the evening, activity in the camp had given way to a muted calm. The children crowded round a young Thaylin Sarra novice, cheering at his juggling tricks. Laughter filled through the air, a salve for weary minds.

Syriem shuffled closer to one of the fires, stretching his hands over the flames in a vain effort to thaw his soul. In the flickering light, Turor seemed to fade in and out of vision as he approached – one moment a flash of orange, the next a shadowy memory. Their eyes met at last and the Rod sang its beguiling song.

"It's time," Syriem stood up, sprinkling dust into the flames.

"The longest part of the journey is over," Turor consoled him, "yet the fourth seal is the most treacherous."

Easen raised no objection when Turor and Syriem ignored Cordal's warnings and took their leave of the camp. He was glad to see them go – it gave him space to think. Turor had kept his bargain, for what it was worth. So Buda was alive – where did *that* leave him?

"Do you think they're still watching us?" Syriem pointed to the lights in the distance.

"I would imagine so," Turor replied.

"Why don't I believe your ignorance?"

Turor stared in surprise, immediately drawn into the seeds of chaos. "Perhaps if you were able to accept the true nature of things, I wouldn't need to ration the truth to accommodate your…beliefs."

"What is the truth, Turor, and when will you trust me enough to share it? I know I lack your exceptional upbringing, but when all's said and done, we're neither of us Thaylin Sarra – that much is clear. And let's not forget, without me you wouldn't even be here."

"No, you're not the same as me, boy," Turor dismissed him. "I doubt you'd have had the strength or the courage to endure what I've been through."

Syriem cast him a dark glance. "You have no idea of the courage that I've had to find."

He stormed off, eager to get as far away from Turor as possible. And as he went, the unseen bind-mark on his chest smouldered. Inner voices stretched the fabric of his reality. He was tired of being treated like this, to be offered crumbs of wisdom and taunted with riddles. He had put all his trust in Turor since Tarsis, and for what?

Well, from now on, he didn't need Turor or any of them. He carried the Rod and the Tablet; he'd encountered the Sekha and survived. Perhaps *he* was the Righteous One – maybe that was what he needed to remember. To hell with Turor, he'd just keep on walking. If the Rod wanted to reach Sarrell so badly, it would have to guide him there alone. "And I know," Syriem whispered spitefully, "just how much you want to go home."

The wind responded to the turbulence of his emotions, buffeting him from every direction. He felt alone, isolated from everyone and everything; an echo of that Dark Night of the Soul when Isca had been taken from him. He steadied his balance as he walked and instinctively reached for the Rod, certain that it would come to his aid. The Rod glinted, shining in the night sky by an ethereal glow.

"Onward, onward," he obeyed, like a call to arms.

The pale moon offered scant illumination, silhouetting a nighthawk as it circled overhead in pursuit of prey. Syriem waved the rod in an arc, no more than a reflex action, and the bird wheeled slowly through the night air, calling to the elements, 'He is here, he is here.'

The beat in Syriem's head rose and swelled until his thoughts subsided, crushed by the torturous drubbing. He swayed, numbed by an unfathomable sound that emanated from within and without, pressing him to the spot. He knew then that if he just dropped the Rod, and kept walking, it would all be over. A few more steps and he would be at peace – an end to all his yearning.

"Syriem, awaken! Remember who you are," she commanded.

He jerked his head up, flashing his eyes open. Reason told him it was his imagination – a twist of memory, nothing more. But instinct knew the voice to be real: Isca had called to him. Her words faded away even as he fought for them.

His first impulse was to run and find her. Only the pain stayed him, seeping through his chest in fluid bursts. She was gone, yet like a guardian she had brought him to his senses. His limbs moved slowly, fear dragging on the muscles like dead weight. He slowed his breathing and tried to reason his position. All he could see around him was darkness and cold, impassive rock. He inched forward, testing each step before he committed to it. Only the updraft hinted at the danger. He gathered his wits and approached the precipice.

"Not thine but mine," he lifted the Rod out over the edge in a demonstration of self-control. He could hear the roaring of a river below, like the mythical Styx, promising passage to the underworld. "One step at a time," he edged back, fighting for breath.

Something grabbed him, wrenching him away like demonic gravity. He screamed, waiting for the dreadful descent as the chasm claimed him. However, the hand that had reached for him held fast, tilting him so that the speckled sky stretched over him in a canopy of stars.

"If you're trying to scare me," Turor held on tightly as he struggled, "you're succeeding."

"How did you know where to find me?"

Turor freed him and he dropped to the ground. "I didn't. I was wandering about in the darkness when I heard someone calling your name. And then the stars all shone."

"It was Isca," Syriem's voice cracked; "she warned us both."

He swallowed his pain, opening his senses to a higher knowledge. This time he pointed and Turor followed his lead. They walked together, companions of the way, across a rocky causeway that bridged the chasm below.

Turor paced methodically until he had measured about halfway across. Then he turned to Syriem, positioning himself so that half his face was bathed in moonlight. Syriem stood opposite and saw not one face divided but two separate faces – each of a different form – and neither fully Turor's.

Syriem settled his mind and consciousness absolved itself. "Who are you?" he intoned to the winds that stirred around him.

"I stand at the Abyss, a Mediator of All. I reflect the twin polarities of manifest existence."

Syriem stepped forward to receive the benediction. He made to speak, but Turor lifted up a hand in judgement. The breeze flowed forcefully, like the breath of the ancients, willing Syriem to submit to an intelligence that would use him for its own ends. And in return, knowledge that was beyond his attainment coursed though his mind. He levelled the Rod across his eyes, and felt Turor's hands pull back the fourth seal. The wax mark cracked and split, yielding up the fourth power of air. Wind and dust converged, in answer to their petition, scourging them with a triumphal roar.

In the stillness that followed, Syriem embraced a universal justice that relied on nothing, was born of nothing and unfolded in great cosmic tides, encompassing all and sparing none. He saw, fleetingly, how everything that had ever happened to him was itself only a tiny sliver of a wider reality – a purpose of such intricacy and completeness that his notion of individuality was little more than a child's empty imaginings. His grief, his anger, his pain and his joy – all were glimpses of truth, each one a distortion of a remembrance of perfection. Tears streamed down his face; they were the tears of the world, of the oppressed and their oppressors. In that moment, he accepted that the world no longer laid claim to him. The Rod fed him the ecstasy of belonging, of moving a step closer towards the final goal.

The breeze scattered Turor's call to the mountains, "Jehovah Elohim."

Cordal stood at his post and watched the fey lights in the distance, noting how they had multiplied since Turor and Syriem had left the camp. He was so absorbed that he didn't spot the two travellers returning.

Syriem walked with his head bowed, cradling memories of Isca as he stepped past. Cordal cast Turor a worried look, concerned that the boy might be bewitched – as *he* had once been. Turor tried to reassure Cordal with a glance because he knew there was nothing he could say – for what the soul had not experienced, the mind would never fully comprehend.

chapter 19

LABYRINTH

A THENNA FOUND Syriem poor company, as they wandered the camp together to no great purpose, killing time until Turor and Easen returned from a survey.

"Do you think we'll ever reach Sarrell?" she sighed, catching him unawares as he scoured the horizon.

"I think it's inevitable," his voice dropped to a faraway tone.

Her eyes brightened. "How can you be so certain?"

He pondered her words for so long that she thought he was ignoring her and coughed aloud impatiently.

"I believe," he shaped the words with difficulty, "that my whole life has been a preparation for this journey. What's happening here is working out of a plan, something bigger than all of us; I think that's what is meant by The Restitution."

He suddenly grew pensive, which could only mean one thing.

"You think about her a lot, don't you?" she moved closer.

"I still feel her presence."

He sounded so old then, so weary of longing that she almost cried.

"I wish someone felt that much for me," she said, blinking several times, as if the words had stung her.

He touched her face and felt a rush of temptation. The realisation startled him and he held out a hand, leading her to the safety of the crowd. Some of the children were attempting to climb a wizened tree, already bowed by the elements. He watched their game, flinching whenever a child swung precariously or crashed into a playmate. The sound of their laughter and screaming, with Athenna nearby, transported him to the past.

He remembered it so clearly, even the roughness of the bricks on the school building. He'd been running from the big lad who had made it his business to torture all the little ones. She'd been the new girl – the pretty one with the long hair and the dark, soulful eyes. He had stood there, mesmerised by her smile and the subtle aroma of spices.

"Hide me," he'd whispered, as Dorron's heavy boots pounded across the playground.

Dorron had already seen the two of them together and wandered over, shy and awkward, swaying from side to side as he plucked up the courage to speak to her for the first time.

"Syriem?" Athenna waved a hand in front of his face. "Are you okay?"

He smiled, aware that patterns had been set in place that first day. Still no sign of Turor; he frowned. He'd become too reliant on him, too willing to seek answers outside of himself. He yawned and rubbed his eyes.

"I'm going to rest up in the Transvector, while it's quiet. Can you ask Turor to come and find me later?"

"Well, I could do that…" she wavered, "…or I could come with you instead."

He stopped in his tracks, unsure how to read the invitation. "I'm not sure your father would approve," he countered in a shaky voice.

"He's not here though, is he?" she gave him a sideways glance.

He studied her face for a moment and then the two of them set off, their hands moulded together. It seemed a long walk to the Transvector, each step perfumed with desire. A voice within him screamed that it was another snare, a deceit to turn him from the path, but the voice fell on deaf ears. Unbridled desire, Isca had once told him, was devoid of morality – it simply took hostages.

The cab door opened wide like a lure. He climbed up and offered his hand. No one outside paid any attention; it was as if they didn't exist. Athenna joined him and their faces almost touched. The cab smelt musty, the stale odour of bodies and spent air lingering like an unwelcome guest. Undeterred, she led him to the warm, dark enclosure of the cargo hold.

They stood for an instant, teetering on the brink. Then he turned to her in the shadowed world of his own longing and kissed her hard on the lips. She let out a tiny sigh and they embraced, body to body. It was insane, he told himself as he started undressing her – what if someone disturbed them? Regardless, he burrowed under a blanket and made space for her.

As their eyes met in the half-light, she froze – as though she were seeing him properly for the first time. "This isn't right," she pulled back.

"It's what we both want, isn't it?"

"I thought I did. Only…it isn't supposed to be this way."

"Then what are you *doing* here?" he glared.

"I don't know. Our bond – it isn't this, Syriem. I can't explain; it's just…"

"Just that I'm not Dorron?"

"That's unfair."

He caught his breath and turned his back to her.

"I'd better go," she flustered, turning her back to refasten her clothes, while he lay there indignantly in a futile state of arousal.

Turor walked a step or two behind Easen, listening carefully to descriptions of mineral strata and their chemical formulae. Clearly, Easen was a very clever man and The Assembly had squandered his talents.

"Any presence of high grade quartz, Easen?"

He quickly located the required samples with a rock hammer. "Here – why?"

"I suspect the quartz deposits are enhancing the lights we've been seeing."

Easen stopped chiselling at the rock-face. "Pseudo-science," he muttered, before continuing with his work.

Turor ignored him and stepped up for a closer look.

"See these veins of discoloration?" Easen explained. "They're iron ore. Any settlement could make use of that."

"There's definitely a settlement in the region; make no mistake."

The old tensions crept back. Even now it was hard for Easen to dismiss the propaganda he'd been fed over the years. *Us* and *Them* – City State folk and Settlers, forever divided.

"You negotiated well at Esilmeor. Settlers can drive a hard bargain."

Easen slipped with his hammer. Turor watched as waves of energy shuddered around him.

"They were very hospitable," he agreed, unaware of Turor's insight.

"You're not the first traveller to have been welcomed so. Judging by the fuel and supplies you managed to acquire, you have the makings of a successful trader!"

"Look," Easen baulked, "I didn't take advantage of anyone if that's what you're implying."

Turor shook his head. "You don't have to convince me – I know the settlements. They have different sensibilities and new blood can be a highly prized commodity."

"New…blood?" Easen repeated, affronted.

"It's just the way things are; nature's way of invigorating the stock."

Easen went back to sampling minerals. It felt strange discussing this with anyone, but especially Turor. It made him wonder whether Turor knew about Alda. He quickly changed the subject.

"Have you seen many settlements?"

"More than you'd imagine!" Turor laughed, as if he too had been found out.

"Do they always practise magic?"

"No, not all of them. Some rely on the Thaylin Sarra for that, but most settlements retain some aspects of the ancient ways. They move with the seasons and natural cycles in a way that most city folk have forgotten."

They talked on, exchanging knowledge and trust. Turor explained how different settlements had their own beliefs and pantheons, augmented by nomadic Thaylin Sarra. He pointed out how practices could be similar and where they differed. And though the Thaylin Sarra loomed large in his recital, he freely acknowledged contradictions there as well.

When they reached the camp, Athenna ran up to greet Easen at full pelt, nearly knocking him over. She swung her arms wildly around him and buried her face in his chest. He sensed that something had upset her – or someone. Out of habit, Turor asked Athenna if she'd seen Syriem and she quietened, muttering that she'd spoken to him earlier and he looked like he wanted to be left alone.

"You know," Easen confided to her as Turor cut a swathe through the crowd, "I think I may have misjudged him."

Turor made straight for Verrsa and suddenly found Syriem a step behind him. Syriem felt the dissonance; something was stirring again. The other Thaylin Sarra gravitated towards them like crows.

Many spoke of their dread at Dastala and of dreams since that augured a transition. Parva Serach's notion of *approaching the starry veil* had taken on a deeper, darker relevance and they pressed Turor for clarity. He made no effort to pacify them; it was left to Verrsa to become the pathfinder.

"Let us meditate on the matter together," she sat before them.

The Thaylin Sarra joined as one and opened their minds to unity.

He leads them as though a beacon were in his hand. Yet the light they follow shines from within – a light he has always veiled. The boy is at his side like a standard bearer. The White Sun rises, cleaving the landscape into brilliance and shadow. And from each of two horizons a flag flutters.

The boy faces the Sun, bearing the Lock and Key, waiting for a prophecy of his own to be fulfilled. Now, from that light, a creature bounds towards him, gathering pace as it closes on its quarry. Its sleek form picks him out, with diamond eyes that see beyond the dream. He kneels, touching the soft, dark fur, and awareness returns. When he has finished the testing, and finished it well, when he is Sarrien – like his mentor – then he will be ready to see and to act. Then he will see her as she wishes to be seen.

"Syriem," Turor gestured towards a flat rock.

He lifted the Tablet free and laid it upon the makeshift altar. The material was torn in four places now, like the skin of an over-ripe fruit.

"Come forward," Turor invited them.

Verrsa was the first. She stretched out a hand, probing the Tablet's aura before touching it. Her fingertips moved delicately over the exposed carvings. The Thaylin Sarra watched as she twitched and blinked, muttering to one another. Her movements subsided and she stood for a while, trance-like. Then a sublime smile filled her face.

"It has consciousness," she replied in wonder. "Alive, as everything is alive in the mind of the One, yet in a way I have never felt before." She sat down next to Turor and Syriem. "Now you," she encouraged the woman nearest to her, ignoring any sense of hierarchy.

They came forward, one after the other, to commune with the Tablet. Athenna had waited until the end. Turor lifted the Tablet up and passed it to Syriem to give to her. He was puzzled, but did as he was asked. As she took the stone, Turor saw a flash of gold around her.

A strange feeling crept over Athenna. As if somewhere, in the deepest recesses of her mind, she had always known that this moment would arrive. Her hand pressed against the Tablet as though she were reaching through to touch some other, inner truth.

Turor addressed the crowd. "You have kept the seeds of your faith through the dark times. Look well upon the harbinger of our deliverance – the Black Rod."

The shift of mood was stark – all small talk and laughter drained away the instant that the Black Rod saw daylight.

"Verrsa?" Turor offered, with a kindness in his voice that surprised Syriem.

She hesitated. What if the tales were true – that Turor had walked the cities and settlements his whole life with the Rod that carried death to the unrighteous? How righteous was she?

He remained still, giving no encouragement – she had to find her own way. She reached out to the Rod and grasped its ancient intelligence in one swift movement. Moments passed and then she lifted the Rod into the air, calling the next person forward by name.

When all present had embraced the Rod and the sacrament was concluded, Turor spoke to them again. "The time for separation is at an end," he stopped, as if he'd heard another voice beside his own, "and we must take our leave of you soon."

"Yes, master," Verrsa bowed as the people dispersed.

Syriem remained by his side, while Athenna waited at a distance.

"*Master*?" he repeated incredulously.

"Her word, not mine. I no more want her devotion than require it."

Syriem narrowed his eyes, but said nothing.

"Believe me, Syriem," Turor's tone soured, "this too shall pass."

The next morning, more people reported nightmares and visions. Syriem's dream focused on Isca; dwelling not so much upon her suffering, as his own. What if she was alive after all and needed him to come and find her? Maybe the dog in his meditation had been some kind of message? Turor listened, as each sentence tumbled chaotically into the next. Half of what Syriem said was lost in the telling, but one thing was clear. Isca's influence on the boy – or whatever she represented – was increasing.

"And what of *your* dreams?"

Turor relented. "I was back in Appra, as a child, with someone I left behind."

Syriem seemed to glimpse more of the man behind the myth, embracing a burden as enduring as his own. "You mean Ursephal?"

He nodded. "It's time for us to go," he said, and went in search of Athenna and Easen.

Turor picked his way up through the narrow footholds, ascending steadily as if he already knew the route. Syriem followed, straining and gasping as he made irregular progress on a path of his own. Finally, he hoisted himself over the ledge and lay there, catching his breath.

For an instant he saw a quiver of energy around Turor, fleeting and chaotic.

"I must have over-exerted myself," Turor turned his head. "Do you feel that?"

Syriem tuned to the pulse with ease. "It's like a sound I can barely hear; I can almost sense it going through me." The Rod sent a burst of energy along his spine. "It's gone now."

"I think not," Turor replied weakly, holding his head.

Behind them a rough track stretched in opposing directions.

"You choose," Turor tried to steady himself.

Syriem pointed the Rod each way in turn to dowse the route; the Rod drew him towards the path with least light. "How far do you think this goes on for?" he disappeared into the gloom, leaving Turor to follow in his wake.

It was the Rod that answered Syriem and he was content to let it lead him, groping about in near blackness, deeper into the mountains. He stopped at the first warm air current.

"You must continue," Turor drew level, leaning against him for support.

Syriem heard a scraping noise, echoing through the dark cavern. At first it sounded like an animal in pain, maybe even a bear – Ces Frayer had once paraded caged bears on Ascension Day. As the tumult grew louder, Syriem recognised the strained notes of a song. He slowed, unconsciously trying to delay the inevitable.

A man emerged, filling the passageway.

"Don't be afraid," Turor urged; "trust in your True Will."

Syriem tried to keep that in mind.

"We are exiles from Tarsis," Turor struggled to focus.

The stranger sparked a flint against the cave wall and lit a torch. The light growled and spluttered, bathing everything in flickering oranges and yellows. Then he raised the torch, revealing a towering figure bearing an iron staff.

"I'm the watchman, so I suppose you'd better come with me."

Turor sensed no hostility. Syriem held back and kept his concerns to himself, noticing rock markings that glistened in the shadows.

"They say they're hundreds of years old," the watchman slowed down. "And some say they are older still."

Turor shivered. Something about the place unnerved him, as though there'd been a deliberate response to his presence. If he'd been superstitious, and the Gods knew he'd had ample opportunity to develop that trait, he would have called them spirits. His mind became swamped by overlaps of the past and present, and myriad pinpoints of light riddled every fleeting vision. He struck out a hand, slamming it hard against the rugged wall, but his head rolled to one side and the ground rose up to greet him.

The watchman picked him up and swung him over one shoulder like a corpse. Syriem weighed up his options. He was alone. Escape, even assuming it were possible, would mean leaving Turor at their mercy. He took a deep breath and touched his talisman.

"Wait for me," he scuttled after the orange glow that had resumed its song.

Syriem felt the path gradually descending, as a grinding tremor jarred at his senses – the few that remained.

"You better keep up or you'll get left behind."

To Syriem's left, a ladder flashed by and then a heavy metal door swung shut, bolting from the other side. As they progressed, other doors slammed before he passed them. Each one blocked out more of the light, closing him off to his fate.

"What is this place?"

"Well, it's home of course," the watchman stopped suddenly, causing Turor's body to bounce against his hardened frame like a stick against a rock. Then he nodded at his own reply and continued on his way.

Syriem reeled as the first waft of searing air hit his lungs. His eyes stung; his breath squeezed through in wheezing gasps. The escort merely laughed and passed him the metal staff to carry, adding to his burden. It was a handsome piece of metalwork that swayed precariously close to the bare rock ceiling, sometimes tapping the wooden and metal supports that shored up the tunnels.

"Three to pass!" the watchman called.

A door opened at the end of the tunnel.

"Who have you got there, Jaco? Send you to check the beams and you bring back hostages!"

Jaco laughed – a thick, guttural roar that reverberated off the walls like a half a dozen men laughing together. Syriem peered past the guards. The grinding and thrashing subsumed all other sounds, pummelling his senses.

The scale of the mining astonished him. Cutting machinery whirled into the rock, grinding out cylindrical holes and spewing back the spoils. Syriem watched as an army of labourers sized the ore and piled it high on wagons, which seemed to move of their own accord once a level was reached. The workers communicated in deft gestures.

"Where is this place?" Syriem shouted at Jaco's face.

"Crail," his brow furrowed.

A woman came over. "Who are they, Jaco?"

"Found them outside. Taller one's out. Reckon they're with the travellers."

"Better bring them through then," she decided, looking past Syriem as if he were mute.

chapter 20
HOSTAGE

A SIDE DOOR unfastened, bringing in a rush of cool air.
"I am Syriem Taulpiris, and this," he pointed to Jaco's cargo, "is my master, Turor."

Jaco set him down.

"You are a long way from home, I think," the woman smiled, bending down to attend to the mage. "Turor," she called softly, "can you hear me? I am Lona," she wiped dust from his face.

Turor heard his name and focused on the sound; the more he concentrated, the more his sickness receded. His sight began to clear – a woman's face, looming over him like a vision. A chalice appeared in her hand.

"Drink this," she lifted the cup to his lips.

He gulped it down and tried to stand too quickly, spilling water everywhere. The cup clattered to the ground and a cacophony of voices rushed in from all sides.

"You need to rest a little longer," she eased him back with a firm hand.

"What's wrong with him?"

"It's nothing serious," she assured Syriem; "just a reaction that many outsiders have when they first arrive here."

"So there have been others," he noted grimly.

"Jaco will stay here with Turor – we are expected," she opened a door on the far side of the room, revealing steps cut into the rock.

"Expected?"

"Once we saw the signs of your approach it was only a matter of time," her voice echoed down the staircase.

"Do you mean the lights? Only…" he began, but she had gone too far ahead. He caught up with her at the final flight of steps.

"Have you eaten?"

"Not so you'd notice," he lamented.

"All in good time; first, there's someone who's very keen to meet you."

The wooden door was polished smooth, its burls and knots pleasing to the touch. A series of recessed spheres and channels depicted the Tree of

Life. Syriem pressed his hand along the curves and turns, wondering at its age. A flood of impressions arose. Many travellers had passed through that doorway – nomads and refugees alike.

Lona waited patiently. When he made eye contact again, she pushed the door and stepped aside. As he entered the room all activity ceased. He crossed to the centre of the chequered floor, oblivious to his own significance. A man, who could easily have been Jaco's cousin, stepped forward to strike a gong.

The host stirred and the room lurched back into motion.

"We welcome you, Taulpiris, bearer of the sacred office."

In his confusion, Syriem reached out, mentally calling upon the Lock and the Key as his twin allies. Words twisted in his head, forming sentences that were not his own. He repeated them, trusting that they were the result of his art and not merely his desperation.

"Behold; I am the past, the present and the future.
All things abide within me and I abide within all things.
I am part of everything, belonging to nothing."

He lifted the Rod free, sweeping it wide to take in the presence of its hosts. The crowd parted like rows of beads, until a single woman faced him. He bowed, compelled downwards by the Rod, so that the act looked forced and graceless.

"You are the messenger?"

He snapped his head up to look at her; she had the bearing of a sage and cruel, raven's eyes. The Rod released him and he stood slowly, uncertain of his next move. A child pushed through the crowd and climbed up on the Matriarch's lap. She settled her and then looked Syriem up and down like a sacrificial offering.

"One verse of the herald's rede proves nothing. You could have learned it any number of ways – perhaps you are the vanguard for raiders?"

He lowered the Rod by his side and sighed – a long, drawn out gesture of frustration.

"If you are a spy then you have a lot to learn about self-control! Come, sit; tell me about yourself, spy."

He slumped beside her and lifted a hunk of bread from the table. If he was going to be interrogated, the least they could do was feed him.

"I'm no spy, just a traveller."

"And how did you avoid the sickness?"

"I don't know," he poured out a measure of water. "My master is ill, but for some reason I am protected."

She nodded thoughtfully. "So it would seem."

The people around her relaxed and resumed their chatter. Syriem leaned back against the chair and pondered how best to handle the situation.

"Tell me, boy," she broke his thoughts, "how far have you come?"

It sounded like a riddle – the sort of innocent inquiry that Turor could turn into something more meaningful.

"We started out in Tarsis City State."

The words hung in the air, draining the colour from her face.

"And when did you leave?" her tone was casual, but her eyes never left his.

He shrugged. "I can scarcely remember a time when we weren't on the move."

"Ever has it been the way of the faith," she nodded, setting the child down.

Isca's words came back to him. "You misunderstand me, Matriarch. There are Thaylin Sarra in our group, but I am not one of them."

The room fell to an icy silence. The Matriarch made the subtlest of signs and everything changed. Guards moved behind the crowd and the Rod responded to their presence, crowding Syriem's veins with adrenaline.

"Not one of the faith? Then how is it that you know of the herald's rede and you bear the Black Rod?"

He reclaimed the centre of the room, keeping his distance. Others edged away, exposing the guards. He glanced about in all directions, unable to find an escape route. Instinct primed him and his mind spiralled upwards, ready to unite with the Rod and the Tablet.

"I want to know about your journey," she pressed, sliding a blade from her sleeve.

"We escaped from Tarsis," he opened his arms wide in protest.

"Go on."

But the Rod did not appreciate its charge being given orders. It was already plotting, even as he scoured the room for refuge.

"After Tarsis, we found our way to a vast forest, near a settlement called Esilmeor. Tarsis City State?" he repeated desperately.

"I know all about Tarsis, boy," emotion choked her words, lending them a bitter edge. "Some of us also lived there, once. Lived and watched as they persecuted and brutalised us. Until we sought our own liberation."

Syriem stared hard at her, caught in the familiar glare of those dark, dark eyes. Gradually they engulfed him, flooding his mind with her memories. Then slowly, inexorably, the two of them became drawn together in a fusion of consciousness.

He saw as she had seen – the unrest and the violence. Targen bringing down peaceful protestors with batons and local officers ordered into the fray; dogs let loose into the crowd to rip and maim and spread terror. But the worst of it, the bleakest memory he touched, made its mark as if it were his own. He saw the raging fires and heard the drowning, fevered screams as flesh bubbled and crackled on the pyre. He shuddered, drawing back to preserve his own psyche. Something was already stirring, awoken by past connections of its own.

Jaco ushered Turor into the room.

"There isn't much time," he glanced at Syriem and then looked away. "Now that we've found you, we must return to our people and let them know we are safe."

"How many of you are there? We have seen the scattered lights all across the highlands..."

"No, Lady Matriarch," Turor replied with deference, "you are mistaken. The lights you speak of are not ours; we are camped in the valley and we watch them as you do."

Jaco folded his arms. "But our watchers have seen the lights for days."

The Matriarch raised a hand in accusation. "Then explain that to me, Syriem Taulpiris."

Syriem looked to Turor and then at the people around him. He felt their fear spiralling in on him like a predator. Yes, that was it, a black dog that would not come when he called it; a ferocious beast he couldn't control – and it was loose.

He span slowly in search of the phantom creature, only for it to fade before him like a mirage. Dizziness followed, numbing his senses, closing him off until only bodily awareness remained. The Rod infiltrated his mind, forcibly curling his fingers around its physical shell, crushing his hand in rhythmic spasms until they were united.

A rasping breath escaped his lungs, like the cry of a creature too long imprisoned. He straightened up awkwardly, the influence unaccustomed to the rigours of physical existence. One arm levelled out the Rod and its living intelligence unfolded, embracing memories from the Tablet. The two entities aligned, collaborating to feed the body their elixir.

He stared directly at the Matriarch, his closed eyelids failing to shield his wrath. "You!" he screeched in outrage, "sought to deny me!"

The people nearest to him scattered to safety and, as if to fill the vacuum, three armed guards converged.

"I want him alive!" the Matriarch decreed.

Syriem shifted position and tilted his head to one side, dog-like. Deprived of vision, the body remained astute, responding to the emanations around him. He moved fluidly, adapting as the guards spread their offensive.

He let out a guttural roar, swinging the Rod laterally in a wide pentagram to generate force and momentum. He connected with the first assailant in a crunch of bone, and the victim dropped to the floor. The remaining guards lifted their swords to maim the wretch – alive, perhaps, but not for long.

Syriem's body attuned itself easily to their emotions. They were overwrought and lacking in experience, his for the taking. He faced his remaining opponents, lowering the Rod with a patronising sneer. The larger of the two guards rushed forward, swinging his sword in a forceful arc to deliver a fatal gash. Syriem twisted low and ducked the blade, resurfacing to smash the Rod into his opponent's ribcage.

The last of the three backed off a little, seeking sanctuary, but there was nowhere left to go. Somewhere deep within his nightmare tomb, Syriem felt the blood surge in readiness for a kill. He called on the Rod, willing himself to be heard, focusing on the intention: *let them live and I will serve you.*

The creature bowed, contorting his lips as it swept the Rod aside. The soldier sheathed his sword and approached to take the prisoner. At the last moment, the creature jerked up, slamming the Rod into him.

Turor looked on in horror. "Everyone out, now!" he rushed in and laid a trembling hand on Syriem's body. He had felt the Rod's malice before, but never like this. Contact brought communion, and then he understood; this time the Rod was the conduit for the Tablet. He rounded on the Matriarch.

"Take us somewhere safe and no one else will be harmed. I give my word."

She glanced at the bodies. "And who is it who gives his word?" she composed herself, rubbing a ceremonial ring on her hand.

"I am Turor Taulpiris, custodian of the Black Rod of Ruin and Sacrifice." Even now he couldn't bring himself to claim ownership of it.

The room crackled with etheric activity.

"Then all will be well," she made a sign of blessing and led them along a corridor.

Syriem followed him, isolated and mute, his arm resting lifelessly on Turor's shoulder. Turor paused at the door, noting a simple carving that depicted the Tablet.

"We will not be disturbed here," the Matriarch assured him.

Turor lowered Syriem into a seat. "The boy is confined," he explained, in a tone that did not invite discussion.

"Will he recover? Will *any* of them recover?"

"Your guards will revive, in time. But Syriem…" he stalled. "It is difficult to say what will happen. I have only known of this condition once before."

The child entered the room and sat opposite Syriem, staring at him as if she could will him back to waking. The Matriarch looked on helplessly.

"Who are you?" Turor turned to face her.

"Very well," she cleared her throat with a soft gulp. "You shall know me and the burden I bear. My name is Buda. I am one of three Matriarchs in Crail. I've long been aware of the Black Rod's existence. It is the Key without a Lock."

"Go on," he said, catching flashes of light around her as she spoke.

She closed her eyes, summoning the strength to finally exorcise the past. "You have the Key, Turor, but it requires the Lock. Back when I lived among the unrighteous in Tarsis, I had a dream." Now she faced him. "For four nights the same image appeared before me, obsessing me and filling my waking hours. It was a stone tablet – the Lock – willing me to receive it.

"I felt the call, but I used what magic I had to deny it – to appease my husband and put my child before my destiny. I decided that although I did not choose the path of hearth and home willingly, I would not cast it aside."

Turor turned to Syriem without comment.

"On the fourth night, the dream released me. The day after that was the day of the riots. I still wonder if I might have prevented a tragedy." Her words dispersed and the room quietened, save for Syriem's laboured breathing.

Turor took a deep, slow breath, certain that another facet of The Restitution had slipped into place. "Then you knew that one day your fate would find you out?"

She touched a thumb to her forehead and her lips. "I have already paid a grave price for my betrayal. Whatever follows now will be the lesser debt. For as long as I have been at the Crail settlement, pilgrims have answered the call to Sarrell. I watch them leave, knowing that my weakness has condemned them to a path that cannot be achieved. And now, as if to punish me further, the Key arrives at last, yet there is no Lock to receive it."

The child screamed. Syriem's eyelids had lifted to reveal two cloudy orbs. She reached forward to touch him, but Buda snatched her hand away. She looked to Turor and found little comfort there.

"I must return to the travellers; Syriem will remain with you."

"Wait," she protested, "you can't leave him here."

"It's the least you can do – you owe him that," he passed his hand over Syriem's face and closed his eyes. "If I don't return soon, others will come for us," he walked to the door, contemplating whether to take the Rod with him.

"Are you so confident of their allegiance?"

"Their *allegiance*?" he rounded on her. "No, not that, but perhaps their instinct for survival. They may not always trust Syriem or me; few though would contest that we've delivered them this far. If they come, they will fight. Not for me, or him – for themselves."

"Let them come then; we are many and you are few."

"Buda," Turor snapped, "what talk is this? The faith has asked so much of them already, torn them from their lives and families. Will you yet deny them?"

It was a calculated attack that found its mark and struck deep.

"Families," she repeated slowly with tears in her eyes.

"You must believe me when I tell you that a higher justice is taking its course."

Verrsa waited until the last of them had spoken their truth. It had seemed wise to gather the people together in unity, but some were willing, even now, to turn tail and head back to Tarsis. She seethed at their forgetfulness and ignorance. How quickly they would return to their enslavers.

So she struck a bargain. If Turor had not returned, or sent word, within three hours, then they were each free to decide their own fate. And those who chose to leave could do so unopposed. Until then, she and the other Thaylin Sarra would tell the traditional stories, and bring them to a clear state of mind.

Her clipped voice carried a sorcery all of its own, riding the breeze like a whisper to the soul. She recounted the legends, half in speech and half in song, delivering each sentence slowly to allow the pictures to form in their minds. And when she sang the songs, as she scattered herbs upon the fires and stepped lightly around the flames, she sang in the sacred languages of Arabic, Latin and Hebrew.

"The tale I tell is from the times *before*; the times – it is said – when the Gods of the mountains walked in peace with the mortals of the sea-lands. And of the village of Maja-Gaia, glistening like a jewel at the shore of the Endless Sea."

The camp fell still in rapt attention.

"Kydira and Arrasse were soulmates, fated to be together by the stars that led them. Yet their love was a difficult love, for the Gods have ever seen fit to mock and test the course of lovers. Kydira had the magic of the moon in her veins and Arrasse that of the sun.

"The Warlords and Chancellors feared that any children of their union would take power, when they came of age. And so, as Kydira and Arrasse answered to none but the Unseen Ones, the Chancellors – those self-appointed makers of earthly law – plotted to forbid their union.

"Kydira and Arrasse were content in their love for one another, but the children of magic are known to wander the land in search of bright deeds. It is a longing that can never been completely fulfilled – for magic causes change and change can only be sustained for a time.

"So laws were passed and – forsaking truth for convention – Kydira and Arrasse parted. All men, from the lowliest servant to the Prince Warlords themselves, loved Kydira. Her smile was as alluring as the moon, and she was lusted after by many."

Verrsa adopted a sultry look, drawing laughter from the crowd.

"Taverns rang with talk of her beauty, of how she could bewitch any man with a smile or a well-chosen charm song. Women adored her too, prizing her as a splendour of womanhood, and scorning any man who looked upon her with desire – all except Arrasse.

"It was said, even in her ordeal, that the Gods looked upon Kydira as their daughter. For she roamed through the world unharmed among the wildest of beasts, protected and nurtured by providence. And in those times, it was Arrasse who wavered between virtue and vanity. For Arrasse enjoyed women, and though he'd never strayed from Kydira, he loved the thrill of new voices and veiled possibilities. Each ardent pledge he extracted rang true to him as a sonnet; each sigh an affirmation of a greater truth.

"The Chancellors watched him and formed a plan. They knew that if they could bond him with another, Kydira would have no claim over him and their love – along with their magic – would be shattered. For magic without love is an empty power. If their scheme succeeded, the Warlords and Chancellors would retain dominion and the world would turn as it always had.

"Blessed are those who keep the flame of faith alive, for faith it is that finds the unseen way. Upon her return, one spring, when her yearning knew no rest, Kydira sought Arrasse out by the banks of the Great Mela.

"'Arrasse,' she lamented, as he bathed in the moon-river of Mela, 'what are we to do with our love? I feel it as the beating of my own heart, but I fear one day you may forget us both in your travels.' And though he protested, Kydira wept.

"'Then bind me to you,' he answered softly, 'and I will love no other.' So she joined him in the great river and there they united, betrothed by the elements…"

Verrsa paused, turning about them as a guardian, drawing on their focused attention to heighten her own awareness, as all Thaylin Sarra initiates were taught. Her audience waited, eager to hear more of Kydira and Arrasse, and Ortha, their first-born – who battled the Warlords at his sister Aysha's bidding.

Turor appeared high above them, silhouetted against the sun. Verrsa and the other Thaylin Sarra turned in unison, as if he were the light itself.

Verrsa let out a cry of exaltation. "Turor has returned!"

She abandoned her tale and began to sing a Thaylin Sarra song of deliverance, swaying her body like a willow tree. Athenna and Easen questioned Syriem's absence, but others, beguiled as a moth to a flame, called upon Turor to show them the true way. He walked among them, receiving their cries of 'Hosanna' with indifference.

"What must we do, master?" Verrsa looked at him with such adoration that her husband felt for the dagger he had carried at his side since Tarsis.

"The mountains await us," he looked for Athenna in the crowd. "We journey next to the Crail Settlement and meet them as our kin."

Cordal waited until Turor was alone.

"How many settlers are there?"

"They are not the enemy, Cordal," he reached out to him.

Cordal flinched back. "Who are you to know my enemy?"

Turor looked beyond him, extending sight and insight into the nameless realm where awareness and guidance merged. An image stared back at him, rising from the formless sea of consciousness: the Black Rod.

Easen trailed after Turor as he moved about the camp – he hadn't mentioned Syriem at all. Athenna read her father's mood in a single glance and targeted Turor like a hawk.

"Well, Athenna?" Turor said kindly, but she was in no mood for kindness.

"Where is Syriem? Have you left him back there as a hostage?"

As the sun faded, the lead Transvector circled to face the mountains. Now, for the first time, beacons dotted the hills, turning the outcrops to red and gold. Motionless figures stood dark against the sky, watching as the two Transvectors moved in a wide arc. Vehicle lights met firelights and two cultures prepared to cross a divide.

"Are you ready, Turor?" Easen paused at the wheel.

Turor thought for a moment, as if he were weighing up the question. Then he looked towards Athenna, bowed slightly and gave his consent.

chapter 21
ANGLES

THE MOUNTAINS swallowed the Transvectors whole. Easen drove cautiously, scanning the shadowy horizon. Something was calling to him, as keenly as desire. He rejected any notions of destiny – that dismal term so beloved of the faithful. This was tangible; he felt it in every fibre of his body, an awareness that called to him like a lover.

He could just make out boreholes above the valley, crude puncture marks in the strata like giant worm casts. And more settlers, at the entrances, watching their arrival.

Cordal sat, silently brooding, staring out of the window. A body count confirmed that they were heavily outnumbered. Crail was larger than he'd ever thought possible for a settlement. He quickly crafted a new strategy. They could raise an army together, travellers and settlers alike, and take Sarrell by force. The fledgling seeds of faith, so recently acquired, faded from his consciousness.

A Thaylin Sarra priestess near to Turor was the first to fall ill – a numbing, violent affliction, so reminiscent of his own that he knew she would not be the last. The sickness was stealthy, progressing rapidly from a mild fever to render the sufferer senseless. It leapt between the two vehicles, striking indiscriminately, until all the Thaylin Sarra were affected. Turor thought about Syriem, protected from one sickness only to fall prey to another.

Easen dismissed Turor's explanation out of hand. As if awareness could make the Thaylin Sarra vulnerable! And, as he was quick to point out, it didn't say much for the deliverance of the righteous.

"Look at this, Turor," he lifted a compass on to the dashboard. The needle circled frantically, seeking an ever-changing origin. "It's very sensitive…"

Turor stared at it blankly, which irked him.

"What's around us is a fluctuating magnetic field; unusual I agree, but hardly mystical."

"Then why aren't you affected?"

The radio flared into life. Others were falling victim, no longer just the Thaylin Sarra. Cordal fidgeted in the cab, twisting his head to avoid the shallow gaze of those in the first stages of sickness. Athenna collapsed, twitching and mumbling incoherently. Turor stayed close and tried to make her comfortable.

Cordal's trigger finger ached as he stretched it back and forth to the rhythm of his thoughts. He was surrounded by the infected and the unclean; Death was stalking them in the guise of his two companions. He'd have to be shrewd; if he didn't get them both then Death would live on to return another time. But if he could get away, Death would be forced to follow him; he could lead Death to the caves and kill it! *Kill Death*! He laughed aloud, rocking with pleasure.

He could see the Hybrolen looking at him from the corner of his eye. *Turn away priest; turn away.* The bodies were everywhere, slumped around him like a demonic larder, but the voice knew what to do. Quickly now, roll them out of the way. Move door; *move*! The handle gave way with a shove and he was free.

"Come and get me, if you dare!" Cordal dropped away from the Transvector.

Turor called to Easen above the howling elements. "I can't leave him out there on his own – I'll have to go after him."

Easen slowed the Transvector and Turor jumped down.

"Keep moving until they tell you," Turor waved them on and started walking.

The wind whipped up the thin blanket he was wearing over his tunic, making it appear like a nomad's cape to those who watched from the vehicles.

Cordal was already receding into the distance, a blur against the dwindling light. Turor narrowed his eyes against the wind and took his first faltering steps into the unknown. He leaned into the squall, heart pounding and ears filled with confusion. Little by little he advanced, resolutely following the last sighting. Intuition trickled through; physical senses alone would be no use here – the land beneath his feet was only the counterpart of a greater reality. He felt the terrain twisting and turning, mirroring his inner turmoil. And in the midst of it all, he recalled Parva Serach's words, cutting through his dilemma.

'Movement comes from stability and not from chaos. Thus, before we can work with higher forces, we must master the lower forces within ourselves.'

He smiled; even now her influence managed to guide him. Or maybe mock him. He bowed his head and controlled his breathing, driving potency into his solar plexus. In his mind's eye, filaments of light extended in all directions. Now he had a grasp on this reality, through symbolism.

He stretched out his hands and combed the energy web as he moved, feeling for his prey. There was no longer any sense of time or place. He kept to a rhythm, walking and then pausing to align himself, secure in the validity of his intent.

"You stay away!"

Turor stopped abruptly. Cordal was a few feet ahead of him, swinging his rifle wildly. He could also sense the presence of Crail settlers high above them.

Cordal levelled the weapon. "One more step, priest, and I'll take your head off!"

Turor opened his arms wide. "Cordal, it's me – Turor."

"You're all going to die," Cordal screamed. "Not me though; I get to cheat death because I don't belong among you."

Turor faced down the barrel, without the Rod or the Tablet to help him. Protection mantras would be useless and invocations to an outside agent unpredictable. No, he would deal with Cordal by his *own* art. Inexplicably, he remembered something his mother had once told him, years before, when he'd asked if she still harboured any bitterness towards their Appren captors: 'Loving your enemy is the greatest test of all.'

He flattened his breathing. In five successive breaths he built the middle pillar, circulating the energy to keep his body and mind supple. Now he became whole and his thoughts flowed like liquid crystal. He focused on compassion, on dissolving his fear by connecting with Cordal. The impressions came immediately. Cordal was physically strong, but emotionally weak – an imbalance he could make use of.

Cordal's aura glowed in torrid rhythms of chaos, and the recent symbols of initiation into the faith flickered to life.

"You're safe now," Turor sensed for vulnerabilities in the energy matrix before him.

He felt the echo, a subtle reverberation at Cordal's solar plexus. Now he knew where to concentrate his efforts. He moved slowly, nodding to reinforce his words.

"Everything's going to be fine," he repeated, over and over, forcefully projecting the first magical symbol of Thaylin Sarra initiation – a quartered circle – at Cordal's solar plexus.

Cordal lowered a hand to his abdomen, unconsciously reacting to the symbol. He wavered and then Turor saw a lunar crescent appear in its place, as Cordal corrected the design.

Turor could feel Cordal's focus slipping; he had to disable Cordal's defences quickly. His hands trembled and energy streamed out of him like a living current. In an instant of clarity, he called from within, from the centre of his being – the reservoir of energy that the Rod had drawn upon so often for its own ends.

He took the last few steps, suddenly projecting the image of a fiery red pentagram with total conviction. Cordal clutched his stomach and staggered back. Turor seized the moment, moving in swiftly to push the rifle away. At the same time, he shifted his weight back on one side before twisting forward like a striking serpent. His fist struck Cordal's jaw, slamming him to the ground. The rifle hit a rock and then discharged.

"And just so you know," Turor hurled the rifle far behind him, "I'm not a priest – I am the Summoner, initiate to Parva Serach. And I summon *you* to awareness." And all at once he knew for certain what he had been hiding from himself.

Cordal slowly opened his eyes, as Turor attended to the psychic wound. When Turor had completed his work, he sealed the aura in potent waves of light.

"What's wrong with me?"

"You reached a crisis – a build-up of the influences that have festered since the Sekha found you."

"Supposing you hadn't come for me…"

"You might have fired at the settlers and they would have killed you. Then they would have probably come for the rest of us," he reasoned, sparing Cordal nothing.

"And what now, Hybrolen?"

"Now, we turn our attention to the others," he helped Cordal to his feet, "and you begin the path in earnest."

They seemed to have walked a mile or more before they found a tunnel. There was so much that Cordal wanted to say, and to know, but Turor's steely gaze unnerved him.

"That was quite a punch," he felt along the swelling that lit up his face.

"I was saving it for a special occasion," Turor replied with a glimmer of warmth.

He lifted a torch from its cradle. The flickering shadows lent the cavern a sense of foreboding. Cordal instinctively felt for his rifle, but this time he would have to rely on Turor.

"Hail, Travellers of the Inner Way."

It was a woman's voice, Turor surmised, before her shadow stalked along the walls towards them. Two enormous guards flanked her, their burnished breastplates gleaming in the amber glare. The woman offered her hand and Cordal took it, pressing firmly to stave off the spinning sensation in his head.

Easen stood as close to the fire pit as he dared. He could see the settlers, watching and waiting, through the long line of flames.

"Will you help us?"

A single water canteen sailed over the fire and landed at his feet. He bent down and grabbed it, opening the top and sniffing at the liquid. Wary, but desperate, he took the bottle and began ministering to the sick, treating others before his daughter to make sure it was safe. Only when a child, in the early stages of illness, showed signs of improvement did he give the dregs to Athenna.

Easen walked the length of the fire and faced a crowd of strangers.

"We need more medicine – most of our people are sick."

An old man came up to him, carrying four more canteens. "Not too much, mind. Too much is as bad as none at all," he warned.

"Thank you. My name is Easen John Minet," he declared, as if he were back in Tarsis addressing an Assembly member.

The settlers drew closer at the name.

"Do you ever get scared, Turor?" Cordal could already feel his mind clearing, as they travelled along the tunnels with the settlers. "Only, Verrsa told me that a true Hybrolen fears nothing."

"Then she's mistaken. Fear is a valuable teacher."

Cordal cleared his throat. "Some of us, we, er…we thought you'd killed the boy. Sacrificed him or something. I guess we should have known better."

"There are many kinds of sacrifice, but he still lives."

Easen was first to greet Turor by the great fires. He showed him to the sick and introduced a few of the settlers, who had ventured across the divide.

"The strange thing is," Easen set aside the bone he was chewing, "I feel as healthy as an ox, but Athenna is still weak. She must have her mother's constitution."

"Of that I have no doubt, Turor acknowledged, stepping through the embers. "I will see the boy now," he told Jaco, who'd made it his business to seek him out.

"Wait," Athenna called out from the ground, "I'm coming with you."

It was more of a plea than insistence and Turor could not find in his heart to refuse her. Especially when he knew what was to follow.

"Easen, would you join us?" he whispered like a charm, attempting to move Athenna on his own and deliberately making a poor job of it.

"Of course," Easen discarded his meal into the flames. "I'd be glad to help."

With Easen at the other arm and Jaco leading the way, they helped Athenna into the nearest tunnel. She was still frail, struggling to stay consciousness, while intimate memories of Dorron swirled about her.

They were together, in the warm comfort of her bed. The scene fragmented when Syriem's voice filtered through the house. She felt his thoughts as though they were her own. He had always known about Dorron and would never speak against him. She lifted a hand and remembered Syriem caressing her body in the Transvector.

Dorron stirred and she was back in his arms, her body aching for his, even as her spirit yearned for its own fulfilment. She lay at the boundaries of ecstasy and emptiness, torn between the two of them. The one who walked like a god, yet knew the world only by the pattern of his shadow; and the other, as wondrous as the rainbows he revered, but whose presence was as ephemeral.

"Syriem?" she murmured. "Where are you?"

"Not far now," Jaco promised, raising his torch before him.

Turor was in no hurry; he dreaded the sight that awaited them. He knew from bitter experience that the Rod would only relinquish Syriem when – and if – it suited its purpose.

Jaco guided them to the chamber. The child had gone and all was still.

"How is he?" Turor asked quietly.

The woman tending to Syriem had her back to them. Before she could respond, the creature within the boy spoke.

"You have returned."

"I have, my lord," Turor touched the talisman at his chest.

"Give me your hand," it demanded, stretching out its own.

Turor stared at the hapless creature. So this was what the overshadowing looked like – how *he* must have appeared when the Rod had used him in the past. The skin was cold to the touch and dry, less human than he had expected.

The Black Rod's consciousness pierced his aura like a talon. "Your path awaits you, Turor."

"The fifth seal is ready; the journey is almost met."

"The renegade shard must be reintegrated and then I shall become whole again," the voice groaned, and Turor felt the first glimmers of warmth from the hand. Again he wondered how to reach the boy.

"Can Syriem talk to us, Turor?" Athenna managed to stand alone, with effort.

The woman knelt beside Syriem shivered at the voice.

"He needs peace," she said.

"Will that be all, ma'am?" Jaco asked.

She flicked her hand behind her, shaking.

Turor spoke directly to Easen and Athenna. "That which was lost is found; that which was taken is now restored."

Buda turned to them and opened her mouth to speak, but the words stuck in her throat. She looked into Athenna's eyes.

"Buda?" Easen stammered. "Is it really you?"

The colour drained from Buda's face. She looked to Turor and he nodded.

Athenna took a faltering step towards her, silent tears cascading down her face. How often had she imagined this moment? How many nights as a child, pretending that it was all a bad dream and everything would be fine in the morning?

"Yes, my child," Buda brushed Athenna's face, pressing her fingers tenderly to her cheek; "the Gods have brought you back to me."

Easen stood before her, unable to speak. She looked upon Turor with such gratitude that he had to turn away.

"Easen?" she beckoned him over, extending an arm.

He touched her hand, and found it strong and tender. This was more than he ever dared hope for; more than he'd believed was possible – yet here she was. Years of pain and separation raged within him, lending his eyes a fiery glow.

Turor intervened. "Easen, why don't you check back on the others; there will be time for talk later."

Easen lunged at the door, glancing back at Turor and the wonder he had worked. Buda held on to Athenna as if she were her life itself, comforting her as she sobbed out the empty years. At that moment, Turor inner sight glimpsed a grave, high on a ridge – a simple tomb marked with a stone cairn. Buda's eyes were on him, willing him to embrace the mystery.

Turor bedded down for the night. Though he doubted Syriem could hear him, he spoke openly, confessing more than he would have done had Syriem been able to comment. He lay there, listening to the clamour outside, catching snatches of songs and laughter as they snaked along the corridor.

In the great chambers, celebrations were taking place for the coming together of two communities and the reunion of the Matriarch and her daughter.

Turor glanced up at Syriem, resting in his chair. "The time will come soon enough when the last seal is opened, Syriem. And what will become of us then, I wonder?"

A rapping at the door interrupted his thoughts.

"Who is it?" he called, though the handle was already turning.

Buda stood before him. "Am I disturbing you, Turor?" she entered the room before he could answer. "I feel I may not have conveyed my gratitude, today; you have given me more than I could ever have hoped for."

"Perhaps I have given you too much?" Turor read the flicker in her eyes. "Tell me, Buda, was there no way you could have taken them with you, out of Tarsis?"

"*Them*?" she gasped. "He would never have joined us. But Athenna – do you think I didn't beg for my child?" And now I have them both again, and the price of one is the burden of the other, what do I make of *that*?"

He paused, as if considering her words. "We wouldn't be here, but for Easen – and neither would Athenna. For that alone we ought to value him."

"Those are easy words for you, Turor; you aren't the one he looks at with hope in his heart and bitterness in his eyes. You do not suffer as we suffer. You have no need of companionship or of family; as free as the wind – aye, and as rootless."

"Part of everything, belonging to nothing – isn't that how it goes?" he scorned her. "Nevertheless, one way or another, we all suffer."

He lifted his talisman from his neck, placing it carefully around a candle. His eyes reflected the flame. "Will you join me in a meditation?"

"I will," she shifted to a space on the floor beside him.

"Later, I would like to hear more about the settlement prophecies. Perhaps I could speak to one of the seers here?"

"You have one before you now," she unveiled her own symbol of office.

The candle flame cast dull reflections off the walls, bathing the room in suffused brilliance. Turor and Buda sat together, facing the flame, while Syriem's clicking breaths heaved and hissed behind them. Incense permeated the room, conjuring shapes like memories. Turor opened his eyes suddenly.

Buda's eyes met his. "Do you feel her presence too? Who is she?"

"An aspect of my past." He watched with trepidation as grey mist spiralled in opposing strands, weaving together. An outline of a human figure began to materialise within the helix.

"What does she want here?"

"Vengeance," Turor answered her coldly; and as he released the word, a pair of amber eyes appeared in the mist.

The eyes glowed in the dusky formlessness. Time and again a face attempted to form, but it receded at the point of manifestation, smothered by grey.

"She is a powerful magus," Buda acknowledged, glancing around at the symbols of protection that adorned the chamber walls.

"She is an Appren high initiate," he explained, "seeking me out."

Buda lifted her necklace clear of the candle, calling like a banshee, "Hekas Hekas Este Bibeloi!" as she cast it at the intrusion.

The string of haematite beads spun in the air, scything through the grey shroud. The helix dissolved and two eyes blinked out of existence, with a shriek of indignation that seemed to come from everywhere at once.

"She won't be back," Buda assured him, stretching forward for her necklace.

"You couldn't be more wrong. Now that Ursephal has found her way here, through the inner planes, nothing will stop her"

"Nothing?" Buda repeated, puzzled.

"Quickly, bring the necklace back while it still carries her emanations."

She wrapped a hand in her tunic and carefully carried the beads to him.

"I think it's time," Turor's face hardened, "for the hunter to become the hunted."

Ursephal opened her eyes, the after-effects of Buda's banishing still ringing in her ears. "Filth!" she glowered, moving closer to the altar fire.

They had cast out her presence like some Appren novice, powerless to resist. The travellers must be close to Sarrell for her powers to be so weakened. It was time to leave the City of Appra and make the journey physically. So be it; she would put her worldly affairs in order. She had only to call his name in the dream worlds to hear the echoes of his screams. He had served his purpose, and now the link had to be severed.

Besides, she was curious to see what he looked like, outside of a detention cell. She picked up a mirror and pursed her lips. A passable likeness of her magical form – one of the more human ones at any rate. She applied makeup sparingly. This time, Dorron would meet his nemesis in the flesh.

A different Treasure House, the third in a week; it didn't do to stay in one place too long. Dorron glanced around at the décor. In the past he would have considered the place a dump, but his standards had changed.

"Hey handsome, what'ya drinking?" the bartender called over, as if she cared.

"Beer's fine."

"Suit yourself," she slammed it on the counter, sending froth down the glass.

He grabbed the beer and slid into a booth, reading everyone around him. A couple of drifters were loitering at the side bar, haggling over some shady deal and being none too discreet about it. He sank into his drink and let the foamy richness soothe his troubles. The beer was a potent brew and by the time the second pint found its mark, the world had softened a little. When the door blew open he didn't even flinch.

"Mind if I join you?"

He glanced up; amused that she was even interested. She didn't belong. Her short hair and spartan clothes were a little too tailored.

"Are you talking to me?"

"You look like you could do with some company and I'm new around here…"

There was *something* about her. He shuffled to make space and returned to his beer. She fetched a drink from the bar, the first bottle that caught her eye, and prowled back. Her eyes feasted on his vacant expression and she felt herself salivating. He was every bit as appealing as she remembered.

"So, is this your local neighbourhood?"

He sighed, irritated that she was trying to hit on him. She liked that – a man playing hard to get. It made a change from the dolts who sniffed after her, like dogs in the rut. Still, she reminded herself, time was short. She had to get him alone and do what she needed to do.

"Look, I'm at a loose end and I'd like some fun," she marvelled at her own audacity. "You won't be disappointed."

"Where are you staying?" he asked, suddenly all eyes and attention.

"No, no," she feigned protest. "My hotel is too risky, but there's an apartment nearby that my husband owns." She leaned over and her moist, pink tongue delivered a promise of Eros.

A short taxi ride later, she unlocked the apartment door. Dorron didn't pounce on her – another surprise. He wavered by the door, as if he hadn't quite made up his mind.

"It's quite safe here, I promise you – we won't be disturbed."

Suddenly it seemed important that he stayed by choice, without influence. She watched his pallid face, wondering whether he'd made the connection. Pity flourished, for a time.

"Come on," she took his hand, feeling his body tremble slightly as she led him to the lounge. "I'll get us another drink."

As soon as she left the room, he slipped away from the couch to rummage through the cupboards. Something didn't sit right. There were no photographs and no personal items at all, yet she evidently knew her way around. She returned, minus her jacket. He smiled appreciatively – it had softened her, made her seem more approachable. He kicked off his shoes and began to relax. She sat across the sofa, kneading his leg with her toes.

"There's no husband, is there?" he reached down to stroke her calf.

"How did you know?"

"No ring and no mark on your finger," he held her hand up delicately. "And frankly I don't buy the rest of your story either."

Perhaps not, she conceded to herself, but you're still here aren't you?

"Look, I don't usually go in for this sort of thing…" she lifted her feet away. "But haven't you ever wanted to be someone else? To just forget yourself for a while?"

Without waiting for an answer, she leaned in to him, losing herself in the moment. Later, in the bedroom, she went to dim the light, but he stopped her.

"No, leave it on. Whoever you are, I want to see you."

She froze; reluctant to let the moment end, as she knew it must. "Promise me that whatever happens, you won't fear me or hate me."

He gave his word, anticipating some body scar or the ravages of age. When she had undressed him, he took his turn, unveiling her pale body with abandon. Then he saw the tattoo on her upper arm.

"You…the one in my dreams…with the monster…" he choked, grasping at shreds of memory. "But that's not possible?" He backed away on the bed.

"There's no need to be afraid. It's different now, just the two of us."

And though she had thought to control him, and to use their coupling for her own magical ends, she decided that she wouldn't stop him or condemn him if he ran. After a tense silence, he reached over and switched off the light.

The cacophony of the city wrestled Dorron from slumber. Ursephal lay beside him.

"I don't understand," he stroked her hair.

"It's very simple; you're free now. No more monsters."

And though he knew he shouldn't have trusted her, he wanted to anyway. "And those dreams are true, somehow?" he struggled to make sense of everything. "You really are seeking the travellers and the Keldies?"

"Very perceptive," she ran a finger down his chest, carefully avoiding his scar. "They took something from me and I intend to get it back. It's mine by right."

She sighed, writhing a little as his hand met her body beneath the sheets.

"So what will happen to me now?" he whispered.

"I told you, you're free; it's over for you."

He propped himself up on one elbow. "Only it's not that simple, is it?" he said, realising that he didn't even know her name. "They're still watching me. Still checking to see if anyone makes contact – they're never going to leave me alone."

Her eyes flashed amber insight as she glimpsed a future for him, a path as tentative as a silken thread. "Dorron, what if there *was* a way out of all of this?" she arced over, feeling the moist heat of his body below her.

Desire muzzled any sense of reason. "What would I have to do?"

"Enlist," she said, delighting in the look of horror on his face. "I'm serious. The Targen are always looking for upright," she paused, "decent citizens. I have contacts in Tarsis; they would sponsor you. If you join the Targen, they'll leave you alone because you'll belong."

He sank back to the pillow. Could it really be that easy? He closed his eyes and took a leap of faith. "Okay, I'll do it."

She rolled back on the bed, pulling him down to her, surprised to find tears in her eyes. How strange, she thought, to be feeling emotions at a time like this.

"And?" Buda roused Turor from his stupor.

He sighed, stretching his neck.

"And…that's it – that's all I see. Ursephal will leave Tarsis soon. And make no mistake, she *is* coming."

"How long before she reaches us – a week? A month?"

"I cannot say. It is difficult to judge the passage of time out here."

She uncrossed her legs and flexed them, rubbing the muscles. "Other travellers have said as much. It must be our proximity to Sarrell."

He stared hard.

"You thought we didn't know?" she replaced her beads around her neck. "Why else do you think I stayed here, awaiting the Righteous One?"

In one explosive revelation, the myth sharpened into focus. The Crail settlers had knowledge of the final journey to Sarrell, but while they had charted the beginning of the path, they could not complete it. Many a pilgrim, inspired by a dream or a vision, had set foot upon the arduous route; few returned.

Search parties, organised by families or the Thaylin Sarra elders, frequently recovered the living – confused and bereft – or else they found the bodies, put to rest without a mark upon them. Many believed that Sarrell was not a realm of their world at all, simply a doorway into the next.

"Some call it the rainbow bridge," she quoted from her texts, "the final journey to unity."

He held his tongue. If Sarrell had no place in the physical world then how could its emissaries have sought him out as a child?

On the fifth day, when storms ranged across the region as if in search of prey, Turor awoke with a renewed sense of purpose. He would break the deadlock by removing the Rod from Syriem's keeping, reacquainting it with the forces of nature and the outer reality of the terrain. Perhaps then the Rod might relinquish its hold over the boy. One thing he was certain of: the fifth seal would require the two of them – the giver and the receiver alike.

When he discussed it with Buda, she offered to be his guide. She explained how treacherous the higher pathways could be for the unprepared and he'd relished her choice of words, reading a double meaning in them.

He also notified the other Thaylin Sarra of the arrangements, since he couldn't be sure of the consequences of separating the Rod from the boy. Easen, meanwhile, had avoided him for days, plagued by vicious talk about Turor and Buda, which did not favour either his disposition or Turor's reputation.

Although the Hybrolen had delivered them to the Crail settlement, where talk of Sarrell was as common as the autumn storms, the boy was still afflicted and Turor seemed to be spending all his time with Buda. Reminiscent, one or two whispered, of his earlier interest in Verrsa, who even now suffered his absence like a bereavement.

Buda took the lead, asking Athenna and Verrsa to tend to Syriem. Verrsa received the request warmly, commending it as proof of Buda's integrity and a counter to her husband's spite. As they talked, it seemed to Verrsa that they had much more in common than a marriage outside the faith.

"Can you not forgive Easen for the past, so that you are able to honour *all* your vows?"

"That may be easily said," Buda conceded, "but I have sworn to obey my True Will above all else, when it makes itself known to me. Each of us must be accountable for our choices."

Verrsa paused awhile and sipped at her glass, tasting the iron rich water thoughtfully. Obedience was not a term that Turor had ever used; it smacked of obligation rather than the joy she imagined True Will to be.

That night, Turor called upon such dreams as might touch his soul; little realising that someone else was seeking the same outcome.

Candles flicker malevolently, tasting the dark, dank air. Vermin scurry under the straw at the approach – heavy, laboured footfalls that pound fear into him. He is cold and shivering; a terrible loneliness shrouds his psyche, isolating him from the one person who can protect him.

"Mother," he whimpers, scrunching up tight in a corner of his cell.

The iron door bolts shriek back.

"You are to come now."

A hand reaches out, hauling him roughly to his feet. He senses no cruelty, only compliance. She pats him down, picking the straw from his hair methodically. It is the closest thing to kindness he has known since his capture.

"Yes, Narl," he answers, standing up straight for her inspection.

"You'll have to do," she smiles, or maybe it's a sneer – he can't be sure.

Then they are out along the corridor, where impressions rush towards him like hungry dogs to a corpse. He does what he always does; squeezing his eyes tight against the onslaught, as he blindly follows the ponderous steps ahead of him.

The doors of the Great Hall open and then he stands before them in rags. The girl is there – nurtured by old ones, who brush at her hair like harpies and smooth down her robe. They preen and fuss over her, shuffling back to the shadows when her patience is exhausted.

"You have only to take it," she tells him, her forced little voice echoing across the room, "and then the next stage can begin." She gestures to a tiny silver chalice glistening in the tallow glow.

There's no telling who or what has shed its blood, or what they have mixed with it, but the thought of it churns his insides. He staggers back, clutching his stomach as the vomit swells and pumps its way up his throat.

The laughter is deafening and high above it, like the call of an exotic bird, he hears Ursephal's delight at his humiliation. He covers his eyes, forcing tears back with the heels of his hands, and silently calls upon 'the voice' to aid him.

It soothes him, telling him not to look at the case where it is confined lest they realise he has already made contact. He sniffs, vowing under his breath that he will avenge them all when he is stronger, and the voice of the Black Rod in his mind swears with him.

Turor lifts his head, meeting Ursephal's implacable gaze with eyes that see beyond linear time. He feels a breeze stirring, a metaphor for a shift in consciousness that freezes the scene. He looks about him, sensing nothing but shells – all bar one.

She coughs to gain his attention. He looks on incredulously as the girl advances towards him.

"It was so long ago, Turor; I thought you'd enjoy reminiscing."

He can feel her hate like a fever, infecting his composure. He flinches and studies his own tiny hand – was he ever this vulnerable?

"The Rod is mine."

The altar plinth is bare and cold. She snarls, clenching a fist in concentration as she tries to build up an image of the Rod upon her astral altar, but nothing will appear.

"Wherever you are, I will come for you. Even Sarrell will be no hiding place, Turor. There is no plane, no enclave of existence where I cannot reach you – remember that."

"Then I await you, Ursephal."

And though her monstrous conjurings have already begun to invade the chamber, he cannot find it in his heart to oppose her and instead banishes himself from the scene.

"I will come for you," she screams, "and then we'll have a reckoning of our own!"

Buda shook Turor awake, one arm up to fend off his flailing limbs. His face was dappled with sweat, eyes wide in distress.

"I didn't know what to do, Turor – you were calling out."

"What time is it?" he blinked swollen eyes.

"Just after dawn. Verrsa and Athenna will be here soon."

"Good, I'll feel safer outside."

"You're safe here – why won't you believe that?"

Turor breathed through his hands to calm himself. "Ursephal took me to her domain; I saw it and felt it. If she can do that with *me* then you're all in danger."

Buda said nothing, but he could see that she wasn't convinced.

"Do not underestimate her. She was always the strongest of the four companions, the Magus…" he stopped at his own words.

Buda was about to say something when she heard voices outside.

"I hope we're not too early, ma'am," Verrsa ventured.

"Not at all. Turor needs air; he has been shut in like a prisoner."

Turor collected the Rod and led Buda to the door. "Don't expect too much of him," he warned Athenna. "Just be ready in case he tries to communicate."

She nodded and went over to Syriem, shifting the blanket around his legs.

"Now do you see what I mean?" Buda whispered as they were made their way outside. "Easen could have come to see us off."

"You judge him harshly," Turor countered. "Give him time."

"I think," she started up the trail, "that ten years was enough time for change."

And before Turor could answer, she took off, ascending steadily towards the sun. The storms had passed in the night. The air was cool, whispering down through fissures and crags. Turor sensed she had travelled the path many times, each handhold and ledge steadfastly receiving her.

"You haven't told me where we're going," he called after her.

"Maybe you just don't know how to listen."

He stopped in his tracks, confronted by an image so sharp that it was almost painful. A cairn dominated his inner sight – the same one he'd seen before. She paused ahead of him.

"Do you understand now?"

"I think so. Out here it's easier to communicate on subtle levels?"

"It's conducive to clarity of perception," she twisted her voice to a parody of Easen's.

"And the significance of the tomb?"

"You'll see," her voice tailed off and she resumed her journey.

The cairn was hidden by a cleft in the rocks, topped with a bush that clung tenaciously to the rocks. He didn't realise it was there until he'd rounded the final ridge.

"A Targen grave?" he responded to the next image.

Buda fussed over the bush, pouring some of her water supply around the base of the trunk. "I've come to say goodbye," she said, and before Turor could interrupt, she pointed back at him. "I've brought a friend – his name is Turor."

She picked at tiny stones and swept them off the ledge. Turor saw frozen images of Buda and the Targen officer escaping from Tarsis, leaving behind the daughter she loved – a life sacrificed for a higher adoration. He opened himself up to the impressions, dimly aware of Buda describing the night that she left Tarsis City State.

"I hadn't intended to abandon them. That night, when I knew I couldn't stay any longer, I tried to reason with Easen. We could have made a life outside; his work could have benefited so many others.

"I told him – *if you won't come with me then I'll take my daughter*. He turned his back on me, said I was as good as dead to him. And when he knew for certain that I'd go, he swore he'd die before he'd let Athenna leave. And if I ever tried to get word to her, he'd make sure that the authorities tracked me down.

"I knew by then that he probably had the connections to do it. I could bear his hatred for myself, but they would have hunted us all down and our supporters – I couldn't risk that."

"From what Syriem told me, he never gave up on you entirely."

"All those wasted years without my daughter!" she shrieked at the wind.

"No, not wasted," he promised her. "Everything that happened is the working out of some greater plan; it has all brought us to this."

Buda pulled the faded leaves from the bush. "I didn't fall for him straight away – Easen, I mean. I'd seen him going into the Central Hall in Qayla; I worked there at the time – I wasn't born to the faith, you see. When we first met, he was charming – shy even. Only later did I find out that he was working for The Assembly. He was one of *their* sons, as different from our kind as night is from day.

"We spoke occasionally, no more than that. Weeks later, while visiting relatives in Tarsis, I was sitting in Keres Park. Suddenly there he was, with some story about working in the area. So one thing led to another and before I knew it we were involved. A long time afterwards, he admitted that he'd had me followed all the way from Qayla – that's the real Easen," she drew a heavy breath. "And I'll tell you another thing, he's dangerous. Ask him some time about what happened to his brother."

Turor knelt beside her at the grave. "What was your friend's name?"

"Pettran," she said proudly, and her eyes were lost in remembering. "It was the smallest of things. I was stopped by a road patrol, coming back from a Thaylin Sarra gathering. Pettran was alone, killing time I suppose. And though the law afforded him powers of authority, he treated me with kindness. I saw him again, quite by accident, a few days after that. He'd remembered my name and we struck up a conversation."

"A risky business where the Targen are concerned."

"Not with him. I couldn't really tell you when it happened or even how; all I know is that by the time we were set on leaving Tarsis City State, Pettran was among us. He took a lot of risks to help us."

"Did Easen know about him?"

"I think he suspected, before I left Tarsis; always commenting about how often I was away at meetings – and how he tolerated my kin. You have to see, I never intended…" she squeezed her palms together. "We all made our way out of the city in secret, but some of the group picked up an illness – Pettran among them. Both our Patriarch and Matriarch died on the journey – I took their place. Pettran only survived for a few months in Crail. He was an incredible man, Turor; he gave up everything for us, and all without the faith to support him."

"You must have meant a great deal to him," he watched her smile at his words.

"We laid him to rest up here. I like to think that he watches over us – it's where I come to be at peace."

"And now?" Turor reflected.

"All that's gone, and I'm back where I was, only…I'm not the same. It's like I've been in a deep sleep. And now, without warning, you have awakened me," she turned her face to the sky. "Sometimes I wish I were still dreaming."

"I know that sometimes it seems as if every step of the path is marked by sacrifice and suffering," he consoled her. "Syriem still grieves for a priestess named Isca, and I too have had my share of tragedy. But is it not the sacred wound that shapes us? And are these trials not the furnace in which our True Will is forged?"

Buda said nothing. The wind howled around the rocks, scattering dust across the two of them. It was answer enough, she felt. She lit a fire and emptied the contents of a bag into a shallow pan.

"So, Turor, now that I've shared my secrets, I want to ask you something."

He crouched low to the flames.

"This creature, Ursephal – is she human?"

He looked up, finding nothing strange in her question. "Yes, though what remains of the person she once was is hard to imagine. She was brought into Appra before my capture, so I know nothing about her past."

"Why were you captured?" she pressed him.

"When I was born, so my mother has told me, I was believed me to be the reincarnation of an earlier Hybrolen. It is said that envoys from Sarrell came to find me. What I do know is that the High Dominus of Appra herself set her minions to the same purpose. My imprisonment in Appra not only deprived me of my mission, it also denied me my lineage."

The Black Rod vibrated against his back, as if to show solidarity.

"You wish to know why Ursephal pursues me – that's complicated." He took a blade and pushed the flatcake around the pan. "They wanted to debase me by degrees, taking delight in my agonies until I wilfully surrendered to them. It was part of a long preparation. Ursephal, although I didn't know it at the time, was the only other child that hadn't died. The High Dominus realised that my mother was sustaining me. The Appren planned to mate me with Ursephal in due course and then use the offspring to house whatever dwelt inside the Rod. They thought they could control it and use its power like a living weapon."

Buda tensed, outraged by the images that came to her.

"They forced us to participate in a ritual, intended to claim dominion over the Rod. It all went hideously wrong. The rite created a schism and a shard of the Rod's essence was released. Only the intervention of the High Dominus herself was able to prevent a greater catastrophe. The Rod's intelligence overshadowed me and through my mother's art we escaped from Appra, taking the Rod with us. It protected us."

"And you left Ursephal behind," Buda touched the beads around her neck. "Left her there to bear their wrath and their cruelty."

He nodded in shame. "How much of that could *you* see?"

"Enough to know that you all suffered. Now, tell me about my daughter," she whispered.

He stared out at the path they had taken. "I have only known her since the Exodus; Syriem is closest to her. She bears *your* gifts without a doubt, along with Easen's reasoning."

"A potent combination that our marriage was unable to withstand."

"Syriem has a special connection with her; I do too, although I cannot fathom it. And you should know that her True Will began to awaken during our journey here."

"Then I will see to it that she is offered instruction – if that's what she wants."

Turor's mood darkened. "What would you counsel me, about Syriem?"

"Only this: follow your True Will. Do not be swayed, regardless of the consequences – to you or to him. Do what you came here to do, Turor – what you have always known, deep down, you were born for. *Fulfil your purpose.*"

The hairs raised at the back of his neck. Her words were stark and uncompromising, and every one of them rang true as temple bells.

chapter 22
THE PORTAL

AFTER DAYS in Crail, while the weary rested and the faithful prepared, the Matriarchs met with representatives from both communities. And together they came to a decision – it was time to leave. Every oracle offered the same advice: movement.

Turor was summoned to give account of Syriem's fitness to travel. Buda had spoken well of him, bolstering his position as a Hybrolen and the Bearer of the Black Rod – the one whose fate was to lead the faithful to Sarrell. Some, however, still wondered about a man who, by his own admission, had spent time in the dark citadel of Appra. Truly, Turor was an enigma.

He arrived with Verrsa at sunrise. Usually he loved the morning, delighting in the pale vistas of dawn. But today he was sombre, as if the weight of the future were bearing down upon him. Verrsa walked quietly beside him, bright-eyed and radiant, still pondering dreams from a night at Syriem's side.

She greeted the waiting elders warmly. Turor entered after her without a word. He didn't appreciate being sent for and certainly not under such secrecy. The chamber had a heightened sense of energy; clearly, much magic had been worked there over the years. Beyond that, he considered, as he looked at the row of expectant faces, the room and its audience had little to recommend themselves.

"You have some information for us," Buda prompted him.

He faced them with a sullen sense of duty and took his place at the table; reluctantly adopting the role that fate had carved for him. "The fifth seal must be released when we are away from the settlement. Then the Lock and Key will combine to activate a portal to Sarrell."

The elders nodded in unison. The seers had all indicated some kind of doorway.

"What of the boy?" Buda took the lead. "Is he able to speak?"

Turor nodded to Verrsa and she cleared her throat.

"Not as yet, although those closest to him can discern the shadow of his thoughts. Where once he seemed irretrievably lost, now he reaches out to us in our dreams."

Buda shifted in her chair. "Why is the Rod keeping him in that state?"

The elders leant forward as she spoke and Verrsa's fearful pallor prompted one of them to offer a soothing hand.

"You may rest easy, my child," she told Verrsa. "Whatever force the Black Rod contains, be it Holy or otherwise," she looked to Turor, "it has no power in this chamber."

Another time, Turor would have questioned that. "I don't think the Rod has ever meant to harm him," he said, bemused to find he had become the Rod's advocate. "I think it's preparing him in some way. It will release him when the need arises."

"This *affliction* sits outside the traditions – how can you be so sure?"

Confronted by their piety, a dark cynicism arose within him. "I have borne the Black Rod and its purpose for most of my life," he took a long, slow breath. "I know of which I speak. It is my path, after all."

Buda rubbed her beads between her fingers. "Then I suggest you attend to it; for now, you are dismissed. You, however," she turned to Verrsa, "may remain – your counsel would be most welcome."

Turor paused behind the curtain on his way out. So, they would leave him to ready the boy, under their authority. And, at the same time, the inclusion of Verrsa would strengthen ties between the communities and make the group mind more cohesive. He closed the door with a smile; there was hope for them yet.

He returned swiftly to Syriem. Athenna was still asleep, lost in a peace he could only envy. He woke her gently and watched as Syriem sank a little when their link weakened.

"I dreamt of Dorron again," she blushed as she glanced back at Syriem. "The woman was there again – dominant and powerful." She rubbed her eyes, sifting memories. "And she was calling *your* name, Turor."

It began in earnest that same evening. All through the day, Syriem had twitched and fidgeted in the chair. Sometimes an arm would thrust into the air, fingers splayed in invocation, or else a hand would slowly turn, lifting the digits in delicate, precise movements.

As nightfall approached, Syriem spoke for the first time; Athenna wept when she heard him. She ran to fetch Turor and although the voice was not fully Syriem's, they both agreed it was a portent of his re-emergence. The words he uttered gave little cause for celebration: Chaos, Sekha, and Reunion.

"What does it mean? " Athenna watched the aura around Syriem pulsating.

Turor closed his eyes in thought. "Go to your mother; tell her that her three soldiers will recover soon. And ready the pilgrims – it will not be long now."

Easen had supervised as complete an overhaul of the Transvectors as their situation allowed, despite Buda insisting it was a pointless task. The Crail metalworkers were masters of their craft, and under his direction they replaced mechanical parts and repaired body panels. He commended their skill as he dined with Buda and Athenna, their strained silences giving way to flurries of stilted conversation. It baffled him that the settlers had managed to develop such industry, separated as they were from the civilising influence of the City States; he said as much to Buda and Athenna.

Buda listened in disbelief and tried to return her daughter's thin smiles of encouragement. Easen continued, with a bone in one hand and a flagon in the other, showering exaggerated praise on the settlement's achievements. He was trying so hard, she could have wept for pity. She smiled, listening to her own thoughts. The world had changed and clearly he had not. Perhaps, in Sarrell, they might *all* be liberated.

The sentry straightened his tunic as the tunnel-train approached the terminus, watching the yellow lights swallow the rim of the tunnel. The train pulled in with a gentle hiss; a single passenger emerged amid the hum of electricity.

"Welcome back, General Ursephal," he saluted, sweat gathering at his back.

She acknowledged him curtly, gladdened by the stifled sigh when she passed. He followed in her wake at a respectful distance, through the security checkpoints and up to the surface. She stared out at Appra City and smiled at the pallid moon, guarding her intent.

Narl greeted Ursephal's arrival with joy, eager to prepare the ritual chamber.

"That won't be necessary. I'll handle this work alone, Narl. And after I leave, no one must enter these chambers again."

Narl looked up, grief-stricken. Ursephal laid a hand on her face. Faithful Narl, who had served her so well over the years; she would miss her. She walked deftly past, unmoved by Narl's sobs as she dragged herself away.

Alone in the silence, Ursephal closed the temple door and crossed the tiles – barefooted, so as not to disturb the rodent – tasting the chill of stone against her soles. She slipped the jacket from her shoulders and touched the dagger at her belt. The rat stirred, turning its cataract eyes towards the sound.

"You are unwell, my lord?" she jeered, watching as the tiny creature tried to stand. "Narl has administered an unusual poison. It will not kill you yet you'll wish for death – even you who comes from beyond the veil."

The rodent gasped for air and sank to the floor of its cage.

"I do not think you so strong *this* time," she baited the creature; "nor I so subordinate. Still, I will release you at last – if you agree to my terms."

She closed her eyes and turned the glare of her awareness towards the cage. She felt the Sekha writhe in torment, trapped and crippled, starved of vitality in an ailing, wretched body. She pointed her dagger and traced out a triangle on the floor. And around it she spun three binding circles, constructing a cage of a different nature.

In a projection of True Will, blue pentagrams flamed against the walls in all directions, lighting the room in shimmering lapis. Now she resonated emotive force, drawing the astral world to her by controlled imagination and desire. The triangle smouldered vermilion as the physical plane retreated.

She focuses, building up power, and invokes the Sekha to appear. The creature struggles, but is helpless to disobey, manifesting within the triangle. She senses waves of dissonance as it tries to breach the boundaries, but her confidence is well founded.

"You have grown strong, my child," it commends her.

"And you have grown weak. I bring you here to make a final pact."

"What is your…desire?" it asks, and the salacious overtone offends her.

"I have only one desire," she replies coldly. "And in that we share a common aim."

The creature floats in the air, a tapered reptilian tail brushing against the floor.

"At your last defeat," she pauses, relishing the Sekha's chagrin, "you swore vengeance on the young Hybrolen who challenged you." She takes a step towards the outer of the three circles. "The magical planes resonate with your shame, but could yet record your triumph. You already have the link with Turor and his underling. I can release you at my bidding – you to visit justice on the boy, and I on the betrayer."

"So be it," the Sekha groans. "I will fulfil your will and then our pact is ended."

"You honour me, my lord. Now, swear thrice by your true name and I shall liberate you."

Ursephal opened her eyes and, to her surprise, the creature's wraith was still hovering in the air. She opened the cage and lifted the rodent on to the altar. The dagger gleamed as she passed it over the wizened body. She held her hand a few inches above the rat and grasped the air. A filament throbbed into view, pulsing faintly between the rodent and the Sekha.

"Be about thy terrible work," she commanded, slicing the air with the dagger and jabbing the point into her outstretched palm.

Three drops of blood dripped against the rodent's fur, and with each scarlet stain a circular boundary dissolved. Then, as the life force disengaged and the rat gave up its last, the etheric triangle blasted apart with an audible *crack*, freeing the Sekha.

"I will avenge myself," it took on the wings of a warring angel.

She poured rich oils over the tiny corpse and watched as it received the flames. The stench of tallow acted as a purgative, cleansing her mind of their association. As the fat and sinew burned away, she read the bones like runes. The Black Rod would be waiting for the Sekha – Turor would see to that. A fitting justice for a creature that had subjugated and abused her, since the day Turor and his mother abandoned her in Appra. Maybe she would grant him a quick death as a dispensation.

She spat into the haze and watched her saliva fizzle. "Rest in torment," she hissed.

Narl was waiting outside the chamber. "Where are we headed, mistress?"

Ursephal embraced her. "Not you, Narl. It is a journey you would not survive; this time I travel alone."

"You're awake then," Turor watched Syriem's hollow gaze as it tracked him across the room.

"Where are the artefacts?" the face tightened to a grimace.

"I have removed them in preparation for the journey."

The body nodded, satisfied, and the essence departed with a shudder. Syriem sagged and after a few seconds he launched into a coughing fit, shaking violently.

"Can you walk?"

"I think so," he pushed down with gaunt arms and slowly found his footing. "We will meet our fate among the elements," he groped for a steadying hand.

"How are you, Syriem?"

"I have dwelt in a psychic wasteland where nothing could reach me – for the most part – except my own tortured reflections. I have revisited every torment and grief, from all sides, until all I knew was pain."

"Perhaps if I had not been so quick to seize upon our meeting in Tarsis…"

"No, Turor, there is no injustice here; no punishment. You found me at birth and Isca pursued that same intent. I chose to follow this path, sometimes consciously, other times by lack of will. I know that any sacrifices have not been without purpose. I don't fully understand the bond between us, but I'm certain this path is only the continuation of a greater journey we commenced long ago."

The tunnels were silent as Syriem shuffled forward, kicking up dust with each step. "Why can't I hear any mining?"

Turor eased him past a wooden post. "They've shut down operations until we leave. Most of the settlers want to remain here, along with some of our travellers."

Syriem heard whispering, as he emerged from the final cavern, and felt the first breeze since his captivity. Voices murmured around him in a chorus of pity. He blinked his clouded eyes against the night sky that Turor was certain the boy could not see.

The Rod stirred, contorting Syriem's face. He clutched at his torso and cried out, but Turor raised a hand to ward off anyone who might come to his aid. Syriem felt himself falling, collapsing back into the void as the Rod's awareness swallowed him. 'Behold,' he heard within his mind, 'the darkness comes once more.'

"The Restitution awaits us," Turor rallied the crowd.

"Light be with you," the creature manipulated Syriem's body to offer a blessing.

The crowd gasped, many having thought it a creature wholly of the chaos. Easen was first to speak, risking Turor's wrath to demonstrate that he still held power. The pilgrims assembled under his instructions, the elders in the lead Transvector, facing a mountain path that snaked into the distance. Buda took Easen's hand.

Turor positioned Syriem next to a window. Other travellers watched, fascinated and repulsed, shielding their children lest Syriem's sickly gaze should fall upon them. The cloudy spheres nestling in his eye-sockets shimmered and, at the first shriek of horror, he turned to Turor with a triumphant leer. Turor closed the connecting door.

As he looked to the boy, Turor felt himself drawn into another reality. Syriem's face dissolved, replaced by the features of a young girl. He felt the scene expanding, gathering pace. He looked again upon her cropped, brown hair and saw her eyes imploring sanctuary, calling silently to him in their misery.

"Turor," Easen nudged him, "Buda's given the signal; we're leaving."

He flinched, glaring up at Easen. Then he forced himself to look back at Syriem. The eyes were closed and the boy's head rocked with each hissing breath, as though he were sighing with contentment.

As the Transvector engines kicked in, a great roar erupted from the crowd. Turor looked out at the line of spectators and their celebratory beacons, buoyed up by their fervour.

Easen leaned over as the Transvector pulled out. "Looks like storms are gathering," he said, trying hard not to make it sound like an accusation.

The rains fell before they'd lost sight of the settlement, the charcoal sky draining in fierce, passionate bursts. The flooding was sporadic and intense, running rivers of mud around the Transvectors and slowing their progress. Syriem sat deathly still, disturbed only by brilliant discharges of lightning, as the terrain flashed in and out of vision.

Hour after hour it raged. Whenever they halted their advance to enable those on foot to take shelter, the storm abated. But as soon as they forged ahead, nature was swift to punish their insolence. The Thaylin Sarra took to singing, straining their voices to be heard above the roar of the tempest. Buda clung to the radio, listening hard as messages crackled back and forth between the two vehicles and the walking pilgrims. She asked several times whether they should turn back, or wait until conditions were more auspicious. Press on, they told her, ablaze like zealots; at all costs, press on.

Sometimes, when the winds fell without warning and the whining hum of the engines faded, the jubilant voices of the throng seemed to be magnified, so that many believed the spirits of the dead now travelled alongside them.

Soon there were reports of light bursts and phantoms, high up on the rocks, conflicting visions that all took to be signs of Sarrell. Each saw only what their mind could safely contain. For some, it was reflections of the past; for others, elaborate enactments of the sacred texts, accompanied by heroines and heroes of old – all witness to the final journey.

"Where are we?" Buda called out to her companions. "This doesn't look like anywhere in the mountains that I've ever seen."

Turor waited, certain that the Rod would not miss such an opportunity to inspire him. "This is where the past and the future converge – the ever-present now."

"Still hiding behind your mysticism, eh?" Easen derided him.

Turor closed his eyes and sought out the Rod. He formed a question in his mind – and received an answer; they would have the truth, whether they recognised it or not.

"Turn the radio off. This is the truth that I acknowledge," he began, uncertain of his next words. "Sarrell is not fully on this plane of existence, but it can be reached through a portal. The emanations increase as the Rod and the Tablet get closer to it."

"And then what happens?" Athenna asked.

"I don't know," he humbled himself. "I seem to have spent my entire life first evading and now abetting this purpose. Perhaps, in the end, faith alone is sufficient."

"This place is barren; there's nothing here," Easen protested.

Verrsa offered a different perspective. "Parva Serach spoke of the journey between separation and unity. Maybe this is the desolate path itself."

Athenna lifted her hand from Syriem's and took a great breath. "I don't think it matters any more what we think individually, just that we complete our journey. That's where we'll find our answers."

"Well said," Turor smiled at her. "Of course, if the Tablet *had* found its way to you, Buda," he noted without judgement, "then the Black Rod may well have come to Athenna."

Buda and her daughter stared at one another, as if they had come to a new understanding.

"And I might be where Syriem is," she whispered.

The visions increased and many people reported hearing voices. Verrsa quoted from a passage she called the *Vale of Souls*, although no one could remember hearing it before.

"Though I walk through the valley of the shadow of death, I will fear no evil. For thou are with me, and thy Rod and staff they comfort me upon my journey."

"Look!" Easen slowed the Transvector. "There's a body out there."

"It's Aschin," Buda touched her heart. "He left the settlement a few days ago."

She peered through the glass at the crumpled mass. Aschin was shrouded in the red blanket she had given him, the sodden cloth edged with symbols of protection and good fortune. She let out a cry of despair at the acolyte who, like many before him, had felt an irresistible calling to Sarrell.

"We must bury him; he deserves that," she turned to Easen.

He hesitated, torn between upsetting her and provoking Turor.

Syriem reached forward, gasping for air. "Take me to him."

Buda picked up the handset. "We're stopping; wait for our signal."

Syriem found his footing with difficulty, clutching Turor's arm for balance. Turor walked on, dragging him along, avoiding his face.

"*Let me touch him*," Syriem stretched out icy fingers to make contact.

Turor stood aside and Syriem placed a withered hand on the unfortunate's face. "Well, Hybrolen?" he confronted Turor, indifferent to the rainwater that poured over his eyes. "Do you see Life or Death?"

"I see Universal Law in manifestation," Turor replied coldly. "That's all I ever see."

"He is weak, yet he lives!" Syriem raised a hand to the sky and drew down a shaft of lightning to the rocky peaks above them.

Turor tried to step away, but Syriem held him fast. "Nothing is without balance, Turor; all things come to a state of resolution."

"And Ursephal?" Turor sank to his knees. "What about her?"

Aschin's body lay before them, pale as death. Syriem placed a hand at Aschin's chest, Turor covered it with his own and together they poured life force into him like a benediction.

Aschin started coughing, choking out rain and mud as he struggled for breath.

"Over here!" Turor waved his arm frantically. "*He's alive!*"

Buda called for blankets and a stretcher, and tried to forget Easen's explanation that the boy had only been in the elements for a short time. She knew that to travel so far, in those conditions, he must have walked for days.

Verrsa remained with Turor and Syriem.

"Only the righteous would have been so rewarded," she told him.

Turor was lost for an answer. But when Aschin began to stir, he made sure that he got to him first. "What did you see?"

"I saw you all," Aschin's face softened. "A procession of lights, travelling towards me. And I heard the songs, just as I learned them as a child. I was in the midst of the Ancient Ones."

"What *happened* to you?" Turor pressed him.

"I wandered in search of the true path and collapsed, exhausted. I awoke in darkness, unable to see or feel. I thought I was back in the womb, ready to be reborn. I clung to my identity and gradually the night lifted. A great figure came towards me. It was Baldor the Valiant, and he held his sword over me to see if my soul sang true – just as the legend says."

"There are many legends," Turor countered. "What did he ask of you?"

Aschin turned his face away. "I was afraid. I ran from his challenges and he called after me, for my return. I was unrighteous before Baldor of the Mountains, and the Gods deepen my shame by leaving me to be found here."

"Listen to me, Aschin, you have served us well. Had you not returned like this, we would still be in ignorance." He marshalled Aschin towards the Transvector with Buda at his side. "This man is a true wayfarer. He has brought us a sign from beyond the veil."

Buda helped Aschin up into the Transvector, to take his place beside the elders. Turor understood now; they were travelling through a realm of archetypes.

Verrsa was first to recognise the outcrop of rock, with its grey monoliths pointing resolutely to the sky. "Baldor's hand," she crossed herself. "As it is foretold."

 "It began here," Aschin shuddered. "That was the last thing I saw; the point of no return."

Five columns of stone thrust out of the bedrock together in a single mass. It was a stylised hand perhaps, but to the Thaylin Sarra there was no doubt: this was indeed the sign of the Ancient Deliverer, Baldor; he who had raised his hand to the light, to receive Ortha's sword of souls, in the battle against the Fallen Ones.

Syriem pressed a hand against the window and whispered a lament, crucified by the memory of Isca's five magical pillars.

The convoy stopped and the rains gradually eased, swept away by a growling sky. They filed out of the Transvectors and waited for the others, massing together at the base of the rock formation. Turor stood back for Buda to lead the proceedings.

"Let us build a fire worthy of Baldor," she proclaimed, orchestrating the rite.

A Patriarch opened with a prayer to the past. The Thaylin Sarra waited with the other pilgrims and all were encouraged to participate; no longer would there be a difference between the believers and the non-believers. The line moved with grace, falling into a flowing rhythm as the fire tribute was performed. Finally, Buda gave consent for Turor and Syriem to approach the flames.

Turor guided him forward, the Rod at his back and the Tablet over his chest. The heat was seductive, reddening Turor's face and filling his ears with a sombre roar.

"What do you see in the flames, Hybrolen?" the Rod tormented him.

"I see change and shifting patterns of perception, and beyond that, darkness."

The creature nodded, breathing in their devotion.

"Will you release him unharmed when the time comes?"

"He made a pact of justice with me and it must be fulfilled. I cannot promise that it will be painless, but his own attachment is the cause of his suffering."

Turor made an offering for them both, watching as the flames consumed the lines of text. Somewhere, deep within those fiery tongues, he thought he saw amber eyes peering back at him. He brushed his hands over the fire, tapping his lips and his forehead.

"It is finished," he declared, bowing towards Buda.

A lone figure stood out on a plateau, ahead of the convoy. She watched impassively, waving a pale banner above her head. In her other hand, a solitary, piercing bell rang out, like a clarion call – or a death knell. Turor sensed the onset of trance and was powerless to resist. He felt his body slump forward and his consciousness ascend, rushing him to another domain.

"Why have you summoned me here?"

Amorphous intent congeals into structure, forming a focus to communicate.

"We are Khorsia. On your plane of existence we are One."

He waits for guidance, aware that he can only experience them by metaphor. A resonance forms, vibrating the molecules around him into a translucent shell. Waves of energy ripple around him, encasing him in a protective pillar of light.

Inner vision pierces through and he perceives the Sekha – unconscious to his presence. It has changed since he first encountered it, augmented by the energies it has absorbed. His etheric body quivers, seeking sanctuary on the physical plane. He plummets, speeding downwards, the different spheres on the Tree of Life flashing by like coloured suns. He connects with the line of pilgrims, heading to their destiny, feeling overwhelming love for them. And he knows that he must face his nemesis.

"What's going on?" Turor shivered in his seat.

"We've tried communicating with her," Buda pointed to the figure on the rocks. "It's as if she can't see us."

He wondered at their ignorance, this far along the path. "She's not present on this plane of reality. She is a guardian and her image reaches us through the properties of the region."

"A holy icon from a bygone age?" Easen mocked him.

"The elders were not privy to this wisdom…" Buda added her suspicion.

"That's because, after you've seen this, you don't usually come back to talk about it," Turor silenced them. "Now, look behind us."

Easen checked the mirror, seeing the second Transvector and, further back, the trail of people as they marched. Beyond them, there was nothing except an inky blackness.

"We seem to be nowhere," Easen glanced around at the terrain.

The rocks shimmered like liquid sculptures, reflecting shifting colours of an iridescent sky.

"I'll wake the boy," Turor pressed his palm to Syriem's forehead. "Are you with us?"

"I think so," he replied wearily.

"Then it is time, if you are willing."

Easen stopped the convoy. Up ahead, he could see the same impenetrable mass, as if the darkness had worked its way stealthily around to encase them in a perimeter of night. The walkers caught up and huddled by the Transvectors, confused and disturbed.

Turor bowed to the Thaylin Sarra and then turned to Verrsa and Buda. They shared a glance and readily conferred their blessing.

"I will see you beyond the veil," Verrsa drank in Turor with her eyes.

Buda gave Turor the Thaylin Sarra blessing. But when it came to Syriem, Athenna came forward and took her place. Their lips touched and a single tear ran down her face.

"Travel well," Buda told them softly, drawing her daughter close.

Turor took a long look at them all – that brave band of pioneers who had entrusted him with their quest. Then he saluted Cordal and turned with Syriem to embrace their fate.

The darkness gradually yielded, and the veil that separated *before* and *after* dissolved, revealing a landscape bereft of life. Syriem groped about in the air and Turor handed him the Tablet, keeping the Rod for himself. He watched, beguiled, as Syriem's eyes glowed against the light of the stars. The cloudy nebula submerged and faded, sinking into twin black orbs. Then, just when Turor began to despair that the Rod had finally overwhelmed Syriem, a pinprick of light appeared in each eye, heralding his resurgence.

"Something is happening," Syriem wheezed in dread.

Energy massed before them, twisting and spinning before it finally coalesced into human form. The Guardian of the Tablet manifested on the plane as a luminous being, covered with myriad eyes that blinked independently, while great wings of energy swept behind it.

"We are here," the creature whispered in many voices. "Now you may join us."

Syriem felt something churning inside him, writhing at the base of his spine. Muscle after muscle relinquished the Rod's grasp as the being worked its way along his vertebrae. Turor took a step behind him.

"Coward," Syriem uttered, as the Sekha appeared.

It descended, pterodactyl-like, resplendent in its malevolence, landing before the boy in a great crash of wings and talons.

"We have unfinished business, Hybrolen child," the Sekha gleamed, extending a claw towards him.

Syriem felt no rage or fear, as Turor gripped his shoulders, only a leaden sense of inevitability; it seemed he would follow Isca after all.

The Sekha advanced towards the Tablet in Syriem's arms.

"You are mine!" it roared, moving closer so its emanations penetrated his aura.

Something within him refused to yield and though he felt as if his flesh were being wrenched from his bones, he stood resolute.

"See how your master sacrifices you!" the Sekha revelled. "Your life is over and when your body is an empty husk, I shall inhabit it and claim my dominion."

Turor felt a burning in his chest; a throbbing, searing scar that flashed across his body like a fault line. He dug his nails hard into the boy, rooting him to the spot, as magical force rippled along his arms like snakes of fire.

Syriem's dwindling magical defences collapsed as the Sekha invaded his body, stripping energy from every nerve ganglion and plexus. As his torso shook, the Tablet rattled ominously in his hands.

The Rod had not moved to Syriem's aid, sequestering itself in the darkest reaches of his being. It awoke like a dragon, uncoiling and spiralling, forcing its way up through the tattered wasteland of his psyche, shattering his fragile awareness in order to separate.

Syriem sensed the two consciousnesses meeting within him. The Sekha struggled to resist, but the Black Rod at last engulfed its renegade shard. White fire raged through Syriem's mind, as the Rod's intelligence rebirthed itself into unity. And the shell that would shatter at its re-emergence would be him.

Turor splayed his hands over Syriem's back, driving vitality into him to keep him conscious. He opened his mind to the flooding energy of The Rod, offering himself as a living conduit for its manifestation. He, who had been part of the Appren ritual that caused the schism, would be the means of redress. A torrent of psychic force flowed through channels of intention, abandoning Syriem as a host.

Turor felt the being's yearning and opened his mind to its needs. "Khorsia!" he called to the heavens, projecting the name with the full intensity of his True Will.

The Black Rod broke free in an exquisite cry of passion, manifesting before them as a shrouded angel. The two great beings, now whole, faced the two Hybrolen like pillars on the tree. Turor released Syriem and stood beside him, breathing furiously.

"Now!" Syriem prompted him.

Turor raised the Rod high in the air as though it were Baldor's sword. He pointed it and focused, charging it with an invocation. The Rod began to glow, changing hue, breaching the visible spectrum and flashing through colours that Turor didn't even have names for. Then, when it shone like a torch forged in the stars, he thrust the beacon forward and watched as reality rippled around it.

The two holy creatures stepped aside and Syriem touched the fifth seal on the Tablet, remembering Isca's words: part of everything belonging to nothing. He smiled, and his soul reached out to that limitless Nothing, from where, she had taught him, all existence originated and returned. His nails made contact with the wax and he felt the symbols rippling beneath his fingertips, conspiring like caged birds poised for flight. He looked at the opening vortex and felt the Tablet being drawn from his grip. He slid his fingers under the cloth and heard the subtle hiss as the wax vaporised. With a great cry of triumph he tore the cloth, sending a shred of material fluttering into the air. It floated upwards, tumbling in the eddy currents. Then the irresistible vortex took hold, drawing the fibres towards it until the fragment disappeared in a flash of silver.

A pale glow formed out of the nothingness, pulsating as it grew. The edges shimmered and then a burst of light hit the Tablet at Syriem's chest: an infusion of energy to awaken the last of its secrets. Turor thrust the Rod into the vortex, watching as energy licked along the Rod to engulf his arm in diaphanous brilliance.

"The giver and the receiver alike," he whispered.

"So shall it be," Syriem acknowledged, leaning into the heat.

A last few steps, shoulder to shoulder – into the Portal and beyond.

Shadow ceases to be; Time ceases to be. Only Light endures – a brilliance that negates all duality and division. For one last instant of awareness, Syriem shares a thought with Turor, a singular expression of everything he is and ever hopes to be. Then it is gone, rendered insignificant beside more complete expressions, themselves fleeting imaginings of the Absolute. And after that, the one eternal revelation: Eheieh – I am that I am.

Chaos and Order are spiralling arms of the first swirlings, the motive intent of Divine Will. Each is composed of creatures – holy living creatures – rejoicing in their magnificence as they blink in and out of individualised existence.

Perception expands to the point where it is the acceptance of Truth – everything reducing to the primary principle: Intention. And when the Summoner and the Messenger can no longer bear even a limited perception of the transcendent presence, then comes the agony of separation. The perilous descent; stripped of Being and deceived with Understanding – drawn from the edge of vastness to embrace their own individuality once more.

Spiritual Will becomes a faculty, a travesty of its true nature – the living garment that clothes the spark. Abstraction decays to a half-forgotten wisdom – a reasoning only glimpsed. Symbols form to harness precious experience, but each one is an imperfect mirror, shielding them from an intensity that would otherwise consume them.

Consciousness gravitates to its own level, diffused by a prism of duality into the influence and the influenced – divided and apart. The one through the many, and the many through the one.

"Turor – are you there? Are we…dead?"

"Would it matter? The fifth seal is released and the covenant is met."

Confusion swept through Syriem's mind. "If this is the next world, why isn't Isca here to meet me?"

The light dulled around him in rainbow bands. Each one condensed and then faded. Turor lifted the Tablet away and Syriem fell to the ground. He called out, over and over, for Isca or for Khorsia. It seemed as if the boy would weep forever.

"What is left of me? Everything I've experienced, all that I've been is gone. I cannot tell reality from illusion."

Turor waited, resolute in his purpose, just as Buda had counselled him.

"This is your initiation, Syriem. Though your True Will has awoken, now you must attain for yourself what was bestowed upon you to meet a greater need."

Syriem leaned so heavily on Turor that Athenna thought he was injured. She ran forward, screaming his name hysterically. Turor felt their awe, as they looked upon Syriem. And he listened as they proclaimed him a worker of wonders. But when Verrsa knelt before him, it was too much to bear. He shook his head sadly and walked away.

"Where would you have us do, master?"

"Follow your True Will and no other," he shouted back, devastated that they had come so far and apparently learned so little.

"What about *me*?" Syriem called piteously.

"Go back to the others," Turor dismissed him. "I cannot help you."

Syriem waited like a lost dog, numbed by the icy rain. If it were death by pneumonia that Turor was after then so be it, they would go together. Turor stopped in his tracks, sensing Syriem's eyes burning into him.

"What do you want from me, Syriem?" he lifted his arms up to the storm. Then he turned and witnessed the hollow fury on his face. He felt the potency of Syriem's thoughts and the desperation that drove him. And he ached with what he couldn't say.

"Turor, I need to know what's real."

"Open your mind!"

Syriem followed his command and the more he held that focus, the more sparks of memory re-ignited within him like lost embers. He reached inside his jacket and took out three strips of white wood, from the blasted tree in Isca's courtyard, and the set of tarot cards she had bequeathed him. He cast them to the wind with the last of his tears.

"Now you are ready to hear me. None of this is real – do you understand? We have opened the Portal and its influence is extending, but we are not safe yet. Why do you think they pay us such homage? They are between realms, Syriem, and they don't even know it – trapped within a web of illusions."

"If this is my illusion then why do I still feel the pain?"

But before Turor could answer, Syriem had returned to the travellers. They climbed back aboard the Transvectors and Athenna made space for Syriem beside her. The vehicles started up and she turned to him, flicking the hair from her face.

It was a beautiful face, brimming with the first flowering of youth. He thought then that he had always loved her, and whatever happened he would never leave her. She smiled at him, sharing his thoughts as her own. Her dark eyes absorbed him and they kissed, years of denial set loose in his blood. His drew her to him and felt the soft yielding weight of her body against his own once more.

"I am yours, Syriem," she vowed, "for always."

And though he wanted to lose himself in her, a part of him resisted – an ancient yearning that would not be appeased. Then he heard Isca's voice, calling from across worlds, as it echoed through the void.

"You have a purpose to serve. Remember who you are."

He brought Isca's face to mind in delicate brush strokes of passion and regret. The memory burned like a furnace, consuming his petty emotions in flames of devotion. For the first time he truly comprehended what she had done for him, and how she had secured his survival and that of her people. In that precious instant he saw her whole and sentient, then he grasped a truth both dreadful and glorious – he began to remember.

The last time Parva Serach's four companions had gathered together, out in the desert. They had sat in a quartered circle drawn in the sand, known now by the names she had given them – the Summoner, the Healer, the Messenger and the Magus – affirming their pact of reunion.

They had looked deep into one another eyes, as if to ensure they would recognise one another in some future life. Then they each took a separate path and never met again.

Syriem wrenched himself from Athenna's embrace, certain that she too was a part of his past and he of hers. He knew that he could stay there with her, but it would only be a lie – and he was tired of lies. He touched the talisman around his neck, the one that matched both Turor's and Isca's, and let his awareness roam free.

He followed a snaking trail in his mind's eye, led by intention and propelled by the wonder of his own discovery. He flashed past Athenna as though she were an ethereal barrier, moving on through her to link with Dorron. His heart leapt at the sight of his friend and he persisted, honing his focus to the present. He saw Dorron marching in step with a cadet regiment, heard the rhythmic crunching of boots and the oath of allegiance to The Frayers and The Assembly. Then, fleetingly, his mind was carried from Dorron to a woman who brought death, the Magus who would betray Dorron even as he sought to do her bidding.

"Enough," Syriem turned at last to Turor. "How do I rid myself of this illusion?"

Turor faced him. "If it is your True Will, express that intent. Allow yourself to see things as they really are – and live with it."

Syriem opened his hands. "It is my True Will."

In a shift of perception, reality cracked. Athenna, the Transvectors and everything around them waned from existence, receding to thought-form shells. Then there was nothing. An absence of light so complete that they were just voices in eternity.

"We have journeyed in the wilderness long enough, Turor," Syriem declared. "Become the Summoner you once were and have always been – take us home."

Turor stared at Syriem, watching as they took on human form once more. He raised his hands in invocation and called forth the power that had lain dormant within him since birth – an authority that his Appren captors had been incapable of subverting.

"I summon the Exodus to awareness," he spoke calmly, as one who understood the source of his authority.

The residual glow dulled to a haze and the physical world gradually came back into focus. A sea of mud surrounded them, fixing their ankles. Syriem bent forward and, with effort, lifted one leg free.

"We're alive!" he cried; the Tablet was still in his arms, close against his chest.

Turor examined the Black Rod and then passed it back to Syriem.

"Well met, Messenger," he bowed, touching his talisman.

Never did Syriem think that he'd look upon Cordal as any kind of blessing. But as he stood there, watching a pistol rise towards him, his heart swelled. Behind Cordal he saw campfires where travellers were huddled together, sleeping peacefully. Buda was a step or two behind Cordal, three small sticks still in her hands. Cordal couldn't resist and fired shots into the air.

Athenna heard the commotion and ran out. Syriem smiled as she stood before him; a grey blanket draped around her shoulders, a little like a magical robe.

"What?" she eyed him with wonder.

"It's good to see you again."

She reached out her hand to him and they stood, transfixed by one another in a dance of stillness, sharing the unspoken connection.

Easen related his account of the storm, shaping his views with little imagination. "It was electrifying!" he laughed at Buda's look of exasperation. "Well, it was! Ball lightning, shafts, forks and distortions of light; the whole area was one gigantic electromagnetic anomaly. If I wasn't a man of science, I'd have sworn that the things I saw were real and not just my scrambled brain."

"My husband fails to do his insights justice," Buda interrupted him. "I know what I saw and felt; it was the fulfilment of the ancient wisdom."

Syriem looked out from the crawling Transvector, on the first rays of dawn, and imagined that same light guiding Isca, wherever she was.

Turor intoned a deep, resonant sound and progressed to an ancient hymn, repeating the opening verses, over and over. Verrsa's voice wove through the prayer like a fine thread. Others added to the form, harmonising together, as they called the righteous to account.

After the first part of the prayer-song, which all the Thaylin Sarra joined, Buda and Turor continued in a strange, lyrical language that Syriem guessed must have been very old. Then they began their litany in earnest. At each response, the other completed; verse upon verse, invoking the forces of Light and Life. Finally, Turor withdrew, allowing Buda and Verrsa to conclude the cycle.

He reached forward and laid a hand on Easen's shoulder; the two Transvectors shuddered to a halt. Turor looked at the lines and carvings that adorned the vault, thrilled to see the sigils crackling like living flames. He laid two fingers on Syriem's forehead, releasing him from his contemplation.

"We have rent the veil and now we must complete the journey."

The cavern was vast, a breathtaking enormity of space. Wrapped in his thoughts, Syriem wondered if this too were merely a representation of reality.

Turor focused his attention on the highest point in the cavern, straining to catch the sound. The cadence affected him deeply, touching the last bastion within that had protected him from the past.

"Do you hear that?"

Syriem nodded, lifting his head to the source. The sound intensified, filling the chamber. He thought that he heard the voices of angels, rich with exaltations. And in his mind's eye, the harmonics took on form, streaming through the cavern as vortices of light. The Rod pulsated in his hand.

"What should I do?"

Turor smiled as the revelation embraced him. "The guardians of the Rod and the Tablet have fulfilled their purpose in bringing us home, Syriem; now we must set them free."

He placed the stone Tablet on the ground and knelt beside it. Syriem nodded sadly and Turor raised the Rod. He felt the Rod's presence as never before, unfettered and limitless.

A sound, like one great in-breath, echoed along the cavern, steadily gathering force as it rushed towards him.

"*Who are you?*" the voice shook the ground.

"I am that I am," he replied, looking upon Syriem with gratitude.

"*Why are you here?*"

"I seek to serve."

"*Are you righteous?*"

"I will make myself so by right action," he bowed his head.

"Then your quest is deemed worthy. It is well."

The pressure on Turor's arm subsided and he brought the Rod down against the Tablet, cleaving it into pieces. When he looked up, two immense figures stood before them. The Guardian of the Tablet took on human form for the last time, a façade for communication.

Syriem faced her. "Where is she – where is Isca?"

"You must find your own answers and then I will come again, Messenger."

The creature raised two winged arms and turned to Turor. "Well met, Summoner," it proclaimed, and then blinked out of corporeal existence.

"I have returned," Khorsia rejoiced. Filaments of light danced about her, intermixing and separating until they became eight shimmering figures, each one characterised by a colour and a form.

Syriem instinctively threw himself to the ground.

"We are not superior," they told him. "We evolved beyond physical expression and ascended the Tree as exemplars of its harmony, but we remain an equal aspect of the One. Long have we waited to be reunited; long have we safeguarded the Sanctuary by our separation. Now the Covenant is fulfilled. From this day forth, a new light joins the world and Sarrell is no longer hidden. But out amongst the uninitiated, your work will be forgotten."

At the far end of the great tunnel, the people of Sarrell waited. Syriem ran ahead, looking in vain for Isca's face among them. A woman greeted them and a babe stirred in her arms. The child, who in a former life had been named Errmoyne, looked upon the two travellers with a strange contentment and fell back to sleep. His mother merely smiled at him, as if she understood, and led them through.

In the early light of dawn, as the sun blessed the land, seven sacred Rods lay on the high altar in the form of the star. And to the right, the White Rod; and to the left, the Black Rod. When the rays of the physical star caressed the pattern of the spiritual star, a time of sleep ended. High above the temples of Sarrell, a rainbow shone – an irrefutable arc to usher in a new aeon.

EPILOGUE

Ursephal carried the body to the pit and eased it into the hollow. Narl had attained liberation on the very morning that Ursephal had planned to leave her. She sobbed as she dragged earth over the shroud. Her fingers ached, but she didn't stop until the body was buried beneath the soil. Then she stood and faced the first rays of the morning.

A rainbow spanned the sky and she couldn't tell whether it was real or a projection of her grief. She straightened up, swearing vengeance upon her enemies as she pressed a triangular talisman against her skin. She was alone again, but she knew the path ahead: Sarrell.

Gareth Knight: I Called it Magic

ISBN 978-1-908011-15-2

The esoteric autobiography of Gareth Knight covers six decades of magical work, tracing his series of legendary Hawkwood workings with Arthurian, Rosicrucian, Celtic and Greek archetypes, Merlin, the Tarot, the Qabalah, the Goddess, Tolkien and the shining allure of Faery.

"If you have ever wanted to glean some understanding of the mind, and motivation, of an adept Mage-of-Light – this is THE book to read. It is the best account of its kind to be published in over a century." — **Inner Fire Journal**

Margaret Lumley Brown: Both Sides of the Door

ISBN 978-1-908011-37-4

The true story of a psychic upheaval the young Margaret Lumley Brown went through in 1913 while living in a disturbed house in Bayswater, London, with her sister Isobel. A casual experiment with table-turning triggered an intense and terrifying haunting, beginning with odd shadows and shapes and soon developing into a full blown poltergeist manifestation. Household items vanished and reappeared, writing appeared on window blinds, bedclothes were pulled off and malevolent presences began to materialise in various disturbing forms, verging on the distinctly demonic. This new edition includes commentary and maps.

Wendy Berg: Red Tree, White Tree

ISBN 978-1-908011-06-0

In this radical re-evaluation of the Grail legends, Wendy Berg brings some meaningful light to the ancient mythology of the British Isles, centred around the marriage of King Arthur to the Faery Gwenevere. Drawing upon Arthurian sources and other related texts, from the Book of Genesis to *The Lord of the Rings*, she explores the magical ritual underpinning of the legends and their connection to the ancient stellar deities of Britain.

"This is the most important and challenging book on Arthurian and Grail tradition for many a long year." — **Gareth Knight**

Rebecca Wilby: In Different Skies

ISBN 978-1-908011-02-2

In the trenches of Loos and the Somme, two disaffected young subalterns, Munro and Tate, struggle to find humour and purpose in a rapidly disintegrating world; brothers unto death – with a firmer bond than anything in their real families. A world away, in another time and place, Katherine is startled when she starts to recover memories – someone else's memories – of the first world war trenches in a series of visions and dreams. These involuntary glimpses into the life of a lost soldier open up a web of inner worlds and a search across the fields of northern Europe for the historical truth behind the visions.

For more quality esoteric books and magical fiction, see

www.skylightpress.co.uk